I0635504

The Siren's Sea

REVENGE

Book One

By Clare Angelica

Clear Angel Publishing

Also By Clare Angelica

The Siren's Sea: Revenge

Coming soon from *The Siren's Sea* Trilogy…

The Siren's Sea: Redemption

The Siren's Sea: Reawakening

For all the Pirates of my heart,
You know who you are...
My deepest love and devotion,
Thank you

A Special Thanks To:

My dear friend and editor, Sharon, for her relentless enthusiasm and constructive criticism, without you this book would not be in print. Thank you for yielding your time, energy and gusto for this book.

My high school English teachers – Mrs. Rushing for our bonded love, some may call it obsession, with Sir William Shakespeare, and Mr. DeGear for pushing me forward in his creative writing class (I don't know how I would have gotten through high school without it!)

My graphic designer, Wheeler Juell, I knew you could do it (and you didn't just do it – you nailed it!)

My go-to-guy, Randy Cassingham, for all of your assistance through this process – another person I could not have done this without.

My dear friends and additional sets of eyes, Kit and Vi, for helping this book along even farther – thank you for the extra time!

My friends and family, who gave me ideas, support, love, and told me to just go do it!

Thank you for the constant faith in my abilities and your consistent support. I love and appreciate you all so very much!

The Siren's Sea
REVENGE

Prologue

———◆———

SNOW FELL LIKE A SHADOW to the streets of the moonlit town, covering the world in its silence. A lone man stalked the alleyway, eyes the color of emeralds peering out from beneath his black cloak. A soft breeze blew the chill of the evening sharply through his bones. Everything he owned, he held close against his body, trying to ward off the wind's whisper against his skin. Methodically, he walked the close-knit streets. Buildings rose high to either side of him. Their stone faces watched him as he sifted through their passageways, barely an arm's length away from their cold faces. Inhaling deeply the winter scents of fresh snow, and promising new life, the stranger entered a weather-beaten door towards the end of the darkening street. The building's entrance was illuminated by a single, white candle. Its flame shrouded within the folds a red lantern. The commotion of the patrons assaulted the man's ears as he entered the small lobby.

The second she heard the clang of the shutting door, the woman's ears pricked up as her chocolate eyes darted towards her newest client. She watched as the man righted himself and relaxed into the warmth of the welcoming inn. She assessed his walk and the bend of his body as he stepped up from the genkan, walking towards her. "Good evening, sir." The woman looked him up and down, licking her lips as if he were a large bowl of milk sitting in front of a hungry cat. "You wish for accommodations? I make it very comfy for you here." She winked at him.

The man swiftly ran his gaze up and down her body as she came around the side of the counter and posed for him, leaning seductively back against the wood counter. He contemplated the ornately garbed woman, watching her red painted lips dance with anticipation. Her black hair was piled high atop her head with gold and jade ornaments stuck in its folds. Her Japanese accent was accentuated with a lisp created by the largeness of her front teeth. "Yes, lady, I seek lodging for the night." Out of respect for the matron, the man bowed slightly.

"Aaawwwwww," she purred. "Only one night? You break my heart, sir." Using her body, she tried to position it into the most enticing stance. Trying to tempt him into changing his mind, she batted her eyelashes and pursed her lips. The unfaltering gaze in which the stranger met her stare unnerved her. The man sent shivers down the courtesan's spine. "Very well," she hustled behind the desk and knelt behind it to retrieve an unseen key. "You pay with cash?" He nodded and divided out the night's stay. The woman recounted what he had given, and then satisfied that she wasn't being cheated, shoved the money into the lock box hidden from view. "I show you your room." Her foreign accent tangled her words and laced his ears. Her smile was not unpleasant.

"Thank you." He gestured with his hand for her to pass, another slight bow in his stance. She giggled, moved in front of him and led him through a door to the right.

They never asked your name at this type of establishment, which led to its appeal. The proprietor could tell by the way you walked, or talked, whether you would, or would not, be one to give information willingly. They also trained their employees not to push when the client was unwilling to give. All the patrons paid in cash, leaving no scrap of information behind. Unless a client's face was recognized from repeat visits, or a wanted flyer hung in the square, the patrons moved like ghosts in and out of the inn, unknown.

Light beamed through the shoji panels, as the lone man followed the woman down the passage way. She deliberately swung her hips enticingly in front of him. The stranger laughed silently to himself. The sounds of merriment brought on by drink crept into the hall. The man could feel the salacious intent of the other patrons behind the thin walls. Their thoughts berated him.

Which pretty lass shall I pay tonight to occupy my bed until the morning's wee hours?

The stranger quickened his step. His foot falls thundered up the well worn stairs at the hallways end, drowning out the giddy men behind the paneled walls. Distance was all he desired from men of such character. The patrons below shared nothing of the stranger's morals.

The innkeeper led him up the stairs, taking a sharp left at the landing, then down the hall to its end. "Here your room, sir." She stood just inside the entrance. His eyes followed her widening, bucktoothed smile, down to her outstretched arm, indicating his lodgings.

The man had been surveying his surroundings with every step they took away from the lobby. Quickly, he examined them again, searching out his exits. The window in his room encompassed the full moon outside. It could easily be broken if he needed to flee across the roof. His room, the last door on the right, was adjacent to an exit, leading out over a balcony with steps at its opposite side winding into the courtyard below.

This would do just fine, he thought.

"Thank you." He nodded for the woman to leave. Her breath caught, and she lingered a little while longer before huffing out of the room. Silently, he closed the door behind her, listening to the woman's solitary banter as she thundered back towards the lobby. He laughed, turning back to face the room. It would do. The comfort of the bare furnishings was all he needed for the night.

The stranger stuck to the traditions of the Japanese life. He bathed before soaking in the outdoor baths. The heat of the water melted his bones, warmed his muscles and started his heartbeat anew. He was almost home. Visions of his family soared through his mind as he settled under the sheets for sleep. It came swiftly.

• • •

"No! NOOOO!!" called the woman in his dream. Their hands ripped apart from one another as she was taken from him. The sea raged behind her tear stained face.

The drifter bolted up in his bed, sweat dripping from his body. He ran both hands over his wet face to bring himself back to reality. Never had he had such beauty taken from him. Usually it was he who took. Never had he had a dream so vivid, so real.

Who was she? His mind raced. He placed a hand over his heart to ease its pounding.

I know her. I can feel her.

He heard it again, the mournful call of a woman from the darkness, screaming for her life. He leapt out of bed, donning his clothes. Grabbing his pack and sword he fled out the door, exiting the inn and slamming into the bitter night.

Where was the voice coming from?

He raced across the ice-covered bridge and slid down the stairs, pausing in the shadows. The woman's voice called to him urgently. He shoved open a door to the left of the stairs and forced his way in. The warmth of the building quickly faded as the darkened hallway left no illusion to the eeriness of this night. His blood ran cold as every muscle in his body tightened. A loud crash, as if something or someone had been thrown, startled him out of his reverie. At the end of the hall, he saw shreds of light escaping the crevices of a door left slightly ajar. He headed stealthily towards it, ignoring the building dread within him.

The man slowed his pace, pressing his back to the wall, stopping against its strength. The door at the end of the hall led back to the outside world. He could see the snow-covered courtyard lying just beyond. He regained his bearings and sought the door just to the right of him. He glided down the remaining length of the hall. Peering through the crack, loomed a rather large and imposing man garbed in the barbarian army's clothing. He was shaking a woman violently within his grasp.

"You owe me! You owe me your daughter!!" the barbarian shouted inches from the poor woman's face.

Surveying the room a second time, his eyes landed on a huddled figure in the farthest corner. The form was female. Her knees were grasped tightly into her chest. She was crying with her head tucked down to shield her eyes, with every harsh word, her body shook with fear. Her hearing could not be stopped.

"I owe you nothing!" The woman's voice brought the stranger back to the reality of what was happening in front of him. His eyes tore toward her. The barbarian slapped her hard across the face. As her head fell back, her eyes found the stranger peering at her from the darkened hallway.

"Help," she mouthed. The words *save my daughter* flooded his head.

The man realized that this woman, this mother, had given up hope for her own life, but not for her child. A sharp pain filled his chest. He didn't want either of them to have to move forward without the other. His mind raced. The soldier far outweighed him. The man was a monstrosity. However, as the stranger watched him, he found the man to be clumsy, a bit of a half-wit. He had to act fast.

The barbarian shot his eyes to the hallway as the man slid back into the shadows. He turned to meet her eyes. "You whore!" He laughed bitterly down at her. The stench of his breath violated her skin. "There is no one here to save you. I picked this inn specifically because it won't open for another month, or more. And by then, your blood will have long washed away." He clutched the woman's throat and brought her ear close to his mouth. "You cannot deny me what is rightfully owed!" He pressed his knife firmly to her heart. "I should let you watch." He inclined his head towards her terrified daughter. The woman gasped as the knife broke her skin. She stared up into the man's eyes, meeting those of the devil. Her eyes grew large with anguish. Releasing his hold on her, the soldier dropped her fragile body to the floor. He clutched at his body, watching the outpour of blood as he felt the sword being removed. Slowly, he turned to meet his vanquisher. As their eyes met, the stranger plunged the sword through his heart, severing this evil from the world. All stood silent in the room as the man slipped from the sword, colliding with the floor, his breath ceasing to rise within his chest.

The stranger rushed to the woman's side, dropping his sword to the ground. He reached beneath the woman to bring support to her fallen body. Her eyes stared, hollow in their gaze, at the dead man before her. "Are you alright?" The stranger spoke staring down at her. "Please, speak to me."

As her eyes focused upon him, light began to twinkle within them. She reached a hand up to cup the side of the mystery man's face, tears filling her eyes. "I am fine, stranger." She laughed softly. "You saved my life. You saved both our lives when I thought only one would be necessary. You have far surpassed my expectations of you." His eyes questioned her, but before she would let him talk, she rolled in his arms to face the corner. The mother spoke to her daughter in their native tongue. Finally, the little creature that had to endure her mother's torture lifted her delicate face. The girl rushed to her mother's arms, sobbing, and clutching at her body as mother held daughter in a reuniting embrace of new life. They had survived.

The man pushed himself backwards to allow them a moment to reconnect. The love and relief were palpable. When they began to stir, he helped them rise together so the link would not be broken. "We must go. I can assist you out of town to a safe place." Looking to the stain on the woman's chest, alarm grew within him. "You're bleeding." He reached for the mother's arm to steady her.

"I am fine, stranger. It's merely a flesh wound." Her English was flawless within the Japanese roots of her homeland. "It will heal in a matter of days. Thank you." Her eyes sparkled up at him from her petite frame. He guessed she must have been around five foot, if that. "I am Kishiko (KEE-SHEE-KO)." She pronounced her name phonetically. "And this is my daughter, Rahn." She took his hand in hers. The hold was light and gentle. How she had withstood the thrashing from the warrior boggled his mind.

"Forgive me. I am Roberts. May I help you out of here? This place and town?" Roberts' voice was urgent. He heard stirrings all around him.

"Rahn?" Mother looked down at daughter as they shared a silent exchange. A reassuring smile spread their lips. The doll-like girl nodded. "Yes, we have family not too far from here in Makizono, Kagoshima. We would be very thankful for your help, Roberts, in getting us home." The last word rolled off her lips in awe, as if she thought she would have never been able to say it again.

"Very well. Once we are rid of this establishment, I will arrange transport." Roberts moved the two women out into the hallway. "Wait here a moment." He stepped back into the room with the fallen man to rid him of his gold, accessories, anything that would fetch a decent price further down the road. Stepping back into the hallway, he guided them silently out the back door, covering them with his cloak to aid in biting back the chill that was consuming the night.

As they exited the opposite side of the inn onto the street, Roberts couldn't help but remark to himself how different it all looked under a blanket of snow. It appeared as though whole buildings were missing or hidden. The market-square appeared to be half its previous size. His mind reeled with how different it had all become. A soft tug at his jacket pulled him back to his task. He looked down to see the brave eyes of a child staring up at him expectantly.

"Right." Roberts led them to an alcove, a safe place where he could keep watch upon them as he scurried through the night.

"He has been gone several minutes, Mama." The small girl clutched at her mother's dress in angst.

"Ssssshhh, my child. Roberts will return soon. Fare is not an easy thing to procure this late at night." Kishiko stood aware and watchful of her surroundings. She trusted this man. She would not have picked a rescuer she didn't. This Roberts would play a large role in a predetermined destiny she had foreseen. He will return, if for nothing more than the mere pull of curiosity.

Roberts scavenged quickly. He did not have much time before the deeds of the night would become noticed. He found an unattended covered cart with two horses. "Waste not, want not." He covered the horses with their blankets before harnessing them to the wagon. He quickly returned to his charges. As he approached the two protected beneath his cloak, he wondered to himself, *how did I get into this?*

Roberts slowed his pace in order to assess their features. He did not recognize Kishiko's from his dream, but the girl, Rahn. Perhaps in her older years, she would resemble the beauty of the woman he lost at sea.

Tragic, Roberts thought to himself. To lose such beauty to the ocean's fury is clearly a curse. He shook his head, startled by his own thoughts. You are thinking too much, friend. It was merely a dream. Now is the time for duty not day-dreaming.

The road to Makizono was long and rough, but peaceful within the sanctuary of the forest. He sought the inn of Kishiko's family. The pair would be safe there, no longer tormented by the demons of their past as the mother would say. A new life awaited them across its threshold. During the long journey, little Rahn swiftly broke her silence, and the dragon's wit and temper that escaped her lips enchanted Roberts.

• • •

Many years passed as Roberts returned to the inn every fall and stayed far into the spring, catching the summer's warmth through the season's change. The inn, and the family that resided there, became his winter wonderland of escape. He watched as Rahn turned from the frightened girl of twelve to a confident teen. As she grew towards womanhood, Roberts saw glimpses of the woman she was to become. The small girl always amazed him. When he looked into her eyes, he could see nothing but admiration, yet, there was a hidden fire smoldering with indignation. The fire would simply take time to unleash. Rahn bore a torch that could not be extinguished. Her fervor for life only grew, and she constantly pushed the limits of her mother's patience and her family's grace. Rahn would answer to no one. Her confidence was as contagious as her uninhibited, heart-warming laugh that could fill the entire room.

With every turn of the season, Roberts grew closer with the Masago family. Nami, Kishiko's sister, ran the inn flawlessly and always had his favorite guest house prepared. The family worked together, and all the while, he envied their closeness. They had a bond he had long ago lost with his kin.

It always amazed Roberts that Kishiko carried no scar of the first night they'd met, physically or mentally. "A wound cut deep, and long forgotten, leaves no scar," Kishiko would always say. The words constantly remained lost on him, but Roberts knew the feeling of their meaning.

On a warm spring day, Roberts was helping Rahn stow winter's covers in the barn. Her eyes studied him. From the moment she had met the man, he had been in her heart. A childish crush one could never squelch. Rarely, it had been broached in conversation that the girl carried feelings for the man who had rescued her. Rahn ignored such comments. She knew that the emotions she felt were more than a mild case of "damsel-in-distress syndrome". Roberts had enchanted his way into her heart with his words of kindness and actions of love. The man was always there for her, come what may. He held no judgment, which Rahn found refreshing. As she grew, the gap in their ages seemed less and less important. Roberts was not as many years her senior as her father had been when he married her mother. Age, she felt, was of no consequence. But, how to convince the man she loved that she was more than the girl he had come to know? How to alter his view so that he saw the woman she had become?

Purposefully, she swayed her hips in front of him as her long, straight raven hair fell down her back, blowing faintly in the wind. Undeniably, she had grown into a beautiful woman. Rahn would be nothing less than stunning as she moved fully into adulthood. The round curve of her face and slanted, up-turned eyes were exotic to him. Their violet hue made Rahn that much more different and striking. She had grown tall, too, towering over her mother at five foot seven. The height, he gathered, had been gained from her beloved father, of who little was spoken.

"Roberts, help me with this." Rahn stood, trying to hoist the large screen above her head into its storage place. She had a mischievous glint to her eye, even though her body was struggling with the task.

"Does never a *please* pass your lips, Rahn?" Roberts laughed, "Always so demanding." He approached her, grabbing onto the opposite side. "Uh-oh, I know that look. You're up to something, and that's never good." Her eyes lingered on him as he lifted the screen effortlessly into its place. He was strong and muscular from days of hard work, tanned from weeks upon sea. He caught her stare. "Are you alright, Rahn? You look a bit pale." He cocked his head to one side, examining her.

Rahn stared transfixed. His eyes soothed her, as they always did. His arms comforted her when she was young as she fell asleep within them to the melodic sound of his voice. He would always tell her tales of his adventures at high sea. She loved to tousle the sandy blonde hair atop his head. Rahn simply had a better reach now. Roberts had changed and morphed, as she had through the years. Now he looked more the man that he was destined to be, than when she had first met him all those years ago. As Rahn grew, Roberts' green eyes disarmed her more and more. She didn't realize until she exhaled, that she had been holding her breath.

It's now or never, she thought. Rahn shoved at his chest with a force that surprised him. Roberts fell backwards into the mound of hay piled high behind them. As his feet left the ground, he reached for her arm dragging her along with him. Laughter filled the air as they collided together onto the soft landing.

The man felt joy at such a childish act, such freedom. But, he swiftly had to regain his composure. Roberts could not let Rahn know what he truly felt within him. Thus far, he had done well at keeping the girl at arm's length. But she was persistent, and he could see the growing affections within her eyes as she gazed at him. Bringing a woman into his life would add a complication he was not ready for.

"You silly girl! You haven't done that to me in ages. I should have known." Laughter lit his voice as he beamed at her, his smile broad.

Rahn rolled on top of him. Her body melded into his as she toyed with the collar of his shirt. The buttons opened to his bare chest.

Oh no. This isn't good, Roberts thought. His body responded far too much to the girl already. "Rahn..." He cautioned her with fear in his voice.

Rahn's fingers crossed his lips halting his speech. "Ssssshh," came out far too seductively for his ears. Roberts had to squelch the moan rising in his throat as she pulled her body gently up the length of his, her mouth lingering inches above him. The violet focus of her eyes was hungry. Roberts couldn't move. His body felt paralyzed and unresponsive to the logic his brain was trying to shout forth. "No one's home," Rahn cooed. "Relax."

Roberts' body felt pinned under the weight of her, and it felt glorious. Pressing against him Roberts could feel her every curve, the thick swell of her bosom against his chest. Rahn slowly ran her tongue out of her mouth and over his soft full lips, teasing him. She cupped the side of his face with her delicate fingers and tenderly brought her lips over his. The innocence of the touch floored him momentarily, although his skilled lips quickly caught up. He slowly opened her mouth and stroked her with his tongue. A soft moan escaped her at the onslaught of the new found pleasure. He took the kiss deeper. His arms, finally responsive, wrapped around her, pulling her tighter against him. Roberts ignored the doubts of his mind, as all the feelings of this moment felt so right.

Roberts rolled on top of her, one hand working its way up her smooth stomach, over the folds of her dress to her full chest. Ravaging her mouth, he rubbed the hard nub of her nipple. Rahn's body responded by bucking up towards his, a moan lost in her mouth. Roberts supported her head and neck with one hand pushing her tighter against him. His other hand began to slide back down the length of her body and lingered slightly above the waistline of her skirt before inching inside. Roberts' fingers cupped her heat causing her body to stiffen slightly.

"Don't stop," the words softly escaped Rahn's lips as a pant. He kissed her again. The feel of her lips on his sent him rigid. He wanted her badly. "Please...," she urged him. He needed no more coercion. Roberts' fingers began to play her softly and slowly at first allowing her to get accustomed to the sensations. He quickened his pace and her body began to shutter with her first orgasm. As the aftershocks of it still flowed through Rahn's body, he couldn't stop kissing her. She grew limp in the safety of his arms.

Roberts raised his head for breath as her eyes fluttered open. "I can't do this Rahn. I should not have done that with you, taken advantage of you so, in this way." The heat from his body left her and she felt hollow as she watched him walk away.

Dinner was awkward. Rahn refused to look anywhere near his general direction. She was mad. Good. The last thing Roberts wanted to do was hurt her. His stomach rolled at the thought of that afternoon. Roberts wanted nothing more than to love her, completely, but he did not want to break the bond of family that had formed between all of them. The man carried to much respect for the Masago clan to disgrace them in anyway. Roberts would not put Rahn in any danger, but by loving her, he feared he already had. He excused himself immediately after the meal. His determined pace slowed ever so slightly as he approached his favorite soaking bath. The warm waters called to him, but he would not answer their plea. He quickly shook off the thought, and quickened his pace heading for his hut, far displaced from the main lodge. It was quiet there. The solitude would do him good, as it always did. He needed to think. He needed to leave. He needed to stop thinking of her, but she had invaded him like a sickness, years ago.

After splashing his face with cold water in an effort to redirect his thoughts, Roberts exited his bathroom. His skin still felt hot in the cool of the evening, and his thoughts were no less contained. As he lifted his head, there she was dressed in his favorite silken robe that he had brought her from India. Rahn stood illuminated by the fires blaze. Her skin radiated a heat he could feel from across the room. He stood frozen in the archway, mesmerized by her pure beauty.

"Will you speak to me?" Rahn paused. "With me?" Her tone, even and melodic, always ensnared him.

Roberts nodded his agreement. "Your change of wording enticed me." He was trying to remain calm and in control.

Her eyes grew in challenge. Rahn disliked humbling herself, but she was going to try. "I know you feel what we did today was wrong, but I am sorry, for I do not feel the same." Rahn's English was as eloquent as her mother's yet even more enchanting within each syllable of her Japanese roots. "I love you," her voice faltered. "I have loved you, for years." Her boldness was back. "I am not asking you anything more than to make my first time wonderful and beautiful. I can think of no other I would want to do this for me. You are one of my dearest friends and confidants. Please grant me this pleasure, Roberts?"

Roberts could tell she was trying. The break in her usual forthwith and demanding delivery had changed. "Rahn... I have loved you over the years. My love has grown from whence we first met. First, seeing the delicate little girl grow, and blossom, into the miraculous and valiant woman who now stands before me. I have not come back all these years simply because I love to see the colors change." Roberts could have sworn he felt her heart beat match his own as she smiled at him. "I just want you to know what you are doing and the consequences that could follow. Age...is of no concern to you? Or honor?"

Rahn's brow furrowed slightly as she contemplated his statement. She raised her head to meet his eyes. "No." Her voice was soft but sure. "It is of no consequence to me. My father was twelve years my mother's senior, you are only eight mine. I see no problem, save for your personal dilemma."

There she was, making it his doubt. "Very well." Roberts' advance on her caused Rahn to jump slightly. "Are you nervous to have me so near?" Their bodies were inches apart as he towered over her.

"No," came out of Rahn's lips, quite shaken. Her hand moved to untie her robe.

"Stop." Roberts hand lingered over hers. "Allow me." He reached a smooth warm hand to her shoulder sliding under the soft fabric. He slid his fingertips over her creamy shoulder and kissed the bare skin that appeared to him. Rahn's knees began to buckle beneath her at the delicate touch. Wrapping a firm arm around her, Roberts pulled her close, supporting her slack body. "I love you, Rahn." He whispered softly in her ear stroking her hair.

Lifting Rahn from the ground, Roberts carried her to the soft bed awaiting them. He gently laid her down atop the piles of linen. He moved to remove his shirt, allowing the light to play off his tanned torso and rippling muscles. Rahn tugged at the waist of her robe and pushed it off her body. She lay naked atop it. The paleness of her skin was radiant in the soft glow of the candle light.

Roberts' breath caught in his throat. "You are beautiful." He spoke as if enchanted by a nymph. Rahn's perfect chest slipped into the curves of her waist, down into round luscious hips. He had always loved her proportions. She was perfect to him.

"I will not be doing this for you, but with you." He took her to bed, softly, sweetly, gently. They both had the climax of a lifetime.

"Pirates are simply sailors,
gone bad."
[JD]

Chapter

1

———◆———

THE WIND LASHED ITS WAY through three lone figures as they stared over the edge of their vessel at the water's impending doom. Clouds grew thicker with every passing breath and swell of the ocean beneath the sky's fury. Today was not the day to seek refuge upon the water's solace, but when you lived and breathed through the sea's torrents, there was nowhere else your soul would rather be to lay its rest if the day happened to be your last. Threatening thunder claps boomed overhead, enforcing their warnings of rage. On a day like today, any other sailor would have held for dear life to solid ground, where their feet could not be shaken. The travelers of today were not like any other sailor, nor were they the typical men who sailed the ocean's waters.

Lights began to twinkle in the far off distance showing sign of the inhabitants who lay beyond, safe from the water's ever changing temper. Vaguely, the crew of the oncoming vessel could make out the shoreline they sought through the ever darkening storm.

"Are you sure you wish to do this?" A woman's voice broke the ebony of the squall as her hands gripped tightly around the helms wheel.

A tall, reed-like girl breathed deeply the ocean's wrath. She looked over the bow of the ship, her blood-red hair dripping across her face. She tried to target the town through the pelting rain, but her eyes were unfocused, distracted by the knot in her stomach. "Yes," she sighed. "It is time to lay my demons to rest with the soul of another." Her fist smashed unconvincingly onto the rail. The words she spoke were nearly lost amongst the crashing of the waves.

The woman at the helm gazed at the lanky, freckle-faced girl out of the corner of her eye. "Very well, we will continue on." She spoke to address the other woman now, dismissing Rowan. "Rahn, prepare the boat for our departure." Rahn carried features as exotic as the land she came from. She nodded her accord to the captain's command. Rahn's jet black hair clung to her face in wet streams as she stared at the petite, rain-soaked woman behind the helm. Dorian was the most unlikely of captains. Slowly, Rahn sauntered off to the main deck, the curves of her body gliding through the air. The woman steering the vessel returned her gaze to the wasp at her side. "Rowan, I make one request of you." Dorian's tone was direct.

Rowan assessed her with wary eyes. Her heart felt heavy within her chest. She feared she lacked the fortitude to see her vengeance through after all these years. She knew Dorian recognized it as well, but Rowan would not allow herself to back down after coming this far. A strand of her crimson hair slashed across her angular face as the wind rose high once more. "Of course, I will grant you anything." The steel of Dorian's eyes pierced her. They always matched the storm in its craze for freedom.

Dorian gripped the wheel, pulling hard to the left as they came about towards shore. "I ask that you not let your emotions rule you in your wrath for revenge. Keep a steady head and an open mind. Do not let your emotions cloud your judgment. Trust your instincts, but allow them to be fully heard before you react. Let your discernment lead you through this endeavor."

Dorian turned to the saddened, bewitchingly green eyes that stared back at her. Rowan, the girl who sought redemption in her captain's stare, had been stricken by a torment that far too long awaited closure. Dorian wished she could envelop Rowan in her arms and take away all her pain, but some torments could only lay at rest when you came to face them yourself.

"Yes, you are right, sister," Rowan paused in her thoughts. "I will do my best to keep a level head about me." With that she turned and rushed down the stairs gaining distance between her and the helm. She could not handle hearing such truth from the woman who stood there.

Rahn ascended slowly from the opposite side in which Rowan fled. Quickly she was beside Dorian again at the helm. They stared together at Rowan's disappearing back. "Do you think she can do it?" Her Japanese accent laced her words with eloquence. Rahn stared at the side of Dorian's face. The captain's blonde hair whipped between them on the wind, slicing the skin like ice.

"By the end of her quest Rowan will arrive at a different outcome. I believe her path will take a different course." Dorian stared forward over the ship's body.

A light laugh escaped Rahn. "In other words, no." She moved behind Dorian looking towards shore. "Ah, well, our sister was never meant for death and destruction anyway. She is better off leaving that to us." A sly smile spread her plump, small lips. Rahn turned back to catch a hint of something written across Dorian's face. "You fear something." There was no question in her words. "What is it?" Rahn demanded as she unconsciously gripped the hilt of her long samurai sword.

Resigning herself, Dorian let loose a small sigh. "I fear a greater force will be released by what we are about to do, one that has been hunting us." Dorian's steel cut eyes fiercely met the violet of Rahn's. "Have you not felt the looming weight on the horizon?"

Rahn felt a wave of frustration with herself. "No, sister, I have not." She broke their stare. She could not withstand the intensity in Dorian's eyes. "What I have felt is that Rowan's little endeavor has held a foreboding menace over me, the source of which I have not yet discovered."

"Truly?" Dorian let fly the word laced with sarcasm. Rahn sliced Dorian with her stare, but Dorian's gaze was lost to the sea. "Soon, I believe, we will all find our roles to fill. It is not necessarily my wish to do what Rowan asks and she knows this. But, I will oblige her. You and I have had more time to tame that which lurks in our shadows. Rowan must learn her own lessons as well. Although, it is not vengeance that I seek, I will play my intended part with gusto." Her smile was devilishly satisfying. Dorian always loved a good game.

Rahn laughed at her delight. "Do not think I have let slide your words, but I will let it go for now. Do you think we have sheltered Rowan for too long?"

"I think Rowan has sheltered herself for too long. Living in the shadows out of fear of what you do not wish to see, only makes you afraid of the dark. This voyage will not be in vain." Dorian laughed at Rahn's expression. "No matter what you may think, I will make sure some good comes of it… maybe even some good for you," she winked at Rahn.

"You always know so much, wretched little woman, but never grant upon others your knowledge!" Rahn relaxed her shoulders and a hearty laugh filled her lungs. Dorian always had the ability to calm her, and Rahn constantly found it annoying. Rahn was famous for brash actions. It was a challenge for her to think outside of her emotions, outside of that gut reaction. Rahn had trouble finding that centered place in which clarity resided. However, Dorian was always there to lead her to it. "Alright, I trust you with my body, my life. Whatever it is that you have foreseen I have faith that you keep it within you for a valid reason."

"You are just displeased because your bullying works not on me." Dorian's smile was honest.

"You know me too well. I shall have to kill you later for that." Rahn teased.

Dorian searched the shoreline for an unseen circumstance that awaited there. "Timing, my dear, is everything." Rahn smiled at her captain's comment. "It is time. The water is calming enough to make our passage clear. Take over the helm." Before descending the stairs Dorian nodded to the men awaiting her and turned back to Rahn.

Rahn had not taken her eyes off her captain and Dorian's stare was unnerving. "Yes," Rahn mocked her.

"My gift of the future is not always certain, for the future is truly incalculable in the present. Circumstances change far too quickly to be counted. No matter what I have seen, it is still my place to let you find the experiences on your own." Dorian continued to speak to her as she stepped down the stairs. "Aren't visions of the future merely guidelines anyway? In the end it's all about timing, choice, decision, and the final outcome of destiny. None of which are as predictable as any of us would like. Patience."

"Aye, sister." Rain pounded around them all as the clouds gave little hope of wandering off. "We must all make the decisions upon our own path," Rahn spoke softly to herself. "But, sometimes it's easier when they are handed to us."

Dorian, although she did not miss the words spoken from her mate's mouth, was far removed by the smash of thunder and lightning continually pounding within her ears. Rahn's greatest trigger was the rage within herself. Dorian would have to take note of it as the fire built within her sister once more.

Balance, Rahn, balance. Dorian thought. *When will you allow yourself to learn it, or to live it?*

• • •

Women aboard a ship are bad luck. Any sailor with a hint of experience will be happy to pass along this helpful advice to a novice, idealistic seaman, who has no greater knowledge of such things. A female brings nothing but strife, discontentment, unsuitable seafaring weather, a nervous ride, an angry sea God, misfortune and angst. The men of old say that to carry a woman on board brings death to those who ride with her.

These be three women, and yet, they be women none at all.

• • •

Clouds hung low and dark taunting the English town within their swell. It was a dreary day that had lead into an even drearier night. Rain banged against the glass panes with a vengeance, threatening to shatter their protective resolve. Window shutters slammed against the hard granite of the buildings awaiting their shattering end. Pillars sagged under the weight of the wild winds. The town of St. Winnifred was encased in gray. Sinister clouds hovered just over head, just out of reach. The brick buildings, built tall to view the sea in all its calm glory and rolling tides, kept all those who sought its shelter safe from the brooding squall. Tonight, few inhabitants journeyed to the city streets. No dog barked to be heard. Light graced every window, yet no happy face was seeking the solitude the storm offered. Each family of St. Winnifred had turned inward, preparing for the anniversary of their town, their pride. It had been many, many years, some say even centuries, since the English had settled in the Caribbean waters, and they intended to enjoy the claiming of this diverse land. Truly, what better a way to celebrate than through the festivities of food, music and drink?

Those sorry souls who had to venture out into the heaven's havoc went nimbly and efficiently through tasks handed down by pleading wives, demanding mothers or guilt driven by mothers-in-law. A small group of girls giggled under the awning of a store front, aglow with the expectations of the evening as their mothers shopped inside. They exchanged excited remarks about the eligible men coming, or leapt to conclusions about who would be the first to marry. Ranging in age from eight to twelve, they spurred each other on in their boy-crazed youth. Rain or shine, the night held many prospects.

If you had glanced across the buildings of St. Winnifred, you would have found a lone man's face filling a rain beaten window. His body was tense as he watched the crashing of the waves pound their punishment onto the land. The man pressed his body into the cold glass, pushing against the storm's call. He glared out over the beaten water and the lands that would one day be his. His resolve began to crack at the weight of responsibility he would soon have to uphold. The man's jaw set tight as a knot grew thick within his stomach. He felt within him the hard pull of the ocean's wrath against his will. It was daring him to play its game of chance, as it sunk deep within his soul. The waters taunted him within their echo as they broke the earth beneath them. The sea called to him far more than his feet that longed to be on solid, peaceful ground. Deep within the recesses of his mind, he felt himself changing into a foreign passenger, a man who fit nowhere, but longed to belong somewhere. A man he didn't know was beginning to surface as his resistance to the call of the sea was buckling. The water always held the last card as it dealt your fate upon its will.

All I need is a distraction, the man thought. *Too long have I forgone a lady's bed.*

His mind flashed to a vision in black, her long golden hair falling in tendrils down her back. Petite, strong shoulders glittered before him as he brushed aside soft curls to kiss her neck. He shivered.

Why can I never shake this illusion from my mind!? The clinking and banging of his friend behind him toiling away over hot coals and steel distracted him.

Christian looked up from the heat. Sweat slowly dripping down his cheek as he recognized the look upon his friend's face. *He is thinking of her.* Christian pulled the blade from the fire and sloshed it into the water at his right. He loved the sound of the steel as it hissed and cackled back at him. *Damn it,* he thought. *He grows restless.* "Aye, aye, Lord!" He bellowed to the man at the window. "Come and have a look at this." Christian stared at his back. "Victor!?" He yelled with a question upon his lips, trying to get the man's attention.

Victor couldn't move just yet. His eyes were transfixed upon the palm trees wrenching back and forth in the wind. *Never had I wanted or longed for anyone before her.* Victor's blue gaze could have burned right through the glass he now pressed so forcefully against. *Something changed within me after her. Something began to awaken from a dark depth. The pixie would not even grant me the decency of knowing her name!* His anger could be palpated throughout the air.

Christian's voice from behind him snapped Victor back to the present. Victor carried with him, as he turned to face his friend, a sense that something was coming his way. A puzzle piece he had longed to find was venturing right to him.

But what!? Victor wondered. He caught the glare of Christian's green eyes and knew he had to appear interested in reality once more. "What have you made this time, Christian?" Victor walked towards the bench they had built together several years back for Christian's father. It was a sturdy fortress of wood that held up under the duress of the men's playful wrath. "Not another bloody pocket knife, I hope…." Victor spoke under his breath as he neared Christian, his fingers unconsciously tracing the nicks and slashes within the hard wood.

"I heard that, you tosser." Christian brought his fists to his chest and spread his feet, taking a boxer's stance. He tossed his sandy, reddish locks out of his eyes to better see Victor. "Watch your words, my lord. I may have a mind to throttle you later." His eyes gleamed with mischief. Although Christian was shorter than

Victor, he was known to be a treacherous opponent. His green eyes sparkled with an invitation for trouble in the soft light of the day's end.

Victor's eyes bore into Christian like sapphire daggers as he matched his stance. "I should have your head for such a comment." The threat loomed between them. "Come on," he badgered Christian. "I love death before a party." His smile brightened the tightness his chiseled features had taken on. Victor charged him full force causing both men to go tumbling across the floor.

Christian wrestled around Victor's body 'til he lay on his side with Victor in a head lock. "You wouldn't hear of such a thing, nor would you allow it. What's a best friend without a head?" Being only one of three men ever allowed to speak to Lord Victor Easton in such an impertinent tone, he reveled in his victory.

With a swift jab to Christian's ribcage, Victor rolled on top of him and pinned him to win the fight. Victor spoke with breathless laughter. "A headless friend would be no friend at all, mate." He helped Christian to his feet. "Where's this new steel of yours then?"

"I've got a mind not to show you now." Christian was wiry, yet deceptively strong.

"Now, now, don't be a sore loser." Victor chided. Victor would never admit an injury to his face, but his body burned in the places of Christian's assault. Not damaging their good looks was an unwritten rule both men abided by.

Christian laughed and patted his friend on the shoulder. "Here, then. Come look upon my art, admire my craftsmanship, oooh and aaahh at all the right times, and be jealous that you did not make it yourself," he goaded. Dodging Victor's punch, he knelt to grab the instrument from its case at the back wall.

Entranced the moment the light reflected off the steel, Victor eagerly took it from Christian's outstretched hands. "You've made this? It's so light." He paused. "The crest is... It reminds me of..." He shook his head. "No." Victor spoke as if no one else was in the room with him.

Christian watched his friend with fascination. Victor's face had taken on a new light even though confusion flooded his features. Christian stopped himself from laughing aloud at Victor's verbal debate. He took Victor's slight invitation to gloat without hesitation. "I've made a new mold for the structure. It's all one piece. The handle stops with the last point of the sword. It has gold entwined throughout it, and gems inlayed within that family's crest." Pride filled the air around him, his chest even rising.

"Magnificent, my friend. Light and deadly. A perfect combination, I'd say." Victor ran his tanned fingers over the crested seal at the top of the hilt. "Whose crest is this? It is oddly unique and beautiful." Images flashed through his mind as he stroked the crest, images he wasn't sure were his to see. Victor shook his head to rid himself of them, but, once again, her face flooded his vision. He could see nothing more than her hair blowing in the ocean's breath as gray sky and crashing waves surrounded her. Somehow he knew her, yet Victor had no recollection of her face, her body, her smile…. She was not his, this woman who haunted him.

Who owns these memories within me? Victor's eyes glazed over and his body slackened as his grip loosened on the sword.

"Are you alright?" Christian's tone indicated that Victor was behaving slightly crazy, heading straight towards mad.

"Yes, I'm fine. Whose is it? The crest…." A shrill obstinacy hit like a stone wall within the room. Victor was determined to know everything he could as the feel of death tightened through his entire body, starting with the hand that gripped the hilt of the sword.

"It's of the family Lily. The man who commissioned the sword died some, oh, I don't know, centuries ago I think. As the years passed, my family could never seem to get rid of it. It just gathered dust in the corner, waiting. The sword has almost become something of a family legend within these walls." Christian watched Victor. His friend was almost coveting the steel within his hands.

"The project has gone unfinished until you?" Victor asked.

"Yes. The project has held a spell over generations, but until me, no one could finish it."

Victor nodded, his eyes still captivated by the woman in the crest.

"I left the crest as a commemoration to him. It was Lily's idea to use a single mold, forge the metal in a different way to make it lighter, stronger. The man was brilliant. My predecessors could not figure out how to do what he asked so the task remained undone. The whole thing was almost all Lily's idea." A twinkle of his emerald eye defied all laws. "Almost," Christian said, a smile spreading his lips. "I came across the plans after my return to the English colony. My father said Lily was a pirate, but a king among them. My ancestors held the man in very high esteem, apparently. Lily did not treat people as though he was a tyrant, nor did he ever talk down to them. His wife, it is said, had the beauty of the ages, transcendent."

Victor was lost as he ran his fingers over the complex details of the crest. A dragon appeared on one side. Its body took the shape of a half moon while its tale wove around to wrap the remaining crest safely in a near circle. The rolling and crashing of tidal waves swam in the center, as the dragon's wings spread far behind his body, open and outstretched. The body of a woman, her lower half wrapped in a gown, wove around the opposite side from the dragon to connect the circle. Her form was delicate and free flowing with movement.

A small chuckle escaped Victor. "Right," he swore he almost heard the crest calling to him. Chills ran through his body. He took the sword in his right hand with the grace of a man who knew how to use it. Victor swished the sword around the room feeling the freedom of its lightness and the ease of his movements. The sword felt like a mere extension of his own arm.

Christian admired the way Victor looked at his sword. He couldn't help but feel a deeper connection to the sword running through Victor's veins. The intensity of his friend's gaze as he looked at the family's crest unnerved him. "Ready for the party, mate? VIC!!?"

The words broke the spell around him. Victor felt as though he had been transplanted from another time, another place, another life. His dark brown, nearly black hair hung teasingly around his face curling at the edges. It made his devilishly blue eyes play games with the Gods. Victor's look was purposeful as he twisted his body back to meet Christian's. He felt alive. "Yes, yes, of course. We mustn't be late, should we?" He eyed Christian. "I need a new mistress as I believe you are in need of new entertainment?" Victor said with a laugh and a smile winding his large full lips. A hobby had evolved as they hunted together and plundered, separately, the beds of their bounty. The good fortune of being such good friends made the game of the hunt that much more fun for the pair. The duo was known for seeking trouble and enjoying all the finer things in life as they zeroed in on their next targets.

A gaze, far off and star struck, entered onto Christian's face. "Aww, yes, indeed I do... And of course you as well." His English accent muddled with an Irish lilt took on an airy tone. He had the face of a soon to be well fed cat. "Right." He slapped his hands together with exuberance. "I'll just be a minute ole chap." He examined his front, "maybe two." He was covered in ash, soot and grease. "I must wash quickly and down my most alluring attire to lure the most attractive set of..." he coughed slightly, "eyes." Christian's quirk of a smile lit his face as he darted back to the stairwell. "Don't injure yourself in my absence. That sword is obscenely sharp."

Victor's voice halted him. "Why do you fiddle around with blacksmithing?" He inquired for the four-hundredth time.

Christian sighed deeply and loudly as he slowly turned back to face Victor, his hands still resting on the stair railing. "Don't I give you the same answer every time, you cockard?"

"Well, yes, mate. But, I was hoping for something with a little more flare to it this time." Victor's eyes mockingly challenged him, laughing all the while.

Christian let another, even more dramatic and exasperated, sigh escape his lungs. "I blacksmith not for a need of money, but for the mere hope that someday the woman of my dreams will waltz through that door, and she will know all the right terminology of my profession to steal my broken heart and make it whole. We will whisk each other away to foreign lands and discover a place all our own. You, being so rich, Victor, will have to pay a fee, of course, to enter our island."

"Of course," Victor laughed, leaning against the table.

"She will be a brazen broad who fights just as well as she loves. Making her my wife will kill my father because she will be all wrong for his sense of etiquette. But, I shall be happy," he smiled, staring straight through Victor. "The old goat I call father said the sword, the one you can't seem to let go of at the moment, was the finest work I'd ever done. Plus, if it wasn't for me toiling away in this hot mess of a place, who would be the lucky sod to fashion your daggers for you? Besides, I need the welcomed distraction. Imagine all the trouble I would find myself in, with my noble sought after bloodlines, if I didn't blacksmith."

Victor laughed a hearty deep throated sound. "That's the closest you've come to entertaining me in quite some time."

"Why thank you, good sir." Christian bowed in a taunting fashion. "I do so aim to please."

"Don't let your head grow to big, it still needs work." Victor cautioned him. His blue eyes bore into the woman of the crest. Her face lay intricately woven into the tale before him. "She ignited a fire I never knew existed. I cannot put it out, nor do I know where it is spreading to." Victor spoke mostly to himself, but Christian did not miss the words as he stared at him from the archway.

Christian felt a twinge as he thought back to the woman who had done the same to him. He, at least, had a name and face to put with his tormentor. Victor's woman was a complete mystery. One he hated to carry. "You must let go and live on, mate. Do not allow yourself to be defined by a circumstance you cannot control. Allow yourself to define your own circumstance and create your own victory." Victor stared up at him blindly, nodding slowly in agreement.

Christian's wiry frame stood still as he smirked before racing up the stairs. He'd at least be another hour. There was no rush anyway. The pair always arrived late for social occasions. They had better things to do than be on time.

"May he never change, if I may pray it so, lord." Victor sat at the table he helped his friend construct and bent under the light to examine the swords hilt once more.

A woman's voice sang to him as his fingers once again traced the intricately laid crest. The sorrow of her words swept deep into his soul as pinpricks raced up his back. Victor knew that somewhere deep within her voice was a story waiting to be heard.

• • •

No citizen of St. Winnifred acknowledged or even noticed the small boat being beaten by the thrashing waters. Reaching the dock after the waters ragged struggle would be a relief to most passengers, most passengers who valued living on land. Three strangers exited the small craft. Two large males and a petite woman stood together at the dock's end. Energy buzzed around them. Excitement filled their very beings to the core as they looked past the dock onto the dampened land beyond them. Pirating was what they did best, and being ruthless had made their reputation. With a sense of sheer exhilaration the trio moved up the plank towards solid land.

"St. Winnifred, it is?" said one of the male passengers, as they approached the docks end. "He is said to be here?"

"That is what we were led to believe. The bloody man's a hard one to track down. If he ain't here, we'll have the scoundrels 'ead who told us false," spoke the other man, a distant accent carried upon his words.

The three looked up at the illuminated town, each keeping to their own thoughts. Beautiful buildings stared back at them with apprehension. They asked questions without answers. St. Winnifred was nicely crafted with wood flowing through the stone structures, adding life to their dull faces. The streets were mildly abuzz with commotion. Townsmen sprinted to and fro, running the day's final errands, as the tears of the storm finally abated. Cobblestones defined the pathways to each establishment. The weary travelers went unnoticed as they blended in with the gray sky and the onslaught of night in the shadows of the fleeting twilight hours.

Searching for a specific sign, the three roamed the streets efficiently. The two bulky male strangers ambled up to the small femme as they tracked down the door to which they desired. With a small nod from the woman, they were off, splattering water down the cobbled path towards their destination.

• • •

Night settled deeply over St. Winnifred. The cloud cover returned to block out the moon's watchful gaze, bringing forth more rain. Soon everyone would be at Lord and Lady Caven's to celebrate the founding of St. Winnifred this very day, centuries in the past. A yearly tradition and excuse to get sloshed in their country's name, that allowed the entire town to behave appalling in public, drink in hand.

The slight woman traveler assessed her surroundings as she approached the imposing door. She stood transfixed on the landing. Night had fallen dark and heavy. No one was out to see her presence. Her gait halted just as her hand pressed the door knob, stopping cold her determination. She shook her head and dismissed her fear, pushing herself forward.

Victor turned as he heard the bell ding from behind him. His breath caught as he examined the woman shaking off her soaked cloak, lightly patting her face to dry it. The petite frame certainly held an elegant figure. Drenched, her lavender dress clung to her body, revealing a tightly toned waist. Smooth, plump breasts peeked out over the neckline of her dress. Droplets of water shimmered off her tanned skin. Her skirts hung against her strong legs that ran their length to the floor. Victor met her eyes. Deep swells of the night's storm echoed back to him. Dampened blonde tendrils escaped to frame her heart shaped face.

Those eyes, he thought. *They have haunted all my sleeping and waking hours for years. Those ocean swells have threatened me with my life.* Victor shook the notion from his mind. He had not yet arrived at the party and already his mind was playing tricks.

"How may I assist you, miss? I do however regret to inform you that the Shop's closed." He tried quickly to regain her attention as her eyes darted around the shop. "But, I'm sure the owner will grant you anything you ask...."

How eloquent Vic. You sound like a pleading child. Victor did a mental head slap. He reveled at her grace. *The riddle before him seemed to float around the room although she never left her place. Why have you suddenly transformed into such a bumbling idiot!? She must have people fawn over her constantly. Don't join the ranks! Get it together man.*

"I do beg your pardon." The woman spoke softly, inwardly acknowledging Victor's inner debate.

Finally, he heard the melody of her voice as she spoke to him. Victor was lost in her eyes. Words for sentences would not form from his lips.

"I saw the light on, so hoped I could find some assistance here." Her voice was smooth and filled with harmony. She immediately sucked him in to her web. "We seem to have encountered some... mechanical trouble, upon my father's boat. I mean ship." She spoke almost to herself, endearing her to him more. "He sent me inland in search of a repairman." Her voice was enthralling, so delicate. Victor just continued to stare at her in wonder so she continued. "Do you know such a man or perhaps where I can find one?"

Her questioning expression startled him from his trance. "Oh, of course," Victor's mind finally caught up with him.

Her father must be a complete numbskull to send his lovely devoted daughter ashore to do his bidding. And in this storm! She could have been sucked under and drown. Victor's mind was reeling in outrage.

Regaining his composure, Victor answered her. "You've come to the right place. Mr. Roberts is an expert in many walks of life and he has taught his son all he knows. I may assure you that he can assist you in such a crisis."

Victor couldn't help but let his eyes roam her. She was stunning, even in her disheveled state. Quite unlike any beauty he had encountered before. She emitted a sheer, palpable confidence that contradicted her outer coyness. The long blonde tresses of her hair were a deep contrast to the steel of her eyes. She was petite, yes, but strong with muscle, and a force that could not be seen. It was rare to have this kind of effect from a woman so quickly, especially with her clothes on. Victor had the urge to utterly devour her. Wiping his hand subconsciously over his mouth, he made sure he wasn't drooling uncontrollably. She caught his movement with a hawk like accuracy.

"You braved this wretched storm alone!?" Victor rose from his seat and then crashed back onto the stool beneath him. "I am sorry. Forgive my brashness. I overstepped my place." His outburst, he noticed, caused her to step backwards in worry. Victor gazed at her again, apologizing with his stare.

I have never seen such beauty matched since... my wife!? The befuddlement that crossed Victor's face caused his companion to stop short. *But I have never been married.* Victor's inner monologue took over his thoughts distracting him for a moment.

The stranger took advantage of Victor's misstep to regain her footing. She had smelled him the second she entered the door. The force of his scent nearly had her slamming shut the portal and retreating back to the dock for cover. In Victor's confusion, she mulled over his body. *The deep blue of your eyes, Victor, must have lured many a girl to your bed only to have them leave a woman.* Victor's white shirt cut his body perfectly, revealing sculpted muscles lying underneath. Victor noticed her stare and smiled brightly, apologizing for his lapse. The woman's knees went weak. She wanted to touch the smooth tan skin that peered out over his collar. He introduced himself as Lord Victor Easton. A name the stranger knew only in passing conversations with bar drunks. But Lord Victor was the bait she sought.

She smiled at him. *What a pity... Capturing you will be such an easy chase.* Victor's look asked for something, her name. *Well, there is no reason not to be honest, she thought.* "It is a pleasure to make your acquaintance Lord Easton. I am Dorian Lily."

Finally, Victor thought, *a name to place with your angelic face.*

"In answer to your previous question, no, I did not make that life wrenching venture alone. Thank goodness." Dorian's soft chuckle was music to Victor's ears. "I brought two of my father's best sailors with me." Dorian held his gaze. "Again, it is an honor to meet you Lord Easton." She curtseyed briefly.

Victor swore he saw a small spark ignite in her eyes at the mention of his name, or was it his title. "Thank you, my lady. It's an honor to make your acquaintance as well, Ms. Lily. I can't believe you were even at sea in this weather." Dorian just shrugged in response.

Victor's smell, that mix of musk and man, was all his own. Dorian's resolve began to crack as a chink formed in her armor. *Damn you gifts,* she cursed herself inwardly. *Why is it so familiar?? The only other man who carried that distinct scent was... No!* Dorian narrowed her gaze on him. *Victor carries the same build almost to a T, but his eye and hair color are completely different. The facial features draw no recognition, although he is attractive. But Victor's smell... Dorian eyed him suspiciously. This task may be harder than I once thought. I had not foreseen this complication.*

"Would you care to wait for Roberts? He has just gone up to change for tonight's festivities, but I am sure he will be down soon." *Yes, he will. When hell freezes over and dragons fly over earth. Please, Christian, give me more time with this enchanting creature.* "May I offer you a seat, Ms. Lily?" Victor pulled out a chair for her at the workman's table.

Roberts. Right. Get your head in the game Dorian. "Thank you." Before she approached the stool, Dorian did another survey of her surroundings. She gathered the other man's smell. She was definitely in the right place. Roberts scent carried the underlying imprint of his sibling. The molecule that bonded him and his sister racked through her senses. "Are Roberts and Mr. Roberts not the same person?" Dorian inquired.

"Roberts is junior, Mr. Roberts is senior." Victor tapped at the stool to his left. "Please, have a seat, my lady."

As Dorian approached him further, her eyes landed on the piece of art under Victor's hand. "What is that lovely piece of metal you are hiding there?" She waltzed up to stand behind him as Victor turned to show her the sword. "The workmanship is incredible," she cooed over Victor's shoulder. "I have never seen such thorough attention to detail." *Yes I have. There is only one man who could have created such mastery and he used to make them for me.* Dorian's emotions did not show on her face. Years of practice had trained her for that.

Victor stared at her in wonder. "You admire such work? I am very impressed, lady." His smile was broad as he gazed back at her. "Did you not say your name was Lily, my lady?"

Dorian nodded. "Yes, indeed, I did, Lord Easton."

"You may find this crest of interest. I do not know how many bloodlines of "Lily" are out in the world. But if you come from the Lily's of centuries old…." His eyes sparkled. "Would you like to hold it, examine it closer? Maybe you could identify the crest?" Victor inclined the sword toward to her. He could smell her. A mix so exotic he felt intoxicated as it laced his nostrils. Dorian smelled of the ocean combined with a scent of her own sweetness. Victor saw the delight in her eyes as she held the sword. *Odd, for a woman,* he mused.

Dorian ran her fingers along the sword's sharpened blade and came to linger over the crest at its head. It was her crest, no doubt about it. She remembered the day her husband, Jason, had commissioned the sword. Her senses darted to the door and the men who lay in wait behind it. Dorian could feel their angst. Far off she sensed the other man, Roberts, finishing his primping. Time was running short. She had to move fast. *Remember your purpose.*

"My friend Roberts constructed it. He says he's found a ne…." Victor's words were lost as his body slammed into the hard table in front of him. His eyes rolled back in his head on impact.

Touching the nape of Victor's neck, Dorian winced. *I'm sorry.* She lowered the instrument to her side, examining his head. He'd be fine. She hadn't drawn blood. The door to her back shattered open, letting in the drenching rain, as two figures were illuminated in the passing lightning that followed the ravenous thunder.

Throwing a discarded cloak their way, Dorian relayed her orders. "Grab him up, boys. Hide his face as best you can in case there are any stragglers out. We don't want even the nightly drunks to catch wind of him missing." The men nodded and swiftly stepped into action. Dorian grabbed the sword's discarded sheath and slipped it into the tightened belt at her waist. *Might as well reclaim what is rightfully mine.* She looked up in time to see the men throw the black cloak over Victor's head, and she felt a small pang as they dragged him up to limp feet.

"Yes, Captain. Did he give you any trouble?" The man's thick Scottish accent muddled his words in a melody. "He may have to have his 'ead knocked on the door jamb as we leave." Seeing Dorian's disconcerting glare he added, "By accident, of course. The aristocrat." He was the taller and broader of the two. The Scottish man searched her face and then faintly smiled as her lips curled up as well.

Dorian moved towards them, reaching down to remove Victor's necktie. Her eyes did not leave the Scott. "No, Grim. Damage by doorjamb will not be necessary. Victor was a perfect gentleman," Dorian spoke, laughing up at the giant. The trio quickly held their breath's as they listened to the impending footsteps echoing from the upper hall. Dorian's face paled slightly. "Get him out of here."

"Aye!" Henry, the second man of similar but slightly smaller build than Grim, whispered enthusiastically.

"Aye, Cap'n," Grim whispered smiling down at the ruthless little woman before him. Dorian always did him proud.

Looking after her men, Dorian watched as they dragged the heir to the Duke and Duchess of Athencourt into the cold night. His limp body disappeared into the angered storm, as it showered them with its tears. Smiling mischievously, Dorian turned to instill her parting gift for Roberts. She removed the nail, hidden between the swell of her bosom, and pounded it into the door with the piece of cloth.

A sorrowful tune broke from her lips, beautiful within its depths of haunting.

"Aaaa Aaaaa Aaaaaaaaaaa Aaaaaaa Aaaa…. Come down, dear sailor, come down…

Aaaa Aaaaa Aaaaaaaaaaa Aaaaaaa Aaaa… Come down, dear soul, come down…

Aaaa Aaaaa Aaaaaaaaaaa Aaaaaaa Aaaa… Come down to the waters to play…" Dorian's voice hung in the air as it softly wove its way throughout the blacksmithing shop to stay, hiding deep within the dark stone crevices. The melody waited patiently for the men to come and find it.

Dorian smiled as she walked back towards the dock. No man could resist the Siren's Call once it had entered your mind and invaded your soul. It was only a matter of time until Roberts, and whomever he brought with him, came to play upon her sea.

Chapter

2

---◆---

FOR A WOMAN WHO RARELY FOUND TREPIDATION, Dorian was terrified. With eyes that could search the devil's soul and still come out unscathed, there was not much she feared. Standing at the bow of her ship, Dorian Lily gripped the railing and stared into the depths of the storm. She loved when the waters raged, and the clouds loomed dark overhead, spilling forth their fury, the ocean threatening to become her tomb. Throwing her head back, she inhaled deeply the smell of salt and anger as it flooded the water around her. The storm's vengeance would soon subside. It could never hold a grudge long against its daughters. The life Dorian had led so far had taught her to be brave and resource-ful, to look fear straight on and surpass it, to master it by her will. Nothing could have prepared her for the mist of a ghost that now hung about her ship.

Although, she thought, *my part is done.*

"Dorian?"

She felt Rowan approaching behind her. *I rejoice too quickly.* "Rowan?" Dorian turned to her. In Rowan's long stride, she elegantly made her way across the deck, coming to stand beside Dorian. The girl fidgeted nervously as her body rested against the ship's railing.

"Dorian, I," Rowan's voice was soft and un-assured. "I... well." She let out a heaving breath. "I can't... Could you?" an exasperated sigh left her lips. Rowan's willowy frame shook slightly. The length of her crimson red hair blew back with the wind's howl, portraying her angular jaw line. Rowan gripped the railing tight and turned to face Dorian. "Now that we are actually executing this plan into action, I need your help. I can't do the violence. You know that I can't, Dorian. You knew it before we even started the venture." Rowan paused. "Why did you even let me go through with it!?" There was hurt in her words. She was angry with herself for her own insecurity.

Dorian inwardly calmed herself before she answered Rowan's words. Releasing anger back upon her was no way to deal with the situation. "Yes, Rowan, I knew of your misgivings before we began, but I truly hoped you'd get past them." Green daggers burned their way towards Dorian's skin, trying to find a point of weakness as Rowan stared her down. "Do you not feel that you have cowered before the feelings and actions of others for too long? Bending to fit into their worlds instead of treading a path for your own?" Rowan seemed so helpless. *That's my Rowan, hates confrontation.* "I had hoped you would come around and find the inner strength that I know resides within you, Rowan."

Rowan stared blankly at Dorian, now scared to respond because she knew she was right. *Where have I gone?* Rowan asked herself.

"Rowan, you are hiding in plain sight, scared to see yourself and all the wonderful things that you are capable of," Dorian responded. "All on your own," she added. "You are scared to surprise yourself with your own abilities."

The tall reed could not help but laugh and break up the embedding fixations of her mind. "I so dislike when you do that," Rowan scolded Dorian, "but I am also grateful." She took Dorian's hand in her own. "Will you help me? Until I get the hang of things anyway."

A sly smile found Dorian's face as she lovingly looked on her sister. Small freckles dotted Rowan's fair cheeks. "Very well, what would you like me to do?"

"What I can't." The black of the clouds only accentuated the deep color of Rowan's fiery hair and the iridescent emerald of her eyes. Her sharp jaw was set tight as she awaited Dorian's answer. "I need you to be strong for me and... fierce. I need you to act as the cruel captain to the mangy, disgruntled slaves," Rowan added.

Dorian's irises swirled with the gray-black of the storm's swells. She was in her element of choice. She just stared forward barely acknowledging the girl next to her.

"I need you to do what you do best." Rowan added.

"Be the enforcer...." Dorian's eyes ran the length of Rowan. Worry seeped from every inch of Rowan's body. Her strong shoulders were rounded slightly in a protective stance. Rowan's straight arms were held tight with tension underneath the blue length of her shirt as she gripped the wood beneath her fingers. The wind sucked at her clothing, pulling it against her thin frame to trail it softly behind her. The belt secured around Rowan's hips told that she had a weapon of choice, a long, deadly sword that she rarely used. The sheath that held the weapon was still firm in its hold, for few battles had it taken part in. Rowan's tight black pants found their way into her brown boots, wet and aged.

"You have a strength within you that is all yours. No one can take it from you nor can anyone else defeat it. You just need to reawaken to it, Rowan. No one's journey is perfect. Strength and determination are the best things to build from weakness and defeat."

Rowan's eyes fluttered at Dorian's last statements. "I know." She spoke as innocently as a child. "Help me, Dorian, just until I get my bearings with this whole event. I have come too far.... I mean you are the Captain, but I need you to...."

Throughout Rowan's speech, Dorian could tell that her mind was jumping to varying scenarios. The girl had not decided on a clear course of action. Dorian would help her of course. "You need me to act the part thoroughly and as deviously as possible?" Dorian felt a slight lift of the weighted conflict that surrounded her friend. Rowan now knew she had an ally. She should have never doubted such things in the first place, but fear will make a person do think strange things. The plan Rowan had ignited was getting to be too devious for her to comprehend and she needed someone to lay out the pieces for her. She needed Dorian's guidance. The reality of what Rowan was undertaking was finally manifesting before her.

"Yes! I will be ready for more vengeance when I see his face." Rowan glared out to sea.

Dorian let out a small laugh. "I don't need you vengeful, jumping from one extreme emotion to the next. I need you focused and ready for whatever happens next, Rowan." Rowan couldn't help but smile. "Do not let your actions be clouded in judgment, whether it is good or bad. Allow yourself clear thinking and the unbiased answers that will come with it. Trust yourself, Rowan."

Rowan sighed. "I know, Dorian. I will be ready. I will be." Her voice faded to a whisper.

"Captain, your *mistress* awakes." The third lady of the ship sauntered up behind them, speaking with contempt about their captive, interrupting their conversation.

"Thank you, Rahn." Dorian couldn't yet tear her eyes from the sea. "Has he spoken yet?"

Rahn came to stand between them at the bow. Her long black hair was a straight contrast to Rowan's full bodied locks. She had secured it behind her in a thick braid. The porcelain finish of Rahn's skin contrasted with the skin of the other two women greatly, but the ivory smoothness only emphasized the violet hue in her eyes. Inwardly, Rahn debated placing a hand of support on Rowan's shoulder, but she felt Rowan would simply shrug it off.

"Sort of, my ladies," Rahn addressed them both. "The man has started to stir and mumble indescribable things. We all thought you had done him in, Dorian." A delighted smile began to cross Rahn's face. She so loved having the upper hand in any situation. "His head has quite the gash on it for 'not hitting him too hard', sister." Rahn had an arrogant smirk as she turned towards Dorian. Rahn's smile wavered as she met Dorian's eyes. "Did you see him, sister?" a tone of graveness entered her once casual voice, as the words barely slipped out of her clenched throat.

Dorian stared back and forth between both girls for a moment. She so loved hearing Rahn speak. The accent of her heritage was beautiful and clear. Dorian took note as the calmness that had entered Rowan's body now fled. Rowan inhaled slightly and held her breath for Dorian's answer. She was beautiful, Rowan had simply forgotten it. "No, I did not see him directly."

Rowan nodded her head exhaling, "I shall take over the helm." She spun on her heels, the wind tearing into her clothes.

"Rowan, there is no 'will be'. There is 'I am ready' or 'I am not'. It is time you decided where your destiny lies." Dorian did not need to look at Rowan to know that she silently nodded in answer to her. Rowan would decide. She would have to. Dorian did not allow room for indecision in matters such as these, and thus far, the captain had been more than lenient. Rowan's mind would not let her rest as her footsteps gently faded into the rain. Rahn met Dorian's face in anticipation of more.

"His presence was everywhere. The man was there, in the building some-where. The pair had been speaking before I entered. His smell swarmed me the second I placed a hand on the door." Dorian turned her face back towards the sea. Inhaling deeply, she closed her eyes. *And the smell of Victor now tortures my senses as well.*

"The timing could have been most inopportune." Rahn turned to stare up towards the helm at the fragile girl standing there. "We need him out in the open and in a place where he can't hide." Rowan had always been lean in her form, but because of the pressing weight of their current venture, Rahn noted, she had lost more of the little curves she had.

"Yes, we need him in *our* open." Dorian emphasized the word and affirmed her meaning by opening her eyes to the dark currents under foot. Giving her attention back to Rahn she examined the girl's essence.

Rahn was clad in her favorite attire. She liked to wear either incredibly bold or softly subdued colors always with an elaborate pattern running over the fabric somewhere. Rahn felt it was a tribute to her heritage and today was no exception. She wore dark teal pants with a matching Japanese style top that hung low over her hips. An intricate lotus flower curved around the front of her shirt to open fully at her back. As always, Rahn wore her belt low to sit over her curvy hips with her pistol and sword strapped at her sides. Her water logged boots came just underneath her knee.

"Will you be alright?" Dorian's voice was subtle but the question was sharply pointed.

Rahn's almond shaped eyes landed on Dorian's face, meeting her eyes. Black strands of her hair clung to her oval face. Her Japanese features made her exotic and terrifying. "I will manage." Rahn averted Dorian's stare out to the ocean's calming rage. "I have waited long for this day. Too many years have I sought him without hope of retribution. It would be a shame to waste the opportunity." Rahn's eyes darkened with her intent as she gazed back at Dorian. "Rowan still knows nothing?" Rahn's voice was strict in its accusation.

Dorian searched her face up and down. The emotions there ran deep under the surface. "She knows nothing. I have made sure of it." Both women turned back to stare at the helm. "It is not my story to tell, Rahn. But secrets… are a terrible thing to try and keep hidden." Dorian's last words wrapped around Rahn's heart and began to constrict it.

"Good. *We* shall keep it that way. Our secret, for now." Rahn turned inward as she focused back to the lulling storm. She began to breathe again. *It has been too long since I've seen you, even if it shall be to witness your downfall, I will not miss one moment of it. You owe me that at the very least. If I'm lucky, Rowan will outsource for your punishment, and I shall grab at the chance to bestow it upon you...*

Rahn felt Dorian's eyes upon her, so she bumbled to find words to fill the void. "I'm not even positive that we have found the true *he.* This man could simply share the same name as Roberts." Rahn lied and Dorian caught every word, every deception Rahn was feeding her. Deep down Rahn wanted the scents of sweet smelling flowers surrounding her and sunsets that gave hope for tomorrow. She wanted these things for everyone, but her hardened exterior would never let them in. Joy was a feeling Rahn had almost entirely lost, and this man, this Roberts, was at the root of her loss. In her mind, he had taken it all away from her, and with a fired vengeance, she wanted it back.

Dorian decided to play along with her. "Very true, my dear. We know nothing for certain. This man we seek to draw out, with our bait below deck, could very well be an imposter. The real Roberts, for all we know, could be long dead." At the mention of Roberts' death, Rahn shivered. Dorian slyly smiled at her reaction. *Nothing is for certain,* the captain thought. *But a true love cannot be stopped, not even by hate.* Dorian's anticipation was well hidden. A journey of adventure always enticed her, but one of reconciliation, whether it is good or bad, was fascinating to watch.

"Although," Dorian continued, "you must consider your feelings. You have felt a menace involving this venture since before it began, Rahn." Rahn nodded. She knew what Dorian was thinking. "You must remember that a vengeance sought is a lot of action put forth for a very little, and mainly unsatisfying, ending." Dorian watched as Rahn lapsed into her own world. She noticed as the girl closed her eyes and let the salt spray kiss her pale skin.

Rahn would consider Dorian's words.

What have I done, allowing all these forms of retaliation? They seem to bubble up at every surface... I may have opened a chasm I will later wish to have not fallen into. Looking back to sea, Dorian made a decision. *I will play my part with fire and see how it spreads.*

Dorian's mood had shifted towards this newest journey. She could feel the colliding of lives as they were coming together. All these lives came together at this point and time for a reason, and Dorian intended to let them explode to their full unrestricted potential. She was ready to embrace the change, come what may...for everyone.

• • •

Christian Roberts, of Nathan and Eva Roberts, was only happiest when he was vying for trouble with the ladies or when he was laboring away at something he loved, putting his whole heart forth. He co-owned "The Master's Blacksmiths" with his father, who in his old age still saw fit to ruffle Christian's feathers and push him to strive that much further towards his goals. Christian carried the height and stature of his best mates, Victor and Sebastian. In essence, that is how the three got paired together over the years. They could match each other stride for stride. Christian wore tanned skin from summer days of play. His sandy blonde locks had streaks of a dark red running through them while his deep green eyes could ensnare anything he so desired. His body profited from hard work as steeled muscles arched in every direction. A warming smile broadened the curve of his lips at the sight of his next obsession.

Christian's jeweled eyes sparkled as he hummed to himself and finalized his appearance. Looking himself up and down in the mirror, he spoke aloud. "Looking pretty good, if I do say so myself." He grinned at his reflection.

Just as Christian turned his head away from the mirror he caught a reflection out of the corner of his eye. He turned back to face the mirror and, in the evening's trick of shadows, his mind created a set of violet eyes staring back at him. The violet hue glowed out of the half darkened face of an exotic beauty. Memories flashed through his mind as he remembered a distant laugh, a dazzling smile.

"You always reminded me of spring. Skin so fresh, it was as if you were reborn every year." Christian's fingertips gently grazed the mirror's surface as the image faded. Another girl entered his mind, one he had let down in a catastrophic way. Her blood rested heavy in his hands, his heart. The loss was a burden he carried in every breath.

Christian shook himself from his darkened thoughts and searched his mind for his favorite tune, a sound that always brightened his mood. He whistled as he exited his bedchamber, smoothly closing the door behind him. He walked the paces down the hallway and made his descent of the stairs from the far right wing of the old brick building. By the time he had reached the final stairwell leading into the shop, his spirits had lifted.

Christian spoke with cheerful optimism. "Alright, Vic, I'm feeling pretty spritely. Wearing my signature black," fussing with his tie on the final decline of the stairs his eyes never rose to the empty room. Christian noticed some scuff marks encompassing the dirt ridden floor. "What the hell? Has that bastard left without me?" His stare echoed across the empty shop. The room was in slight disarray. The once inhabited stool was knocked over with a leg broken. Christian cautiously moved to the table. Blood had seeped into the untreated wood. He could still feel the warmth of it on his fingertips. It had been shed recently.

"Shit." Christian walked quickly across the smooth floor and flung open the door. A neck cloth whipped against his face as he did so. Chilled through, he examined the door. The necktie was pinned with a large nail made of steel embedded deeply within the wooden portal. At the head of the nail lay the crest of the doomed, a skull and cross. The nail said it all. He had been marked, and Victor had been taken as collateral to ensure that Christian would seek them out.

Finally, Christian thought. *My foes have caught up with me. But which ones?*

"Bullocks!" he yelled pounding his fist against the door. "Think, Christian, think!" He paced just inside the entrance of his shop, as rain began to beat the ground near his feet. "Sebastian! He is of able body and mind, not to mention he loves the adventure that calls to him from the sea. He will help." Christian donned his cloak and stepped onto the landing still shielded from the awning of his storefront. He turned. *Sebastian loves proof.* Christian placed a hard grip on the large nail in his door and yanked. The object did not budge. "The power of ten men must have pounded it in." He spoke annoyed. Tightly gripping the nail with both hands he tugged – nothing. "One more try..." he yanked, landing flat on his rump with the nail in tow. "Good lord, I pray that when I meet the one who marked my door with this curse, they are weakened by illness. For, I would not like to convene with them in their full strength." Christian scrambled to his feet and raced off into the night holding the ice cold steel in his hand.

• • •

Watching Victor sleep sent raw shivers of fear down Dorian's spine. Could he be the missing puzzle piece surrounding the tragedy of her life, oh, so long ago? Victor carried the scent of him unmistakably. No other human being had that intoxicating smell of pure man that affected her so. And the scent was so exact. Dorian hadn't smelled his scent in years. Nah, centuries. But now, Victor walked around with it on his skin. The scent played in her body, rushing heat through her water logged veins.

WHY!? Dorian grew angry with herself. *Who is this man? Who was he?*

Flitting between sleep and wakefulness, Victor sensed the moment another human was near him. His head ached and slowly he reached up to feel the sticky drying mess of blood in his hair. Inhaling, his nostrils were filled with the salt of a well worn hull. The smell was intoxicating to his every sense. Rolling to his back, Victor braced his body as he meekly opened his eyes. They came into focus on Dorian's black trousers. Victor noticed that the pants fit her as a second skin before they disappeared into knee-high, brown leather boots, soaked from being topside. His eyes traveled up to her vanishing waist line concealed by a long white tunic. Dorian's belt rested low on her hips, holding her weapons. Victor observed that the sword Christian had fashioned now hung in Dorian's sheath.

Have I reached heaven or am being sent to hell? Victor wondered.

"What do you want of me?" Victor's voice was dry and cracked. His gaze ran up her buttoned blouse revealing beneath it the confines of her corseted chest. He lingered over the pendant that lay in their small swells. Victor could feel Dorian's ominous demeanor in the stance she took over him. He wouldn't let her have the satisfaction of avoiding her eyes. He was no coward. Pulling his eyes away from her necklace, Victor shifted to stare at her face. Dorian's gold tendrils fell freely around her. She almost glowed in the dim light of the cabin.

You look like a sprite, my lady, a very deadly one at that. One that cannot be trusted.

Dorian smiled at his thoughts. "Want of you, my lord? Why, I want nothing of you, Victor." Calmly and smoothly, her voice glided across his skin. She took him in, sensing the change his energy took before she saw it transform physically. Victor's hand was pressing against his forehead to ward off the pain from the inflicted injury. He bent one leg to the ceiling. Victor's face slowly shifted from fear to anger as Dorian's words seeped through the mist filling his mind. His eyes opened wide to his surroundings.

Moonlight filled the cabin through the round portholes. The ocean was rocking soothingly after the storm's wake. Wood rose from the floors in a dark, honey-gold finish, surrounding them on all sides. Victor lay upon a plush bed, taking it all in. Although smaller in size, and save for the prison bars bordering one wall, the room had the appeal of a captain's quarters.

Watching him observe his room, Dorian felt a growing despise for Victor. *How could someone like you carry the scent of him?* Death had come back to vex her in another human form. *You are not half the man, nor anywhere near the formidable opponent he was. You are too disgraceful to carry his mark.*

Victor's scent carried an all too familiar calling card that Dorian had long thought gone. Centuries ago, she assumed the mark that Victor now carried had been laid to rest in peace. Either someone was playing her, or unfinished business was knocking at her door.

Seeking out Dorian's face once more, Victor's pulse quickened. "You want nothing?" He rose to sit up on the bed. "You *want* nothing!" Victor was on his feet. Before Dorian could react he pinned her to the bars of his cell, crushing his body against her. Shock registered on her face, before Dorian masked it with a glare of ice. She did not fear him, even though he held her throat in his hand. "You have beaten me! You have taken me from my land and home, you have kidnapped me! And you have the audacity to say you want nothing of me!?" The heat of Victor's anger radiated off his body like ignited fire to flame. *How dare she!* "I do not believe it! Why go through the trouble of taking me if you wanted nothing from me?"

Closing her eyes briefly, Dorian inhaled his rage and found solace within it.

Fine. If this is how you wish to play the game, Victor, I will oblige your actions.

"I'll ask you," the words slipped from Dorian's clenched throat, "only once to release me. No more." Dorian's jaw tightened as her eyes opened upon him. "You would be smart to do as I ask."

"Ask? Ask!? You do not know the meaning of the word! All you know is orders and demands. You take." Victor's pulse beat rapidly, palpating the stifling air. The slate color of Dorian's eyes abruptly consumed him. Victor couldn't think within their gaze. He had to look away.

The little wench did not falter beneath my gaze as the many that have come before her, and most of them were men! I have challenged the bravest among them, and they have faltered, but not her! Not this tiny little woman whose life is at my disposal.

Dorian's passive attitude only fueled Victor's oncoming madness. He tightened his grip around her neck and came down to whisper in her ear. "Why should I release you, lady, when I could kill you right now and rid myself of this place?" Victor felt a sharp pang against his chest. Cold steel cut into his exposed skin and wound its way up to the left side of his jugular, digging in. He let up his grip on the leech's neck. In turn, Dorian brought her lips close to his left ear, a warm sweet breath against his cheek.

"You would never make it off my ship alive, Victor, if your threats were sincere and your actions carried out. If you did succeed in killing me, which is highly unlikely, my men have skills the likes of which your small mind has never seen nor could ever comprehend. And the ladies aboard this vessel have gifts you can't match. Gifts no human can fight." Dorian smiled as she felt the shiver run through Victor's spine.

"No human?" Victor's face creased at her side. Dastardly visions raced through his mind. *What are you?*

Dorian's breath was still warm on his skin as she spoke. "You are at my disposal. In truth, we do not need you alive to carry out our plan, but, in theory, your rescuers will want to see that you still live." Her voice never wavered nor did it harden. Dorian spoke very matter-of-factly. "You are simply a minuscule piece in a very large game, utterly expendable."

Victor felt as if he was no longer in his body and that another source was leaking into his mind and streaming through his memories. Dorian's body grew stiff as he grabbed onto the bar just by her head for support. "Stop what you are doing." Victor demanded short winded.

The storm in her eyes questioned him. "What is it that I am doing, Victor?"

Dorian asked.

"You are... I'm not entirely sure what you are doing, but stop rifling through my mind, for it feels like you are."

Interesting, Dorian thought. *He can feel me. Humans usually can't, but there is always an exception to every rule, isn't there? Hhmmm...* Turning the blade of her knife into Victor's neck, he finally released all holds he had on her, but he did not make the step back in distance Dorian would have liked. As her eyes cut into his soul, she saw the glimmer of a supernatural life. *So, you aren't human after all... how amusing.*

"Next time you seek revenge, sire, heed this." Dorian pointed the knife directly into his throat walking him backwards until his legs bumped the bed, and Victor fell to sit back upon it. Dorian bent toward Victor so she was close to his face, capturing his eyes. "Do not disturb the water, sir. You will not want to know what lies beneath." Her eyes turned as black as the deepest crevices of the sea. Victor could almost swear her teeth had even taken on a sharper glint. "Do you understand me, my liege, or do you have need for me to make my meaning more clear?" Dorian was bold in her approach to him, too bold.

Victor could feel the trickle of blood that now ran down his neck to the dip of his collar bone. Tilting his head slightly to look up at the imp who now held all his cards, he steadily nodded in accordance.

"Good." Dorian's eyes scanned him, breathing him in. As she bent towards his neck, all of Victor's muscles froze. She ran her tongue directly over the cut she had given him in warning. Dorian heard the release of his breath as she moved away.

As Dorian backed away, Victor quickly grasped a hand to his neck, protecting it. He felt the last remnants of his injury before they simply faded away. *What magic is this? Can this woman heal the body and control the mind?* He wondered. Regaining his senses, Victor stopped her exit. "May I ask my captor's name?" Victor steadily and harshly intoned his voice for effect and to show he had not let her beat him just yet. The woman before him utterly infuriated him. Yet the very essence of her, this Dorian, intrigued every inch of his body, mind, and soul. *Who is she? What is she?* He kept asking himself. Victor watched as she twisted her torso to face him at the cells entrance. He could now see where it was that she hid her dagger. *Saucy little minx.* Unconsciously, Victor reached up to dab at the blood flowing from his neck. The blood's flow had stopped, and all he felt was skin, not even a mark where he had been cut, no raised scar upon his skin.

As Dorian watched him she answered one of his silent questions. "Victor, do yourself some good and remember that I can give life, as easily as I can take it away." Her stare bore into him, immobilizing every thought as fear crept into Victor's core. "Once I've taken your last breath, I won't give it back."

"Your name!" Victor demanded with hoarse words.

Dorian smiled, "Indignant little fellow, aren't you?" Her eyes unsettled him. "You really must pay better attention." Dorian's eyes twinkled at him with her charming smile. "My name is Dorian Lily, and I am Captain of this ship. Welcome aboard." She was gone in an instant with an unparalleled grace.

"Well," Victor sauntered towards the bars and stared after her, reclaiming some of his lost strength. "That at least explains why your skin has been so kissed by the sun, my lady." A smile built on his lips. "Remarkable." Her lips reminded him of a mouth he had long ago kissed and a body he had once wanted to hold forever. "Dorian…. The name suits you." He spoke aloud to himself. "I will soon find out what that plump bottom lip of yours tastes like, even if I do kill you afterwards, Captain." Victor saluted her. He began pacing his cell, not out of anxiety, but out of astonishment that a woman would be brazen enough to hurt him, to make *him* bleed. "She will pay for the embarrassment. Yes, yes. You will pay greatly, Captain Dorian Lily, whenever it is that I can get my hands on you." Victor stared at his reflection in the mirror hanging from the wall. His body tensed as he registered the emotion of shock across his face. The realization set in that he was shocked at how quickly, and easily, this woman had gotten beneath his skin and built settlement. Her voice was echoing inside his head, as the visual of Dorian's smile replayed on a loop through his brain.

"You are a virus, Captain…. And I will not rest until you have been extinguished." Victor stared at his face, he didn't recognize himself anymore.

Dorian's face flashed against Victor's memory. A debilitating pain followed and he gripped his temples for fear that his head would explode. Visions he did not recognize raced through his mind's eye. Victor watched as another person's life passed before him. A life of wealth, happiness, and adventure…. It almost felt as if it were meant for him.

The sideboards of the ship disappeared along with the portholes as they melted into the ocean's lapping waves. An apparition of a young girl with flowing blonde locks, a heart shaped face, and clear gray eyes ran in front of him along a sandy shore line calling, "Victor." Her torso turned towards him, as her left arm trailed behind, floating on the gentle breeze, bidding him, with her thin fingers, to follow her. The garments she wore pulled tight against her form as the gentle winds blew them behind her. She smiled brightly and then faded softly into the waves, his goddess gone. Her voice was a sweet melodic memory.

A man came to stand beside Victor, transparent, but lean and strong. He, too, looked after the girl. Victor looked forward to search for her, and, there she was, standing, facing them both, a bright smile lit her every inch of being. Victor looked over to the man who was staring at him now and jumped as the man walked right towards him. It felt as though the man entered his very core, fitting perfectly into his body. Victor gripped his heart, as he turned back to the girl. The sun was setting and its rays cast reflective light against her skin. She glowed under its praise. The man inside of him called out. Victor felt, in every inch of his body, the love and adoration that this man felt for the woman standing in the distance. It ripped through him. Victor's body burned with the other man's heartache. An all consuming anguish filled him. This man, he knew, had lost his love. He would never hold her again.

The man inside urged Victor's physical body forward, Chase the girl, *he said.* Find her. Bring her back to me. Bring her back to us. *Victor moved, no longer in control. He rushed forward to grasp the girl before she disappeared, once again.*

The pain of his shins running into the bed's frame brought Victor back to reality. He rubbed his hands over his face and mulled over the illusion he had just taken part in. *Why was I shown this?* Pain surged through him once more. He felt as if his brain was being ripped in two. Then, again, came the voice of the man from the beach. Victor's head shot up, and his eyes sought the reflection of his face through the port's window. "This ship will be the death of me," he declared. Through his reflection, Victor found half his face and half the face of a stranger staring back at him.

• • •

Rahn paced the fore deck, wind lashing through her robes as Dorian and Rowan approached her. She yelled at them in a fury.

"How are you so sure that Christian will come for him!?" Rahn demanded. Her ebony hair blew straight in the high winds as she lengthened her stride. The violet of her eyes was damning to those who came close to her at this moment. Her small pert mouth was turned into a thin line of outrage. "If he doesn't come we are stuck with a snobby, know-it-all, rich boy who doesn't know the right end of a stick." Rahn threw her hands up towards the heavens, "Please, Lord, let me be the one to push him off the plank!"

"Rahn," Dorian had her full attention. "Pull yourself together. Now." Dorian's glacial eyes zeroed in on her and she shrank in size. Rahn stared at the shock on Rowan's face as the two women's energies swam around her.

"What are you not telling me?" Rowan's voice sounded small to their ears. "I have a right to know what is going on with this journey! What is going on between the two of you?"

Rahn could hear Dorian's voice inside her head guiding her towards strength and composure. *Tell her or don't, but pull yourself together.* Dorian instructed Rahn.

"You won't push my brother off the plank!" Rowan puffed up in her stance. "I'll be the only one having that honor. I'll be the only one to give those orders. This is my plan, not either of yours."

Rahn's face twisted with disgust. Rowan's shoulders caved around her. "You...." Rahn extended a hand towards her bringing a foot forward with her stance, rage rolling off her body.

"Rahn," Dorian tried to caution her.

Rahn merely pushed past the captain's warning. "You, who planned out every detail, every meticulous little for-instance, every tiny thing that could go wrong... You, Rowan, who spent years planning revenge upon a man who left you for dead!" Rahn got right up in Rowan's face, glaring into her emerald eyes. "And now that your final plan is being executed, you have Dorian and me pulling all the weight!? But, yet, you say nothing goes down without your go-ahead!? Do you not see the idiocy in this plan?" Rahn was fuming. "Foolish wench," she spoke under her breath as she moved away.

Dorian could simply watch. Rahn's irrationality was at its shining moment. The war within her was building, the two sides tearing her apart. Unfortunately for Rowan, she got the receiving end of Rahn's force. Rahn's anger had nothing to do with either of the women around her, and everything to do with a conflicted past of unresolved darkness she had no way of coping with.

Tears streamed down Rowan's face. She knew in her heart what she really wanted, but how could Rahn understand that? Rowan despised conflict, or simply hid from it out of fear and self protection. She longed to use her words. The words Dorian was still encouraging her to find. Rowan used to use her weapon only in dire moments of self-defense. She used to often, desperately, think of a life past pirating. Yet, she didn't anymore. Dorian's way of life had become what she knew. Pirating was in her blood now, by conscious choice. Rowan was still becoming one with the strength within her, and it grew stronger every day. She still wanted everyone, and everything, to get along and for all to be right in the world. A farfetched hope, but hope nonetheless. Yet, as she matured and grew with greater knowledge of the lineage she was a part of, Rowan wanted what was right for her, and she allowed the needs of others to drift away, while her needs bubbled to the surface. Rowan wanted a life of completeness with the Siren within her, and she was going to get it.

Rowan threw her head back and screamed her frustration to the only one who would truly hear her, the sea beneath her feet. A gale came up, bringing with it the sea's vengeance, knocking Rahn on her back, drenching her through to the bone.

"This is why I have you two sisters! You will help me through the hardest parts as I have helped you. Do you not remember, Rahn!? I ask that you be on my side! That you help me with no hidden agenda for your own advancement! He will come! Of this I am sure. Yes, I was hasty in stating that this is my venture alone. It is not, and I do ask for your guidance, but not your demands." Rowan bore into Rahn's eyes as she still lay on deck, her cheeks rising in color. "I will have my revenge when I see the bastard's face, at that moment when I steal his last breath of air! But until then, leave me be. Let me do this my way." Rowan spun on her heel and stormed off to her quarters.

Rahn's face was slack and her jaw hung agape in astonishment. Never had Rowan had such an outburst.

The captain simply whole heartedly laughed down at the soaked passenger. "You utterly deserved that." Dorian reached down to offer Rahn her hand. "That was a long time coming. You two fight like night and day, rarely agreeing on anything. She was bound to one day snap and score a point at your own game, Rahn." Dorian hauled Rahn to her feet and rested an arm against her to steady her sister's shivering body.

Rahn's blurry eyes finally came into slight focus upon Dorian. "You didn't do anything to stop her." She spat water out of her mouth. "What about all that kinship bullshit? We need to stay on each other's side etc, etc."

Dorian's eyes sparkled with mirth and she laughed. "Like I said, you had that one coming. We are Sirens. We are our own brand of ruthless. Our nasty, mischievous, spritely side must come out from time to time…." Rahn laughed, she knew Dorian was right. They could never mask who or what they were. "Be easy on the girl. She will do what needs to be done by her, my Water Lily. This is not our fight, remember?"

Rahn eased into Dorian's embrace and she wrapped her arms further around her. "You're right. Killing him is truly the farthest thing from my mind. I hope she decides against it." Rahn paused for a moment, her eyes settling on the rocking waves. "Yet, I don't."

"Is this the root of your rage, your own indecision?" Rahn reluctantly nodded as she eased further into Dorian's hold. Rahn knew that Dorian, as captain, was always thinking in a much grander picture than anyone else. Her view was not blocked by insignificant boulders and reefs.... She had to see past them. Rahn knew that Dorian had no other choice than to see life this way, for many lives were held liable by the captain's actions upon every vessel.

Dorian looked out over her ship. The sun was high, illuminating the world for a new day. The storm had settled late into the night making way for clear waters. She respected the crew, the men below who would die for her. All of the men were busying themselves upon the deck, making repairs, sharpening blades, keeping a watchful eye on the horizon. She admired her ship and how effortless it was to keep afloat and the crew upon it happy. The dark mahogany of the wood had all eyes drawn to it when its ivory sails were flying high in the wind. Or it could have been the woman carved at the bow? Her arms opened to the ocean while her breasts fell free, her hair blew in the wind, her hips wrapped in cover twining her legs. The lady of the ship, mandate of safe passage, broke first the waves of each journey.

"Rowan is of as strong a will as you or I." Dorian smiled up at the girl in her arms. "She is as stubborn as you or I and she will reach her own conclusion, no matter how painful the journey ahead of her may be. You should know better than any how much we like to make our own mistakes rather than learn from those of others."

Rahn hugged tight Dorian's waist. "Save for you. You are the ultimate observer, Dorian. Always at ease, never hasty, and always with a back-up plan or exit strategy if need be."

"Aaah, 'tis nothing more than my longer years of trial and error to which I owe my patience, skill, and keen observations before action."

"I wish I had your countenance of serenity."

Dorian looked back over her men, admiring each and every one of them. "Practice, my dear, and an actual desire for change will bring forth a more perma- nent calm." Rahn watched the side of her captain's face as Dorian's stare became distant. "When are you going to tell her?" Dorian paused, "Rowan has a right to know where your hostility is coming from regarding our soon-to-be acquired, revenge candidate."

Rahn laughed. "Well chosen, sister." A tired sigh escaped her. "I suppose I will have to tell her soon enough." She brought her hand along Dorian's face. "Water Lily," Rahn paused, thoughtfully contemplating the English translation of her name. "It has been a long time since anyone has called me that out of affec- tion." She laughed. "It is time for me to fully reclaim the name and stop hiding from my past."

"As you will, my dear, make peace with our sister. She needs *our* support." Dorian searched the tall Asian's eyes, a moment passing between them.

"Yes, I will go speak with her." Rahn turned to leave, but couldn't. "Just give me some time to collect myself," her violet eyes met Dorian's, and the captain nodded. "Good," Rahn shook her head before walking away.

Rahn walked up to the ship's bow and knelt down to pass a hand over their guardian. *If Rowan can play with the sea's winds, then my next trick will be to send forth its creatures.* A smile crossed her face, lighting her features. She so loved the hunt, and she could smell it on the winds. Rahn sought the horizon. Their destiny was on its way.

• • •

"Are you alright?" Dorian saw Rowan nearly jump through her skin. She stood close behind her as Rowan steered the helm.

"I hate when you do that. You're too damn quiet." Rowan let a large sigh find its way down her body, releasing the tension of her muscles. "I'm fine. I actually feel exhilarated. I took a stand and survived!" She burst out laughing. "Rahn's temper is so intimidating. She only wants you to see her way. There is no middle ground with her." Staring straight to the horizon's edge, Rowan regained her composure. "I know what I want to come of this. I've told Rahn and now I will tell you."

"I am all ears, Rowan." Dorian came to stand beside her, looking straight to the horizon line as Rowan did.

"I want him scared, but not dead. If he does turn out to be the bastard I intend to find, then I want him shaking. Although, I have no idea what to expect. I have in my mind a perfect scenario, but we both know dreams and reality are not quite the same thing. I will know when I see him whether I still want his head on a platter, metaphorically speaking, or if our broken bond is worth mending. I will follow my emotions from here, listen to the feeling." Rowan glanced at the side of her companion's face. "Tell me something…." Dorian arched an eyebrow her way. "Why is Rahn acting this way? Is he of some importance to her?"

Dorian's face creased with confusion. *The two of you have talked, yet Rahn still skirted the most pressing issue…interesting.* Dorian stored the knowledge for later. Rowan was still completely in the dark, and the captain couldn't comprehend why. Rahn would not reveal the truth to Rowan.

Dorian had to navigate her words carefully. *It is not my tale to tell.* "We both know how Rahn can be when it has been too long between lovers. She is irritable and quick to anger." She winked at Rowan, "...too many skeletons in her bed. Do not worry. You did well, Rowan. Standing up for yourself adds an ethereal glow to your skin. Don't let go of your confidence because someone else's convictions are banging on your door." She turned to leave her.

"Where are you going?"

"To check on our guest, he is most intriguing." Dorian began her descent of the stairs.

"Dorian, be careful with that one." Rowan turned back to stare at her, her eyes wide, evading emotional distress. "He smells just like...."

"Don't!" Dorian cut her off quickly. "Don't say his name. This I must figure out on my own." Thundering down the stairs, she headed straight for the entrance to the hull.

Rowan surveyed the ship, landing on Rahn's stare from the bow. The women nodded at each other and shared a breathless truce. The swords had been dropped for now.

• • •

Victor was restless. *Why have I been kidnapped if not for ransom? Because of my money and title? What does she mean she wants nothing of me!?* He stared out over the ocean's lull. The figure of the girl from his vision drifted past him. This ship was making him mad.

Walking the distance to the end of the hall, Dorian slowed her step. She cautiously peered into the cell on her left, having her body slowly follow her eyes. Victor's back was to her. She could feel the assault of his mind, as he was lost to his own world of turmoil. "Scouring for your rescue vessel, my lord?"

Her voice had startled Victor's thoughts as he leaned against the porthole, staring pointedly at the dark waters, but truly seeing nothing. The incoming sun gleamed off his muscled shoulder blades. His blue eyes jumped as he heard her words. Victor hadn't heard her approach. His eyes lingered on the water, then, he gradually turned his torso to face her, assessing her appearance. She wore a corset-fashioned white top that left little of her curves to the imagination. A long black skirt hiked up high on her right thigh revealed muscular tanned legs that melded with her knee high black leather boots.

Why did she always appear to be glowing? Victor wanted to reach out and caress her bare shoulders as they shimmered in front of him, but the thought made him physically shudder, it wasn't his.

"So now that you have me prisoner aboard this ship...." He still hadn't met her eyes, the heat of his blue gaze raked across Dorian's body. "Your ship," Victor spoke with breathy words, finally meeting her moonlit gaze. "What do you intend to do with me, lady? I appear to be of no real importance to you, so I am very curious as to my proper role in your game."

Dorian ran her hand lightly against the cell's bars as she stalked their length, back and forth in front of him. "Hhmmm.... That is a very amicable question, milord. What to do with you indeed...." She stopped parallel to him bringing a delicate hand to her mouth and tapped her fingers against her chin.

This woman was completely toying with him, she was testing him, and Victor was allowing it. He was succumbing to weakness as it entered into his system. His usual resolve of stone was breaking. Dorian was edging her way in. Victor hated himself because of his own lack of will. It was dissipating before his very eyes. His self-control was leaving him. No matter the dire situations he had been placed in previously, Victor never cracked. He always kept his head level and stayed on guard. Yet, this woman was breaking him. He couldn't understand why. Victor did not recognize the feelings within him. Nor did he understand them. The loss of power was utterly foreign to him.

"Your head does hold a high reward, but I fear my intentions are debts held closer to the heart." Her eyes taunted him, pulling him out further from his stone walls.

How could her eyes be such calm serene silver pools one moment, and then black cavernous depths the next? Victor wondered. The liquid of her eyes was luring him in. He fought back the horror of drowning in them.

Disconcerted, Victor was standing against the bars, his body trying to push its way through to the other side, to her. The man inside called to him, but he ignored his pleas. Dorian captivated Victor's eyes. Her voice spoke sweetly in his head, controlling his movements. Victor's mouth went dry, as he tried to fight her inward intrusion. "What do you speak of, wench?" The words finally escaped, hoarse and brittle from his mouth.

Dorian's expression acknowledged him blandly. She appeared bored. "You are a strong one, aren't you? There's something you've been hiding for a long time." She gently touched his face, her eyes unfocused. "A secret."

"What?" Victor pushed against the bars, backing away from her across the room. He wanted nothing more than distance from this fiend. Dorian's hand still reached out for his face with a curl of her fingers that he recognized. "What are you, witch!?" Victor couldn't breathe.

This creature of a woman crawled beneath his skin. *Could she not also see inside my mind? What if she found the other man lurking there!?*

Dorian laughed at him. "You shall soon have all your questions answered. But, the real inquiry is, will you be the answer to all of mine?" Dorian lightly gripped the bars for support. This man hid something deep within him she would need time to draw out. Victor was not aware of what he was, or what he held within him. Her face creased as she looked beyond him. "Ah, I see you shall know one answer sooner than I thought."

Chapter

3

———◆———

HOW COULD I HAVE NOT KNOWN, how could I have not sensed them!?
Christian raked through his memory for any sign of his opponents coming for
him. He could find none.

Drenched from the storm, Christian slowed his pace as he approached the
Caven's residence. *Pull yourself together. Don't bring attention,* he thought. He
quickly walked through the imposing oak double doors, pausing on the landing
to allow the attendant to take his drenched coat. He searched the faces below.
Pinpointing his friend's location, he descended the stairs. People waltzed around
him, dazzling in the ornately-carved, gold-encrusted hall. His image bounced
back to him from every mirror, mocking his movements.

"Lord Roberts," a drunken debutante flung her body against him, crashing
into the dancing couple behind them.

"Sorry, my lord," Christian turned to apologize to the couple, "…and, my lady."
He righted the girl who had landed in his arms. The debutante clung to him for
support as her body felt the spin of alcohol.

Christian was slightly appalled as he grasped the girl. Her body was slack and
waving in its place limp as a rag-doll. But then he remembered himself, his past.
He was in no position to judge, however, he was in no mood for the situation.

"I believe you owe me a dance, Lord Roberts, Christian." She pointed a
drunken finger in his general direction.

"Yes. Right. You look…peaked this evening, Daphne." Christian looked
over the bumbling girl. She would quickly forget his absence. "I'll be right back,

Daphne. May I get you some more wine?"

"Oh yes, please. Do make a haste-full return." Daphne giggled mindlessly behind him as he made his way back into the crowd.

"Seb. Seb!" Christian tried to keep his voice level but he knew he didn't have much time. He spoke to his friend's back as Sebastian talked with some mates from school.

"Oh, Christian. Sorry mate, you know...." Sebastian started to gesture towards the other men, but was quickly cut off.

"Yes, yes, I know everyone. Hello. How are you?" He grabbed Sebastian's arm and dragged him away from the group. "I need to talk to you."

"Alright, alright!" Sebastian turned back to the group and apologized. "What is of such big importan..." Christian thrust the nail against his chest stopping his speech. "Oh. Ooh. Where did you get this?" He scrutinized Christian's face.

"It was nailed to my door. Victor's gone. Taken by force, I am sure. There was fresh blood on the table." Christian was trying to remain calm, but within his eyes lurked a grave anxiety. In a very cut and quick manor, he relayed the information of the night.

"Can never leave that boy alone for a second, can we, without trouble finding him.... So, you have no idea who these assailants are, or who they could be?" Christian shrugged. "I see. Why have they pinpointed Victor?" Anger began to boil up in Sebastian's throat. *Who would be so stupid?* "Do you think this has anything to do with Victor specifically, or he was just the pawn? Right place, right time?"

Christian thought hard. "Yes, I think he was in the right place, but at the wrong time. If Victor had been the target, this," he pointed towards the nail Sebastian held, "would not have been laid in my door. When I stopped pirating I burnt no bridge and have since kept up with all my contacts, just in case." *Just in case I wanted to re-enter that world.* "I could contact a few people and see who could have done this, but it would take too much time. I do not know who holds this vendetta. I left that world on good terms, and those I left with a bad taste in their mouth I made certain would never find me."

"I see." Sebastian examined his friend. "Everyone?" Christian's eyes were intent on Sebastian's, and his nod was brief. "You had more in you than I've ever seen. Hhmmm..." Sebastian studied the nail once more. Christian was too panicked to be offended by his friend's jab. "Can't leave Victor alone for a bloody minute," Sebastian said again, feeling the nail in his hand, assessing the droop of his body that corresponded with the weight of the mark. "Why would these adversaries have taken Victor?" A warning chilled his voice.

"Collateral. These people need to know I'll come after them, and they must have known taking Victor would do it." Christian shouted in exasperation. "We can't leave him in their hands, whoever they are."

"What about Victor's enemies, Chris? Surely he has acquired plenty of those throughout the years." Sebastian's eyes mocked him. "What if this is not all about vengeance towards you? What if Victor burned some bridges of his own?"

Christian thought about it. Sebastian had a valid theory. "No. Like I said before, if Victor had been the intended target the mark would have been left at his residence, not mine. You are doing well, thinking beyond the box, but this is a threat against me, not Victor." He paced slightly in the darkened corner. "I just don't know the *who* in this equation."

"You are certain of this?" Sarcasm oozed from Sebastian's body. Christian gave him a look you would dole out when dealing with a petulant child. "Right. I am sorry to doubt your knowledge." Sebastian's tone became zealous. "I am so envious of the life you used to lead and its freedom."

"You forget about the damnation that follows such actions of freedom," Christian added. "You are labeled an outlaw by everyone who once knew you, and all those who will learn of your name in the future. It alters your entire world. An alteration you can never come back from." Christian stopped with Sebastian's full attention egging him on for more. "I loved every second of my first life, but my second life is none too shabby. Less adventure, save for now. The transition from one to the other was confounding until I found my rhythm."

"But you have come back from such an alteration.... Far better than most," Sebastian butted in.

"I had no choice, Seb. I had to redeem myself, for my sister's memory alone. Having new roots in a foreign land where the name *Roberts* does not come with a black flag, and the promise of a hangman's noose, made the transition all the more easy. My father's good-name helped me rebuild what I feared had been lost," Christian paused as his friend waited for more. "My second chance at redemption, Seb, without my family I could have never done it."

"I see, the eternal ghost..." Sebastian could not speak her name. For this ghost was the reason Christian suffered so.

Christian nodded, fully understanding his friend's implication. "There's something else...." His eyes wavered as he looked at Sebastian.

Excitement blazed through Sebastian's eyes. "What?"

"The song," Christian's words lay heavy in the air.

"The song.... What song?" Sebastian's head came closer so he could hear

Christian's whisper.

"The Song of the Siren…. It lingers still in the shop." Christian looked at his friend's face and the utter confusion almost made him laugh out loud. "What the women of the sea would want with me, I have no idea. It played in my ears the entire way here. It still lingers in my brain, soft and sorrowful in its beauty." Christian's eyes glazed over as the voice consumed him.

Sebastian placed a hand on Christian's shoulder and shook him out of his trance. "The Sirens have taken Victor you think?" He paused long in thought. "I have heard that song, but only once in my life. Sorrowfully beautiful, it ensnares your every sense. It holds you captive to its will. It is their weapon, their drug that infects your being, wrapping it's talons around your heart." He spoke in nearly a dream like state, mostly to himself.

Christian openly gawked at his friend, throwing Sebastian back a step. "If you think the song is the only gift the Sirens have, you are more naïve than I could have ever thought."

Sebastian waved him off. Christian was being irrational because of the whispers in his mind. Sebastian knew. He had been ensnared once himself. "Thank you, friend. Consider me warned. So what do we know?" Sebastian began counting a list on his fingers. "They do not seek Victor. He is merely a pawn of some sort to them, most likely of little importance." He laughed. "Ole Vic will be furious once he figures that one out, being the self-important man that he is." The male companions shared a soft chuckle at their captured friend's expense. "But," Sebastian continued, "What they do seek is your blood on their waters. How are we doing so far?"

Christian laughed. "Yes, mate. You are putting it all together nicely. But, damnit! I did a damn good job of making sure no one would ever find me. I disappeared after I quit, faded into the shadows. You, of all people, should know you always eradicate the most lethal target first. I believed all of my foes to be vanquished, years ago. How did they do it, these women?"

That stopped Sebastian's brain full on. "You mean to say that you have killed all your rivals!?"

"Or had someone else do it for me, yes." Christian was all business now.

Sebastian stared at him wide-eyed. "Masterful, if it's true. Let's think of it in another way," Sebastian paused, lost within his thoughts. "You have vanquished your foes, but, perhaps you forgot about the women in your passage of broken hearts. Could one of them have been a Siren?"

Christian froze at the thought. Sirens were the rumored terrors of the sea.

Few men saw them and lived to tell the tale, as the stories go. Sebastian survived only because of his age. He was too innocent to slaughter at the time he heard the song of seduction, as his story went, but he never actually saw a Siren with his own eyes.

"Sirens are women of myth and legend. The only place their stories lay is in that of fables." Christian would not meet his friend's eyes. *The song was real...* He had been a sailor long enough to know that, upon the sea, nothing was certain and anything could happen. He was scared to share the water's secrets with his friend for he held far too many of them.

Sebastian held a hand up so Christian couldn't speak anymore. "I am putting this all in line for us. Sshhh." He paused, almost brooding. "Did you not just imply that these Sirens are of dastardly prowess? After such a statement, from your lips I might add, you doubt that they are capable of finding you, that anyone is capable of finding you? You need to get your story straight. I know there is a certain brand of women, that exists, that merits being labeled a Siren, but I also know that these women are no less real than you or me. I know that they do not possess gifts beyond that of our physical beings, they are human, Christian. Yet, you seem to imply that there are women in our world that have magic..."

"Do you believe what you are saying, Seb?"

Sebastian nodded. "To openly admit to magic is to allow its force to consume you."

Christian thought hard about this. "But, you do believe, don't you?"

Sebastian's stare was penetrating. "I do," the words were barely a whisper.

"It is a dark memory that keeps you from wanting to believe, but the song still lingers in your consciousness daring you not to."

Sebastian shook his body, reliving the past as it was now becoming his present.

Christian nodded. He would not press the subject of Sebastian's past any further. "As sailors, we know a greater world is just outside our reach, but to acknowledge it means to admit that there is more than human life outside of our mere realm of being." Christian looked his friend square in the eye. "You are a sailor, Sebastian. You know that the sea holds many a mystery, and that magic is not as farfetched as it may appear."

"You are frightening me, Christian." Sebastian spoke with a smile. "I fear you are going to ask me to venture into a tale of myth..."

Christian nodded. "I have a plan, but I need you to help carry it out." Sebastian raised his arms in protest and slightly backed away. Playing up Sebastian's love of the sea and naval training skills, Christian continued. "I'm good, but I've been out of the game for a while. I need your nautical capabilities, Seb, and your ship."

Sebastian just stared at him. His heart raced with adrenaline at the mere thought of voyaging on his beloved sea. And the promise of a battle made the deal all the more enticing. He was going to hold out until Christian was begging. Inwardly, Sebastian had already agreed to help far before he had been asked. To be a good sailor you had to be a smart gambling man.

Sebastian thought of his past. *I would love to see one of them...* He looked at Christian, pacing beside him. It had always been easier to forget his past and say he didn't believe in such things. But, any good sailor knew, you spoke about the reality of myth in the company of fellow believers. The Queen's Navy had never believed, so Sebastian had conformed.

"Damnit! I need your help if we want Victor back alive and not chopped up for shark bait." Christian was desperate. He wouldn't be held responsible for another death especially if it came through piracy. That's why he had gotten out. He'd lost too much to be redeemable.

"Easy, mate. We both need to calm down." Seeing the onlookers, Sebastian calmed his friend. "Both our voices have become too high for the ears that are longing to hear them, our excitement is showing." Sebastian looked into Christian's eyes and they both had a mutual feeling of deep unsettling fear. Sebastian laughed, dissipating the moment. "It is not the first time I have heard your words spoken to me. Many a woman has wanted to use me for my abilities, and ship..." His eyes gleamed. "Are we truly going after the Sirens then!?" Sebastian had the exuberance of a school boy.

"Sirens do not exist. However, pirates do, and that is who we are looking for. Pirates are nasty, treacherous, vile people. They have no scruples and will kill as they see fit. No second guessing. They make split decisions and don't think twice. We need to get to Victor sooner rather than later. I don't want another person's blood on my hands." Christian spoke in all sincerity.

Sebastian searched him. "How can you say that?"

"Say what?"

"That they do not exist?" Sebastian spoke firmly. Christian shook his head at his friend, not understanding. "Sirens!"

"Sebastian, please. By acknowledging their existence, we are saying that we believe in something unbelievable. I do know that there are women in this world that one does not trifle with, as you have already said. We both know that there are women who can use a firearm better than us, and that they will fight to the death. But, do they have magic? No." Christian tried to reassure himself.

Throughout his life he had seen many unexplainable and miraculous things, but to have to admit to the actual existence of Sirens added a whole new dimension to life that he was unprepared for. Christian knew what he knew, but to acknowledge what he knew was terrifying.

"But the song...." Sebastian pleaded.

"The song is a warning."

Sebastian reigned in his emotions. Taking a deep breath, he calmed himself. "You asked if I *believed*. We are both standing here, skirting around an issue we both know is not a fantasy."

Christian opened his mouth to respond, but stopped himself. He just shrugged his shoulders and shook his head.

"Fine," Sebastian sighed. He was giving up the battle for now. "I'm just off of probation from the last lolly voyage Victor took me on." He mulled over the consequences in his head. "How shall we approach this?" he spoke, smiling.

"Let us ease our way out of here and back to the shop."

Once they reached the outside, Sebastian's ears began to ring. "What is that!?"

"Keep moving, push through it." Christian instructed him. They raced through puddled streets and pouring rain.

As they shook off their cloaks just inside the shop's entrance, Sebastian noticed the hole, and the spreading crack in the door. "Whoever pounded that nail in came with the force of ten, strong men. You'll soon need a new door, Christian." Standing arrow straight, his body froze in its place.

"That's *exactly* what I said!" Christian looked up to see his friend's form stone solid and unmoving. Sebastian's dark brown hair hung straight about his head and his hazel eyes stared forward, unseeing. Christian moved to stand in front of him, Sebastian's piercing gaze burned right through him. He saw nothing. "Sebastian." They stood eye to eye. Their bodies mirrored each other, save for Christian was built wiry and lean with muscle, while Sebastian's stature was thicker and larger. Christian placed his hands on Sebastian's strong shoulders and shook him, softly calling his name.

Sebastian's eyes came back into focus. "I hear them. I hear their song."

Christian nodded his head, a grave expression upon his face. "Shall we get to work now?" The unexplainable had just reached an audience of two.

"It is more potent than the last one I heard. This must be a strong Siren." Sebastian was still in awe of what his ears were feeding into his body, his mind, his soul. He felt the pull of his will wanting to be taken over by this haunting voice that now called to him, singing sweetly in his ears.

"Sebastian! Push through it. If you give in so easily, the Sirens will call you out to sea and drown you for your soul." Christian watched as a violent shiver ran through Sebastian's body, pulling him from the spell. "They like a challenge, and we will give them one."

"You said you didn't believe in them." Sebastian stated dreamily.

"Just because their existence is masked by myth does not mean I completely disregard all respect for them. Sirens are a legend sprung from the seafaring man. Show respect to the lineage and it will show respect to you. The song is derived from a deep-rooted fear within us." Christian placed a hand over his friend's chest to reiterate his meaning. "The ocean senses this and sings to us, drawing us out. It is said that each man hears a different song, yet they all reach the same fate. When water is angry with earth, the elements collide, creating the song of legend that we now hear."

"Is that how the stories go, justifying the Sirens' song?" Christian nodded. "Huh, I'd believe there are women who possess the powers of Gods before I'd believe that tale." Sebastian laughed at his own pun.

Christian retorted, "What do we know of legend and myth, Seb?" The other man shrugged his shoulders. "That every tale has a root as real as the sunrise and as dastardly as the calm, glowing moon before a squall." Sebastian smiled at his friend's words.

The two men schemed long into the night about their plan of attack. They had the connections and clout to round up crewmen and ruffians alike to set sail alongside them with a few hours notice. The men the pair sought longed for the ocean's threat of death as much as they did. Their love of her ever-changing waters consistently pulled for their hearts upon her waves. As Christian and Sebastian finalized their plans and readied the ship under the clouded night, the Siren's soft call sung faintly in their ears, tempting them. Their departure was set for dawn's first light.

They had come to a mutual understanding about the Sirens and both men prayed the women of lore stayed just there, safely ensconced within the written page. Christian and Sebastian hoped the song was brought on because of a long-ing for the sea, or desire for adventure. The waters call to them could simply be a trick of the mind that wanted them to function in fear of the beings that could live within its depths.

When it came to sailors, everything was magic and superstition. Fables became laws that each man revered. No one questioned the other of his sight or experience upon the water's edge. Each man returned with a story to tell, and

God be helped if he didn't get to tell it.

• • •

Just as Christian and Sebastian were blowing out the last lights of the night to take their rest for a few hours before leaving, a visitor burst through the door.

Lord Athencourt filled the doorway, slicked with rain. His face was shadowed beneath the brim of his large hat. Lord Caven wasn't far behind. The men made a fine pair. They had been best friends for years and always sought trouble together. They thought the chastising from their wives was better dealt with as a united front instead of solo. So far their plan had elicited survival.

"Christian, Sebastian." Lord Athencourt acknowledged each boy, as he still saw them in their youth, not yet grown into men. He hung his cloak and hat to dry near the door. He walked the floor's distance to the table and took a seat overlooking the map that had been laid out. Lord Caven followed suit.

"Where was my boy tonight? Surely he did not find the refuge of a woman before even attending the ball?" Lord Athencourt addressed them with impatience. Victor disappointed him from time to time and he felt fit to take out his mood on someone, anyone.

Christian and Sebastian looked briefly at each other, saying nothing.

"Cat got your tongue is it? Very well. Tell Victor to come to me for his hide whipping in the morning." Lord Athencourt snorted.

"Sir," Christian leaned forward over the table as the men moved to leave it.

"Yes?" Lord Athencourt waited. "Oh, what is it boy!?" He demanded losing his patience.

"Sebastian... Do you have anything to say?" Lord Caven was only mildly annoyed. Mostly he found the antics of his old friend Athencourt humorous, he truly only came along for a good laugh. Lord Caven had known the old codger long enough to know that his current brevity was just an act. Lord Athencourt always wanted to elicit respect from people and he got it mainly through fear.

"No, Da." Sebastian's Irish lilt came out with the last word.

"Sir, we venture to find Victor tomorrow, at dawn's break. He is leading us on a treasure hunt you see, and..."

Lord Athencourt cut him off. "That damn boy and all his fancies. Has he given you a heading?"

Christian shook his head. "No, well, not exactly."

Lord Athencourt sighed. "Very well, let's beat him at his own game then shall we? You shall take my fastest ship and head straight for St. Saul. Once there, you shall make inquiries regarding my son. Is that understood? I want him home, at the very latest, in a fortnight. I will send orders to Eric to stock your ship, Sebastian, with more food and supplies than you could ever need and a more able-bodied crew." His face mocked their abilities. "I trust you both, but wish to have Captain Forte at the helm for he is a worldly sailor and a confidant of mine. I trust you shall respect my wishes?" His eyes dared them to question him on any account. The same blue fire as Victor's bore into them as Lord Athencourt moved from face to face. "Now, Lord Caven will agree with me, I'm sure, when I say that our wishes are for all a safe return." Christian knew the only reason he had brought Lord Caven out with him was to sway Sebastian into silent approval. "I have every faith in you both with Captain Forte as your guide. Do not despair. Lord Caven and I will think of everything you need to best my son at his game." He uncrossed his arms from over his round belly and stood to leave.

Both of the younger men began to open their mouths in protest, but were silenced with a swift hand. "Do not question my…" Lord Athencourt looked to Lord Caven, "…our, judgment boys. Forte will relay the rest of our wishes to you when you board ship." The older men donned their garments. Lord Athencourt perked up his ears and stared straight into both boys, searching their souls.

Lord Athencourt's eyes locked on Christian's, and the young man heard his voice in his head. *Beware the Sirens who now sail this sea, Christian. They are not to be underestimated. Bring my son home safe, as well as yourself and Sebastian. There will be no rest if you all perish. I do not know why you have been marked, but you both carry the sign. We will not worry Lord Caven or the company with this news. I will merely say, when pressed, that it is indeed a treasure hunt of men.*

Victor's father's eyes were filled with worry. Christian knew he could not let the old man down, even if he died trying. The fact that the Lord was worried was evidence enough that something far larger than Christian or Sebastian could have imagined was in the making. Christian stared at him in bafflement. Never had he known the Lord to do such a thing. Victor had certainly never mentioned it.

Lord Athencourt gave the boys a stern, foreboding look. *Mark my words boy.* And with that, he released Christian's eyes, jolting him. "Goodnight." The pair of lords left in a cold, dark wake.

"Well that was interesting." Christian stared after Victor's father. *Everyone has a secret,* he thought.

"Shit." Sebastian exploded into the silence. "Captain Forte doesn't know port from starboard let alone which direction St. Saul is!"

Christian was still contemplating what had just happened between himself and Lord Athencourt. *I had no idea that the Lord possessed some sort of gift. Maybe Victor does too?* Then he flashed to Captain Forte. *Why had they chosen such an incompetent man to take Sebastian's place at the helm?* Christian pondered this new change of plans. *Forte has Athencourt under his thumb and we all despise it.* Christian pondered the strong, independent man who had raised Victor. *But how...how did Forte ensnare Lord Athencourt to his will? The Lord clearly cannot see that Forte is evil walking amongst the earth.*

Christian pulled himself from his reverie. "You did not hear anything?" He questioned Sebastian.

Sebastian leaned over the map marking the Caribbean Sea, his dark hair falling over his face. "Have you gone as mad as Lord Athencourt too? No, Chris, I did not hear anything except for the haunting song already filling my brain. Pull yourself together." Sebastian glanced up at him. "I say we take the crew and let Forte sleep in." His hazel eyes were alight with a new thrill.

"Aye, good friend. Aye." Christian came around the other side of the table to look at the map. "I knew I picked the right man in you. We need to go here." His finger landed on an island south, but neighboring St. Winnifred.

Sebastian followed his finger. "There?" Christian nodded his head. "They'll be that close!?" He raised his head in question.

"No, but they will meet us there."

"How do you know?" Sebastian was in awe.

"It struck me while Lord Athencourt was speaking."

Sebastian waited with baited breath for his friend to finish, but by Christian's expression it looked as though he had gotten lost within his mind. Sebastian knew the ins and outs of naval sailing. Service was all he knew in his naval career, that and the regulations and standards a soldier must uphold. Christian knew of the pirating laws upon the sea, or lack thereof. Pirates upheld an unwritten code between one another that they either chose to abide by or bent to their own needs, as they saw fit.

"Christian!"

"The markings within the skull are a map to the destination of barter." Christian stared down at the map for a long moment. "You'll take care of Forte?" He spoke as though he had never paused.

Sebastian grinned wide, "With pleasure. But first, show me."

Christian met the sparkle of his friend's eye. He picked up the nail and talked Sebastian through the coordinates. Training his naval friend to see what wasn't there, preparing him for the future. Only a soul that did not walk on the right side of the law could read the destination map placed upon the sign of the marked. The skull and cross ridiculed Christian in every turn of his lesson.

• • •

Rahn gripped the railing of The Lady as she peered out over the crystalline waters. Her heart raced. His body, his scent swirled around her. He had gone in search of his sister years past and the moment Rahn had met her in the present, she knew the girl held the key to utter demise or unstoppable salvation, the likes of which had not been revealed to her as of yet. Rahn's heart hammered as she felt his descent into the clear water. He was bringing formidable allies.

What a pity, she thought. *Good men are coming to die. I hope they at least put forth a good fight before their deaths at the hands of Sirens.* Rahn laughed to herself.

Rahn's eyes sought Rowan as she spoke with a crewman underneath the aft deck. She had to tell her, but how? Rahn was terrified at the notion of having the words cross the threshold of her lips. She, Rahn, was the entire reason Rowan was who she was today. No action or remittance could change that. What she feared most was Rowan's wrath, and she would certainly have every right to unleash it. Rahn had taken someone from her in the moment they were needed and in doing so altered the course of Rowan's life.

Rahn's mind surged back to an ancient memory. One she had hidden from herself for many years. The vision came forth as she watched it from the other side, the place of an observer. The fear came back to her all too clearly.

Snow fell silently to the streets of the moonlit town as she lay in her bed peacefully staring out her window. Rahn loved the smell of the snow as it lay fresh and calm against the earth. After her mother and father would tuck her in, she would scurry up to her floor-to-ceiling window and crack it open, ever so slightly, to allow the new scent in. Falling into the slumber of her night, Rahn had images of a man in black with green eyes glowing from beneath his hooded face. Usually she filled with fear at such images. After all, it was a large, imposing man in black who had killed her father in the spring of the New Year. But Rahn felt nothing of the sort. She felt safe within the mystery of his eyes. The man's green stare became her focus as she drifted into a deep sleep.

Distant screaming pulled her into a half-wakened state. Glass shattering and the banging of pots and pans flying startled her. Rahn shot up in her bed.

"Mama..." Rahn meekly called out.

"What are you doing here?" Her mother's voice was firm. "Leave! Get out of here!" She demanded.

Rahn could not understand what the man said when he spoke to her mother, but she recognized the roughness of his voice.

"The man in black..." Rahn spoke softly to the shadows.

"How did you find us?" Her mother pleaded.

"Quiet, Kishiko!" Rahn heard the thump as her mother was slammed into the wall. "Stay there or I will kill your daughter right now, in front of you," the man stated.

Rahn sat huddled in a ball in the center of her bed, staring at the door, waiting for him to burst in.

The door was flung open, shattering as it hit the wall behind it. "Hello, little one. Come with me now and nothing bad will happen to your mama, ok?" His voice to her ears was repulsive. Rahn nodded her head and remained silent. The brute grabbed her by the neck and dragged her out into the kitchen where her mother still lay slumped against the wall. Rahn didn't scream, she couldn't. He threw her against her mother and she collided into her arms.

Rahn held her mother's face in her hands. Are you alright? She asked, silently.

Yes, my love. I am fine. We will be alright, Kishiko promised as the pair communicated through a shared connection of the mind.

Rahn closed her eyes tight, sending the image of the man into her mother's mind so she could see him. Can he help us mama?

Kishiko shrugged her shoulders. I am not sure. Take my hand love and do not let go. He is going to take us somewhere.

"Rise," the barbarian ordered. He tied a rope around Kishiko's waist and tugged forcefully so she was right beside him. He put his arm around her. "See, now isn't this nice? We are going for an outing. Stay still." The man stepped behind them and blindfolded both mother and daughter. He then draped a cloak over them so their identities could not be seen. "Carry her." Kishiko felt for her daughter's waist and lifted the small girl into her arms.

"Tokutaro, if your family could only see you now, and how you have fallen." Kishiko spoke with strong words. Whether her life continued or death became her, she was not going to let this delusional man break her spirit.

"Watch your tongue, woman, or I shall kill you like I killed your husband." Tokutaro puffed up his chest.

"Torture?" Kishiko questioned him. "Have you forgotten the meaning of the name you carry?" She could feel the force of his anger, for she knew he was staring at her blinded face. "Virtuous son… I do not think you are worthy of it."

"Push me farther, Kishiko, and you shall see what I am capable of." Tokutaro ripped Rahn from her mother's embrace and pressed a blade into the girl's chest. "I shall end your lineage right now, Kishiko, if you continue to defy me." The mother heard her daughter's whimpers.

"Giver her back, I will do as you ask."

"As I thought," he threw the girl back into her mother's arms.

Kishiko hugged her daughter close, feeling a wet liquid soak into her breast. "Has he cut you?"

"I am fine, mama. The cut is not deep." Rahn answered.

"Quiet!" Tokutaro demanded as he pulled the blindfolded mother and her daughter into the cold night's air.

Who is the man, Rahn? Kishiko questioned her.

I do not know mama. I saw him in my dream. He felt safe, Rahn pleaded. Try, mama, try. The pair spoke to each other without words. Their captor could not know what was said between them because he would never be pure enough to grasp their power.

They did not know where the man was taking them, but it was cold with the onset of winter, and its winds. Kishiko searched the present for the man in black that Rahn had seen, but she could not find him.

Rahn he is not here. Where did you see him? Kishiko spoke tersely in Rahn's head.

He entered a building, mama, in the 4th quarter. Rahn tried to keep the desperation she felt out of her voice.

Was anything different, Rahn, than it is today in your vision of the street? Kishiko was searching through time for the man, but coming up short, his face could not yet be found.

Rahn thought long and hard, her head resting on her mother's shoulder. Yes! The building was lit with a white candle in a red lantern and the entrance was new. Not how it is laid out today. The inn was finished.

Kishiko searched further into the past, looking for any change in the building. She stumbled upon the first construction of the place, but nothing else. Her mind cringed as she sought the man in black. Where is he? She thought, Who is he? Finally, she found him in the future. He had been waited on by a Geisha she had never seen before and she was giving him a room on the ground floor.

That won't do, Kishiko thought. The soldier is taking us to the same inn.

Kishiko entered the mind of the attendant and willed her to change the man's room.

Kishiko watched as the man's gaze searched up and down the body of the ornately garbed woman in front of him. Her face was powder white with a red pout painted in the center of her lips. Her black hair was piled high atop her head with gold and jade ornaments stuck in its folds. "Yes, I need a room for the night."

Kishiko surmised he was completely uninterested in this woman, but that she was going to try and vie for his attentions. She laughed to herself.

"Aawww, only passin' through... What a pity." *The Geisha knelt down behind the desk to retrieve his room key. Her hand grazed over the last room key for the ground level and then it jumped to the last room on the second story. She shook her head and grabbed it.* "I show you your room." *Her foreign accent tangled her words and laced his ears.*

"Thank you," *the stranger said, as she moved in front of him and lead him through the door to the right.*

Light beamed through the shoji paneled doors as Kishiko followed the stranger and the Geisha down the passage way. The sounds of laughter and merriment brought on by drink crept into the hall. His foot falls thundered up the well-worn stairs at the passages end drowning out the giddy men behind the paneled walls.

Kishiko noted that when the soldier who had taken her and her daughter brought them to the same inn, it was silent. Gaps of centuries between people will do that. The inn which they were now entering and the inn in which the stranger was to sleep were the same establishment spaced through time. Their inn was quiet and unopened, still under construction. The stranger got to visit it in all its glory. The comfort of noise surrounded him.

Kishiko had to act fast. Their footfalls echoed against the stone hallway. The soldier ripped Rahn from her mother's arms and flung her into the farthest corner of the room they had just entered.

"Rahn, I am going to use your image of when you are older to draw him in." *Kishiko spoke to her daughter's mind.*

The girl sniffled and tried to wipe away her tears. "Ok, Mama. Make the bad man go away." *Rahn answered her without a sound.*

With her daughter's aid and permission, she called to the stranger, entering his dreams. Kishiko warped her mind to create a portal in time for the stranger to enter. She called to him, for life, or death, depended on it.

The stranger was sleeping soundly after his long journey. A wild sea began to swirl around him as his feet left the comfort of the sand. He was being drawn into a whirlpool and could see nothing but gray and black skies surrounding him. The body of a young woman reached out her arm to him.

"Help me..." *She spoke to him as if he were her last prayer. Her violet eyes enthralled him and he reached for her.*

"I will save you. Give me your hand." *Her form was lush and perfect. The garments she wore hung down into the sinking pit, swirling with the waters rage. Her long fingers gripped his and held onto his wrist. The stranger had never felt such smooth skin.*

The woman's eyes pleaded with him. "Help..." *they said to him.* "Help."

"I will," *he promised. Her smile encompassed him with hope that they would both make it out alive from the spinning currents.*

"No! NOO!!" *called the woman in the stranger's dream. Their hands ripped apart from one another as she was taken from him. The sea raged behind her tear stained face as she disappeared, encompassed by the thrashing waves.*

The stranger bolted up in his bed, sweat dripping from his body. He ran both hands over his wet face to bring him back to himself. He had never had such beauty taken from him before. Usually it was he who took.

Who was she? *He placed his hand over his heart to ease its pounding.* I feel as though I know her, *he thought. He heard it again, a woman wailing in the darkness, screaming for her life. He leapt out of bed donning his clothes. Grabbing his pack and sword he fled out the door, exiting the inn.*

Where was the voice coming from? *The stranger wondered as his eyes raced along the layout of the inn, searching. His mind vaguely registered that the inn had changed since he slept. The urgency of a woman's words pulled him past his present thoughts and his only goal was to find her.*

The stairs lead down to a darkened hall which left no illusion to the eeriness of this night. He heard a loud crash, as if something or someone had been thrown. Down at the end of the hall was a door slightly ajar, light escaping its crevices.

The man slowed his pace. Pressing his back to the wall, he paused. The door at the very end of the hall led to the outside world. He could see the snow-covered courtyard lying just beyond. The screaming reached his ears once more. He walked the remaining length to the door. Peering through the crack, a rather large and imposing man garbed in the barbarian army's clothing appeared within his line of vision. He was shaking a woman violently within his grasp.

"You owe me!! You owe me your daughter!" *he shouted inches from the poor woman's face.*

Surveying the room a second time, his eyes landed on a huddled figure in the farthest corner. The form was female. Her knees were grasped tightly into her chest.

She was crying with her head tucked down to shield her eyes, with every harsh word, her body shook with fear. Her hearing could not be stopped.

"I owe you nothing!" The woman's voice brought him back to the reality of what was happening in front of him. His eyes tore towards her. The barbarian slapped her hard across the face. As her head fell back, her eyes focused on the man, the stranger, peering at her from the darkened hallway. "Help." She mouthed. "Save my daughter."

Her captor shot his eyes to the hallway as the man slid back into the shadows. He came back to meet her eyes. "You whore! Think you can deny me what is right-fully owed!" He clutched the woman's neck and brought her ear close to his mouth. He had his knife pressed firmly to her heart. "I should let you watch." She gasped as the knife broke into her skin. The woman watched as the devil's eyes grew large with anguish. He released his hold on her, dropping her to the floor. He clutched at his body, seeing the outpour of blood. Slowly he turned to meet his vanquisher. As their eyes met, the stranger plunged the sword through the soldier's heart, severing him from this life.

He rushed to her side, reaching his arm under her back to support her. "Are you alright?" the stranger asked.

The woman reached her hand up to cup his face, tears filling her eyes. "I am fine, stranger. You saved both our lives when I thought only one would be necessary." The woman turned in his arms to face the corner and spoke in her native tongue to her daughter, whose eyes had finally lifted from the shelter of her knees. The girl rushed to her arms, sobbing and clutching her mother's body.

He helped them rise together, so the link would not be broken. "We must go. I can assist you out of town to a safe place." Looking at the stain on the woman's chest, alarm grew in his heart. "You are bleeding." He reached for her arm to steady her.

"I am fine. It is merely a flesh wound. 'Twill heal in a matter of days. I am Kishiko (KEE-SHEE-KO) and this is my daughter, Rahn." She took his hand in hers. The hold was gentle and light.

"Forgive me. I am Roberts. May I help you out of here? This place and town?"

"Rahn?" Kishiko looked down at daughter. A reassuring smile spread their lips. The girl nodded. "Yes, we have family not far from here in Makizono, Kagoshima."

"Very well, allow me to arrange transport." He led the woman and child out the back door and covered them with his cloak to ward off the cold. He stepped back into the room with the fallen man to rid him of all his gold, accessories, anything that would fetch a decent price. Rejoining the women, he left them hiding in the

shadows of the alley where he could keep watch upon them.

"He has been gone several minutes, Mama." *The girl clutched at her mother's dress in angst.*

"Ssshh, my child. He will return soon. Fare is not an easy thing to arrange this late at night." *Kishiko stood aware and watchful of her surroundings. She trusted this man. He would play a large role in a predetermined destiny she had foreseen. He would return, if for nothing more than the mere pull of curiosity.* "You did well, my daughter, in assisting with calling him to us. I was too distracted to fully use our art."

Large doe eyes looked up at her. "I was in panic, mother, but I would not see you die tonight."

Oh how Rahn loved her mother. She would go home and visit her after this journey's end, she thought, as she continued watching the story of the past unfold before her.

"You did well, my daughter. Someday I believe you will far surpass my mastery of our gifts."

"No, Mother, I..."

"Sssshhh, my child, he returns."

Roberts had found an unattended, covered cart and the two horses to pull it not far in the shed. "Waste not, want not." *He saddled up the horses and quickly returned to his charges.*

Rahn watched as the years passed and the man she only knew as Roberts returned to the inn every fall where he had reunited the mother and daughter with their family. Roberts always stayed far into spring, Rahn remembered. She got to see now how he had watched her grow from a frightened girl of twelve to the confident girl of her teens, bowling boys and men alike over in her wake. Roberts grew close with her family, the Masago family. Nami, Rahn's aunt, ran their inn flawlessly and always had Roberts' favorite hut prepared. Occasionally, Nami would let Rahn help get it ready, for his visit came every year like clock-work. The family worked together. It always amazed Roberts that Kishiko carried no scar of the first night they'd met, physically or mentally.

Rahn often heard her mother saying to Roberts, "A wound cut deep, forgiven, and long ago forgotten, leaves no scar." The complete meaning was something Roberts could never quite grasp. Rahn could always tell by his expression afterward that the words still bewildered him.

Then it came to Rahn, the next connection in her life.

The first of spring's warm days filled the air and warmed the spirits. Winter's snow melted away, filling the grass up with its drink. Rahn could almost smell the pure scent of the flowers as they wafted in the scene before her.

Roberts was helping her stow winter covers in the barn. He watched as her hips swayed in front of him, her long straight raven hair fell down her back, blowing faintly in the wind.

Rahn assessed the vision of herself, the sight of a girl she had long forgotten.

She had grown into a beautiful woman by the age of seventeen. She would be nothing less than stunning as she gracefully entered into adulthood. The round curve of her face and slanted up-turned eyes were exotic to Roberts. The violet of her eyes made her that much more unique and beautiful.

For the first time, Rahn could clearly feel Roberts' emotions towards her. It only aggravated her more.

"Roberts, help me with this." Rahn stood trying to hoist the large screen above her head into its storage place. She had a mischievous glint to her eye.

He approached her, grabbing onto the opposite side. "Uh-oh, I know that look. You're up to something, and that is never good." Roberts' tone played with her.

Rahn's eyes lingered on him as he lifted the screen effortlessly into its place. He was strong and muscled from days of hard work, tanned from weeks upon the sea. He caught her stare.

He was beautifully built, *Rahn thought*, as she stared at his image from the past.

"Rahn? Are you alright?" Roberts cocked his head to one side, examining her.

Rahn remembered that look. She loved that look. He was always filled with fun and mischief when he looked at her like that. She remembered many fond adventures they had as she grew up.

It's now or never, she thought.

Rahn could hear her own inner dialogue, as if she could have forgotten any detail of that day. Yet, it was streaming in front of her. The tale was forcing her to remember details from both sides of their story.

Rahn shoved at his chest, causing him to fall backwards into the hay piled high behind them. As his feet left the ground Roberts reached for her arm, dragging her along with him. Laughter filled the air, as they collided together onto the soft landing.

"You silly girl, you haven't done that to me in ages. I should have known." Roberts' voice was alight with mirth.

Rahn rolled on top of him, her body melding into his. She toyed with the collar of his shirt.

Oh no. This isn't good, *Roberts thought.* My body has responded far too much to the girl already. *She was his friend, favorite companion, and occasional fantasy, although he would never admit it.* "Rahn…"

For the first time, Rahn heard what Roberts was thinking that day. She hated it. She didn't want to hear it, but the vision left her no choice. This was knowledge she couldn't out run. She wasn't sure if knowing and feeling what Roberts' was going through that day was an asset for the present, but the vision was not done with her. Rahn had to continue.

Rahn's finger crossed his lips, stopping his speech. "Sssshh," it came out far too seductively to his ears. He had to squelch the moan rising in his throat as Rahn pulled her body gently up against his. Her mouth lingered only inches away. The violet of her eyes focused on his emerald oceans. Roberts couldn't move. His body felt paralyzed and unresponsive to the logic his brain was trying to shout forth, "We are far from the inn and all its inhabitants. Relax, Roberts."

Roberts' body felt pinned under the weight of her, and it felt glorious. Rahn slowly ran her tongue out of her mouth and over his full lips, teasing him. She cupped the side of his face with her long, delicate fingers and tenderly brought her lips over his. Roberts' mouth took no time to respond. He slowly opened her mouth and stroked her with his tongue. A soft moan escaped her at the sensation of the new found pleasure. He took the kiss deeper. His arms, finally responsive, wrapped around Rahn, pulling her closer and tighter against him, as if she was his last drink of life and he was going to drain every drop.

Roberts rolled on top of her, one hand working its way up her smooth stomach to her pert bosom. Ravaging Rahn's mouth, he rubbed the hard nub of her nipple. Rahn's body responded by bucking up towards his, a moan lost in her mouth. He supported her head and neck with one hand, pushing the kiss deeper. His other hand began to slide back down the length of her body and lingered slightly above the waist line of her skirt before inching inside. Roberts' fingers cupped her heat, causing her body to stiffen slightly.

"Don't stop," escaped her lips as a pant. Roberts kissed her again. The feel of her lips on his sent him rigid. He wanted her badly. His fingers began to play her softly and slowly at first, letting her get accustomed to the sensation. He quickened his pace and her body began to shudder with her first orgasm. As the aftershocks of it still coursed through her body, Roberts couldn't stop kissing her. Rahn grew limp in his arms.

Roberts raised his head for breath, as Rahn's eyes fluttered open. "I can't do this. I'm so sorry, Rahn. I shouldn't have done that with you." The heat from his body left her and she felt hollow as she watched him walk away.

Rahn remembered that feeling perfectly and despised that she was being forced to feel it again, to relive its anguish. The images flashed forward to dinner later that evening, giving her no time to pause and regroup.

Dinner was awkward with Rahn not even glimpsing Roberts' way. The entire table noticed her disposition.

How could she have been so naive to act that way? Rahn did a head slap as she watched herself being so insolent on that day in the past.

She is mad, good. *Roberts thought. He didn't want to hurt her. He excused himself immediately after the meal, walking straight past his favorite soaking bath to his hut far from the house. It was quiet there, the solitude did him good. He needed to think.*

Rahn held her breath as she recollected what happened next.

As Rahn watched Roberts leave, she inwardly cursed him and herself. "May I be excused?"

Her mother looked at her. "Of course, my lily, go get some rest. Tomorrow will be a big day for all of us."

"Thank you. Goodnight, Nami. Goodnight, Mama." Rahn looked around the table. Kishiko had remarried, and truly he was a wonderful man, but with Rahn's mood all she could think about was that Torao was not her father. She looked to her uncle, Yemon, and then to the rest of the inn's guests. "Goodnight, everyone." Rahn quickly disappeared.

Rahn rushed up the flight of stairs behind the kitchen and fled to her bedroom, sliding closed the shoji panel. "Rrrrrrrrrrrr!" She released her rage on the inanimate objects around her. Resting over her desk chair, she saw the robe Roberts had brought her from one of his adventures. "I must give it one more try." She stripped her clothing and put on the robe over her bare skin. The silkiness of it was cool at first, but as the rush of adrenaline flooded her, she didn't feel it anymore.

Rahn blew out the candles in her room and stepped out onto her terrace. Her room was at the back of the building, all by itself. It had the prettiest view of the grounds and she could occasionally see Roberts on his walk home. She slipped down the stairs as quietly as she could manage, and, as her feet hit the ground, she took off in a dead run. As Rahn approached Roberts' hut she slowed her pace and slyly peeked inside the windows, seeing the soft glow of candlelight. He wasn't in the empty room. Rahn heard the pour of water into a basin and knew he was in the bath. She quietly pushed open his door and slipped inside.

Roberts exited his bathroom after washing cold water over his skin to try and focus, and there she was. Dressed in his favorite silken robe, Rahn stood illuminated by the fire's blaze. Her skin radiated heat that he could feel from across the room.

He stood frozen in the archway, mesmerized by her pure beauty.

"Will you let me speak?" Rahn's tone, even and melodic, touched his ears. Roberts nodded his approval. "I know you feel what we did today was wrong, and I am sorry for that for I do not feel the same." Her English accent was enchanting with her Japanese roots. "I love you, have loved you for years. I am only asking that you make my first time wonderful and beautiful. I can think of no other I would want to do this for me. You are one of my dearest friends and confidants. Please, grant me this pleasure."

Rahn heard herself speak the words, and could not remember the last time she had been so open and trusting with someone.

"Rahn… Over the years my love for you has grown, from a friendly love to something much deeper. I have not come back all these years to see the colors change. I just want you to know what you are doing and the consequences along the way. Age… is of no concern to you? Or honor?"

Her brow furrowed slightly as she contemplated Roberts' statement. She raised her head to meet his eyes. "No, age is of no consequence to me. My father was twelve years my mother's senior, you are only eight mine. I see no problem, save for a personal dilemma."

"What dilemma is that, Rahn?" Roberts was making sure she knew what she was doing. Rahn looked him square in the face, disconcerting him as her stare always did. She does always know what she wants, no matter how fleeting it may be, *Roberts thought.*

"I trust you, Roberts. Which, you should take as the highest of compliments, for my trust does not come easily. I know what I am asking of you, even though you may think it is coming from the will of a child. I am ready for this, and I want you to be the one to help guide me through it."

In all of Rahn's recaps of this event in her life, she never remembered actually speaking the words to him. She remembered thinking them. *My will, a power greater than simply me, is changing the courses of our destinies, once again.* Rahn watched to see what else was going to change. She shivered knowing that Roberts' memories would change as hers did.

"Very well." Roberts' advance on her made Rahn jump slightly. "Are you nervous to have me so near?" Their bodies were inches apart.

"No." The word came out shaky. Rahn's hand moved to untie her robe.

"Stop." His hand lingered over hers. "Allow me." He reached a smooth warm hand to her shoulder, sliding under the soft fabric. He slid it over her creamy shoulders and kissed the bare skin there. Rahn's knees began to buckle beneath her

at the delicate touch. Wrapping a firm arm around her, Roberts supported her limp body. "I love you, Rahn," he whispered softly in her ear.

Lifting her from the ground, Roberts carried Rahn to the soft bed awaiting them. Roberts gently lay her down atop the swells of linen. He removed his shirt, allowing the light to play off his tanned torso and rippling muscles. Rahn tugged at the waist of her robe and pushed it off her body. She lay naked atop it.

Roberts' breath caught in his throat. "You are beautiful." He spoke as if enchanted by a nymph. Rahn's perfect, plump chest sloped down into her curvy waist, and round hips. He had always loved her proportions. She was perfect to him.

He took her to bed softly, sweetly, gently.

Rahn now remembered it all with a cruel clarity. She shook off the vision, even as her body responded to a phantom touch she hadn't felt in years.

"I need a new lover, now. It has been too long. Let me forget his face, his lips, and the weight of his body atop mine. Let me see instead how he will die!" Thunderously Rahn shut herself in her quarters sealing off her heart for now, trying to keep out the haunting memory of her past.

The changes in her vision however could not be undone. What changed for her also changed for Roberts. He finally heard what Rahn had wanted to say all along. It also came back to him in memory. At his distance, he too felt the shock. The unspoken words between lovers were now shared, hiding no truths. Each now knew the other's thoughts without a doubt from those passing days.

● ● ●

Dorian's eyes never left the sea as she stared out over Victor's shoulder. "Your friends are catching up with you."

Victor turned to see nothing but wafting blue outside his window. He couldn't see what she did, but he didn't doubt her vision. Softly, as if time stood still in that brief moment, he saw a speck of white breaking the horizon line. *Act quickly,* raced across Victor's mind. Turning with regained precision, Victor grabbed Dorian's arm with his left hand and yanked her against the bars. He pulled her sword from its sheath and brought the sharpened blade to her neck.

"Have you been preparing for battle, my lady?" Victor spoke with acid-laced words, twisting her arm farther into distortion. Dorian's body winced subtly with pain. Victor watched as her chest rose with a sharp inhalation as he ran the blade against her sun bronzed neck. "Your instrument is sharper than I remember Christian leaving it."

Dorian met his ice cold eyes. "Do you really wish to do this?" Her body was rigid as stone.

Folding her arm against the hot bars, Victor held her tight as he scoured her folds for the keys to his release. She hadn't moved an inch since the cool of the blade had kissed her skin. Just because Dorian had magic running through to her core, she was by no means invincible. She waited. Life is, after all, all about the timing, and Victor had determination in his eyes. Dorian was apprehensive to test it.

Victor had a triumphant smile as his hand found the skeleton key at the captain's hip. Placing the key in her left hand, Victor ordered, "Unlock the door."

"No." Dorian fidgeted slightly as the blade cut into her skin. She burned hot with fury. *Victor, you do not want to push me. Life and death are always at stake, and it will not be mine!* Dorian's gaze scorched across his body. Victor could barely keep his grip upon her as the heat radiated off her body, scorching his hand.

Victor dug the blade harder against Dorian's neck, ignoring his flaming skin, and watched as he broke the barrier of Dorian's flesh. "Unlock the door," he spoke slowly now, and commanding. He noticed as she diverted her eyes for the first time. *Was she worried now?* He laughed silently to himself. Victor's eyes found their way back to her neck and the faint stream of blood that escaped there. *How is the wound already closing up?*

Dorian watched him tentatively. Victor's face furrowed as he assessed her disappearing wound. She felt his countenance shift. "As you wish, milord." Victor was back to full attention at the sound of her voice. The keys clanged in the lock rattling down the deserted hallway. The cell door opened with a thud as the lock dropped. Removing the blade from her neck, Victor pulled the door to him, grasping her wrist tightly so Dorian had to walk with the opening gate.

"If your wish is to imprison me in my own cell, I must say you will have some difficulty and quite the price to pay." She stopped at an arm's length, waiting intently. Then she felt it, the slightest loosen of his grasp. Her stream of words had surprised him. Dorian yanked her arm free and brought her leg level with Victor's chest, kicking him dead on. He flew backwards, stunned and hard of breath, crashing into the furniture behind him. No one had ever hit him with that type of force.

Dorian moved to block the doorway, watching him. Cautiously, Victor rose to his feet, not trusting his balance. She packed quite a punch. He brought the sword he still held in his hand even to the rise of her chest. "Lady…." It was introduction to a challenge. Dorian nodded. Victor transferred his sword and lunged at her grabbing her open hand.

Shit, she thought. *He's quicker than I would have anticipated. Whatever is lurking within you is spreading its poison into your movements.* Dorian lost her breath as Victor crushed her body to his. Victor bent his head to her lips and savagely assaulted her mouth. She bit down, hard. With a grasp on his lower lip, she smashed her boot down onto his nearest foot. Jerking away, Victor released her. Dorian punched him hard in the jaw shoving him backwards.

As he stumbled back, Victor's sword sliced into the other side of her neck. Victor stared down at the fresh blood that lay at its tip. "I see you do bleed, my Lady." Dorian held her neck, the cut reaching farther than the last. Victor wiped off his bleeding lip. "I do so lavish in your reaction to my kiss, 'tis not my normal response." Victor stared at her. *Did she not feel it? Most women would be scream-ing by now and running the opposite direction.*

Her expression didn't even change. Dorian held her composure. "Everything that's living bleeds, Victor. Do not bait me with your words, it will not work." Victor touched his wounded lip. "Although, my wounds shall heal faster than yours." She pulled a dagger from her side.

Centering on her gray eyes, Victor said, "I hope you've got more protection than that, my lady. You'll need it if you wish to see tomorrow's sunrise."

Dorian's laugh was vicious to his ears. "It's a pity I'm not the one who should be concerned with personal protection." Victor felt his stomach flip. Somewhere deep within he feared she was telling him the truth. He wouldn't be beat by a nymph with a superiority complex. "You've started a fight you are no match for." Dorian's words were cold steel. She lowered the hand that held her neck and transferred the dagger to it, blood seeping into the handle. "I have allowed injury once, you will not be granted the privilege again, Lord Victor."

Hostility boiled inside him. "We shall see who breaths the mornings air, my lady." Victor advanced forcing her to enter the sun lit hallway.

NOOOOO!! Cried a voice from within him. The man who had melded into his body was trying to stop him. The tip of Victor's blade pressed between the indent of her breasts and he physically could not push the blade farther into her skin, or he wasn't allowed to. Victor stared Dorian down. The knowledge with which she gripped her knife worried him. He warded off the man inside.

Be quiet! Victor demanded. *This is not your fight. Stand down, now.*

You are right, Victor, this is not my fight. It is OUR fight, you scoundrel! The man inside challenged him.

I'm going mad. Victor was lost. He did not want to believe that the vision he had had anything to do with him and his future, or past.

Dorian's lips curled into a half smile. "As you wish," she said seductively taking the stance of battle. Victor mimicked her movements still holding the blade to her chest. He moved out of the cell his back facing the window at the hall's end.

Dorian parried his forward advance and swiftly moved down to the end of the hall. A crewman's footsteps could be heard thumping down the steps filtering the sunlight with his well worn trousers and dirt stained shirt.

Victor slowed his pace meeting the man's eyes. "So this is how you win battles, bring in your crew and retreat to your quarters?"

Dorian's eyes were haunting as they turned upon him. A simmering fire blazed within her iris. "How little you think of the captain of this ship! I couldn't have gotten the title if I wasn't the one skewering heads from time to time." Her eyes didn't leave him, but she reached up her hand to the man at the stairs. "I would be much obliged for your sword, Canon."

Canon eyed Victor. "My pleasure, Captain." Meeting Victor's gaze he gave the man a valid warning. "She'll soon be taking that back, Sire." He gestured to the sword in his hand. Dorian's hand clasped the steel as it entered her grip.

Victor swore he saw a flash of sympathy cross the man's face as he turned away. *A crewman feels sorry for me, why?* He had no time to find the answer. Coming within blades length, Victor taunted her. "Your men won't fight for your honor. How loyal a crew can they be?"

Dorian held her crewman's sword, running its length along the edges of her sword seized by Victor's hand. A slicing sound echoed the silence. She smiled as he flinched. Playfully, she cocked her head to the side and mocked him. "If I were in any real danger you would no longer be standing." She slowly approached him and brought her lips to his ear, whispering, "nor would you be breathing, Victor."

Her scent scraped its way through Victor's body, clawing at his insides. Everything inside of him urged Victor to stop his pursuit.

The man inside was furious. *Do not injure her, you coward!* He screamed, hoping Victor would listen.

Victor couldn't help but breathe the captain in more deeply a second time. Her smell was deliciously intoxicating and he wanted more. He wanted to know what she tasted like. "Don't underestimate me, Dorian." He pushed back the inner voice and regained control of his body. Her hand had rested on his chest and now, she shoved him backwards. He swung to counter her attack. The clash of metal on metal rang out.

Noooooo!! Victor heard the man inside him whine, but Victor was too stubborn to listen, his pride too wounded.

Life is reason enough for living, but when we get in our own way with selfishness, or ego, or pride, we forget that life happens for a reason. We forget to tame our inner-selves of destruction so that our successes can shine through. Victor was listening to the caustic voices of self instead of to the wise words of his true-path. Timing had brought Dorian into his life, but life knew the agenda for the meeting, and death was not included. Whatever the case, the man inside watched in vain as shot after shot was struck upon the woman he loved. Victor's mind would not listen, but hopefully, soon, his heart would. For the heart was what would bind the soul of a man to the spirit he lost.

• • •

Dawn's break approached. Christian and Sebastian had their group rallied and making the final preparations for the voyage. Adrenaline hung in the air like an itch that needed scratching. Sebastian's pride was named The Alastar, meaning defender or helper of mankind. He was proud to man the helm of his own vessel on this expedition. He would be sailing under no one else's colors but his own. The pride Sebastian felt filled his chest.

Sebastian searched out over the main deck for Christian and finally spotted him at the dock's end, staring out over the currents of night's last dance.

Christian watched the open water at the edge of his feet. "Don't get too close. The Siren's Call will tow you under." Sebastian pulled him out of his memories. Christian looked back to watch his friend's approach and slapped a hand over his shoulder.

"Has it been taken care of?" Christian questioned him. Sebastian nodded in response. "Good. Shall we see what the ocean has in store for us today?" The men watched as the sun began its rise from the sea's final end. The orb burst from its resting place, bold and aflame with life. "We shall have clear water, at least for today."

Sebastian couldn't speak. He had to tear his eyes away from the other worldly creation of God as Christian tugged at his shoulder. The men turned their backs on the sunrise heading for The Alastar's deck.

Both men still had the faint, distant song drifting through their heads. In truth, they could not ignore its call even if they used every inch of their being to refuse. The fire would eventually find them. At least this way it could be slightly within their own terms.

• • •

Dorian had her back pressed against the wall, her footing steady as she walked backwards up the stairs. Victor had begun to sweat. She could see the gleam of his skin at the approaching sun from the top deck. He had nicks and cuts across his body, nothing long running and harmful, but enough to get his attention when she needed it. Blood melded with sweat as it ran its course to the top of his pants.

Victor sliced into her upper thigh as she moved to pull farther away from him. "Why do you keep running away from me? I only ask that you let me kill you!" He lunged again. The man inside caused him to lose his footing and trip on the stair as she made the final climb through to the upper deck.

Dorian ran a hand over the wound feeling its depth. He had landed a fine blow. Her eyes reached him at the doorway. "Your aim is very poor for a man of your ranking," Dorian taunted. Her eyes roamed his body through the shadowed light. Toned muscles and a strong back waltzed its way into the sunlight. "Perhaps we could make this a lesson?" Dorian could feel Victor's rage at her dismissal of his skill and station.

Victor stared at the blood trickling down from her right thigh as the liquid seeped into her boot cuff. The Lady's crew paused all around them, unsure whether to take action in their captain's defense or watch the game unfold with mirth. They appeared as shocked as Victor was at the sight of Dorian's blood.

She did not even flinch when I inflicted the injury... Did she not feel pain or is her black heart immune to it by now? What burned through her veins that made her so impenetrable? The questions in Victor's mind zinged off all corners of his brain.

She's not human... came the answer. *Nor are you, Victor.* The man inside responded.

Victor was becoming very irate at the man within him. *Do be quiet, sir. If I want your opinion I will ask for it!*

Jason. My name is Jason. The man answered him.

Well, Jason, if I want your opinion I will ask for it. Understood?

You cannot berate me and treat me as someone below you. I have the answers to questions you are dying to know! I am inside your head, your soul, your body, Victor! You cannot ignore me. You cannot be rid of me!

"Let me take him..." Victor didn't even notice the approach of another person, another woman, but he felt the steel against his jugular. A wispy reed stood next to him. It was the eyes that caught his attention, eyes the color of a deep green sea. He stared long and hard at the woman. She was tall and thin with lean muscle. She had sharp defined features that accentuated her frail beauty. Her skin faintly glowed, regardless of the sun's bright rays beating down around her. *The same shimmer as...* His mind jumped back to Dorian as her eyes laughed at him.

"Are you sure?" Dorian inclined her head to the girl, never breaking contact with Victor.

"Yes. I think it will help get me in the proper mood. Don't you?" The girl looked towards the captain.

Dorian nodded her approval. "Lord Victor, may I introduce Lady Rowan. She is a whole new breed of green-eyed monster." Dorian's eyes lay directly on his, fathomless. "Enjoy." She smiled as she turned towards the helm, leaving him breathless.

A shout from overhead made Victor turn up to see the speaker. "Don't kill him. I'd like to have a go!" Dark hair floated in the wind's breath. A tall curvy silhouette gazed down at him. Her features were too far away to be defined, but the accent was easily placed. The third woman was of Asian heritage.

"Bloody hell," Victor breathed the words, but no ear aboard missed it. *A ship wheeled by women...* But he knew *women* wasn't the right word. *She-Devils would have been more appropriate. They must have magical powers to have so many male crewmen aboard, taking orders from them. Witches perhaps... Damn it.*

"We are not *She-Devils*, as far as I know, but then again... to some we may appear that way," called Dorian as she walked away. She paused, not turning to face him, but her words floated to his ear. "You greatly underestimate the inhabitants of this ship, Victor. All the souls placed upon this deck, by circumstances of their own, are here upon their own volition. I do not take the free-will of others," her eyes now turned upon him. The gray held him captivated. "That is why you still have the will to fight. That is the difference of you being captive upon The Lady. Your mind is still your own, as are your actions." Dorian began to walk away again, "Choose wisely, Victor, for if your intentions are to do more harm, I will, for the sake of the protection of my crew, inhibit your freedom upon this vessel."

Victor stared after her speechless. He knew he would not like the way in which the captain would inhibit his freedom. His mind reeled.

"Shall we begin?" The tall redhead actually bowed to him slightly before attacking. Rowan parried his retort and responded with a riposte.

They know what they are doing. Victor was hard of breath and being moved all over the deck. Both the women he had fought had skills he had never seen before.

Not even from his fellow male competitors had he seen such accuracy and fluidity while handling a sword. *These women look like moving art with lethal extensions.* If he wasn't busy fighting for his life, he would have taken time to admire their form. They fought like no one he had ever met. The lady's aboard this vessel adhered to the rules of engagement, but shed no time in taking their own creative liberties.

The duel progressed over the entire deck. Victor lunged, trying to place a fatal blow to Rowan's body. He could see the humor reflected in her eyes as she, simply, swayed away from him. *She is enjoying herself!* Outrage shuddered through Victor's body as Rowan pinned him to the bow of the ship. The man was at a loss, and there was one more who wanted a go at his defeat.

Rowan held her swords point straight against his neck. She felt better and more confident of her skills. She knew she could do what she needed to if the time came to make that type of decision. *This man is child's play,* Rowan inwardly mocked him. *Compared to what I will have to do next, he is nothing. I don't want to completely drain myself.* She proved to herself that the Siren within her could fight, and win. Thus, she had tired of the game of cat-and-mouse.

"Next," Rowan called out as she stared at the pride-stricken man. She would not admit that Victor was more than an admirable adversary. The man had gotten in a few good jabs. Her clothing masked the trails of blood well. He also knew what to do with a blade.

"Rahn, I believe it's your turn." Dorian looked at her as she manned the helm.

Her violet vision turned down. "No. He looks boring. This cat is all your fight." Rahn smiled.

Dorian laughed. "Very well. I deserve to have a little more fun, do I not?" She made it down to him with a speed and agility Victor couldn't follow.

Rowan departed as Dorian filled her place. The blood thirst was radiating off of the captain. The Siren lineage is one of vicious tales, and predetermined traits a woman of the line cannot disregard. Blood lust, a well known characteristic throughout the lore of the ancient bloodline, is brought forth by the woman's fury, fueled by the adrenaline as it floods the woman's body. Sirens are ethereal, beautiful beings with souls of condemned women.

"You know what's interesting?" Dorian's voice startled him. "You have the same set of skills as we do, yet you do not know how to use them. They lie dormant within you. Males of our bred are rare, and though they be a scandal to our Siren name, to deny the powers of an Elemental gift is futile. You should awaken to your gifts, Victor." Dorian subtly inhaled, deeply the aroma of the ocean and the fury within her faded. A Siren's heart is as ever changing as the sea in its fluidity. Thus, the predetermined traits can be soothed by the ocean's voice.

The silver gleam of Dorian's eyes distracted Victor. Serenity echoed throughout their stare. Victor's mind raced forward at her words. *She is clearly mad.* "I know not of what you speak." Slowly, Victor approached her. The pair began a dance as they circled each other. Victor walked towards her. His eyes, turning into blue chasms, filled with the intention of drawing the captain into their drowning depths. Dorian backed into the V of the ship, their places swapped. He stalked toward her vehemently, forcefully. His pace was otherworldly as all time slowed around his threatening demeanor. Victor wished her harm. Death would have been too swift a reward. "Tired yet, my Lady?" Dorian felt the warmth of his breath brush against her skin, his spare hand rested around her neck as the duo came to a halt, the world stilling around them.

She heard the rasp of Victor's breath as it ran through his body. He was tired. "You underestimate me if you think I'm finished." His eyes jerked towards her as she spoke. Gently, Victor bent down to kiss the crook right underneath her ear. Dorian's entire body froze. *No one, but* him *knows the location of that spot!* Her eyes were charged with centuries of bottled-up energy as she scorched Victor's gaze. His eyes burned with her intensity, but his will was not his own, and he could not look away from the blaze.

Damn it, Jason! Victor chided the inner man. *Stop making me do things.* A laughter not his own bounced across his brain. *This harms us both!*

NO! The kiss was to remind her, Jason responded. *However, her anger harms you for you are denying who and what you are! I feel your pain as my own, but I know what I am, I know who I am, and I know the woman before you is what I have lost.*

You will take the pain? Victor meant the words more as a statement of realization than that of a question.

I would take all the pain, of the entire world, for I am deserving of its wrath. I have felt nothing but hollow-emptiness since our first death. To feel anything, makes me alive, it makes us one, Victor, as we should be. Jason was calm, but Victor could feel the inner man's anxiety.

Very well, for at the moment, I have no choice but to endure this woman's vexation.

WE, Jason added. *We, Victor, have no choice but to endure.*

Victor could close out his mind, his thoughts, from this other man. Or at least, for the moment, he thought he could. He pondered Jason's use of *'we'*. *Who was 'we'? Who was 'I'?* Victor didn't know any of the answers, nor the line that defined them.

Dorian's skin began to flame as she recognized the gesture as a term of endearment her husband used to reward her with. When the married couple was at parties her husband would sidle up to her, wrap an arm around her waist and kiss the same crook beneath her ear. From Victor, it simply infuriated her that he would do the same thing. *How did he know? Why did he pick that spot!?*

Victor pushed against Dorian's body, breaking the searing pain between them, stumbling backwards, he stood erect. His skin felt charred from the inside out. "Well, if it is my fate to die at the hands of a woman, I would not have it be to any other, than the one who stands before me, Captain." His voice trailed off when he noticed her flinch. *You are a face that I once knew, but from where I do not know.* Victor flashed upon an image from the past, unrecognizable to him through the hazy vision. Then it was gone, as swiftly as it had come.

You are accessing my memories, Victor. Jason's tone was one of doubtfulness. He could not understand how Victor could be transitioning so quickly.

Damn it! Dorian thought. *The power that courses through his veins is one I can feel... one I have felt before. But who?* As she assessed him, neither one of them moved, giving her more time for thought. *The only way to bring it out faster is through anger. The creature within you, Victor, likes to be pushed, much like you. Very well, if that is how it must be.*

Dorian surged towards Victor. Their swords clashed as they exhibited dance-like movements across the deck, heading towards the stern. The fight was imminent as they cut and sliced each other the entire way. Breath heavy, slashed and bleeding they stared each other down. Dorian raised her sword high above her head gripping it with both hands, her skirt floating softly around her. Walking straight up to Victor's face she got in close as his hands fell flat at his sides.

"You have no idea do you?" The hilt of Dorian's sword smacked hard across his face, dropping Victor to his back. Dorian fell onto his chest pinning his arms with her knees and brought her sword horizontal with his throat.

"Bitch," he spat in her face. Victor's emotions were so conflicted and disturbed he knew not love or hate. At this moment, every fiber of his being was rebelling against this woman.

Don't be such an insubordinate child. Show more respect. Jason cautioned.

There, Dorian felt the dragon stir within him. "I see I've hit a cord. Lovely." Ice slicked her words. "You are a fool."

Victor looked up at her slim body covered in dirt and dried blood. The gash on her thigh was raw, her skirt in ruins. "You will repay me the insult, sooner or later." Dorian lifted her face to the sun's light and ocean's breeze, ignoring Victor's warning of retribution. The illumination hit the planes of her features accentuating her bare beauty.

With her eyes still closed to the sun, Dorian spoke, startling him. "It must be hard having a conflicting voice inside your head. He leads you another way than you wish to go." Victor stared up at her in terror. "The question is who is he?" They stared at each other in silence. Looking up, Dorian nodded. As she lifted off of him, two men took hold of his arms and raised Victor to his feet.

"How did you know?" Victor asked of her in earnest. Dorian just looked at him as though she was seeing right into him, to his very soul.

"He'll need some doctoring to his wounds, Cap'n." A large man he didn't recognize spoke.

"I tried to warn ye." Canon stated, as he patted Victor on the shoulder, shaking his head at the man's ignorance. "Poor fools never listen," he chuckled to himself.

"Grim, you'll see to what he needs?" Dorian asked.

"Aye, Cap'n." Victor noticed Grim had the audacity to wink at her. Grim and Canon laughed as they hauled him back beneath the deck. "You should 'av listened. Only a fool would go up against one of 'em." They set him back in his cell and locked the door. "I'll fetch the doctor, shall I?"

"Aye, and I'll go to the galley in search of some bonded-jacky, eh, eh..." Canon nudged Grim's arm as Victor listened to their banter.

"Ahh, yes. I'll need me some of that sweet, sweet tobacco after this." Grim added. As they walked away their laughter faded into the distance.

The pair left Victor alone in a pitch-black room. He knew not who he was, what he was, or what he stood for in life. His entire being had been uprooted and transplanted into a place he did not know, or understand. He paced his cell, flooded with foreign feelings. His body, his mind, his soul was lost to a darkness that was brought on only by the clarity of the light.

Chapter

4

———◆———

THE ADVANTAGE OF LORD ATHENCOURT having named Forte the captain he wished to man their voyage was simply that every goat and ninny for miles around knew Forte's weakness.

Sebastian snuck in through the servant's entrance of the kitchen, the weakest point of the house. If anyone saw him, they would have thought it was one of the vagabonds the chef fed behind the master's back. The chef was quick to feed anyone in need, no matter what their status in this world. Food was always at the ready, and word was spread that no matter the time, an empty belly could always come get its fill. Respect was shown and advantage had yet to be taken. Sebastian surveyed the corridor leading away from the kitchen. The rock hallway was empty, save for the echo of his pounding heart. He took a steadying breath before he entered the moonlit passage. The corridor was a servant's maze that allowed them to move through the house undetected. Forte wished his workers to remain as anonymous as possible, thus the chef's rebellion in sharing the wealth of Forte's full pantry. The master of the house was well disliked. His demeanor frightened most into an attitude of submission, and for those he couldn't scare, they either quit or were punished until they complied.

Sebastian shivered as he mounted the stairs leading up to Forte's chamber. Something about the man always had him on edge. Whenever Sebastian was in Forte's company he could feel an underlying presence beneath the man's skin. Although Forte always played the part of the fool, Sebastian sensed it was an act of pure entertainment for the man. Every move Forte made was deceptive and for his own personal gain, yet men and women alike fell for the man's charms, disregarding his motives. Forte always seemed to get exactly what he wanted and it irked Sebastian to his core. The man was filth, but it was hard getting others to believe him.

Reaching the top of the stairs, Sebastian was consumed in darkness. The windows ended far below the portal, leaving the man in a state of disorientation. The sailor gave his eyes time to adjust. As the minutes ticked away, Sebastian slowly, and soundlessly, opened the door to Forte's bedchamber. He crept inside, pausing just inside the room. Sebastian froze, holding his breath as he heard the mumbling of a sleeping man. Softly, he exhaled his constricted breath. Sebastian listened closely as Forte fought with a woman in his dreams.

No matter who you are, Sebastian thought. *Women will always consume you.* He smiled, shaking his head, as he swiftly moved past Forte's canopy bed towards the windows that lay facing the rising sun.

Forte had strategically laid out his bedroom so that the sun's first light would flood him as it broke the horizon. Without the sun to raise him from his sleep, waking the man was like trying to raise the dead after morning's first light. The task was frankly impossible, yet, today, it was a simple cure to an ailing problem for the crew of The Alastar.

Weakness, in any line of work, is a terrible thing to have divulged. If hated, the people surrounding you will exploit your faults to their advantage. They will exploit and manipulate you to the full extent of their cause, causalities guaranteed. Forte's flaw was discovered after one of his servants came to tend his laundry while he slept. The woman gathered up his things, and, taking pity on the man as he tossed-and-turned in his bed, she drew the curtains closed to allow him a few hours extra sleep. As the next day awoke without him, a lord stopped by to call upon the captain. The house was in a frenzy as person after person tried to awake him. The lord eventually rushed upstairs to aid the help in reviving their master. As the noon bell chimed over the waters, resonating off the wave's peaks, Forte bolted up in bed, eyes crazed, he searched the faces of those around him. No one breathed, for they feared his oncoming wrath. Forte's body, which moments before had felt cold, and heavy with death, was now tense with life as anger rolled from his shoulders, touching all those surrounding him within the force of his fury. The story of Forte's incident spread throughout the town like sin.

Sebastian's grin was prominent, and wide as he shut Forte off to the world. He pulled the heavy, thick draperies together leaving the sleeping man in utter darkness. Sebastian laughed to himself as he left Forte's room. *Silly man,* he thought. *Tomorrow, the sun rises without you to greet it,* and as silently as he arrived, Sebastian departed. *Only high-noon will wake the man who cannot rise without the sun...*

What neither Sebastian nor Christian knew was that Forte had two lives, one ruled by the day, the other by the night, and that Forte was just sitting in wait for an opportunity to unleash his oncoming hurricane that would collide the forces of the sun and moon in one united strength. Forte smiled as his room went blacker than the night outside. His time was fast approaching.

• • •

"We approach an unmarked ship, Captain!" The resounding call came from Sam in the crow's nest of The Alastar. Sam was a little boy who knew all the dirtiest, seediest places of St. Winnifred, and still lived to tell about them. Sebastian trusted the little weasel. He was a good spy to have when need be, and he was loyal as the day is long.

"Thank you, Sam!" Sebastian yelled up to the boy. "That boy has impeccable sight," he spoke to Christian. Pulling out his telescope to see for himself, the sight surprised him. "What do the rumored *Sirens of the Sea* have against you, mate?"

"It is true then? Sirens?" Christian looked at his comrade with resignation written across his face. "So be it." His tone was one of a man who was on the verge of surrendering.

Sebastian couldn't help but laugh at him. Never had he seen such submission in Christian's eyes. The look was comical. "Was the lingering Siren Song not convincing enough? You need more proof that these women hold a vendetta against you?"

"The song is an illusion, Seb! Give me that thing." Glancing skeptically at his friend, Christian raised the scope to his eye. The carved sentinel at their opponent's bow stared back at him with open arms inviting him into her watery clutches. "It cannot be…The Dark Lady? The so called, Calypso of the Sea? Why would they have reason to seek me out?" He raised and lowered the scope from his eye numerous times during his query. "I don't know any of the women who ride upon that vessel!" Gazing through the glass once more, dread encompassed him. "Goddamn it! Goddamn it!" Swiftly, Christian began pacing. "If we are attacked by them in open water we will be obliterated. Our ship is no match for theirs. Here, look. Look." He shoved the scope over Sebastian's eye. "They have a double row of revolving canons as well as guns at the bow and stern of the ship."

Silence fell between them.

Sebastian stared at his friend in all of Christian's crazed glory. "For a man who used to sail as a pirate, and was fearsome among them, you are acting as if you are a terrified virgin holding a woman's hand for the first time." Sebastian's gaze was piercing.

The man sighed. "You are right. I have been out of the game long enough to forget how it's played." Christian grabbed the railing and breathed deeply in and out. "I must remember the rules of the undefined game."

Sebastian laughed. "I did not know that once that life was in your blood it could be forgotten." Christian wouldn't meet his eyes, so Sebastian let it slide. "They obviously wanted to meet us on the open sea or we would never have caught them." Sebastian remarked. "By your surprise, mate, I take it that you know of other Sirens, and that these women never came into play?"

There was Sebastian's instinctual, naval logic kicking in. *Always calm in a crisis situation*, Christian thought. "You're right, mate. I can't believe I didn't think of that." Christian did a mental head slap. Pacing as he spoke, "When I thought of the Sirens that could have had a hand in this I did not think it would be the three who lead the way for the rest. You are right in your assumption, Seb. I know them only by reputation." He paused gathering his thoughts. "Let it be known that I use the term *sirens* loosely when speaking of women. They are all dastardly vixens in my eyes. However, those three, are the real thing."

"What?" Sebastian couldn't believe what he heard his friend say. "The *real thing*?" he repeated.

"I never thought that my foe would be a woman, or women," Christian laughed. "It seems fitting." He sighed deeply. "I was looking for an overburdened man or muscled miscreant. The women aboard that ship are some of the first-ever women pirates to set sail amongst men. They are ruthless, powerful and vindictive. You do not cross them lightly. If you can help it, you do not cross them at all." Christian's heart beat was rising. From a place deep within his body, he was ready for the fight, thrilling within the idea of being beaten by the empresses of the sea.

"Those three are the source for Sirens amongst us?" Sebastian had heard the stories. Any man with ears had heard tales of the women who had no sympathy, but he did not pay much attention to them. Women weren't as strong as men nor as determined he had been told over and over by higher-ranking officers.

"Yes, but we call all women *sirens*, for one reason or another, not because they hold special gifts, but because women will always hold a special power over us, over men – whether it be for love, or money, or lust, or destruction… the list goes on-and-on." Christian's eyes glazed over as he stared at the sea. "However, there are specific women we call *sirens* because they match the moods of the women of fables who lure men to their death with the waters' chill. They are more beautiful and vexing than most. Specific women truly earn the right to carry the name of *Siren*," Christian stared at The Lady, "and they are aboard that ship. Those women are different. They are living embodiments of lore."

"You say this because the women of The Lady are magic, or because they are as brutal as any man?" Sebastian was trying to follow what his friend was saying, and he was trying not to believe what he was hearing between the lines of Christian's words. Belief would be admitting to another side of life, a side one couldn't always see.

Every pure and true sailor knew that possibilities beyond their control existed. That the unbelievable became real upon the treacherous sea. If sailing was your way of life, you would become one with the ocean and her moods. Her unpredictability became your new normal. The game of life and death was prominent throughout one's entire day, for a sailor never truly knew if they would live to see the end of it. Men thrived in the ocean's ever changing currents. Yet, upon the water's will, many a soul was lost, never to be found. Lives were altered forever when a monster of the deep, whose name was only spoken in hushed tones on dry land, surfaced before you. Beings of imagined powers became real while magic swirled in the currents below you. Stories spread of miraculous recoveries and more than tragic ends. At the heart of every sailor slept a dreamer, but with a mind that refused to believe in otherworldly activities. To believe in more than the body of a man would take an incredible feat the world was unprepared for. Therefore, the true stories, of the true sailors of the sea, were passed in secret and the listeners were given free choice whether to take heed, and believe, or be reckless, and abandon the warnings to the wind.

Christian stared at his friend, pondering his response to the question. "I advise you that caution should be shown at all times when dealing with the women of The Lady." He looked away from Sebastian. "They are more brutal than any man you have ever met, and they never fight fair." Christian made eye contact with Sebastian. "They manipulate the mind in ways one could have never imagined."

Sebastian was dumbfounded. "Why on earth were you marked by them? What could you have possibly done!?" Fear entered into Sebastian's voice. He tried quickly to smother it.

Christian could feel Sebastian's eyes bearing into the side of his face, searching it, exploring it for answers. He let out a long sigh. "In all honesty I cannot say. I used to be involved with Blue, but," he trailed off into a past memory of a small girl with bright eyes and a smiling face, a girl who trusted him with her whole heart. "Once I heard of my sister's death I cut all ties to the pirate world. I eventually discontinued my search for her. I came back home to my ailing father and made amends, as my sister would have wished it. You know the rest. The old buzzard won't die." Christian laughed. He truly loved his father and all his devious habits. "We now work side by side in his blacksmithing shop bickering about proper and improper protocols and procedures." Both men laughed.

"He is an ornery old buzzard." Sebastian added having known firsthand the chiding Lord Roberts senior could dish out.

"Yes, it was how she would have wanted it, and ultimately, it is how I wanted it too. To have such strife within your past that reverberates into your present, unresolved, holds you back from every step forward." A long pause defined their conversation. "Alas, I have no idea why the She-Devils of the sea would want my head. My qualms do not lie with them. And what they want with Victor is still to be determined fully. Although he has made excellent bait, has he not?"

"Victor got us out on the sea in search." Sebastian added placing a comforting hand on his friend's shoulder. He could feel Christian's life force waning. "I am sorry, Christian. I know you loved your sister very much, but there was nothing you could do. You know that. You must stop punishing yourself for a fate you cannot alter. For a fate that was not yours to alter. We all must walk our own path, come what may. You know this better than anyone."

Christian pushed forward, ignoring the pain he still held in his heart for the loss of his sibling. "I fear for Victor's life." Christian spoke from a world away as he stared out over the water. "I fear another must die at my expense." *Another piece of my heart must be taken from me.* "Why I have been targeted after all these years is baffling." He scoured through his memory for any event that would bring clarity to the situation. *Why would these women want me?*

"We shall soon find out. The Lady is advancing on us," Sebastian stated.

The wind shifted, assaulting their bodies with its gusts. Imminent clouds gathered high overhead. The water stilled around their ship, inhibiting its progress anywhere. With the approach of the opposing vessel's sails in their direction, the pirate flag was dropped.

"Our ship cannot withstand an attack from The Lady. We will be utterly decimated." Christian's tone was as if he were chatting over tea, not standing at the rail of The Alastar seeing his impending death heading straight towards him.

"We must ready the men." He began shouting orders. "Lift anchor! Prepare the guns!! Get ready to fly!"

"Chris, come have a look at this." Sebastian leaned far over the railing staring down at the water surrounding them. His speech was airy as Christian approached him from behind. "The water's current has all but stopped around us. It appears we couldn't flee even if we had faith we could out run them. Look," He pointed far off. "The water remains calm around our vessel, stagnant. You can see the breaking point there. That shouldn't be possible with a wind as fierce as this."

Dread filled them. Christian eyed the swift approach of the so named *Dark Lady*. "Hold on mate. We have entered their war now. The captain aboard that ship isn't called Calypso for nothing."

• • •

Rahn and Rowan flanked Dorian as she held tight to the helm. Dorian had not changed from her duel with Victor, time had been short. Her stance was intimidating. The winds whipped her skirt behind her and sliced through her blood stained corset. A dried trail could be traced down her right leg to the stained rim of her boot. Soot still lingered on her exposed skin. What better a way to be a pirate than to look it?

The other two women mirrored the captain's commanding, dominating air. Rahn, attired in skintight black pants, a white short sleeved blouse and mid-length red silk vest, automatically placed a hand on the hilt of her sword. An instrument she had been given by a master of the craft in Japan. She had trained with Ayumi Ito (Ah-yoo-me Ee-to), a legend of her own time. Ayumi was exact in her art of samurai. One of the few women worthy of practicing the craft, she taught Rahn well and helped her to channel her anger elsewhere, to be centered and prepared; a practice Dorian tried to reignite within her. Rahn was never far from her samurai sword and the destruction it promised. Her eyes were set straight ahead, menace radiating from her being, as she stared down her adversaries.

Rowan's face looked just as lethal as she glared down the approaching vessel. Her hands rested on either side of her, loosely grasping the low-slung pistols at her belted hip. The black of her pants hugged muscular legs as her white tunic moved faintly with the wind. The wind swept through her hair as the fury built, electrifying the air. Rowan was awash with a tidal wave of emotions. She could not decide what she needed to do, even though the feeling was prominent within her, she pushed it aside. Anxiety was high on her list. Crimson waves blew around her sharp jaw. The green within her eyes had never been so bright. Slowly, Rowan had regained her space of calm as she stared at The Alastar. When she needed to fight, Rowan entered a place in her mind where no limits restrained her, no fears scared her and nothing stood in her way. She brought forth a personality that dwelled within her, that pushed her while she did nothing. Fighting she could do. Wrecking her brother's character? She wasn't so sure.

Dorian inclined her head towards Rahn, meeting her eyes. A brief nod passed between them, and Rahn was down from the bridge giving orders to the men on the main deck within seconds, preparing them for battle, if need be. The three women had been successful thus far in their career as blood-thirsty pirates. Men and women feared them and the wrath they brought forth onto their enemies and oppressors alike. A reputation built through forceful word of mouth, spoken by the lips of the meek. Everyone loves a good ruse and their stories were where myths could be made. They really needn't do much else.

"A night of battle could be approaching…depending upon how many of our shipmates can keep to their word. Are you prepared?" Dorian asked Rowan.

Rowan leered at the oncoming vessel, her stomach beginning to turn. "I have waited many years for just such an encounter, Captain. I have no intention of letting anyone down." A soft smile came across her lips. "Especially myself," she spoke with authority.

Dorian turned to face her. Her eyes, like silver pools, searched the girl's body, her face. She could feel Rowan's resolve. Rowan would push forth regardless of her misgivings. She had already come this far, far enough not to be able to turn back. Dorian sensed the imminent result, but she would allow the girl to speak it herself. However, she would enjoy playing along 'til then.

"I do fear, my dear Rowan, that you have been thoroughly and utterly corrupted into seeing things my way." The sparkle of jest shone in Dorian's eyes. They both laughed, dissipating the spell of menace. Returning her attention back to the sea, "I don't need you vengeful, regardless of what Rahn says. I need you focused and assertive. Can you do that for me?"

"Yes. I believe I can." Rowan spoke, self-assured.

"Good. Do not let the cloud of hate storm your judgments." Rahn's eyes peered up at her captain from the lower deck as the request entered her thoughts as well. "Hate does no one good. Clarity, even towards one's enemies, is the only way to ensure a straight and honest victory."

I shall try, Rahn's response entered into Dorian's mind.

Rowan stared down at the petite woman manning the helm. Dorian may have been small in stature, but she commanded the entire ship with a no-nonsense straightforward air. The crew knew what was expected of them and they knew the consequence if they did not perform what was asked. Despite stories of her famed maliciousness, Dorian carried the love, trust and devotion of every soul upon the ship. To know her was to devote a life to her. Common threads banded all the crewmen together, but loyalty kept them strong and an abominable united force.

"Aye, Captain," Rowan responded.

One did not often question Dorian. For, most of the time, her words and actions were dead on target. Dorian had lived in this life, this form, much longer then either Rahn or Rowan. When it came down to it, you simply did not question your elders.

● ● ●

"Hold your fire, men." Sebastian commanded. The ship was alive with the pulsing of anxiety, fear and excitement. Each crewman held a charge of exhilaration in wait of what would happen next. "Do not fire unless fired upon!" came the final order from the captain. "This is most intriguing," Sebastian turned to Christian. "They are but yards away and do not attack." He was purely baffled. He had anticipated blood-lust and hell's fury from the women of The Lady.

"I do not understand it either. This is not their normal protocol from the events that have been relayed to me of The Lady's advance. I think they wish to play a game of cat and mouse." Christian suggested.

"Then by all means let us play." A sly smirk crossed Sebastian's face.

"Why do you feel a confidence I cannot seem to find within myself? Please share...." Christian urged his friend.

"They have Victor yes, but what do we have, huh... huh? I'll tell you. We have a desire to retrieve our friend as well as the skills and thinking patterns of pirates, thanks to you, and we have nautical skills and training that they and their crew could not exceed. It will be a fun fight, hopefully not too much bloodshed, but isn't that usually just a formality?" Sebastian looked back towards The Lady. "Someone's always going to die."

Christian blankly stared at his friend. He dearly loved this man, but he was crazy. He forgot what a cocky-ass he could be at times. He would soon learn his lesson. "I think you underestimate these women greatly, Sebastian. We are talking about *pirates* here, mate. They know the sea as well, or better, than you, and *pirates* never fight fair. Not to mention, you are disarmingly naïve, to the fact that just because they are women, you think they are incapable of beating us."

Sebastian glared at him. "You seem to be putting extra merit in their gender, but you forget they are just *women*, Christian. They are not sea monsters from the ocean's depths. Is it not known that women are not as strong as men, not as skilled with a blade or rifle, have more sense to panic, and rather flee than to stay and fight? Those reasons, and more, are why men are put in place to protect them!" Sebastian's eyes begged Christian to challenge him. "I must admit, that regardless, I am highly interested in what they are truly capable of."

Christian sighed, exasperated. His friend had a very old-fashioned mindset when it came to family and order. Sebastian felt he had to protect everyone, and that women, had no greater means of protecting themselves without men to do it for them. Partly learned behavior, partly how he was raised, Christian guessed.

"I know not the caliber of women you have come in contact with, but I hope the women of The Lady aid in shoving the rest of your foot in your mouth." Christian stared at the approaching vessel. "To be so ignorant as to assume that women, in general, are of a meek and timid caliber, simply shows me how unprepared you are for this venture, and for life." Christian was having trouble listening to the audacity of his friend's statements. Sebastian really didn't understand a thing. "They are *Sirens*, Sebastian!" Christian was annoyed with Sebastian's utter belief that these women couldn't harm him. *If it comes to it, I will enjoy seeing you get your rear handed to you, you delusional man.*

Sebastian laughed at him. "A sailor such as you has told me time and again that Sirens do not exist outside the realm of books. What is there to be afraid of? Women with swords? Folly!"

They stared at each other, silently. Christian knew far more of myths than he would have ever admitted. He knew that powers of the supernatural lurked just outside one's realm of sight. His days of sailing taught him that otherworldly occurrences happened. Not only did they happen, but they were as real as the two of them staring face to face. Unexplainable things happened all the time. Christian merely chose to ignore them, or to pretend that another world where myths were made did not exist. He stored them in his mind for safe-keeping. He guarded the information with his life. He had seen too much, and once your line of sight had altered, there was no going back. Strange things seemed to come your way more often, once you had borne witness to nature's inexplicable side. Christian had argued with everyone that things outside of normal did not exist. He wanted to keep nature's secret a secret, for as long as he could. But, on a day such as today, as they approached the Siren's vessel, he could no longer keep his fellow men in the dark. Christian had to prepare those around him for the impending tidal wave. He was the first to break the staring game with Sebastian.

"Shall we bet on the outcome then?" Sebastian smiled. Christian just sighed and chose not to respond to Sebastian's bait.

• • •

Dorian slowed her ship as it approached Lord Caven's naval vessel. The wind began to dissipate as she pulled The Lady alongside The Alastar's side and commenced her wait. The air hung still between them. No shot had been fired, no word spoken. Only the lapping of the waves between the boards broke the silence.

A calm breeze gently flowed through each body as the crews of good and evil, saved and damned, stared each other down. Melodically a voice rose above the anticipation of battle, speaking with the cool breeze.

"No blood need be shed this day if you only give us what we want." The woman who spoke stood in a tattered skirt and stained corset on the rail of the ship gripping the ropes.

"And who are you, Lady, to negotiate such a deal? You look as though you have just been sent from Hyde Street's cheapest... and filthiest, brothel." Sebastian answered back, assessing her from head to toe.

Dorian laughed at his statement. "Yes. I assume I do look the part rather famously, thank you…. Very well, let me put it thusly…I shall be your death's angel or life's sweet salvation. The choice I leave to you, Lord Caven, for you are *captain* of The Alastar." Her voice was captivating, entrancing with its slow steady speech. Two women stood directly behind her to either side. "And as captain, you should make your choice based upon the best outcome for your crew and yourself."

Christian could feel Sebastian's mood shift as the woman spoke. She was trying to tempt him, bend Sebastian to her will. "Seb…"

He placed a hand to Christian's arm, stopping him. "Alright, Lady, I'll entertain you." Sebastian was amused and thought that if this was the imp and her accomplices who had taken down many a strong vessel he had nothing to fear. He could snap her in two, gifts or no. "May I have my adversary's name?" Sebastian stared her down.

"My name is Dorian Lily and you, sir, have just entered uncharted territory."

Sebastian could feel the weight of Dorian's smile as it was aimed for him. "What is it you would negotiate for safe passage through your waters, Lady

Dorian?" Sebastian inwardly scoffed at her. *The legend of The Lady overpowering all who cross her path is rubbish. Those men were weak, and surrendered openly to a pretty face. If the stories are true at all, the cowards were just ashamed to admit their own incompetence. I will not repeat the offense.* He was oozing with confidence now that he had seen his opponents. Dorian Lily was a name he had heard before from the lips of drunken men. Yet, at every mention of it, their eyes filled with fear. Sebastian was thrilled to have the chance to meet her himself. He did not believe in the reputation of this woman.

Christian could feel his friend's assurance after his assessment of the three. "Watch yourself, Seb. You do not know what they are capable of."

"We are not merely pretty faces, Sire. You shall do good to remember that." The second, and tallest of the three, had long black hair and spoke with the same mesmerizing tone, a foreign light to her words.

Can they read my mind? Sebastian felt his confidence falter.

"Every thought you think is damning from where you stand right now." Rowan answered him. Sebastian's hazel eyes touched her and were immediately enchanted. She had blood-red hair and soft skin that glowed under the sunlight.

A chill went straight down Sebastian's spine as he reassessed his situation.

Chapter

5

———◆———

DORIAN LAUGHED. *This is going to be more fun than I had initially antic-ipated. These men will grovel at a pretty face.* The captain smiled as she looked at her prey. *Both of them have taken a liking to a lady aboard my ship. Lovely.*

Dorian reached out to search the emotions of the men. Christian had not recognized any of the women aboard The Lady, yet. His inner conflict was vast. Christian so desired to share with his friend all that he knew about this world, however Christian wished to keep the secrets of the supernatural safe. He wanted to shelter Sebastian from the knowledge that no one is who they appear to be once the line beyond reality is crossed. All Christian's shadows lay in the world of magic.

Then there was Sebastian. Dorian held back her laughter. He was so eager and ready for a life outside constraint, to break free of the patterns and habits that bound him. He was right on the verge, but he didn't know how to jump. All of Sebastian's feelings about women lay in his breeding. Dorian could feel that the sailor no longer wanted to speak such words of belittlement. Sebastian didn't truly believe what he was saying, but he was conditioned to regurgitate the information instilled within him. She could feel the freedom Sebastian longed for. He wanted to experience everything for himself. He was tired of rules and regulations that had to be followed, and protocols that had no end. Sebastian was ripe for adven-ture, for love, and everything in between.

Perfect. Dorian's wolfish smile spread across her face.

"Lord Sebastian underestimates me. Let's show him what his lack in judgment shall yield." Dorian shouted across the water to the rival ship. "Lord Sebastian

Caven, I do believe I have changed my mind." She let her words sink in and recognized as shock ran across his face. Sebastian was not used to things going according to someone else's plan. "All I wanted was the return of a seditious man to my possession to be dealt with accordingly. Yet, now I would rather take him by force." Dorian coyly waltzed in front of Sebastian on the rail of her ship. "Congratulations, Lord Sebastian, you have inspired my widely known venomous streak."

Dorian's smile instilled pure terror in Sebastian, yet he also saw pure beauty. *What do these women possess that makes them so compelling?* Although he couldn't fully see the depth of Dorian's eyes, he could feel the strength of their power. She was smiling at him. *The arrogance of that wench!* Sebastian heard the words bounce across his mind. In a place he dare not acknowledge, he knew The Lady's captain could free him from the unseen ties he could not break himself.

Moving forward, his mood altered once more. "As you will, lady. I much prefer it that way!" Rage had replaced any of the doubt Sebastian once held.

Christian was watching. "Damn your pride!" Christian grabbed Sebastian's arm. "You do not know what you're getting into, Seb. They have skills that will chill your bones. Let me go over of my own volition and it will all be over." Laughter echoed back to them. Christian held Sebastian's attention. "This does not simply involve you and your ego."

"I will still take you, Roberts, willingly or no, but I shall not miss out on a chance for fun." Ropes were cast and the crewmen of The Lady flooded The Alastar like insects taking prey. The clash and clang of steal heightened in the air. "After you, ladies," Dorian gestured for her sisters to take flight first.

Each woman grasped a rope and glided effortlessly through the air, landing lightly on The Alastar's deck while their crewman followed. The Alastar's crew stopped and gaped at such quick, fluid movements. The air seemed to slow around the women as they rose from their crouch. Their garments drifted around their bodies as their hair floated on the air. The three women stood at the center of the main deck amidst a savage takeover. The men who gaped at them reveled at the Siren's grace.

"Advance on Christian and Sebastian first. I want them mostly unharmed and in our hull's quarters after capture." Dorian's words broke the still of the battle.

Rahn moved first. The men's movements around her were subdued, making her attack smoother and more efficient. She lunged at the officer approaching her, knocking him unconscious. Death was not the goal here, as much as she had protested it. Fluidly, Rahn made her way through the throng of crewmen to the stairs leading toward the upper deck. With her target in sight, she did not anticipate the slash of another crewman's steel against her skin from behind. One foot upon the stairs, Rahn stopped and pressed a hand to the blood flowing out of her side. The sailor watched as her warm violet eyes darkened with rage. Holding the young boy's gaze, she raised her sword in challenge. He physically quivered against her threat. Bringing her sword level with his eyes, she inquired, "How old are you boy?"

Dread began to take the place of fear filling the young boy's eyes. "I am ten and seven." The sword in his hand trembled.

"Pity, you show much potential." Rahn swung swiftly towards the boy and he parried her attack. "You are lighter on your feet than I would have expected." She smiled down at him. "Wonderful." Steel cut against steel as Rahn lowered herself from the steps, backing the boy around the corner towards the captain's quarters. She rammed the boy with her body, causing them to crash through the double doors, as they tumbled over each other.

"Woman! Leave the boy alone!!" A stern male voice called from behind them. "It is me you want, is it not?" His voice roared into the shadows of the room. "Get off him. Allow him to reach his next birthday."

"Whether this boy sees a new year or not, I believe, is entirely up to you." Rahn's body lay atop the boy, crushing him. She winked at him and brought her mouth to his ear. "You have played your part well. Make way to The Lady." A hidden smile lit the boys face as Rahn pushed off his body. She turned on the man behind them, her energy pushing him out into the sunlight.

Sebastian felt the heat of her mood bearing into him. He would need to be more calculated than he had thought. *These women hold a world of secrets.* "Why not play with someone more your skill level, lady? Or do you fear defeat?"

"How quaint, you are trying to bait me. Well…" Rahn started waltzing in front of him. "You are not my target, as much as it pangs you to hear it. You are of no consequence. Still, it shall be my pleasure to bestow upon you a lesson in the game, Sebastian." With swift movements, Rahn forced him to back against the stairs, climbing them in retreat. A fast glance towards the bow and she located her sisters. Both were otherwise engaged and free of visible harm. "I hope you can present me with some semblance of competition."

"You are quite the little tart, aren't you? Do you search for aid in your final hour? Don't think I missed your glance over my ship." The man's Irish lilt twined his words, making her heart stop. Sebastian took her in. Cool violet eyes stared back at him. Rahn did not seem in anyway impaired by the cut to her side. In fact, it seemed to have already stopped bleeding. *How?* He thought. Her abundant curves portrayed strong legs and a toned bottom. Sebastian's eyes scanned the arc of her hips, lingering at her well endowed bosom. Rahn's skin sparkled under the sun's rays, but he could not explain the glimmer that emanated from it. The rounded features of her face showed of exotic lands. Sebastian froze once more in his approach, captured again by the intense gaze of her purple-hued eyes. *She is no doubt beautiful, but beautiful for someone else.*

Rahn felt his assessment of her. She lavished in his gaze. *Let him look,* she thought. *One last bit of luxury before the darkness and someone should damn well enjoy it.* "Lord Sebastian, may I introduce myself?" Curtseying deeply, her eyes never left him. "I am Rahn Lily and the pleasure is all mine." She advanced so fluidly that he hadn't had time to think before his body was pressed to hers, his sword pointing up towards the heavens. Rage flushed his body. Sebastian pushed her off and their war began.

"I can tell by the suggestive way you look at me, Rahn, that you think I find you attractive." Sebastian spoke through rushed breath. "Or that is simply the manner in which you accomplish getting your way."

His words burned her. Rahn laughed wickedly, ignoring the pounding of her chest. "Do you not find me presentable, Lord Caven? I have been around the ways of men long enough to know what they want."

"I am sure you do." Her sword came dangerously close to slicing open his core. "I am also sure that you manipulate it to your full advantage." It was Sebastian's turn to laugh. Rahn's face had registered shock. "I look because I am a man and that's what we do. We appreciate women for their... assets. While you are beautiful in your own right, you are far from my personal liking." He had thrown her off balance. Opening a window for attack, he took the advantage he had been hoping for.

Rahn collided with the support beam of the stairwell, snapping it in two. "You lie!" she shouted from the wreckage.

Sebastian had anticipated that she used her body in ways other than defense and she was proud of it. Knowing that he did not fancy her provoked her to misstep.

"Ha ha, no I speak the truth, fair lady." Sebastian spoke candidly. He almost enjoyed the banter created between himself and Rahn. She was a firecracker with a cutting response for anything you threw at her.

Rahn laughed at him. "Well, if you don't fancy me I will definitely have to kill you." Their swords caught once more in battle. *I almost like the squirt. Pity.*

As their metal clashed, Sebastian inwardly praised Rahn's long sword. He had no doubt it had been manufactured just for her. Its intricacies were impeccable.

Rowan followed Rahn's path with her eyes, noting that she was heading towards the stern. Rowan quickly advanced in her own direction, opposite that of her sister. *Remember your goal...* Her eyes rushed through the faces of the pirates aboard, searching for one specifically. Eyeing her charge, she forced her way towards the bow of the ship.

You can do this, you can do this, you can do this... was the mantra flooding Rowan's head, pushing her forward. *Go to your other place, your place of survival.*

Christian was battling a man twice his size and besting him every chance he got. "Might I cut in, Aldus?" Rowan asked the giant Viking. Aldus was large bodied, willfully strong, and deadly loyal. His uncovered sculpted upper-body gleamed of sweat. He was enjoying himself.

Pinning Christian with his forearm, Aldus looked down at Rowan. "Of course, Milady," he grinned down at her. "I was just having a bit of fun 'til you got here." He knew Rowan could hold her own, but sometimes lacked the instincts of Dorian and Rahn. He would not stray far.

Aldus lumbered behind Rowan and took on another attacker. Rowan watched as Christian struggled for breath after the near choke of Aldus's bulk-weighted arm. She drew her sword to his chest.

"Christian Roberts, what a pleasure to see you after all these years." She could feel the betrayal and hatred build within her. Rowan focused on his eyes and willed herself to become calm or all could be lost.

Still gasping for breath, Christian did not recognize the woman in front of him as anything more than another assailant in the fight for his life. He lunged with all his might and met the force of a champion. Christian gawked at the thin woman in front of him. *How could she pack that much punch?* He was astounded. As an inkling of recognition entered Christian's muddled brain, Rowan attacked once more throwing him off balance.

Dorian looked after the courses of her sisters to make sure they would come to no harm. Standing her ground at the center of the ship's deck, boys and men alike tried to overthrow her, all failing miserably. She was in her element. The adrenaline of battle surged through her veins. Even Rahn, with her lust for life, couldn't match Dorian in her will for a good fight. Though the end of this battle had already been predetermined, the women had given no orders to hold back on either side. They just wished that no one need die this day for there could be a better use for them later. Every soul had potential.

With the thrill of battle pounding in their hearts, neither Christian nor Sebastian noticed that not a canon was being fired, nor a gunshot was heard ringing out over the waters. As each man paused, individually scanning the destruction taking place, they didn't notice that every man who lay slain was not dying, or dead.

As a group of men advanced on Dorian she brought her pistol to the air and fired. *Enough of this act. Let's get on with the show.*

Every sword was now turned upon a crewman of The Alastar as all activity abruptly ceased aboard the vessel. Dorian sashayed through the captive men, sidestepping the fallen.

Rahn held Sebastian at gun point, her pistol held to his head. He raised his arms in defeat as his sword clattered to the wooden deck. Aldus held Christian, blood seeping onto his bare skin. Rowan stood inches away, leaning against her sword, a smile upon her face, proud of herself.

"Take them aboard!" Making eye contact with Grim, Dorian stated, "No survivors." He nodded his accord.

Sebastian moved forward. "Let my men go! You have no reason to kill them. You have what you came for." His voice was pleading. Dorian could see it was hard for him to beg, especially to a woman. Sebastian heard the click of the pistol held to the back of his head as it engaged.

Sebastian cringed as Dorian laughed at him. "Are you the captain of this ship?" Her gray eyes filled him.

"Yes," Sebastian answered with caution in his voice.

"Tell me then... Do you take orders from anyone aboard your vessel?" Taking in his face, Dorian got her answer. "I thought not. Then I ask that you not question my commands. I will do my own will, either way…with or without your approval." She could see the pain cross his features. Turning to face the mass of her crew, she shouted "Kill them all!" Dorian sought out Christian and Sebastian's eyes. Focusing again on Sebastian, Dorian said, "The outcome of their lives is held on your head. Death always lays heavy on the heart of a captain. I gave you a choice and you chose incorrectly." She had made up her mind. Looking to their keepers, Dorian nodded. Her mocking eyes were the last thing both Sebastian and Christian took in before losing consciousness.

• • •

Christian awoke to the gentle sway of a ship gliding over steady water. Darkness filled his vision as he opened his eyes. He didn't know if it were night or day or how many days had passed since his ship was overtaken by pirates.

Pirates, Christian thought. *To think I used to be one of them.* Moving, Christian could feel the pull of bandages against his bare skin. Pirates now revolted him. *How could a person be so callous?* Within every journey, he found a heart and a mind of redemption. Bloodlust and fury were merely a front to hide the emotions of a human deep inside. Every man he sailed with had hope and love within him. Loyalty was a tough bond to forge and nearly impossible to break. Christian hated himself. He knew what man was capable of and yet, he knew that the reason was generally sound. Right and wrong were so far blurred that bad was good and good was bad.

"Sebastian," He whispered to the lightless room. "Seb." Christian had endured many wounds in battles throughout his years and the movement of the sea always made him dizzy afterwards, no matter how smooth her current was. He lightly ran a hand over his face, feeling the bump on the side of his forehead before the darkness took him again.

• • •

Awakening to the distant call of his name from the shadows, Sebastian slowly pulled himself up. The upward movement tore at his head. Quickly he reached his hand up to apply pressure to the sharp pang beating into his skull. His eyes opened to blackness. The room held no record of night or day. Days, weeks, could have elapsed through time as he lay in the darkness. Twisting his body, he felt the tug of doctoring to his wounds. His war-sore body was beginning to heal. Faintly, Sebastian heard his name being called again.

"Christian," he couldn't think rationally. "Christian!" Although the words felt as a shout passing Sebastian's lips, they were barely audible above the lap of the ocean. "Ouchhh." He had twisted too far. *If they plan on killing me, why fix me first?*

The door to his cell swung open blinding him in light. A curvy silhouette moved to block the light, and Sebastian lowered the shield of his arm from his eyes. The captor lit a lantern just inside the door, illuminating the sadness of his room. Baring down on the figure, her oriental features came into focus. She wore gleaming black, accentuated only by the straight hang of her hair around the elegance of her face. Rahn appeared to be lighting the room all on her own, a glow that grew brighter upon his appraisal.

"Do you like what it is that you see?" Rahn asked him.

Sebastian was infuriated. "What is it I see, my lady? The saint or the sinner... I believe it to be the devil." His stare darkened. "My answer remains the same as when we engaged in battle. I do not find you attractive."

Rahn laughed. She thought him funny. "Oh, you have no idea, my poor boy, how closely the devil and I dwell. Pity your soul was in the wrong place at the wrong time... for now it is condemned." Rahn watched him. "I was hoping you would have changed your mind since we took you captive. 'Tis a true disappointment to learn otherwise."

Now he remembered. "What has become of my men!?" Sebastian demanded.

"Yes, your men. Well they had all crossed a line far in the past and chosen a loyalty not even the bartering of souls can break." Rahn delivered her words slowly and with precision. Sebastian felt the impact of them as they floated on the air in front of him, taking shape.

"You will pay for this! Good men died this day." Sebastian moved to reach for her and jerked back as the clang of the metal holding him in place echoed throughout the cabin. Peering at Rahn through his anger, his body steeled. "I will avenge every last one of my men. They deserve a better fate than dying at the hands of you petty whores." Sebastian heard himself speak the words and immediately regretted them.

Again, a shrill laughter mocked him. "Whores! Whores of which you speak so harshly while comparing them to the women of this ship, however, let me remind you, you have spent many a night of pleasure with a whore in your bed. I do not think a complaint ever crossed your lips then!" Rahn's Japanese accent was more pronounced the more heated she became. "However, I do believe you misunderstand me. No blood was shed this day save for those drops that occurred by accident or in pirate play."

The rage of betrayal built within him. "You bitch!" Sebastian was on his feet straining to get to her. Rahn could see the muscles harden in his bare chest as he fought against the chain. His physical attributes held no appeal to her, but Rahn could see his potential. "My men will fight for my honor once the bewitchment falls from their eyes!" He growled in frustration. "I do not believe they are so disloyal as to betray me to the likes of you!" Sebastian ran his eyes swiftly the full-length of Rahn. "If the betrayal is true, I disown them for choosing such poor camaraderie over mine, or over anyone else." Holding her gaze, Sebastian felt his entire body calm in Rahn's violet pools.

"Harsh, harsh words, my lord. What a pity they have no effect for my heart has long been made of stone. I shall also say that if your aim is to break me, I have already been broken. The pieces of my soul scattered across the seven-seas. I have nothing to lose." Her voice was the smoothest sound Sebastian had ever heard, and while he should have found comfort within her tone, terror encroached upon him. Coyly, Rahn inclined her head towards him, toying with the nervous man. Her eyes never left his eyes. For if she had broken their bond, the sense of calm Rahn was filling the prisoner with would leave, dispelling the energy around them back to Sebastian's rage.

Rahn questioned him. "Did you not wonder how we captured you so easily, without the deadly blows of battle?" She reached out and lightly laid a hand on the side of his face. Sebastian had not realized her advance. His body froze. As her skin rested against his, Sebastian's mind began to slow and order threaded its way back into his consciousness. He could feel the calm spreading from their point of contact. Silently, he was grateful for the peace.

"Mind you, we did tell the men not to hold back to make the battle appear more authentic, but we had no need to kill any of the men aboard your ship today." Rahn's voice rang clearer through his ears.

Sebastian laughed. "Of course and aboard my own vessel!" He met her eyes once more. "I should have known that some trickery was afoot. I recruited mostly men from the street. Of course their allegiance would have already lain at the foot of the devil's bed." Sebastian searched her. "My lady, I think in another life, we could have been great friends."

Rahn slowly removed her hand from his face. She had looked into his soul.

"You challenge me, but I can see the light in your eyes. You push the limits with no caution or fear. I also see that you do none of this with the intent to harm." Sebastian stated.

Rahn was surprised at how observant the captain was of other's traits.

"Please tell me," he continued. "What are you?" Sebastian requested.

Rahn was touched by his honesty. She was moved to tell this sailor the truth. "I am a Siren." She slipped from his side so swiftly it couldn't have been human. "I believe you are right about our friendship. You need to be pushed." Her swaying hips and outlined form was the last thing Sebastian saw as Rahn closed the door on his darkness.

Sebastian placed a hand over where hers had lain against his cheek. The skin that lay beneath it was hotter than the areas that surrounded it. He stood in the same spot. The reality of what Rahn had said sunk in and a fury grew deep within him.

Sebastian had been had. The men aboard his ship held no allegiance to him, or to the crown, or to the bond of country. His contacts had been good, his men proven loyal. *Loyal to someone else*, he thought. Many of them he had used before.

He trusted them.

A smile spread across Rahn's lips as she made her way down the deserted hallway. The walls around her shook with the pounding rants of a man betrayed and caged in a shroud of darkness.

"Don't worry, Sebastian, you will soon be over the betrayal and on to new adventures." Rahn smiled as she continued her paces down the deserted hallway. "I believe we will be good friends, with a good push in the right direction of course."

• • •

"Have both men's lives been accounted for? Neither one died in the night, or anything wretched like that?" Dorian's eyes never left the horizon line, nor did her heart.

Rowan had not sensed their sister join them as she and Dorian stood at the helm. She was not as adept as the other two in wielding her Siren gifts, but she was learning quickly. A smile spread across her angular features.

Rahn came to stand on the opposite side of Dorian at the wheel. "What a pitiful state those two are left in. Your brother doesn't know which foot is left and Sebastian is in a right mood, after the acknowledgement of the betrayal, of course." Neither man suspected that the men selected to serve alongside them, men once thought loyal to the Queen's Navy, had already allied with the enemy."

"You put forth the information about the mutiny?" Dorian questioned Rahn.

Rahn knew Dorian's words were more statement than question. "I'm sorry... I couldn't help myself. Heat of the moment and all that, but..."

"Both men are alive and breathing, although their mental states are in query." Rowan answered with lightness to her voice. "Has anyone checked on Victor?"

Crashing back to the present, Dorian gave a slight physical jump. "Oh dear." That pretty much said it all for the other two women. Dorian had bid everyone steer clear of him while the battle was being staged to avoid any persuasions of being set free, which would only lead to another brawl, or the risk of a breakout. Rapidly she scanned the mulling men above deck. "Grim!"

Turning upwards to acknowledge his captain, Grim smiled broadly to the ladies of his ship. "Captain," he yelled back.

"Take Victor back to his original cell." Having Grim sent to do her bidding, Dorian returned her attention to her forever-waiting mistress with her smooth waters.

Rowan and Rahn looked back and forth between each other and drifted into the shadows. They decided to let Dorian be. She was at her place of peace.

• • •

Victor sat in darkness. He listened fiercely for cannon fire and gunshots, but none rang out. *Perhaps I am too far below deck to hear them. I could be leagues beneath the water level for all I know,* he thought.

Victor knew that The Lady approached another ship because of the ocean's currents beneath him. Vaguely, he could just make out the shouts of men, men whose voices he recognized. Fear filled him and utter helplessness, for he couldn't do anything to alter their fate. The Alastar would be taken and all its passengers slaughtered. In his mind's eye, Victor could see the sails flying gallantly through the wind with his mate, Sebastian, at the helm, and Christian alongside him. He brought to memory their faces before they became severed from their bodies. Then all that encompassed his thoughts were the steely gray eyes of Dorian Lily.

• • •

"Where are you off to?" Dorian caught Rowan trying to slink away.

Rowan froze in her silent decent of the stairs. She felt like a child who had been caught doing something naughty. "I am off to the galley, Dorian, to see the cook."

"Oh yes, I s'pose it is about meal time, is it not... Will you tell Snow to make me something divine for lunch?" Dorian sweetly requested.

"Of course. Rahn, would you like anything?"

"No thank you, Love," Rahn answered. *My stomach is too knotted to even attempt to fill it with food.*

"Very well." Rowan was gone swiftly. After giving Snow Dorian's lunch request, and stealing a roll or two, Rowan turned in the opposite direction of the stairs leading to top deck. She was on a mission of reconnaissance just for herself.

Chapter

6

———◆———

ROWAN STARED AT THE MAN as he lay on his back gazing up at
the ceiling. His torso gleamed in the midday sun. He had not yet noticed her,
although she could feel the inner turmoil of his mind. It felt as though he was
warring within himself, a fierce battle at that. His smell wafted to her. She was
certain he carried the same scent as he who Dorian would not mention.

But why? Rowan pondered. *Every individual walking this earth has their
own aroma. No other would ever possess it.* Her thoughts drifted to the day she
was rescued aboard Jester's ship. Dorian had saved her that day from the many
cruel fates that had awaited her upon Jester's vessel. Rowan cringed. Jester's voice
was full of threats. Far worse than the final release of death, was the torture that
always followed. As the mist began to clear from the gunfire, a man stood very
near her, his body parallel to hers. Rowan stared at him as he looked off towards
the sea. The ice of his eyes finally turned to meet her. A swift breath caught within
her chest as she assessed him. The man's body was opaque, blurred around the
edges. Rowan remembered the way her body felt, paralyzed within his gaze, she
could do nothing. The scent of his spirit wafted towards her upon the winds. She
could smell his sweet cologne, as well as, feel his every heartache and triumph
within it. The spirit smiled at her and drifted through half of her body, chilling her
bones. As she turned to follow him, the man disappeared into the mists. That day
was forever embedded in Rowan's mind. The man's face was one she could never
forget, nor the smell of his love and sorrow.

"So tell me..." Rowan's voice startled him. Victor bounced up on the bed and sat staring at her. "Why do you feel such rage towards our captain and little to none towards me?" Victor just stared at her, confused. "I can sense your emotions. They do not carry the same weight as they would if you were to be looking at Dorian, instead of me, right now."

Victor laughed. "I do not know why she aggravates me so. I feel no charge towards you, of that you are right. I feel as though she holds the key for something that I need unlocked…" His voice drifted off. "I have never needed a woman for anything more than their company for a night." His eyes blazed down at his hands. "It infuriates me."

"Interesting." They both rested in silence. "Perhaps it is time you learn to seek guidance from others outside yourself. It is hardly possible for one person to hold all the answers, Victor. Especially before they have allowed themselves to ask the questions." Rowan assessed him. "You know, I feel I know you from another time, but I cannot place the recognition."

"I'm sure you are right, but I will not admit that to myself just yet." Victor looked up to her. "I have always solved everything on my own. I have never needed…"

Rowan cut him off immediately. "I hardly can believe that is true!" Her eyes settled upon him, searching for answers. Victor was strong-willed, destructively independent and would rather die before asking for another's aid. The man was unused to someone else having the answer, particularly when the answer was his own.

"You are blind, Victor, to the world around you because you are so headstrong. No one has ever been without the help of others in one shape or form. It's impossible to get through life *all* on your own." Rowan knew this better than anyone. She could not have lived, if not for others helping guide her back from the darkness.

"You know that all too well, don't you?" Victor startled her.

Rowan tried to laugh, but failed. "Do you have gifts of telepathy, Victor?"

He shook his head, surprised by his own action. "No, it was a feeling." When Victor's eyes met hers, they were the wounded eyes of a child looking for hope. Rowan's heart went to him. "I can feel that you have suffered great pain, and that you still carry it." Rowan nodded for him to continue. "I can feel the turmoil of your heart. There is a part of you that is scared to move forward."

Rowan didn't realize she had been holding her breath until it forced its way out of her tightened chest. "Yes…" she spoke hoarsely. Clearing her throat, she continued. "There is not one person aboard this ship, or walking the Earth for that matter, who has not felt pain. What matters is, how one carries-on." Rowan turned to leave.

"Are you?" Victor's words stopped her, bringing Rowan back into his line of sight.

"Am I, what?"

"Carrying-on… or simply getting by?" Victor's voice sounded broken as he spoke the words.

Rowan sighed. "Both." As their eyes met, the pair laughed. In order to move forward, one had to simply get by at one point, and carry-on at another.

"I feel the same." Victor spoke with his head down. "I feel as though I have known you from another time and place. The memory is long and distant." His head rose, "Fitting, isn't it? Two wandering souls meet again."

Rowan nodded. "Do you also feel that something lies dormant within you, because I can see that it does." Rowan lightly gripped the cell's bars and leaned in against them. Her precociousness mirrored that of a child as she stood before him. Thick waves cascaded around her face. The crimson of her hair accentuated the emerald of her eyes.

"I've been hearing that a lot lately…" Victor's voice was a whisper of sarcasm. "I'm not sure *dormant* is the correct word." He stared at Rowan. "Answer me this then. If it is true that I am not human, why do I still bleed as humans do?"

Rowan smiled down at him. "Because your dragon still sleeps. Once he has fully re-awakened, you will no longer be who you once thought you were. Life as you know it shall be altered into a different course, a grander one than that of simple old Victor, son of Lord Athencourt, heir to the fortune, blah, blah, blah." She laughed at him. "You know, Victor, I think you are confusing the gifts of the god's immortality with being an Elemental. If we are living, we all bleed."

"That's basically what he said, too." Victor looked disappointed that Rowan could not give him more. "Elemental? What's that?"

"He? He who?" Rowan demanded lightly. The mention of *he* was the spark of knowledge Rowan had been waiting for.

"Oh," Victor searched his hands. "No one, no one, forget about it."

"The *he* whom you were warring with internally when I approached?" Rowan was excited she may be getting somewhere. "Did you have a brother in the Lily bloodline?"

"The what?" Victor was astonished. "No. I am an only child. Always have been."

"Curious. Only direct bloodlines can share a similar scent or marking as you do… Are you quite sure?" Victor nodded. "Hhmmm, the mystery continues as to who you are." Rowan turned to leave him once more.

"Rowan…" She turned her head to look back at him. "What of the passengers upon The Alastar?" Victor asked her patiently. Demands would get you nowhere with these women.

"They all live," Rowan began to walk off, "for now."

Victor moved to stare after her, his heart heavy. "Rowan, wait! What of Elementals?"

"I am an Elemental, Victor. A being born or created of nature's force," Rowan continued to walk away. "Whatever, or whomever, lies within you are also of the Elemental gift. Be careful, Victor." She mockingly warned him. "You may need to ask for help in understanding what you are to become."

That was all she needed. Rowan was now ready to face another captive aboard The Lady, and Victor was more confused than ever.

• • •

Rahn sat at his bedside wiping the sweat from his brow with a damp cloth. Her heart tore her in two directions. She loved him and hated him. She wanted him dead and wanted to hold him tightly in her arms. Rahn's memory couldn't forget what he had done, his betrayal. She would love him silently and pray for his quick death.

Rahn's eyes darted towards the door as she heard the creaking of someone coming down the stairs. *I have tarried here too long.* Swiftly, she got to the door and opened it. Slowly peeking out, Rahn saw nothing, but she sensed someone coming for this room. Rahn stepped out of the cell, soundlessly closing the door, and slipped into the shadows beneath the easement of the stairs.

Watching as Rowan entered, Rahn could feel the girl's emotions bubbling over. Rahn backed from the shadows towards the upper deck, her mind ablaze with accusations.

I owe that man nothing! Rahn spoke within herself. *He does not deserve the type of sympathy I was about to bestow upon him. He deserves nothing!* She paused at the end of the hall, staring at the closed door. *I should have killed him.* Reason tried to leak into her thought pattern. *What would that have accomplished? Death is only the ending of a part of your story. My life would have continued on in… agony…happiness…accomplishment…God knows what, for having finished the vengeance he is due… Ugh! I do not know.* Rahn began her ascent to the main deck. *I will get the chance again and next time I will not be so forgiving.*

• • •

Light called to him from the dark. Slowly, Christian opened his eyes to find the room softly illuminated. The air felt suffocating in the small enclosure. He felt as though all the oxygen was being sucked straight from his lungs crumpling his body against its weight. Christian sat bolt upright, grabbing at his throat and gasping for air. He felt like his wind pipe was closing of its own accord. An unseen force was crushing the air within him, threatening his life with one last breath.

Rowan stood propped in the doorway intently burning into his skin. As Christian finally noticed he was not alone, his eyes changed focus to the visible air drifting towards her. His air. Carefully, Rowan lifted her head, lighting her countenance, releasing some of her grip. Air rushed back into Christian's lungs as he labored for breath, physically jumping with the burn of air in his once empty lungs.

Christian felt the grip of hands leaving his throat. "What are you, woman?" For the first time he looked at her fully. Christian took in her leather knee-high boots, aged from the water's torrents. The long, sky-blue of her skirt floated around her body, slicing up to her thigh. She wore a white blouse with a mid-length brown vest atop her thin frame. The features of her face bore a resemblance he couldn't grasp. But her eyes, now those he did recognize. Rowan could feel him as he lapsed into memories long past. Christian's face creased as he looked deep into her face, her eyes.

Feeling her own malice, Rowan sunk into repentance. *It is cruel to literally suck the air from him.* But, of all the learning Rowan still had in her new life as a Siren, the manipulation of the sea's air was one she had nearly mastered. *And what better a way to awaken a man you loathe than by stealing his breath?* She cringed at her own thoughts. *This is a man you once loved...*

The coolness of her voice broke both through the air. "I thought I would feel more vengeance towards you, more hatred." Rowan's voice trailed off as she took him in. Christian sat on the edge of his bed, body slumping forward, carrying the weary weight on his knees. *Beaten and defeated by a woman.* "But all I feel is loss."

Christian's memories dawned on him. "Rowan?" Disbelief clouded his vision. The ghost nodded in front of him. "But you... but you... you've..." Christian stopped and started himself many times trying to find the right words to say. "You've been among the living for all this time?" Christian stared at Rowan in awe. His entire life had just been altered.

Taking in the sister he lost, Christian recognized her build. She was built just like him, lean and tall with muscle. Her hair had altered and any remnant of the sandy blonde locks she once had were replaced fully with the dark crimson streaks that Christian also carried. They had the same sharp features, save for his were more masculine while Rowan's were softer and feminine. She had grown into a beautiful woman, no longer resembling the girl Christian left behind.

"Yes." Rowan's voice was cool.

The single word stabbed at Christian's heart and he began to bleed. "I searched for years for anything, any glimmer involving your life. For any word that you still lived. Then came the stories," he stood searching Rowan for emotion, "of a young girl's death aboard Jester's ship..." He couldn't stomach telling her the rest. Christian's chest began to tighten at the remembrance of the tales. Christian raised his eyes to meet hers.

They were as cool as the breeze staring back at him, a perfect mirror. "You weren't still pirateering then?" Rowan's words were loaded with deep pain, and deceit.

Astonished by the force of Rowan's rage crushing into him, Christian could barely answer her. "*No.*" His voice was soft and meek.

"They lead me to believe you were still commanding your own ship and that you deserted me." The truth of all the lies Rowan had been fed finally shattered through the blackness.

Why had I believed the words of treacherous pirates!? All the fueled rage Rowan had built up, the vengeance, evaporated as the mist dissipates over a clear lake. Tears began welling in her eyes and gliding down her rose-colored cheeks.

"I was so beaten down and... abused that I let them..." Sobs poured from her. "I let them tell me their version of the truth... and I believed it in my broken state. And after all these years I sought revenge on a lie..." Rowan became less and less coherent as the reality of her past smashed into her. "How could I have been so stupid!?" She was furious with herself.

Christian was scared to go near her. *What if she doesn't want my comfort?*

"Jester told you I deserted you?"

Rowan looked up at him with tears dripping down her face.

"I searched for years for you, Rowan." Christian's voice was firm and harsh. He wanted his sister to hear him. Christian clenched his fist in anger. "If that bastard wasn't dead already I'd butcher him myself. I traveled every inch of sea in search of you, dead or alive. I sought any word of your life." Finally, Rowan met her brother's gaze with red-stained eyes.

"After hearing of your death, I cut all ties to the pirate world. I continued my search for any scrap of information on you I could find. Finally, I returned home to make amends, because there was nothing to find." Christian spoke with softened words. "Any trace of you was gone, long before I could get there to find it. I knew you would have wanted for father and me to reconcile. Everything I have done these past seven years has been for you, Rowan."

Rowan rushed towards him, openly weeping, and leapt into his arms. Christian crushed her to his chest, hugging close the sister he thought perished long ago. Rowan collapsed into him, letting Christian nurture the little girl inside of her that she had long since abandoned. The little girl who had suffered at the hands of a crazed pirate lost in a world of debt, lust, and power-hungry madness.

The ship Rowan had thought held the promise of a new life was targeted as a Queen's vessel and taken by force to reap the bounty of the monarchy. She had been among the few allowed to live. Her young naivety had saved her life.

"Young, pretty virgins hold the highest price at market," Rowan would always hear the men say.

Rowan cringed at the memory of her beatings. Christian only held onto her tighter, making her feel finally safe from those haunting demons. Gently rubbing her back, Christian urged Rowan to talk about her experience, to release the horrors she held. Rowan wiped her eyes and centered on him.

Melting into Christian, Rowan decided, *I will tell you my story and I will tell you what I have become.*

"I have lived with this tale for so long, and held on to such denial, that it barely seems real anymore." Rowan looked at her brother. "I am sorry," her voice caught. "To think of all that I have missed."

The experiences Rowan went through had made her timid and scared. Life was waiting at her door, begging her to join in, but she couldn't, or wouldn't, allow herself. With the help and guidance of Captain Dorian, Rowan slowly began to trust and learn about her new body, her new gifts, and her second chance in life. In order to push through her past, Rowan would detach from her present and access the fear. Fear pushed her to fight. It taught her to defend her Siren rights. Rowan was still haunted by the sailors of her past aboard Jester's ship of blackness. The experience had left its scar deep within her, causing the life of her inner Siren to remain repressed, and barely vocal. Luckily, the awaiting *mistress of the sea* within her was a patient one.

Rowan's voice shook. "It began the day our ship left port. It was the last day of my life." Christian held Rowan's gaze urging her forward. "As you know, I was on my way to London to attend Mrs. Bristole's finishing school for young ladies..."

Christian nodded, "If I had only come back when I said I would, none of this would have happened. I would have been there as I said to escort you to school." Christian despised himself. Briefly his mind wandered to the small girl and innocent woman he had saved at the same time Rowan was being captured. He cringed. Duty had called to Christian that night in Japan, a duty that he felt he had to fulfill. Yet, the duty to his family, his blood, went unfulfilled. The unfinished promise still weighed heavy in his heart.

"It is no fault of your own." Rowan placed a comforting hand atop Christian's. "Father insisted I leave earlier rather than await your return."

"What?" Shock crossed his features. "Father made me believe..." Christian was distraught. *No wonder father behaved the way he did, especially in his actions towards me. He was guilty too.*

Rowan squeezed her hand atop Christian's, comforting him. "I know." Emerald stared into emerald as they silently understood each other. Christian nodded for her to continue. "I can see it all as if it had just occurred... The sky was overcast and the air hung heavy around us. The captain called out the approach of another ship, one unmarked by any party." Rowan looked down to her hands fidgeting in her lap. "That was the last peaceful moment of the day, and the marker for the last day of my first life."

The oncoming vessel unrolled the red death flag. The opaqueness of the skull and cross mocked its prey. An alarm went up throughout the Queen's Vessel. Cannon fire began pounding out between the ships. Wood splintered and pieces of debris flew past the heads of passengers. Shrapnel killed most bystanders. Bodies lay fallen all over the ship.

"Surrender yer vessel, Cap'n, and there need be no more bloodshed." Captain Jester's cruel voice sang clear in Rowan's memory.

"Take what you want, the jewels, the money, take it all. Leave the remaining souls aboard unharmed," Captain Mitus spoke in a frantic air. He wanted the destruction and death to stop. He was a good captain, but couldn't stomach much blood. He never could quite make it as a full-blown military man.

"Aye." The captains of both ships shook hands. Jester fluidly pulled Mitus close spearing him through. To trust a man such as Jester, how wrong could anyone be?

"I've re-thought our arrangement, it didn't suite me." Jester spoke into the dying man's ear as he fell to the deck in a pool of his own blood. "Men, grab all the bounty you see and take from the maidens everything you wish!" His wicked sneer made ice run through your veins.

More bodies fell around as a small Rowan hid behind a pile of wreckage on the aft deck. Women's last cries soaked into the sea as their bodies were ravaged and then silenced forever. As the noises upon deck began to lull, Rowan thought that she could almost make it out alive and unnoticed. Jester's silent approach from behind surprised her. Rowan gasped in fear as more tears ran down her face.

"What 'ave we got 'ere, mates? Looks like a scared lil' bunny." Jester ruthlessly pulled Rowan to her feet by the collar of her dress to show his men the frightened little girl. He hauled her down to the main deck. "Round up all the remaining untouched girls, the pretty ones who will land me a healthy price at market." Cheers rang out all around Rowan as she stared at the disgusting men. She was smacked and dragged over to Jester's ship along with several other girls and women, pushed and shoved the entire way. Two of Jester's men held her back from climbing back over the railing to reach her friend, still aboard the Queen's Vessel.

"Sadly, I'm glad to say they did. As we sailed away, the Queen's Vessel exploded, killing all who had been left tied aboard." Rowan shuttered at the memory of the last cries of the remaining souls, and then the silence left by the explosion.

"From then on, it was just a series of beatings and malicious treatment. They never hit me above the neck, said it would ruin my beauty for when I was sold at market. It continued like that for weeks, perhaps months... They never raped me or... anything like that. But they did cruel things to me and threatened to rape me if I didn't behave. Only a handful of us survived the months aboard Jester's ship, and an even fewer made it without being raped and murdered." Rowan's hands dropped to her lap as she finished gesturing with them while she spoke.

"Then one day," Rowan's voice broke slightly, "my fate changed again.... Cannon and gun fire began hammering above deck. I remember how we all huddled together in a corner of our cell and began to pray. We gripped each other for life and strength." Rowan's eyes glazed over as she brought back the memory of that day. "Bullets shot right through the side of the ship, denting the cells door enough for us to get out. We ran to the top deck, wading through the bloody mass of bodies. A man fell on top of me as he was pelted with gunfire. His body blocked most of the bullets, but a few found their way into my skin. His blood mixed with mine." Rowan paused, remembering the moment when her course in life was utterly altered forever. She could never return.

Looking up to the sound of Christian's voice, Rowan just stared at him, tears threading her face. "You were so brave when you shouldn't have needed to be. If I had come home...I would have been there.... I would have been there." Christian shook his head, "None of this would have happened!" His voice was distant, as though he spoke only to himself, reprimanding himself for his past choices.

The pain of his father's grief and animosity towards him had lain heavy within Christian for years. Christian never knew the true source of his father's anger, but today he found it wasn't because he was late at coming home. It was because his sister's departure had been earlier than planned. That was why his father had held him responsible. Their father had never wanted to admit his own part in the disappearance of his daughter, of Rowan. What parent wants to own the part they played in losing a child? Christian finally understood, after all these years.

A slight smile spread Rowan's lips. "You needn't feel all heroic, brother. I now know you loved me then and you love me now. That is all I need to know. I was fed so many lies upon that vessel that I began to believe them." Rowan shook her head in disbelief. "I can't believe I've already gotten my vengeance. I had it all along. I can't believe it's taken me so many years to find that I already got what I wanted." Her body steeled at the memory. She turned to meet her brother's eyes, and with hesitation, Christian held her stare. "The man who lay atop me was Jester, still breathing. His eyes focused on me with the intent to kill because of the hatred built in his heart and the threat of being under attack. I grabbed the knife that was always fastened at his thigh and slit his throat." Rowan's jaw tightened as she inclined her head away from Christian. *My first kill,* she thought, *for self preservation.*

Christian took his sister's hands in his. "Rowan..."

"I was rescued that day." Rowan spoke matter-of-factly, the trauma having passed.

Emotions raced across Christian's face. "What? By whom? Why wasn't the family or I notified?"Anger twined his words as he searched the depths within her eyes.

She paused, taking him in. "By Dorian Lily, the captain of this ship, The Lady."

Christian's brow creased. "What? The women aboard this ship saved you?"

"Wo*man*." Rowan emphasized, "And the men, of course, the crew. Dorian is the petite blonde on ship. I was told our parents had died and that you wanted nothing to do with me... I was so battered and weakened that I believed it. I never sought the truth for myself." She sounded so broken. You could hear the self-disappointment in the inflection of her voice.

"Rowan..." She raised her hand to silence him. She knew his words. "Alright," Christian continued. "What of them? Who are these people!?" Christian wanted to know, his tone demanding answers.

"Dorian inherited The Lady from her husband, Jason Lily. He was killed in battle long before I was rescued. I have heard a great many things about him and am saddened I never got the chance to meet him. Dorian took Jason's place as captain several months after his death. He trained her well." Rowan's smile was mischievous as she thought of her captain's skills. "Dorian couldn't resist the call of the sea. In a way, it was her service for the loss of her husband. Dorian can't sit idly by. She doesn't know how. And Rahn, to my knowledge, has never had a husband. She had not joined league with The Lady at the time of my rescue."

"Rahn..." Christian's voice was light with dream.

"Yes, she is from Japan and only joined us... Let's see what is it now? Several years back is the closest I can give you. She's a real bull's head," Rowan added. "Dorian and Rahn had crossed paths many a time, but, finally, Rahn decided to join. Adventure called to her, and The Lady offered her the most excitement."

Christian pondered the ship he had been captured by. *Men roamed the planks but they held no certain place aboard it. The Alastar had been taken by a vessel led by women. One crewed by the She-Devils of the sea, no less, and his sister was one of them.* He stared at Rowan fascinated. The only women, who had ever brought him down, lived and breathed upon this vessel and bled along with its men. "Continue..."

"In a way, Jason became my salvation that day, just as much as Dorian. It was his cause that placed Dorian in the waters in the first place. Jason was trying to rid the world of pirates, although he himself was one. He held an honor I have not heard matched by anyone." Rowan lapsed into a brief silence. "Jason had a mission. He was trying to exterminate the evil, malicious bastards of the breed. I guess you could say he landed on the side of good rather than evil. Jason Lily came from a wealthy, privileged background. That's how he met Dorian, on one of his crusades back home to become a civilized person amongst society, though he could never shake his pirate's heart... or soul. It truly is a way of life that consumes you." A smile fell across her frail lips. "Dorian was his junior in age, but matched him tit-for-tat in everything else. There was no challenge he could throw at her that she couldn't surpass. They were equals in many ways, I have been told. Jason's love for her caused him to reflect upon his life's choices." Rowan paused, remembering the love in Dorian's voice as she talked about her lost husband. Nothing could match that feeling.

"I don't yet understand the connection, Rowan. This man, it sounds, had been long deceased." His sister spoke of a man whom had been dead for many years by the length of her tone. Christian understood that Dorian had saved her, but he wanted to know why Rowan spoke of her husband, Jason.

"Jason's mission was to go after the deadliest of his kind and eradicate them as best he could. Pirates have a good heart and are more loyal than any man signed by contract, to those they see fit, anyway." Rowan shook her head, "Perhaps they aren't loyal, they change alliances based solely on convenience..."

Christian chimed in, "Not all of them. When a man finds an alliance worthy of his blood, he does not betray it. Pirates play an entirely different game, one worthy of the highest intrigue. Take note, sister, that nearly all motives have a hidden agenda – regardless of the man's social rank and colleagues."

Rowan nodded in agreement. "I have never known loyalty like the crew aboard this ship, Christian. These men redefine all rules," she paused, adding, "These women redefine all rules." They stared at each other in a mutual under-standing, and awe.

I am amongst the people I need to be, Christian thought. *I finally feel home.*

"Anyway," Rowan continued, "Jason believed that evil had no business upon the sea. Pirates, well, were pirates... freedom seekers, liberators of goods, rebels. Men who redefined all rules," she added with a smile. "But, when the death tolls began to rise and ships were being captured and destroyed without being plundered, the inhabitants burned alive for the sake of the battle, Jason wanted to change the course of piracy. He wanted to reclaim the heart of pirateering. Yes, you raided, but you didn't kill to kill." Rowan's voice faded. In her heart, she knew what her captain had told her was true.

...A true pirate heart is one of rebellion and change. A true pirate heart is freedom.

We fear nothing, for fear holds us back from our destinies. No, we do not follow the moral code of man and country, but we follow the rules of our heart. Our impulses and actions carry consequences, but without forward thinking and motion, how would progress ever be made? Without mistakes, how would we learn and prosper?

To be a pirate is to be part of something more, something earth-shattering, and something new. To be a pirate is to look adversity in the face and say, I will overcome you, and then, I will surpass you. To be a pirate is to be a liberator – of mind, body and soul. To be a pirate is to release yourself from the bonds of societal standards and choose your own path, come what may.

Choose to be a true pirate heart, my dear...

Dorian's words played across Rowan's mind from time to time. Her captain had a much different outlook on life. Dorian loved being a pirate. She loved the freedom it allowed her, the liberation. Yet, Rowan also knew that Dorian was speaking of self-choice and discernment. She was stating that to think for one's self is a choice, not a habit. Rowan understood Dorian's love of the pirating world, but she also understood that Dorian's vision far surpassed it.

Rowan continued. "As Dorian mended from Jason's loss, she grew stronger and even more willful. She did not want to finish what he had started, per se, but she felt she owed it to him to give it a shot – to remember where pirates had started. Steadying her feet atop The Lady's planks helped Dorian move forward with her life."

"Dorian wanted retribution," Christian's voice was more statement than question, but Rowan still heard the wisp of hesitation.

"Yes," she answered.

"Seek no greater wrath than a woman scorned," Christian stated.

"Exactly. Dorian knew that Jester was selling girls into the sex-slave trade, so she went for his jugular." A long, forlorn grief entered Rowan's body. "Many girls were killed during the battle, I am thankful to be among the saved. After I was aboard The Lady, I was tended to and bandaged accordingly. When Dorian inquired as to my family, I said I had none." Meeting Christian's hurt eyes, Rowan continued. "I was led to believe that my whole life was ruined, that no one would claim me as kin after being aboard Jester's ship. I was so worn down mentally and physically, that I had no sense of what to believe as true anymore. Jester told me swells of lies, that my family, you, wanted nothing to do with me, that he tried to barter for my return and you snubbed the offer as if you didn't have a sibling, as if our parents didn't have a daughter."

Christian moved to speak, but held his tongue. *Let her get this out, she needs it. She needs me to understand,* he thought. Christian simply shut his mouth and nodded for Rowan to continue.

Focusing harder on his eyes, "Jester built a rage within me that I have been unable to extinguish," Rowan became livid.

Christian could feel it, the full force of Rowan's fury. He also felt the moment she began to let it go, to let it heal from within her. He took her hands gently once again. "I have always loved you, Rowan. I will continue to love you until the day I am no longer allowed to draw breath from this world's air. I wish I could take all the pain you endured away, so you would never have to think of it again. I wish I could right all the lies that held you captive all those years." He cupped her chin, forcing her to look at him. "All I can offer you is the love I still hold for you, and a hope that I can serve you as best I can, from now until we part ways in the afterlife. I will not leave you again, Rowan."

Rowan laughed. "I accept!" Rowan wiped away the tears trickling from her eyes. "I hope that I can do the same for you as well, my brother. I cannot say that I would wish a different path in my life. All my experiences have made me who I am today. I am proud of who I've become. All I could ever think to change is that you had been by my side earlier." Her childlike laughter lightened the room just as her skin began to glow with more intensity.

Christian laughed at his sister's joy. "Thank you, my sister." He hugged her close, overwhelmed by his emotions, he had no words.

As the moments passed, Christian wanted to hear more of Rowan's story. He wanted to know everything he had missed.

Releasing her, Christian held Rowan at arm's length. "Tell me, how is Dorian captain?"

"Dorian," Rowan laughed. She could hear the awe in her brother's voice. He had never met a woman captain before, although he had certainly heard of them. "It was all a matter of circumstance and timing. Dorian would not hear of being left behind, ever. So, when Jason was alive, he trained her and always watched out for her on the excursions they took. Dorian got to the point where she could handle herself, her name growing with reputation. Dorian was captain of the ship, brother, the day I was rescued. It was a terrible thing, her husband's death, for she can never find a true love again." Rowan's face filled with sadness at the thought of never being able to hold true love in your heart again.

"What?" Christian was astonished with his sister's words.

"Jason was her match, her mate for life. Dorian will never find another to fill the void his death left within her," Rowan said the words sorrowfully. "Dorian never fully wanted to finish out pirates. She is one and loves every minute of it. She only has one name on her vendetta list and she is still searching for him."

"The man who killed her husband, Jason?" Rowan nodded. Christian shook his head remembering his sister's other words. "Has she tried to find love again? Surely this Jason cannot be *it* for her." Christian tried to find hope in his sister's eyes. He couldn't believe that such a perfect love existed and, once lost, it was lost forever. *Inconceivable.*

Rowan contemplated what to say. "In our life, there is one perfect match. You can either live wholly with them or have a life half-filled without them. To find their love and lose it is better than never having known the joy your match could bring you."

"What do you mean?" Christian was confused.

"More on that later, we have all the time in the world now, brother," Rowan beamed at him.

"Fine. What happened after the rescue?" Christian longed to know everything about his sister. He had missed her so.

"Oh, many marvelous and strange things..." An odd expression crossed Rowan's face, yet she spoke with the enthusiasm of a child. "Dorian recognized the signs in me before they took life, and since I claimed no living relatives she brought me back to her home. I fell in love with Dorian instantly. She is so vivacious and free. I could see in every inch of her being why her late husband had loved her so madly. He was a very handsome man, from the..." Rowan looked up at her brother, fumbling her words, remembering a distant encounter. "From the paintings I've seen, of course." She sighed, and smiled, nervously. "Dorian allowed me to enter into one of the finest finishing schools known, when I was ready. And until then, Dorian brought the finest tutors to me."

Christian let out a breath of relief, and wonder. "I should give this woman my life in exchange for all she has done for you, Rowan." He gripped her hand. "She has taken great care of you." His tone edged on regret as he heard of all the wonders Dorian had bestowed upon his sister. This woman, truly, had done right by her. His heartache is that he wasn't there to see it with his own eyes.

His memory recalled the youthful gleam of the captain's face. "Dorian did not attend school with you? You two look to be about the same age."

"Dorian is a few years older than I," Rowan spoke the words reluctantly. "Dorian is actually several centuries older than I..." Rowan slowly enunciated her last few words. "Dorian placed before me the finest tutors, educational schools, extra courses in arts, swordsmanship... She gave me anything I wanted when it came to my education."

Christian stared at his sister with a slack-jaw. *Centuries? Did she really say centuries?* His mind was hung-up on the word.

Ignoring her brother, Rowan lapsed back into a love story that was not her own, awe in her voice. "Dorian and Jason had been seeing each other for years, in her first life. The life before she became a Siren. I believe he fell in love with her when she was twelve. They grew together and when she came of age, both parents consented to the marriage. Jason was her senior by perhaps five or six years, nothing really, in the grand scheme of life. A love match with all the right societal connections, as Dorian's parents would say. Dorian and I became very close and she helped me through all the milestones of my new gifts. I entered into a world of beauty and trust... and love. A world I hadn't felt since my capture at twelve. Someday, I hope to find what Dorian lost."

"I am sure you will, my sister. To me, it sounds as if you have much more life experiences ahead of you. I know you do." Christian placed a hand over his beating heart, trying to calm it.

"Are you alright, Christian?" Worry was written across her face.

"I am sorry, my mind is racing, Rowan." Christian paused with more on his tongue. "What gifts, Rowan? Why do you keep talking of gifts?" Christian didn't understand. "And centuries, truly?"

Rowan sighed, loudly. *Now or never...* "I am a Siren, Christian." Rowan answered him. "An Elemental."

"A what?" Christian couldn't believe his ears. "Aren't those the things in myths that no lone soul should ever want to meet, for death is certain of them should they seek it? Are you sick, Rowan?" Christian felt her head for fever.

"No," she laughed. "I am not sick, or delusional, or mad." Softly, Rowan removed Christian's hand and held it. "Do you not feel the heat radiating from my skin? Do you not see that my skin's glow changes with my mood? Did you not feel the air being sucked from your lungs in my first fury?"

"That was... How did... How did this happen?" Christian rubbed his face in his hands. "I have heard stories of seamen being caught by beautiful women of the sea, Sirens. They invade their ship and take everything they want. Men stand no chance against their wrath. These women can control the water's currents, the sea's air and the creatures that lie beneath the darkness. I thought them merely myth and lore. An illusion brought on by stress and being miles out on heavy water with no land insight, nowhere to go, nothing to do but imagine."

"As did I, until my body began changing and morphing into something else, something inhuman, I thought at first. There are several ways to take on the life of a Siren. I will tell you how it became mine, I will not tell you about the other women's transformations, however."

"Why not, Rowan?"

"Did you not hear the song?" Rowan questioned him. "Each Siren has her own story to tell. It is not my place."

"I did, but all I thought of Sirens was merely to be a powerful sort of witch, not capable of much save for a man's strength and agility with the sword... or a higher knowledge of manipulation than most. I know not the full extent of who, or what, they are. One hears many a sailor's tale and experiences some of your own, but you think it a fluke or... irrational thinking due to exhaustion and fatigue."

"Most people's fear stems from a lack of knowledge, understanding. Our powers or gifts if you like, are greatly underestimated, for people don't believe in them until they see them first-hand. Sirens do exist and believe me there are things scarier than us out there. I was given my gift through blood. Jester was an Urchin, a male Siren, so named because males are an anomaly in our bloodline. When one does appear, the men do not possess the same influence or power that the women do. Urchins do not have the same skill set, so to speak, as Sirens. However, many years in any life will yield more power, no matter the sex.

Throughout history, Sirens were women, until they began breeding with the human male. How they procreated the bloodline before I have no idea. Once they began breeding with human men, Urchins began popping into existence, half human and half Elemental. In time, full-blooded Urchins mated with Sirens, making for stronger male offspring than their half-human counterparts. Jason was an Urchin as well, a full-blooded Elemental, I think. The day Jester was killed his blood mixed with mine. Upon his death, his Elemental life-force transcended, making my body its new home. No two Elementals can share the same blood and still be living." Rowan stared at her brother's confused face. "Only one can continue on. It's the law of magic that two people can't share the same blood supply indefinitely because they can never be whole to access their full potential. One must die so they can unite the separated soul into one whole being to continue on living. Do you see?"

Christian nodded then said, "No, not really. I understand more the women, but Urchins, the men, are a mystery."

Rowan nodded, understanding filling her eyes. *This knowledge is a lot for anyone, brother. I have faith in you.*

"Jester's blood saved my life that day and altered my course forever." Rowan stared off into her memories. "As for the Elemental powers it is true that we can manipulate the sea's air, waters, and creatures but we cannot control all three. Each Siren, and Urchin, bonds with a specific element and can have power over all its different nuances. However, Dorian is a slight exception, I think, because of the bond with her husband. She is very intuitive and can call forth hell's fury if she wishes. Dorian, I believe, holds something within her besides simply her Siren gifts." Rowan spoke about Dorian mainly to herself but Christian still listened, confused. "It's almost as though there are many rules and guidelines to this lineage, yet exceptions to everything that it entails. I'm constantly learning." She laughed to herself.

"Sirens have two souls?" He was completely playing catch up with a world he knew very little about.

"No, only Urchins do, and not even all of them." His sister smiled reassuringly. *You'll get it eventually.* "Don't think of it as two souls. Consider one soul that has been split in two. The two halves inhabit two different bodies and in order to live forever in the gifted form, one body must die so the soul halves can reunite, thus reaching the soul's full potential in one combined life and body. Again, this is yet another irregularity in the male side of Urchins that occurs occasionally. I think of it as inbreeding." Rowan smiled.

Since his mind was about to implode with all the new knowledge, Christian changed the subject to something simpler. "What is your gift?"

"Air." Rowan stared into his eyes, unflinching. *No fears in there, thank goodness, just demonstrative curiosity on overload.* She could trust him with anything. "Only near the water's edge, or on top of its currents, can I bring forth my gifts of its manipulation for I am slow of study."

Christian's mind was reeling with questions, but he remembered to breathe and ask one at a time. "Why? On dry land could you not control the air there?"

"I can, but have not mastered it yet. My power is strongest when I am atop the water or directly in my source of power. To use a fable term, Sirens can be thought of as fairies that have bonded with the element of water. We have at our disposal many of the same traits and talents as the fairies of lore. Reading books of myths and legends is almost like reading our direct history. All myths have a basis in reality and some, more than others, know what they are talking about." She winked at him.

"Are there land Sirens... fairies?" Christian was amused with her tale.

"Yes. We mostly just call them fairies. They have a different driving power source than we do. They use air, plants and creatures, as we do, but their source is the land, the earth. They do not have control of water as we do, and we do not have control of land as they do," Rowan answered.

"I see. I'm sorry. This is all a lot to take in…" Christian rubbed his hands across his face once more.

"I know, brother, and I am sorry for the weight of information I am instilling upon your shoulders, but…" Rowan lifted Christian's head to look into his eyes, "I wanted you to know what I am. I wanted you to know what you are up against being aboard this vessel. We can talk more later, when your mind has rested with the information and the questions within you have formed more precisely." Her smile was more genuine and heartfelt than in anyone Christian had ever seen. "I am part of an ancient bloodline where ageless immortality is a gift, beauty is ethereal, a life force of power is vibrating at my finger tips and the elements are my guide." Energy surged around her.

"Sounds right. I am racing with this insight. My mind feels like it can take no more, but I've always been one for more punishment. Answer me this, sister. I am not asking how the other women got their gifts, but I want to know what they are, so I am aware of all the dangers of the ship." Christian's eyes sparkled with laughter.

"Of course, that is an honest question, given the magnitude of what you now know. Rahn, the tall Asian girl..." Rowan searched him. "You have a history with her?" She asked softly, without accusations, although she could feel them building.

Rowan's tone was soft. Christian felt she could read his mind. "I am not sure if it is one and the same. The girl I knew was just that when I met her. I have not looked upon her in many, many years, nor do I know what she would look like now." He was lying and Rowan probably knew it.

Rowans eyes burned into him. *So this is what Rahn has been hiding from me.* "Very well. Rahn bonded with the sea's creatures. She has many friends in dark, low places."

"Rahn. That would sound right of her, actually, dark, low places." Christian caught the accusation in Rowan's stare. "I just mean from what I have seen of her, Rahn, having seedy friends seems quite fitting. What of the captain, Dorian?" Christian flashed on the face of a woman he loved long ago, a woman who took his heart with her when she left his life. *No,* he thought. *Rahn couldn't have morphed so drastically, could she?*

Oh, they didn't want me to know... but why? Rowan thought. *What is the big secret?*

Christian stared into his sister's face. *The gift that now coursed through her veins has changed her physically. It could have done the same to her... to Rahn. Rowan has only become more beautiful. Her hair is no longer the sandy blonde that dominates mine, but crimson in its waves. The same must be true of all the women, the transition changes them somehow.* "Continue...what of Dorian?"

"Dorian controls the water and its storms, although the two go hand in hand. Together, we can make one dastardly storm." They both laughed.

"Incredible." Christian raised his hand to Rowan's mouth as she began to speak again. "Please... no more. My world cannot take any more today. Let this settle within me first. I have one remaining question for you...." Rowan's face creased in questioning. "Does this mean I can go atop deck?"

They both laughed as Rowan pulled her brother close. She felt the strong connection once more. A connection that's loss she had once mourned deeply.

"I have not changed as much as you think I have, brother. I am only more of what I would have been in a human existence. My beauty is only more accentuated because of my confidence in this life. I am more agile, and I am stronger because of the experiences I have gone through. Becoming a Siren does not change who you are or how you look, it only accentuates it." Rowan nestled into the safe comfort of her brother's arms.

Christian hugged her tight and whispered, "I am proud of you, Rowan. No matter what now runs through your veins, you are mine and I am yours. I shall always be by your side whenever you need me, dear sister." As Rowan hugged him tighter in happiness, Christian could feel the full force of her strength and it made him smile through gasps of air. She was becoming someone new. Christian silently hoped that his mortality lasted long enough to see all of what Rowan would become.

Chapter

7

———◆———

INHALING DEEPLY THE SALTY AIR of his home, the lone man stood gripping the bow of his vessel. Clad in navy pants, a matching navy vest, soldier's boots, and a tailored gentleman's shirt, Captain Forte's gaze tore across the horizon. The weight of his black coat bellowed behind him with the morning winds. His peppered hair blew in wisps around his face, while a few days stubble rounded his hard set jaw.

Directing his words back over his right shoulder, Forte spoke to his second in command as he approached from behind. "I can smell them on the winds. The Lady is close within our grasp!" He beat the side of his fist against the railing.

"Aye, so close. But, why do we take her now, sir, upon first sight? Surely she cannot outgun us." His cadet, Nicholas, spoke with a certainty of knowledge he did not posses. He had not had the occasion to see the women aboard The Lady's planks. His captain had only told him stories about the Dark Lady of the sea.

"Outgun The Stallion…no, no, no." It had been many years since Forte had seen The Lady in all her glory and he couldn't quite recall the number of guns she carried. He had only borne witness to the previous captain's command of her skills. Jason Lily had been a man Forte envied, envied until the day Jason died.

"But, alas Nicholas, we cannot take The Lady in these waters. We can only hope to surprise her and instill an irrevocable fear." Forte spoke grandly with his hands, as he always did, punctuating his point into the air surrounding them. "This is why we send in someone expendable first, for they will surely be slaughtered," he paused. "And they should do some slaughtering of their own to make our ascent easier," Forte began to laugh, a cruel sound rising from his chest. "Unless our little crew of diversion carries a *lady of luck*, they will not see tomorrow. The idiot puppets stand no real chance against The Lady and her crew." Another deep chuckle rose in his vexed throat. "We will take action once The Lady has reached the haven of her home port. After all, no one has been able to find the home of the Sirens, and with Blue's incompetent attempt at conquering The Lady, the women will lead us straight to it. Blue as my little decoy poses the perfect distraction. The man is abysmal." Forte physically cringed at the thought of the pirate.

"Are you sure, sir?" Nicholas questioned.

"I am positive. Any battle, no matter who is fighting it, will leave the survivors battered. The Lady will be weakened and in need of repair, as will her crew. The best advantage is to strike at the weakest point, and then she will be in our winds."

Nicholas began fidgeting, nervously.

"What is the matter, man!?" Forte spoke with ferocity. His temper was never far from escaping the thin confines he tried to contain it in.

"I mean no disrespect, but are you so sure of the pirate's incompetence?" Nicholas spoke with reserve, treading lightly. "I simply mean, you sent a man with a hate-filled vendetta directly to its source. I cannot help but outweigh Blue's short-comings for the settling of scores. He despises those women. You mean to scare them, but you may have paid for their death sentence." The crewman knew he had stepped too far. He could feel the anger of his captain boiling up to the surface.

"You think I have killed the one person I vowed to love for eternity!?" Outrage filled Forte's voice. "You think that Blue will astound us all and fight harder because of his hatred?"

Nicholas nodded. "Hate has made people do far worse things...." his voice trailed off as he watched his captain's eyes fill with black.

Forte laughed, "Nonsense, nonsense, Nicholas. However, I think you underestimate me. Of course, I sealed the deaths of the other women, I need only one." He sighed. "Blue will do what I ask him to do because fortune breathes louder in his ear than vengeance. I will make him a very rich man if he carries out my wishes accordingly, my damsel safe from his sword."

Forte's mood was so volatile Nicholas exhaled a silent breath of relief. His captain had snapped back into sanity. Nicholas loved this man, but Forte was crazed from an infection long within his blood stream.

The captain and his mate stared out over the tempestuous waters in preparation for the oncoming squall. The will of the ocean, secretly, controlling them all within the beat of their hearts.

"I cannot believe that the little ninnies thought shielding me from the light of day would discourage me from completing this mission! They do not know what is at stake, nor that I have been awaiting this moment for many, many years." Venom dripped from Forte's lips. "Those three simpletons do not know what lies in store for them. Sebastian, Christian and Victor will be punished for their moronic deed."

"Sire, is it not Victor we are rescuing?" Nicholas looked at his master. His scrawny muscled frame held strong against storms. The hollowness of his face was attractive, yet daunting to look upon, as one fell into the depths of his eyes. Evil lay deep within him, for Nicholas strived to embody Forte at all lengths. His face was long and narrow, portraying the rat he truly was.

"Of course, dear Nicholas, but she will never come to me if Victor lives. That alone justifies the torture and impending death. These men are of no importance to me, merely a means to an end. Christian, Sebastian and Victor are simply pawns in the last corner of my game, utterly doomed, no matter the course of action they follow." Forte said the last of the three names with a dripping contempt. He hated Victor and all his privilege. Forte hated who Victor was and the potential of who he could become. Forte had to ensure that Victor never made it to the full reconciliation of his identity. The man, Forte decided, was best left in the dark of death, where he belonged.

Nicholas laughed. "Right, sir," and stared at Forte.

"What amuses you?" Forte asked, annoyed.

"That they thought hiding the light could dissuade you," Nicholas giggled. "Nothing dissuades a captain as good as you, Forte."

"You know better than any, I thrive off the day light hours in my current form," Forte placed a palm against his chest. "I leave the night time hours to my second nature, Seth. We switch lives at daybreak and sunset. Although after this whole escapade I am hoping to be done with the softer side of my soul. Seth is too tepid. He does not share my will for punishment!" Forte pounded his fist into the railing of The Stallion, causing the crew around him to jump and gasp at his action. "Alas, because of the circumstances surrounding our entry into the Elemental life, Seth and I cannot exist living side by side, ever." His smile's berth was wide and wicked. "Thank God. Unfortunately, we both grow tired, living side-by-side, and it drains our will. Therefore, he sleeps during the day and I the night." The man paused, respectfully. "It is sad, for sometimes I think I would dearly like to keep him around." Forte gazed out over the open waters. "Alas, one of us must eventually die to give the other the chance for immortality." He laughed brutally. "Perhaps when we are reunited as our one, whole, soul, our maker's blood gift will mend the craze within my veins." Forte's mind drifted to his counterpart. "That damn boy, he carries none of the madness I do!"

Silence fell between them. Nicholas knew the tale of Forte's rebirth into the Elemental realm and he knew of his challenges. The crewman understood Forte's deep respect, and jealousy, of Seth. Seth had not been infected as Forte had. Seth's birth into the gifted world was pure.

Nicholas turned to Forte in awe. Forte was everything he wasn't. Nicholas was human, Forte was not. Their minds grew alike and shared a common will, a common purpose. Nicholas had a heart of evil that matched Forte's perfectly. The captain had promised him immortality for his loyalty and Nicholas was going to see to it Forte kept his word.

"Right, sir," Nicholas' voice dispelled the silence. "Seth is not half the Urchin you are. He will never be able to conquer the seas as you will. Anyway, Seth seems too preoccupied with his lady love to notice you are coming for his will." Nicholas chided him. "His mind does not see the bigger picture of which he plays no part." He couldn't wait to witness the merger of a reunited soul. The force alone was sought after as the power of the union would fill everything for hundreds of leagues. Magic could be palpated in the air. Nicholas hoped to feel it within him, to save some for himself.

Rare occurrences always happen in nature, love, and life. Male Sirens appeared, gaining the name of Urchin, a feat never thought possible in a bloodline strictly reserved for viperous women. Although, Urchins cannot match Sirens for power, years of immortality will make anyone strong and formidable. Forte was ready for the test of his centuries in Urchin life, but he wanted all the power for himself. He knew he could not go up against his adversary at half knots, he needed full speed ahead. He needed his second nature's half of a soul, an event that would have to take place one way or another. A soul cannot carry on living unfulfilled.

"All those bastards did was delay the swap for a few more hours. Soon enough, Christian, Sebastian and Victor will see the errors of their ways. Appearing foolish and directionally challenged has been only to my advantage all these years." Forte stared out to sea, searching the sunset. He knew the waters beneath him better than he knew the structure of his face. "All these years I've waited... too long. My love is upon this sea. She is distracted, and has been so for too long. She knows not that I come for her. Nevertheless, she will soon enough. Those idiots who surround her… they will pay, dearly." He paused with his eyes settling on the water's calm. "Seth is now in the perfect position for taking. Love makes one vulnerable and easy to exploit. No one is safe in its game. I know this better than any," he spoke his last sentence softly, to the listening ear of the wave.

"Aye, sir," Nicholas rallied beside him.

"But you are right, my dear friend!" Forte grew animated as an idea took shape within him.

"What?" Nicholas was scared. If Forte was only kidding there would be a colossal whopping in his future.

"*Ziah,* Nicholas, Ziah. She is the key to carrying out our plan." Forte expanded in his excitement.

Whew! Nicholas was relieved he had said something right. "Aye, aye, Captain." His eyes twinkled at the thought of Ziah. *This will be fun.*

What Forte truly new of love was little and warped. The full depth of the word was lost on him completely. Obsession was his love because he could not distinguish the difference. Forte's mind was as simple as a child's and just as impressionable and impulsive. He wanted what he wanted, now, until he no longer wanted it, the fancy gone and discarded, moving on to something else. But the woman he sought had evaded him for years. She held the spell of a promise he lost and would do anything to get back. His love was not true. His love was not substantial. His love was not returned. In his obsession, Forte felt he held all the cards and this woman would fold under his pressure.

What Forte did not know of love was its protection, its loyalty, its honesty, its nature of giving and receiving, its patience, its steadiness, its resilience and its inability to fold under pressure. The woman Forte treasured knew the true meaning of love and in that lay the upper-hand neither one of them knew was held.

• • •

Rahn nearly jumped out of her skin as she watched Rowan and Christian emerge from the dark of the descending stairwell. She quickly made herself scarce.

I am not ready for this… I know not whether I hold love or hate for this union. Rahn's mood bore into the pair as she walked away. Everyone had a motive and normally it was for their own personal gain. Rahn was no different, except she was more self-centered than many. She did not like the union of the siblings before her because, mainly, it had not been a decision she made. When outcomes didn't go her way, she got angry, an occurrence that was appearing more and more frequently.

• • •

Rowan emerged topside with Christian not a stride's length behind her. The cool breeze of the night cleansed her senses. All eyes of the crew followed the pair as they made their way to the captain awaiting them at the helm. The crew held their breaths in anticipation of what the unleashed captive would do. Murmurs of Christian's pirate days filled the vessel. The crewmen wanted to see if he was made of what the tales implied…they wanted to hear of his knowledge.

As Rowan approached, Dorian's eyes did not leave the course of the vessel. Dorian's senses reached out. She read the situation and inwardly laughed that Grim now owed her money against their bet. The silly man should know better than to bet against the Siren Captain of the Sea.

Rowan paced slightly behind Dorian, as the captain waited for her to finally speak. Christian stood silent and calm behind her.

"All lies," Rowan blurted out. "I cannot believe the magnitude of my own naivety." Rowan stared at the side of her captain's face. Dorian's expression was steady. It did not stir from its purpose. "You know, I really find it quite unfair how hard you are to read. I must learn how you completely shut people off to what you are feeling… and thinking. Speak before you aggravate me to tears, Dorian."

Dorian had summoned Grim to her. As Grim's first foot was placed on the bridge, she spoke. "Take the helm, Grim." Her eyes smiled at him.

Grim laughed. "Yes, my lady. We shall settle our debts later then…" Matching his broad smile, Dorian nodded.

Grim took his stance behind the wheel, gripping its strength in his hands. "I love my life," he whispered to the ocean's ears.

"Come," Dorian instructed as she descended the stairs. Rowan and Christian followed Dorian into her chambers.

Rowan was regaining her calm after the frenzy within her heart. Her mind could not decide what she feared more, Dorian's acceptance or her own indifference.

"Please, sit." A subtly exquisite sitting room lay before them. Christian admired the simplistic style and beauty of the few pieces chosen. "Tell me, how did your reconciliation come to pass?" Dorian inquired.

Dorian's voice was music within Christian's ears. He could feel himself being drawn into this woman's magic. *Why do Rowan's words not have this effect?*

"Rowan is related to you by blood," Dorian's eyes sought him. "In your shared genetics lays protection, mortal or immortal…." Christian nodded, smiling at her inner intrusion. "Rowan?" Dorian did not pause long.

Dorian listened intently as Rowan conveyed what had taken place between her and her sibling. The mention of Jason from Rowan's lips caused an unseen inner pang. Never skipping a beat, Rowan plowed through to her conclusion. With every word the binding chains of her past broke and freedom glowed from Rowan's skin. The pair now waited in silence for the oncoming verdict of the captain. Dorian had not said a word. Christian thought he saw a hint of pain in her eyes with the mention of her past, but Rowan was too oblivious within her own euphoria to notice. He let it slide.

Why bring to life an already haunting ghost? He kept to himself.

Rowan had already told Christian that Dorian and Rahn's opinions were all that mattered to her. Her sister's words were none to be taken lightly. However, in such decisions upon The Lady, Dorian held the final voice.

Speaking directly to Christian, holding his eyes, Dorian commanded, "Tell me the truth." This surprised him.

"Of course," Christian answered intrigued. *Whatever you want to know…*

"I hope that's true." Dorian searched his eyes and found her answer waiting there. She also saw the forming of a question Christian didn't know quite how to ask. Stretching herself, she felt the mutual love and devotion emanating from the pair. Rowan had found her way home at last. Now, her brother could help guide her to a new fearless life where she held the key to her own destiny, to a place no longer controlled by the ghosts of others. Christian was vital to his sister's growth and inner strength. She needed his support in many ways, and only he could give it in the way Rowan needed.

Unnerved by the intense fire he felt emanating from Dorian's eyes Christian merely sat silent waiting for Dorian to address him. Out of rebellion he never broke from the eyes that probed him, shining through him like gray pools of moonlight. He had to show strength. He had to prove that he could withstand the winds aboard this vessel. Christian could feel her search within his mind. He was not afraid to let Dorian find his secrets. They were for anyone to know who sought the truth inside the tale. Staring at the women, Christian felt she was the only one to truly unlock him, to fully decode his past. Dorian was a creature of myth, far more than any other alive. He felt she held her own secrets that no one would ever discover unless she wanted them too.

When she was finished, Dorian curtly smiled and nodded to Rowan meeting her emerald gaze. Relief flooded over the sides of The Lady.

Rahn felt it too, even at her distance. The relief quickly transformed into a deep unsettling fear within her veins. *Bullocks. Now I am stuck with the pair of them and allied, no less. I know not what to do!*

Turning back to Christian, Dorian didn't speak immediately, but let him hang in anticipation.

You are far wiser to this game than I would have ever expected, Dorian spoke to him, the words filling his mind. *Remember to follow through with such intuitions.*

Christian tried not to gawk at her. Dorian knew what he thought of her, of her secrets. He knew she was telling him he was right. Her secrets were long and buried deep. Holding her gaze, he nodded, for he had no words.

"As I see it, good sir, you have two choices." He waited attentively for Dorian's next words, moving forward slightly to the edge of his seat. She held up one finger, fisting the rest. "Become an ally of The Lady and all her inhabitants, or..." She paused, raising a second finger, "run the risk of losing all protection and face a tormented death upon revealing the secrets of this ship. The choice is yours, Christian. No ill-will will follow your decision," she lowered her hand. Dorian's voice never wavered, nor did it become harsh or threatening.

Christian was simply bewitched. Even at the sound of torture and eventual death he felt drawn to this woman. Dorian's words slipped around him covering his body with their melody.

"Dorian..." Rowan was mad at the effects of Dorian's words over her brother. "What?"

"Release him," Rowan demanded.

"You have never complained of the use before... it is only because it is your brother. I have no real hold over him. You know, as well as I, some aspects of the gifts cannot be fully controlled, they just happen. He is not under any control but his own." Rowan crossed her arms against her body, brooding. "Does not your voice yield the same effect on others?" Dorian questioned her.

Rowan glared at Dorian. She knew she was right.

Christian turned to Rowan without fully seeing her. He shook his head softly and regained his senses. "My loyalty lies with my sister. If hers is with you, so shall mine be." He fully smacked into the real world with the help of his own voice. "I wish to join the crew upon The Lady." He made eye contact with each woman.

"You wish to join my men?" Dorian stared at him, thinking. "Now, that I hadn't expected. I thought you were out of the game," Dorian stood and began to slowly pace in front of the small party. Her petite form was clothed in black from her boots, sliver buckles shining, to her deeply v-necked shirt. She moved as if she had no earthly constraints. Stopping finally to meet Christian's eyes, she waited.

"I understand you ask my loyalty, as an ally, to The Lady, but I wish to pledge more. Looking at you, I can tell, you are as infected as I." Her brow furrowed at his last statement, but Dorian kept quiet, listening. "The pirate life is in your soul, infecting all it reaches."

Dorian gave a slight nod as she understood his meaning. Pirating is a way of life, a choice one makes for oneself. Although, once it is made, the person can never turn back. The call infiltrates your blood stream, never to release you.

His eyes held hers, desperation within them. "The call has never been dormant within me. It has taken all my will to silence it the best I could. I have never succeeded in ignoring it. Please," Christian's voice was pleading, gently. "Please… let me stay. Allow me the honor of serving beneath your colors and the tribute of getting to know my sister in the world we all love."

Dorian's smile was wolfish. "Well, you were rumored to be quite the pirate back in your glory days. However, I know, it has been many years since you sailed the seas. Can you remember?"

Christian's eyes sparkled. "Can I remember the wind against my face? Can I remember the roar of the cannon fire? Can I remember the feel of the ship over the water's currents?" Christian spoke as if in a dream. "I will try to not find insult in your question, Captain." Dorian looked at him with alertness in her eyes. She was hearing what she had hoped too. "I remember. I remember it all as if yesterdays did not exist and my life had never left the sea's call."

Dorian's smile widened, encompassing him.

"It has not been all that long," Christian winked at her, his smile charming. "My blood runs thick with the pirate's promise." He sighed, "I have not been as honest with others as I have myself. I hid from…" Christian stopped himself.

She stood and declared, "I know." Dorian smiled at him, a truly beautiful sight to behold. "I would be honored to have thee, Christian Roberts, serve upon my vessel. My men will be glad. Many were displeased with me when I spoke of your probable death. Everyone knows what a fine sailor you are. They thought it a total waste to kill such talent." She extended her hand and Christian rose to take it. "No harm shall befall thee while you choose to serve The Lady, and the Sirens of the Sea."

Christian clasped his other hand atop hers. He felt the slight angst before Dorian relaxed into his motion. "I am honored. Thank you." Christian bowed his head in reverence.

The steel in her eyes cut him. "Do not prove me wrong, Christian," her right eyebrow quirked with a small smile. "Shall we announce the news?" Dorian eyed Christian. "We have very few secrets here, and if they do so exist, they are hidden deep for a good reason." He nodded, taking Rowan's hand. "Good, come…."

Brother and sister followed behind the captain as they exited Dorian's quarters. She continued onto the helm as the pair paused, looking up to the bridge, to their captain. All eyes aboard watched them closely.

Dorian's voice filled the vessel, telling all her men that Christian had joined them. A roar of approval surrounded them. No *man* was sad to see him join their ranks. If the captain agreed to the union, so did the crew.

"Welcome aboard, mate." Grim heartily slapped his shoulder. "We are proud to have ye."

Rowan laughed. Pulling her brother close, she whispered in his ear. "Dorian would not have tortured and killed you. If you had wished to leave, she would have let you do so willingly because of our accord. However, if you do speak word of The Lady's secrets we all will join in your demise."

Christian looked deeply into Rowan's eyes, "you think so little of me already? Please, give me more time to earn your disgrace." But, he nodded. "I will not betray you or the crew aboard this vessel, Rowan. If you are to hold anything dear, make it my word." He began to pull away but she wouldn't let him.

"A word of advice…" Her eyes twinkled as Christian returned to her. "All these men revere you, but take note that none aboard this ship is without secrets. You are entering a crew where humans are not the dominating race."

Christian intently looked at her. "I will heed the warning, sister, for twice now it has come my way. Thank you." He winked at her and she winked back. *No one is without secrets,* he thought.

"Come on, mate, I'll show ye around a bit. Introduce ye to the crew." Grim took Christian under his wing. If his captain was happy, he was happy too.

As he was led down the stairs, Christian looked back. Far behind The Lady Sebastian's ship was following, steady and fast. He laughed to himself. *Never underestimate your surroundings.* Christian had to remind himself continually of that aboard this vessel.

"I will take my leave of you. For all the trouble this has cost my nerves, food has been far from my reach. Finally my stomach wishes to be full." Rowan spoke with a full heart.

Dorian laughed. "Very well, be gone out of my sight."

Rowan turned back to her. "Thank you, Dorian."

Dorian felt the full force of Rowan's praise. Rowan now knew what Dorian had known all along. "You are welcome." As Rowan began her descent, she laughed at Dorian's parting words. "What fun would life be if I did not let you figure some things out for yourself?"

Dorian watched her sister depart with hope. Rowan had become gaunt and frail. Stress did not agree with her. In the new found relationship with her brother, Dorian had faith that the weight would return to her bones and allow the curves of her womanhood to reform. Though Rowan was still tall and thin when she was at her happiest, her body was fleshier and full in the best of ways.

"Where have you been hiding?" Dorian asked, as Rahn approached from the night's shadows.

As Dorian stood alone at the helm, reveling in the still peace of the evening, Rahn came to stand next to her. The deck below held few souls as the twilight of the evening faded to black.

"The water. I could not endure her decision. Christian still lives. Rowan must have softened at the sight of his retched soul and allowed him to meet the dawn once more."

"You speak in such haste, Rahn," Dorian cautioned.

Rahn cut her off. "No! I do not. I speak in earnest."

"You hold a grudge that is all. At one time you lost your heart to another. You must not forget that. First of all, you gave it willingly. It was not taken from you. I have watched you, through the years, as you have grown vengeful and malicious at its breaking." Dorian looked at her. Rahn was strong, and far too guarded, which is why her heart remained broken.

"Do you not admit it? Can you not learn from this and add forgiveness and trust back into your countenance? Rowan has learned to forgive, to see the truth of her emotions and fears. She is growing away from her darkened past. Why can you not do the same? At the least, you could speak with the man and settle on some terms, or ground rules, so you can work together upon this vessel."

"You are asking that I compromise?" Rahn's voice was rife with accusations, and pain.

"I am asking that you remember that we are also human, and held to mortal laws and emotions. I am not asking for compromise. I am suggesting a chance at salvation." Dorian was calm in her delivery.

"You want to save him!" Rahn was outraged.

"I want to save you, Rahn." Dorian paused, "Better yet, I want you to save yourself. Give him a chance, he may surprise you."

Rahn scoffed. "No one has managed it yet, sister."

Dorian was patient as she spoke with Rahn, but truly she was getting fed up with her willful antics. "His departure is not an option, Rahn. Rowan needs him more than the air needs to make the wind rush through our sails."

Why must you always know my thoughts! Rahn screamed her fury forth. "I *hate* when you speak sanity back to me. I am torn between love and loathe. Life would have been easier if Rowan had chosen revenge over redemption. I could have let my emotions die with Christian as he sunk to the bottom to meet Davey Jones."

"You wish Christian dead so you can continue running from the things you are too scared to face." Dorian stared at the girl. "That is true childishness, Rahn. His death would change nothing for you, nothing within you. The same emotions would still swirl beneath the surface of your skin until you resolved them and let them go. Only you can do this, no one else." *Stop fighting. Stop running,* Dorian thought as she stared at Rahn. Her words were closer to demands than suggestions.

Rahn was quiet for many strokes. "Fine. I will settle my emotions for him, but I will not, I will not, allow him back into my company."

"What you think is best surely is for you." Dorian looked at her with resignation. The fire within Rahn's soul was a scorpion clawing and scratching to be free of its old skin. "I am sorry I chastise you for your emotions, but, do you not think it is time you moved past this and released some of this venomous anger you have been holding? You have grown very bitter, Rahn, and resentful. You have grown more and more untrusting of men. It has been hard to watch." Dorian paused, "As long as you see them as villains you remain a victim."

Rahn was startled by Dorian's last statement. "A victim…." The word stung her as her voice fell.

Dorian nodded. "Yes, you remain a victim until you no longer see villains within their faces."

Rahn swallowed hard. She had done this to herself. She had made herself the victim within their eyes. "I no longer want to see such faces." Her voice cracked as she spoke, the veil beginning to crumble. "But, you are also saying my mistrust has carried over into my interactions with you and Rowan?"

Again, Dorian nodded, but she did not respond.

"I forget the effect my mood has on those around me. I have merely been thinking of myself. I have been living blinded by my fear, the victimization I placed upon myself." Rahn paused, feeling the full impact of the truth Dorian had spoken.

Dorian's cool gaze met hers and she simply nodded.

Rahn nodded back, feeling a pang in her heart. "Right," she responded softly. "My mind needs to work this out. Until then, I refuse to see him for fear that I will take too brash a course of action." She stared at Dorian's face. "Thank you for the searing truth within your words. I will heed it. I no longer wish to see life in this way, but it will take time. Habits do not like to let go once they have built a path within you."

Dorian laughed. "What a scary thing from you, reason," she observed.

Rahn laughed at Dorian's teasing. "I will try." Finally feeling the weight beginning to lift away from her, Rahn noticed that Dorian was hiding something as well. "Something has been bothering you greatly. I have seen that through my cloud of self-righteousness since Christian's arrival."

"Damn, I was hoping you'd missed it," Dorian remarked with a smile.

Rahn smirked. "What is it, Dorian?" Rarely did much effect Dorian. She retained a calm head and dealt with what came her way. Rahn was worried.

"It is Victor," Dorian stated.

"Victor!? Another bug I would see squashed." Rahn gestured with the crush of her fist, the calm leaving her as fleetingly as it had come. "Why?"

"He bares the scent of my husband. A fact I cannot find a conclusion to." Dorian stated. "Our world does not share imprints."

"But... the only way one can carry the scent of another is to be blood-related or to be an Urchin's matching form. Yet, the scent marking is rarely ever exact." Rahn validated.

"It is never exact." Dorian's eyes held the dagger's sharp edge within them. "Jason was an Urchin, but if he had been one of the Two-Natured disposition I would have known it. He would have told me. It's just the smell is so precise... I cannot place its reasoning." Dorian was confused.

Rahn comfortingly touched Dorian's shoulder. "Dear sister, I fear we will have met our match with the men aboard this ship. Hopefully, it will not be to our demise, for I think I have many more years of play left within me. I will leave you with your quandary and I am off with mine."

"Fare thee well, sister. Our demons will soon be brought to light," Dorian added.

"I am sorry I cannot be of more assistance," Rahn paused. "I do not understand all the complexities of our world."

Dorian laughed, "Nor do I, Rahn. Thank goodness finding out is always an adventure."

"Right you are." Rahn's eyes twinkled as she thought of all she still had to discover. The women smiled at each other, knowing they would have life no other way than uncharted.

"Do you feel that?" Dorian grew alarmed in her speech. Looking out over the ship, her eyes widened.

Rahn followed Dorian's gaze, nodding. "The wind has shifted. Trouble will soon break the horizon."

Dorian stared at Rahn. "Someone is coming."

"I will be awaiting your call." Rahn stated.

They both knew that when the currents changed and the winds began whispering chants of warning to their ears, blood would be shed. When The Lady was sought, it was not in friendly company.

"Where are you going, Rahn?" Dorian questioned her sister as she stepped away.

"I cannot be aboard this ship. I am going to swim with my creatures and try to find reason, as you say. I know I am in need of it," Rahn's smile was bright. At that, she was gone with the subtlest splash into the dark waters below them.

"Fare thee well, sister. Find solace with your monsters," Dorian advised.

Rahn heard her sister's last words as her body slipped beneath the ocean's surface. *I will rest well here. These creatures always give me relief.*

Rahn had the will to befriend the darkest of foes and many of them lay at the bottom of the ocean. Her favorite was Serpentine. His body was long and snake-like with coils. He had the head of a dragon and four legs with webbed feet. Serpentine was ferocious with the wail of a banshee. Rahn loved him. He was large and powerful, yet with great peace in his heart. She sought him for her hideout beneath sea. They would swim and talk beneath The Lady's passage.

• • •

Victor awoke as the subtle dawn nudged him from sleep. He rushed to the window, relishing in the oncoming light of day. Too many days he had spent in darkness, captive somewhere far below deck. His senses were overloaded as the light reflected off the mellow waves of morning.

"Good morning, Vic. Glad to see you are well."

Victor's body quickly twisted to find the source of the voice. He had heard no one approach. With only the dim light of morning to light the hall, he could not see anyone either. He shot to the bars of his cell and stared straight across as something moved from the shadows. Sebastian leaned against the cool bars, gazing out the window at the halls end.

"Seb! How glad I am to see you still draw breath," Victor exclaimed.

Sebastian turned towards him, "as I am glad to see you too, Victor. I have spent many days in darkness and delight in the suns soft rays of an approaching day." Their conversation halted at the approach of footsteps advancing from the corridor.

"Christian." Both men said in unison, the same stunned expression plastered on their faces.

"What the bloody hell are you doing waltzing around like you're a free man aboard this vessel of death!?" Sebastian was outraged.

"Have you sold your soul to the devils?" Victor chimed in.

Christian looked back and forth between the men he felt as kin. They were both pressing against the bars as if at any moment they would squeeze right through them to freedom or pain.

How will they ever forgive? Christian thought as he stared back and forth between his friends.

"I did not sell my soul to anyone. It still rests safely within me, although I am now a crewman of The Lady." Christian watched as their faces dropped in shock, disappointment and anger. "Before you reprimand me, hear this... My sister lives. Rowan is a lady of this vessel and I have sworn to protect her from now on, to never leave her side, come what may. Her loyalty lies with the captain and crew of The Lady. As does hers, so shall mine. I shall never let what has passed befall again." Christian's emotions ran deep and fiery.

Victor and Sebastian both understood his meaning, even if they did not agree with it. Christian had long suffered over the death of his sister, and now was his time to make amends. Truly, they were both happy that he could reconnect the pieces of his shattered life.

Victor looked him up and down. Christian had been supplied with new clothing and weapons. He wore his new shirt tied round his waist. He gleamed from the splashing waters of topside.

"Get us out of here then, Chris! I have been caged long enough." If looks could kill, Christian would be a mass of dead flesh on the floor. The intensity of Victor's anger came seething from his body, but it wasn't aimed at Christian. He was just in the way of its path. "Surely they have no more use of us. Let us free," Victor demanded. "You stay silent. Don't you agree, Seb?"

Sebastian toyed with a bar of his cell. He was envious. He wanted to be a freeman aboard the pirate vessel. He wanted to sail beneath its colors, as Christian would. "Actually, the place is quite growing on me," he teased with the truth he felt.

"You unbelievable man!" Victor was on a roll.

"Freedom, Victor? Have you looked around you? Where are you to go?" Sympathy filled Christian as he looked at Victor. Sebastian would be fine he knew. *Sebastian always keeps a level head, but Victor, has a crazed glint in his eye.* Christian laughed. *Sebastian probably wasn't lying with his statement.* "I can do nothing. I am sorry. The only way to ensure your release is to make a deal with one of the ladies. Only they yield the power to set you free. I do not know why you are both still here. They have what they came for." Christian gestured to himself. "I do not know their plans for the two of you."

"They have bewitched you with their beauty and charm, insolent, weak bastard. If I was not caged so, I would throttle you myself." Victor banged his fury on the bars.

"Do as you wish, Victor. It will do you no good." Christian stated, staring at him calmly.

"Hhmmmm..." Sebastian observed him. "I fear our friend will go quite mad, and soon, if he is not released. Best get on that, Chris."

Christian laughed. "Truly, I can do nothing but give an opinion. Your fate is in your own hands, mates, not mine," he paused for a moment, contemplating their current circumstances. "Nor is it in the women's hands. Pick your actions wisely, for they will surely give you away quicker than your wit."

Victor glared at each of them in turn. Focusing on Christian, he spoke with heated words. "How are you so sure those women have, to quote you, 'what they came for'? You know nothing about their real plans, only what they have chosen to show you, Christian."

Christian was speechless as his eyes held Victor's for a brief moment. He could not hold Victor's stare. His gaze was too intense with a clarity of truth that was beating to be free. In a place he was resisting entering, he knew Victor was right. The women of The Lady had many secrets and hidden agendas that Christian, as a mortal, knew nothing of. He did not know his true place in this new world of magic. Christian could have simply been a pawn in a much larger game, but he didn't know, and wouldn't know until the time was upon him. Christian was scared. As he thought about his fate a chill ran down his spine.

He shook his head. "Bide your time, good friends, bide your time." Christian looked over his shoulder at the noises behind him. "Ahhh, a lady comes to deal your fate as we speak." He winked at both of them before departing. "Choose wisely..." he spoke, the words trailing over his shoulder as he walked away.

"Bloody *pirates*!" Victor's voice trailed after him. The caged men's eyes met and a hearty laugh lifted the gloom of their spirits. Victor would need more coaxing, but Sebastian was ready, come what may.

"We just don't understand, Victor, the call of freedom that nestles itself inside your heart." Sebastian spoke, still staring through the shadowed hall at Christian's fading back. Excitement buzzed around him.

Victor gazed at the side of Sebastian's face. "I know it... it infects your bloodstream like a disease that will never be cured," he spoke softly. "The call of a pirate's heart upon the ocean... is unquenchable." His soft voice faded to nothing.

You will feel it again, Jason answered.

Victor shook his head. *But will I want too?* He questioned his counter-part. *Look at what I lost...* Victor's memories were a mash of old and new, his own and Jason's.

Sebastian continued, not hearing any of what Victor had said. "I want that freedom," he added, still looking after the shadows.

The old saying lies true...

Once a pirate, always a pirate. It's in your blood. It's in your head. You can't escape the call of the ocean's winds once you have held the ocean's heart.

• • •

Feeling the warmth of the waking sun on her skin, the grip of the smooth helm in her hands, the captain of The Lady felt at ease upon the crystalline blue of the rocking waters.

"Shall we venture inland, ladies? Shall we return home and let the men below decide their fate?" Dorian's ivory skirts gently floated behind her in the soft breeze. A matching ivory corset snuggly wrapped her upper body allowing the sun to kiss her tanned shoulders. Her golden hair fell freely down her back.

All three women were attired in light-flowing skirts and corsets. Rahn had regained some of her resolve and reboarded The Lady. She stood serenely next to Dorian, wearing her trade mark of bold colors. The deep royal purple of her clothing offset her regal features. Rahn's winter skin became all the more enticing with the sun's kiss of light upon her. She stood proudly, not allowing the fact of who now rode freely upon The Lady to disturb her.

Rowan tended to favor blues and greens for herself, and this fine sailing day was no exception. She had on her favorite summer green with matching top with criss-crossed white lace to cinch just between the small swell of her breasts. Short wisps of a sleeve fell down on either side of her shoulders, lying lightly over her smooth, freckled skin.

Rahn moved to stand beside Rowan, to Dorian's left. She wrapped her arm around Rowan's thin waist. The pair rarely saw eye to eye on any given day, but the unbridled love they shared was stronger than any words of hurt or misunderstanding they could inflict upon each other.

Rowan embraced Rahn's gesture and rested a hand over hers. "Home," Rowan spoke dreamily as she gazed out over the horizon.

Rahn lingered in her sister's embrace with joy, but then was quickly lost to another world entirely as she stared down the main deck at the man working there. His muscles gleamed with sweat in the sun-dried air. He arched and lowered in his task. She unconsciously licked her lips and bit the bottom corner as he bent once more. Rahn felt a hand squeeze over hers and jerked herself back to the present. Her straight black hair caught in the ocean's breeze. Rahn's violet eyes darted back and forth between the women staring at her, waiting.

"What?" Rahn's voice was dry in her throat. She cleared her throat to make it more responsive and, again, questioned them. "What? What is it you vultures want now?"

Dorian turned away from her, smiling. Grim approached the top deck to take over at the helm. He looked back and forth among the three of them. Looking upon his captain's face, he couldn't help but laugh.

Rahn's emotions were displayed openly across her features. She had come back, startled, to the present world.

Dorian met Grim's eyes in mock laughter. There was little that Grim didn't know concerning the three, especially his captain. The pair are confidants. Life would be exchanged for life if need be, no questions or hesitations. Grim would die for Dorian and she would die for him.

"Thank you, Grim," Dorian touched his arm as they exchanged places. "Your turn," she winked as she walked towards Rowan and Rahn.

Grim smiled at her. *No man, or crew, could ever be so lucky as to be aboard this ship,* he thought.

Red flushed Rahn's cheeks as the two stared her down, waiting for her to speak. Rahn rarely blushed. Many a lover she had taken and she never thought more of them when she was finished. Although a ripe mood always followed at the bad end of an affair, going too long between lovers would make Rahn cynical and harsh. She had yet to find a balance between the two lives. She knew the two women staring at her had already determined she had a new interest. *But who* was the question on at least one of their minds.

Make it a gift, or a curse, that men found the three women deadly desirable. Such men would stop at nothing to share their bed. The after effects of romance would only lead to violence, professions of undying love, or fanatical actions at the affair's end. Men could not let go of the notion of the Sirens, clinging to their beauty. The mystical women haunted their dreams long after they had gone, driving some causalities mad. Nor could men find another to deaden their lust for some time to come. Once bedding a Siren, the men could not forget the burning fire beneath their skin…

Rahn glanced back at the man she had been watching. Coolly she answered her sisters, her face regaining its control over the inner heat. "I do not know why you accost me so… I merely long to be home and the sweet dreams of my bed call to me."

Rowan stared her down. "Who is it that catches your eye now? Lust is clearly written across your face. Who? One of the travelers below deck?" The temperature of her gaze heightened against Rahn's skin. "Is it… I dare not say, my kin!?"

Rahn turned to meet her, fire in her eyes. "Of course not! How dare you think such a lowly coupling of me. I would never dream of it. We are none the same and share no common bond between us. Christian knows not who or what I am nor of what I have become." Ice held her gaze. "He does know what we are, you have told him!" Rahn stated as she stared at Rowan. "Very well, I guess you have the right to do so." Rahn said peeking into Rowan's thoughts.

"He is my blood. Of course I told him what he is up against being upon this vessel. I did not think it would infuriate you so. I am sorry for the offense." Rowan was apologetic.

Rahn calmed herself. *I need to tell her, but…* "No, I am sorry. I spoke too quickly in anger. I… I must watch myself." She stared back down towards the deck. "Oh, look, he's doing it all wrong." With that she pushed past the women and marched down the steps to the flailing man neither of the other girls could find.

"Are you fair?" Dorian asked.

"Indeed," Rowan followed Rahn's movements 'til she disappeared below deck. "She speaks as though she hates him, although they have never before met. Rahn certainly puts forth the proper amount of loathing on Christian's behalf, constantly belittling him," her voice dropped off slowly.

Dorian turned Rowan to face her. "You of all people should know, my dear, there is a very thin line between love and hate. Most people do not even know where it lies, nor when they have crossed it. The only tell is when they have landed upon a side." Dorian sighed before continuing. "Do not forget that our sister is a fierce protector over that which she loves. Rahn, in her own way, is trying to shield you, to defend you, Rowan. While her intentions are not always clear, they are most often good."

Rowan nodded, understanding.

"We each have our own path," Dorian went on. "It is not my place to say what Rahn is experiencing but heed this," Dorian stepped in front of Rowan, placing both hands on her shoulders. "Rahn has evils to conquer within her, the same as you and I. Allow her space and time to work them out. All will be revealed upon the proper occasion, when it is ready."

"Yes, you are right. If she withholds something from us it is only with the best of intentions." Rowan eased out of Dorian's grasp, and stepped away, coming to rest against the bridge's back rail. "What shall we do with the imprisoned men? They have no true value to us now that the lies about my brother have been proven false." She dropped her head, and squinted her eyes at Dorian, as a look of utter delight crossed her face. "Dorian!?" she scolded.

"I was only going to suggest…" Dorian's hands went up in surrender as she spoke.

"NO!" Rowan cut her off. "We are not going to harm them or hold a bounty over their heads. *Dead or Alive* the papers will read, with our faces plastered on them. Do you hear me in there, or are you going into full captain-mode?"

Dorian dropped her hands to her sides in defeat. "Oh, alright! You are no fun in the revenge business. I suggest a parlay, then. You take one and I'll take the other," Dorian offered. "We might as well get rid of them in one way or another. They are just filling space, wasting time, below deck."

"Now this sounds like fun," Rowan rubbed her hands together with enthusiasm.

Grim couldn't help but boldly smile out to sea. He loved when his women were being devious. It made them all the more endearing to his heart, intriguing and human. He never quite knew what to expect from them.

"Be nice ladies, we have no need of a return for retaliation once they are freed." Grim cautioned.

"Who said anything about them being permanently freed? We have need of more handy men aboard," Rowan spoke as she and Dorian both smiled at Grim. He laughed at their jest and turned back to steering.

"You make an excellent point, sister." Dorian smiled, surprised by Rowan's sudden statement. "Perhaps there is hope for you yet in the field of revenge," she teased.

Rowan grabbed Dorian's arm as they passed their quarters on the main deck. "But, what of Victor? I know I said neither of them held any importance, but that is not entirely true. He's different."

"I feel your concerns. Victor's dragon responds to force and is triggered by anger within him. The only way to set his true nature free is to come at him so... Alas, he inspires such feelings in me as well. Once I know his path has been reawakened, he shall be free to go," Dorian smiled half-heartedly. "It is a pity to have an Urchin around who's unknowing of his gifts. I do our kind an honor."

"Do our kind an honor? Ha!" Rowan joked with her. "You are going to have far too much fun with this." Dorian stopped Rowan with a firm arm against her chest. "What is it, Dorian?"

"You spoke with him," Dorian's eyes turned on her. "Why?"

"How did...." There was no point. Dorian had attuned her talents over centuries. She could discover any knowledge she wanted. "I merely sought answers. I feel a familiarity with him, from another life.... I wanted to see it through to conclusion," Rowan said.

"And? Did you find your conclusion?"

"No." Rowan flashed to the day of her rescue, to the lost soul that turned her blood to ice. Her eyes glazed over, so Dorian gently grasped her arm, awakening her. "Victor feels the same about me, he recognizes me. It's like we know each other from somewhere else, but neither of us knows from where. He holds no hostility towards me, as he does towards you." Rowan searched Dorian's face. "It's fascinating how his emotions differ so greatly."

Dorian nodded. "So my premonitions have been proven, thank you." Dorian rested her arm against her side. "Shall we carry on then?"

Rowan nodded, but she wanted to know more. "What premonition?"

"Victor is of the Two-Natured. He is a sleeping Urchin. His soul not yet united back into one." Dorian spoke over her shoulder as they descended below deck.

• • •

Victor and Sebastian could hear the hushed exchange down the darkened hall as Christian passed the oncoming tyrants.

"Damn pirates." Sebastian said mildly. "They think they can just keep us here, hostages forever."

"Oh come now, Seb, I see the fire in your eyes at the word. You envy them, do you not?" Victor challenged him.

Sebastian smiled broadly, "Aye, mate, a part of me longs…" his voice went soft as two sashaying figures glided into the streaming sunlight.

"Gentlemen, I hope we do not disturb you." Dorian looked back and forth between them. She could feel Victor's pulse begin to quicken with rage and Sebastian's with excitement. "We could come back if you need a few more moments to end your discussion." She appraised them. "No? No?" Dorian looked from Victor to Sebastian. "We have come to determine the terms of the remainder of your visit aboard The Lady. Whether you remain here amicably or no, until we can dispense of you accordingly, is entirely your choice." Turning her head, Dorian faced her silent partner. The pair shared a silent exchange and nodded in agreement. Each moved to pull at the wooden handle to slide the privacy wall into place to shield the other man from view.

"I request word with the captain," Victor appealed. His companion just stared at him with a slight shock written across his face.

"Why do you think I should grant such a demand? I am not inclined to secure the terms of your surrender because that is what you wish. I have not built my reputation upon requests, Lord Victor," Dorian answered him.

Victor's blood began to boil, but he kept his voice in check. "I believe the negotiations will do us both good, my lady."

Dorian sighed. "You exasperate me. However, I will indulge you. You did ask it of me so sweetly." She could feel Victor's true mind. He was growing furious.

The women resumed pushing the walls into their hold.

"What are you doing that for?" Sebastian asked, stepping back from the wall to avoid losing a finger.

"To ensure you don't hear the terms of the other's stay aboard this ship. Each term will be different and we don't want clouded judgment on your parts because of hearing the other's wishes." Rowan spoke with a zest in her voice.

Sebastian felt Rowan's words float on the air, coming to envelop him, releasing all the tension he held in his body. Her voice was sweet, gentle kisses on his ears. Sebastian jumped as she approached the door, turning it closed behind her, locking them away from the world for now.

"Lucky me," came out in a rush from Sebastian's lungs.

"What?" *I couldn't have heard him right,* Rowan thought.

"I just mean that…. Not that I would have minded the captain, but Victor nixed that." When Rowan moved into the stream of sunlight Sebastian's throat went dry at the radiance of her shimmering skin. He followed the path of her delicate freckles.

Rowan felt his eyes on her. What rich pools of hazel they were. Cocking her head slightly she inquired, "Why do you feel you are lucky, Captain?" Rowan surprised herself at the flirtation that came out in her words. She liked it. She had not felt this way in many, many years.

Rowan stood in front of Sebastian, filling his vision. Her silhouette formed in the sun's backdrop, the rich green of her dress sharpened her features. His eyes ran the length of her long, lean frame. She was beauty he'd never encountered before. All the women aboard this ship were rarities in their stance and exquisiteness. *But her,* he thought.

Finally raising his eyes to Rowan's, he found his voice. "I merely say..." he gestured with his hand.

"My name is Rowan."

A fleeting distance look crossed his face. "Lovely," Sebastian spoke ever so softly, but not an Elemental ear for ten thousand leagues would have missed it had they been listening. "I merely say, Rowan, that I much prefer you be the dealer of my fate, life or death, than any other aboard this vessel. I fear you will be the fairest and most lenient."

Her eyes sparkled. "Please sit." Rowan pulled out the chair of the desk for herself and gestured for him to sit atop the bed. He did so immediately. "So what is your will then... to die? It can be arranged."

"What!? No, no. Of course not! I wish to live. I wish for a long and happy life, milady. I pray someday to see my children grow strong, and tall and have a lovely wife alongside me. I do not wish to die now." Sebastian sat waiting.

Rowan's body gave no hint of even having the slightest interest in what he was saying. She looked bored. "Alright, you have very much stated you do not wish death. Where does your allegiance stand, Captain? Does it lie with the Queen of England or does it lie within you?"

It aggravated him to have her call him *Captain* when he was caged as an animal. Sebastian did not show his disdain.

"I hold a certain loyalty to the crown for she has served me well within my years of service to her cause. Although, my true allegiances, as you call it, lies within the depths of my heritage, my homeland. It 'tis a land of rolling green hills, cliffs that dive to reach the ocean at its end, a sweet air of crispness and winds that whisper of the tales of old." Sebastian's voice lapsed into a dream, one Rowan couldn't see.

"Do you wish to go back home? To your wife and family?" Rowan's voice stirred him with its melodic tone.

"Yes, someday. I want to build a life there and settle down within its safe harbors. However, you misunderstand me, Rowan. As of the current moment I have no wife or children, milady. It is simply a dream of the future to attain such things. I have no intention of going back, just yet, anyway." He smiled at her with warmth. "I feel I have at least a few more years to sail the seas before I return home to Ireland and plant my roots."

Rowan had to hide the blush of her cheeks, so she allowed her eyes to drift out to sea. The sunlight once again claimed her face only to accentuate its planes. Her skin's glow of Sebastian's praise did not go unnoticed.

"I feel in your heart you have a wildness that has been hard to tame. I ask this only once and if you refuse there shall be no hard feelings. Would you have a disposition to join this ship and crew?" When he remained silent, Rowan turned to meet his eyes. "I know of your past, Sebastian, your brief stint as a pirate. Once you have that thrill of life, it's embedded within your blood, always pushing to be set loose again." Her eyes stayed on him. He was a large man, bronzed from days aboard ship or long days of play and leisure. Sebastian's hands showed signs of wear. He did not fear the work for his daily bread, even with his noble birth.

"How did you? No one knows about that." Finally, Sebastian's mind settled on fate. *If the woman in front of me can discover my best held secret then I must stick around to see what else is to be found.* "In my heart, I feel this ship and its crew are not of utter malice and destruction. An effortless reputation born through the fear of men, easily attained. Do I stand correct in this?"

Rowan nodded in accord. "You must know, of course, that not all the stories are a counterfeit adaption. The crew of The Lady is not one to be trifled with. All tales eventually air on the side of truth."

It was Sebastian's turn to nod. He had heard many a bone-chilling tale of life and death of those paired against this vessel. Through observation, he had begun to assimilate what he would find himself mired in if fate brought him back to The Lady. She was a terrifying new breed. "I have no real life waiting for me at my return home. My home has always been the sea. I shall never stray far from her side."

"You accept then, Captain?" Rowan awarded him with a vibrant smile.

Sebastian smiled. "On one condition…"

Rowan quickly regained her outward composure, although her stomach remained full of butterflies. "Yes?"

"I beg of thee, please, no longer refer to me as *Captain*. The phrase holds nothing but angst for me."

"Why?" Rowan questioned.

"I was not a free captain while the name was given me. I was a pawn in a very long chain of command, just like everyone else around me." Sebastian answered with heavy words.

"But, to be given the title of *captain* is a great honor." Rowan responded.

"Not in the way it was given to me. I have listened, and watched, and observed the workings of The Lady. Dorian is free. She is not held under any loyalty but to that which she chooses. She is the head of command, not a middle man. I was never allowed such choice over my actions when manning a Queen's Vessel."

"I understand your meaning, but from what I know of the varying branches of service..."

Sebastian cut her off, saying simply, "Forte."

"Forte?" Rowan's mind was beginning to spin.

"Forte. The man controlled everything, his fingers in every pie." Sebastian spoke with contempt.

"I see," Rowan paused, taking note that she would have to tell Dorian about this new insight. "Well, Captain is off the table. How about Sebastian?" The man smiled at her, nodding, glad to have the conversation diverted elsewhere. "Wonderful. Sebastian, you are henceforth placed under the protection of The Lady. All information you are privy to shall remain yours alone until you find yourself in grave. Is that understood?" She was solemn now. Sebastian nodded, of course. "Good. No secret has ever reached outsiders ears without death soon to follow."

"Truly?" Sebastian asked with surprise.

"How do you think we keep the mystery of our vessel's enchantment?" Rowan paused, "No survivors."

"The stories are true then, all of them?" Sebastian became giddy.

"No, not all to their full extent.... But, who better to remain in lore than the three women who are descendants of its birth?" Rowan rose from her chair in one fluid stroke. The dead bolt dropping echoed throughout the room. She sauntered out leaving the door gaping behind her. Sebastian rose on his feet to follow, but paused at the doorway and bent his head around the corner. Rowan stopped before the hall to stare back at him.

Sunlight encompassed her body. The soft wave of her thick red hair shone in bright reflections. Rowan was stunning. "What lies aboard this ship?" was Sebastian's last query.

Rowan smiled coyly before responding. "You are within the lair of the Sirens, beings of myth and fantasy, with powers thought only true in fairy books. Relax with the knowledge that everyone aboard this ship holds a secret and set of skills all their own. Do not cause offense or you shall see firsthand the gifts of those who wield them." Rowan disappeared into the darkened hallway. "I'll see you topside. The men will be glad of your joining, for word of your naval skills has spread far." Sebastian heard her distant footfalls as Rowan re-entered the world outside.

To say Sebastian walked to the stairs would be denying his lust for the salt air. He ran to the sanctity of the sunlit world and was surprised at its embrace of him.

Rowan had flown to the helm the moment she left the stairs so she could watch Sebastian on his way out unnoticed. Grim just laughed at her, but left her alone.

Does he really like me!? Rowan questioned herself. *He is too handsome for me and too nice. I could not deserve someone such as him...* Rowan watched as Sebastian was immediately swarmed by the crew, questions flying his way as he entered the lion's den.

• • •

Dorian watched as Rowan shut the door behind her and listened for the clang of the lock. *Rowan can handle herself. Plus, that man means no harm to her.*

Debating when to enter, Dorian stood still as stone, gazing over her surroundings. *This is my ship! I know where the exits are,* she thought. She had to bring forth hatred for the man behind the closed door. *He had asked to speak with me! Perfect.* Dorian smiled at the notion that had at first worried her.

Victor reminded her too much of a long distant memory, one that held her love and loss. *Impossible to even consider that he knew him, but why does he carry his markings if not... Ugh! I do not know. My centuries of life fail me in a most crucial hour. Be calm. Allow him to think he has caught me unguarded. I need to lay bare what lies dormant within you, Victor. Unfortunately, it only stirs at my provocation.* Dorian's mind wandered back to the tete-a-tete between them. She had enjoyed it. It was always fun to parlay with prey, the hunt made all the more enticing. *Lord Victor Easton of Athencourt, who lies hidden beneath your skin?* She entered the now enclosed cell with caution on her lips.

"Dorian." Victor addressed her directly from his seated position. His head rested against the back wall for support. He was waiting and ready.

"Victor." Hearing his name from Dorian's lips quickened the blood coursing through his veins. She could feel his pulse beat within her head. *Maybe I need not put physical force on him. Perhaps it can be through seduction... That would be fun.*

Dorian smiled wickedly. "A bold move asking the Captain to deal your fate, is it not, Victor?"

Dorian's smile unnerved him. Victor's confidence began to shake once more. "Have you decided what to do with me? I am of no further use to you, as I see it." His tone was dry and lifeless.

"Quite right, of no use at all." Dorian seated herself in the chair at the end of his bed and looked out to sea. "Shall we throw you overboard and be done with it? See if you sink or float as they do in the witch trials?" Dorian could feel the constant gaze of Victor's eyes. They never left her. "We need to make an accord," she stated, as her calm, gray eyes met his. "Tell me what it is that you wish and I shall tell you what it is that I want."

It took Victor a moment to gather the meaning of her words. *No matter what I say she will come to her own end.* "You ask me what it is that I want?" Dorian nodded. "I want vengeance, my lady, on you. You have taken me from house and home and I want retribution. You have filled my mind with thoughts of you, of your body against mine, the feel of your kiss..." He was standing now, towering over her. "I want amends for the time you have taken from me!" Dorian watched as the sun glistened off Victor's torso. The sight caused an up curve of her lips. "Do you mock me!?" He grew livid at her physical response to him.

"No, sir." As Dorian stood, Victor felt a concealed force push his chest to the back wall. He lay flattened against it, unable to move. The brilliance of his sapphire eyes glared at her.

"There," Dorian's eyes sparkled as she stared into his eyes. "There is the serpent that slinks beneath your skin. He burns bright in your eyes. Do you not feel his heart beat match your own?" Dorian gently placed a hand on Victor's chest, directly over the rhythm of his pounding heart. Eyes like silver pools held his. The ice formed within him began to melt. "Shall we try another way to stir the beast?" She did not wait for an answer. Dorian lifted herself on pointed toe, wrapped an arm around his neck and pulled Victor's lips to hers.

The man inside watched through Victor's eyes as Dorian approached them. His heart beat quickened inside Victor's, making them beat faster as one. As the feelings of Dorian's lips raced through Victor's body, the man inside latched on and took over.

Their lips melded perfectly as heat raced through both their forms. Victor longed to clutch his arms around her body, but the unseen powers Dorian possessed still held his arms firmly to his sides. The kiss deepened in its sweetness as Victor and Jason tasted Dorian's tongue. Slowly, Victor's arms loosened from their hold and he brought Dorian's body even closer to his in a grasp as firm as iron. She fit perfectly against him. This was unlike their first kiss. For one, there was no bloodshed, and second, there was mutual agreement of its taking. Victor felt he could live forever within this one moment.

You can live forever, Victor. Let me help you. Let us become one and reclaim our life! Jason spoke to him. *This feeling we are sharing right now is how life is supposed to be, without separation. Quit fighting me.*

At this moment Jason and Victor had nearly become one. Nearly one heart, one soul and one mind. In this one moment they both loved the woman in their arms. To truly be one united soul, there will be no difference between the memories of your past and the feelings of your present. The Urchin will be one united force, with no second voice within their head.

A wretched scream ripped them apart. It tore out from Victor's body, a voice not his own. Out of an uncontrollable reaction, he pushed Dorian across the room. Bending forward, Victor gripped his head in pain.

Dorian steadied herself. "Are you alright!?"

"I...." Victor staggered towards her but he was knocked sideways as a cannon ball flew through the room, missing him by inches.

I guess you aren't quite ready. I will take our transition slower. Forgive me... Jason felt remorse that he had pushed Victor to the brink. Victor's body wasn't ready, nor was his mental state.

Dorian rushed to Victor as he lay fallen, shattered glass from the mirror by his head. She ran her hands over his upper body checking for cuts and bleeding. A reflection in the glass caught her attention. The reflection was not his own. She held the shard closer to his face.

"Who are you!?" A tear ran down her face in agony. In the distance, she could urgently hear her name being called from the deck. Ignoring her instinct to run topside, Dorian brought the broken glass closer to Victor's skin moving it over his face and as it reached his eyes it shattered in her hand, dissolving on the wind. "I have no time for this. Are you stable?" Victor nodded. Dorian rushed through the hanging door and flew up the stairs.

Victor heard her speaking to someone as her footsteps raced towards the upper deck. Two thin men, very short in stature, entered his cell and examined the gaping hole from the cannonball. They spoke in tandem. Their movements matched each other's as they nodded. One pulled from inside his coat a small dark vile and handed it to the other. Taking it in hand he poured it over the splintered wood. They watched as the liquid bubbled and the wood warped itself back together healing the wound. As Victor's eyes came fully into focus he noted they were twins, exactly the other's match in every way. They spoke in quick unidentifiable words to each other as they stepped over him and left, his existence barely noted.

Victor shook off the scream from the man within him, the pain beginning to dissipate from his mind. Slowly he moved to his feet and regained his footing. "If Dorian is the cause of all of your suffering, Jason, I will see your cause through to the end." He spoke into a shard of glass at the reflection waiting there.

Noooo! Victor, you misunderstand me. Victor didn't hear Jason's plea.

The pain Victor had just suffered had been unlike any other he had felt in his lifetime. It was worse than the agony of a broken heart, more debilitating than a fatal bullet wound, more unbearable than the grief of losing loved ones, and more piercing and raw than being stabbed through the heart. It was every ache and pain one could ever feel coupled with every woeful emotion that came with heartbreak. Victor's only consolation was that it didn't last long.

As Dorian burst onto the main deck, smoke and gunfire blurred her vision. Her skirt floated around her as she searched for the cause of the attack. She did not sense Victor behind her, but she felt his hands as he grabbed her. They tumbled to the deck missing the cannon fire aimed directly at them. Victor covered her body on instinct. Dorian gazed up into his eyes, softening at the blue pools that awaited her. Wood splintered from a bullet near her head.

"We will discuss what happened later. Grab anything you can find to fight with!" Dorian instructed him as she pushed Victor up. He dragged her to her feet, 'til they were both standing.

"Fire all!" Dorian's voice roared over the cannons. Without hesitation she ran across the deck, grabbed the nearest rope and flung herself across to the opposing vessel. She recognized it immediately.

Victor gawked after her. A sword was thrust at his chest. His eyes followed it up to the hand that held it. Sebastian nodded, encouraging him to join the battle.

"Of course," Victor spoke to himself. Sebastian was already racing off to find a foe to fight. Victor laughed and shook his head. No man was safe from these women's allure.

Dorian landed in the throngs of bloodshed. Rahn and Rowan flanked her on the descent. Christian stood protectively next to his sister. Although, thus far seeing her fight, he feared more for himself.

"Leave Blue for me!" Dorian called out. The four fanned out, joining their men in fight and slaying those who stood in opposition.

Captain Blue stood perched over the railing on the aft deck, saving his strength and tracking the advancement of the ladies aboard his vessel. Dorian scaled the steps to meet him.

"My lady, I see you are in fine form. How nice of you to wear white to this co-memorable union. It suits you well." Blue let his coat fall to the deck revealing his soiled clothing. The stench of him assaulted Dorian's senses. He drew his sword and raised it high above his head in challenge. "Let me see if I can't leave you scarred and dying." His yellow stained and missing teeth made for a sad smile. "Unless of course you wish to surrender that gorgeous body of yours to me now and we can skip all the dismemberment..."

"I would sooner die, but since we both know you won't be able to bring me death, shall we proceed?" Their swords crashed against each other in wrath. "I must ask who would be more inadequate than you in a fight, as to make someone send you in their stead."

"Your discount of my abilities strikes my heart." Blue looked almost sad at Dorian's words. They fought ignoring all others. This was not just a fight of captain to captain. It was fueled by hate, with both parties bent on destruction. "You may know the man who paid prettily to find you."

Dorian laughed at him. "Well, obviously, there was a higher hand in this. You did not find me without help, nor would you seek me without a promise of bounty. You are too yellow-livered to do it yourself."

"Your mockery only fuels my determination to see you dead!" Blue yelled.

"Dead? Ha!" Dorian smiled. "Whoever instructed you to find me, I know, would not want me dead." She spoke slowly and with punctuation.

"So you do know who seeks you?" Blue paused, standing a second too long against the starboard side railing, as he looked in awe behind The Lady. He hadn't expected the Sirens to have another ship in convoy. *The women usually only traveled on The Lady without allies.* Blue's employer had said nothing of it. There was never any mention of *two* ships. *The second ship wasn't part of the plan.* Dorian relieved Blue of his sword, misjudging the hand that already lay on his pistol. She stabbed Blue through the heart as a shot rang out above the lower deck. Both Dorian and Blue's bodies collided simultaneously with the deck. Blood stained Dorian's white corset.

The heaven's broke forth, crying their insult upon their fallen child. The tears of their pain tried to wash away the blood of death from the ship's wooden planks.

Chapter

8

———◆———

RAIN POURED FORTH over their heads, drenching the world in its wrath. Black clouds consumed the sky, hiding the light of day. Men could not move after the sight before them. Never had they seen a Siren of The Lady fall in blood. As the bodies of the breathing men quickly chilled from the oncoming rain, their senses regained control over their lost thoughts. A flurry of activity pursued. All the men who sailed under Blue's reign lay broken. Never more shall they rejoice in the breath of day. The Lady always brought forward victory, but one could never wager in the cost.

Grim was the first to reach Dorian. The bulk of his body knelt over her and gently caressed her head in his large hand. His body sheltered her from the rain. "She has very little breath… but it is there." Carefully he gathered Dorian's limp body up into his arms and whisked her back to The Lady. For such a big man, all who watched him considered his movements graceful.

Rahn and Rowan followed behind Grim. "Blow it up!" Rahn ordered, her back turning on the vessel, never wanting to see it again. Even through the rain, Blue's ship ignited as The Lady sailed away. The flame assaulted the awaiting sea as it took it down to Davey Jones, with nothing more than a smoldering heap left behind, as it faded into the distance.

The women knew that Grim would kill everyone before he ever considered leaving Dorian's side. He would take the words as a slur if he was asked to step back. Rahn thought quickly as she searched the crew frantically, constantly readjusting with the ships movements as it fought the looming storm.

"Sebastian! Yes, come here." Rahn waited until he was closer at ear. "Will you sail the vessel home?"

"Of course...but...."

Rahn cut him off. "It knows the way, but it needs a man at the helm to guide it there. You will feel the fight of the waters as they try to tear you off course. Allow the wheel to lead you. The Lady will not steer you wrong, Sebastian. Follow her. Quickly! We have little time to waste."

Sebastian nodded and was off to the helm in a flash. Sebastian had seen the burn of Rahn's eyes and knew not to tarry long before taking on his task. His heart became tight within his chest, a fear he seldom felt. *I do not want the captain to die...* His mind raced as he placed his hands on the wheel. *How does it know the way home?* The battle began as the wheel took on a life of its own at his mortal touch.

• • •

Rahn grew uncomfortable with Christian's proximity, not to mention his attitude. His fervor filled the air, making it toxic. She leaned close to Rowan and whispered in her ear. "If you do not get your brother out of here post haste I will personally see to it that he drowns after his fall overboard!" Rowan stared at Rahn and moved away.

"Calm yourself brother! You are not helping matters." Rowan spoke hushed words at Christian's side.

"I do not understand!" Christian paced in front of her. "How? How is that girl still breathing? Siren or not, a shot that close to the heart.... It grazed an artery!" He was speaking through years of anxiety. Not to mention the numerous cuts and scrapes that lay across Dorian's body, did she not feel them? *I do not understand how the human form can survive such a fatal wound lying next to, if not in, the heart. All my days of sailing the ocean and I have never seen such a lucky survivor.*

Grabbing Christian's arm, Rowan dragged him out of the room. "Dorian needs doctoring, not you brooding over her! Come with me." They entered a closed door at the end of the hall. A lavish canopy bed lay against the far wall. Faint light streamed in through the open windows. Beautiful dark wooden furniture carried the theme throughout the suite. Rowan ushered him to the couch within the seating area to the left and pushed him down to sit. "You need a good stiff drink."

"No. Explain to me how Dorian is still drawing shaken breaths!" Christian was demanding in his questions.

"Yes." Rowan shoved a glass filled with an amber liquid in his hand.

Christian took a long sip. "Why is it pirates always have a supply of rum and little else?" Rowan smiled. Christian continued as if he hadn't skipped a beat. "I have never seen any man live through such a wound. They usually die on impact." He finished his drink and leaned the glass towards her to be refilled. She took it and rose. "Don't give me that snide look and turn away from me Rowan... I am thrilled she lives, but my mind cannot understand why."

Taking a deep breath, Rowan drew on all the strength that still remained in her body. Exhilaration still quickened her pulse, and she thrived on the adrenaline rush, but Christian was beginning to drain her. "When I spoke of Jason's death...."

Christian harshly cut her off. "What difference does a man's death make!?" His body was tense with the aftershock of battle.

Rowan took a deep calming breath and started over. "When I spoke of Jason's death, I didn't tell you everything. You need to know more of that day, brother. The day he died was also the day Dorian lost their baby, a son. Dorian had gone into premature labor and it was killing her. She fought long and hard for the child, but..." A tear streamed down Rowan's cheek. "Dorian lost the boy and because that child was Jason's, it carried Urchin blood. In its dying, it passed its life, its gift, onto Dorian. She has lived many long years, I'd say close to four hundred. However, none of us truly know her age, for she will not tell it. An Elemental only grows stronger through their life span. I fear I could not survive the shot Dorian took today. I have only been gifted as an Elemental for a handful of years in my total of two-and-twenty. Nor could Rahn and she has at least a century on me." Rowan paused letting her words find a way into Christian's mind.

"A *century*...." The word hung on Christian's lips as memories of Rahn's adolescence filled his mind's eye. *How is that possible? How could I have known her youth if Rahn is truly more than a century older than I?*

Rowan did not hear her brother's words, for they were spoken no louder than the breeze. She continued on, undeterred. "Our gifts, by no means, make us infinitely immortal, yet they procure the ability to heal quickly and mix with nature to pull strength, specifically from water, for Sirens. The waters rage outside our windows because they know a Siren is in pain and they offer their form and strength to serve them in recovery, if fate would have it that way..." Rowan paused calling on the ocean's strength for some of her own. "Somehow the Siren's genetic disposition has made our lives impenetrable to humans. Mortals cannot kill us." Christian began to speak but she stopped him. "Humans can injure us greatly, but they cannot bring about our death. Some law of nature few of us understand. However, what Dorian was shot with today was a laced bullet from another worldly creature. Blue knew what he was doing when he loaded his gun with it. His intention was to kill today."

"I am sorry, Rowan." Christian was sincere. "I hope that Dorian pulls through." His thoughts were now occupied by other questions, questions his sister could not answer.

"Me too." Rowan wiped tears from her cheek. "The bullet was venom laced. I'm glad she killed him. Blue deserved to die. He was lazy, incompetent and cruel."

Christian laughed. "My dear Rowan, I don't think I have heard you speak so ill of another before." As he met the cool of his sister's eyes, all feelings of joy fled him. "But yes, Blue certainly appeared that way." Christian stared at his sister. He could see her hurting. "So, that is Dorian's birth into your so called fantasy world. She was given the life of another as you were?"

"Yes, but the bond of love is tougher than that of hate. The child's soul had the knowledge that it would not seize the life it was coming for and so it passed its form onto its mother to give her life once more, to give her a chance."

"She lost child and husband on the same day...." Rowan briefly nodded in response to her brother. "Is her transformation stronger than yours?" Christian continued.

"Bonds of love make everything stronger. Dorian is different," Rowan's eyes drifted as she spoke, and Christian could see that no one fully understood their captain. "Her transition was different in that being was transferred to being, soul to soul, life force to life force; it was a direct transference of *life*. Mine was taken by blood. There are few ways to become a Siren. None are better than the other. None are necessarily stronger, just different. Dorian has a better chance of survival because of her years of growth within this life and form that is all." Rowan sighed.

"Gifts that make you so strong and agile leave room for human error still... Your world is fascinating." Christian searched her eyes. "Is Dorian's body now the house for the unborn child? When the transfer took place, did Dorian die so the child could live on?"

Rowan was amused by her brother's acute curiosity, she laughed. "No, brother. The child, the being, gave its gift directly to Dorian, encompassing and filling her completely so that her life, her soul, her body and mind could live on. The child's fate was to surrender its gifts to another."

Christian nodded as he listened, biting his thumb nail, trying to take it all in.

"Why did you tell me of Dorian's life, I thought you were not…"

Rowan held up her hand to silence him. "Dorian gave me permission. She thought it would enlighten you to a facet of our world, or at least remove your presence for a little while. You were aggravating some of the other crewmen. None of our stories are tightly held secrets, but they hold significance all their own to us, me, Rahn, Dorian, becoming who we are, what we are. Dorian thought the tale would entertain your nerves."

"You read my mind sister. Did Dorian tell you this while she was lying near death on her bed?" Rowan nodded. "You communicate through your minds then…" Again she nodded. "Why ever have use for speech?" Christian asked.

"Because, we like to hear our own voices," Rowan meekly smiled at him.

Christian laughed. "I am sorry." He moved to console Rowan. "I am awash with questions and your captain lies in wait of life or death. Forgive my ungovernable behavior, sister. My mind just could not comprehend what I was seeing."

Rowan grasped his hands within hers. "I can tell you time and again who and what I am, what we are, but you still doubt your own eyes, brother? Dorian lives for now… Is that not enough justification that a world unknown to mortal man exists?"

"Yes, yes it is proof. It is more than proof. My mind simply refuses to see it for what it is. I have seen you fight, not as the little girl who used to spar with me, but as the woman who can kill without blinking. I have sworn to protect you, but I fear my duties will fall short and it will be I who needs the protecting," Christian affirmed.

Rowan stared at her brother with understanding eyes. "Someday, I have faith, that you will not see the world as being so small. That you will look upon its realms with new eyes, and see the vast possibilities it truly holds."

Christian pulled her to him, hugging her to his chest. "You are quite the fighter, Rowan," he kissed the top of her crimson head.

She hugged him tightly for a moment, "We are not all fighters. Sirens are in lore because of their vengeance, cruelty, love of the human man, and his certain death in their hands. Loyalty is strong and rarely broken. Sirens are the most beautiful monsters I have ever seen or heard of. We truly are wicked creatures." Rowan laughed softly at the thought. "The bloodline binds us in a family, one in which we truly do protect each other, no matter the cost," she finished nuzzling into his embrace.

He laughed heartily, startling her. "You say you are not all fighters, and then list off all the reasons that make you a worthy adversary."

Rowan playfully put a fist into her brother's ribs. "What I meant was that

Sirens are as human as you. We feel loss, pain, betrayal, love, happiness, regret, hurt…we feel it all – only magnified. Sirens are all the same, yet we are all different. From what I know, our lineage has given humans the benefit of the doubt, only to be wronged, again and again. It is part of our heritage to claim that which we want upon the sea, as we do. Besides, if it wasn't for Sirens, who would the sailors fear?"

"Each other," Christian added.

"Mmm, but it is much more fun to fear something other than yourselves." Rowan chided.

Christian looked at the girl in his arms, the sister he had lost. "Serene," he spoke soothingly.

Rowan blew out a loud breath of air as she smiled up at her brother. "Busted. All Sirens carry a certain need for vengeance, or retribution maybe a better word, although it is greater than that. We are all peaceful until provoked."

"Ah-HA!" Christian had her there.

"Any Siren can out-fight any man of training. Desire and ambition, goals, make a Siren seek another way of life. When we grow tired of our bloodlust and gain calm through centuries of life, when we tire of this seductive, life taking part of our nature, we can always go home."

"Home?" Christian asked.

"Home. It is a hidden sanctuary, a place all our own. Many Sirens reside there and watch this realm through pools of sight. I do not know what I shall do now. I have no more need of fight, although the currents still call to me, and will continue to do so. Pirating still holds a place in my heart. The thirst for freedom is unquenchable. You can ask either Rahn or Dorian. I have never been much for the pirating business, but it calls to me…." Softly, Rowan laughed.

"What of your ancestors then?" Christian wanted to know more.

"The oldest Siren still in life resides there, most of the time," Rowan had a twinkle in her eye as she spoke her last words. "She is old, far beyond her years, although she still looks sixteen. Sirens are immortal until killed. Our frailty of life is not much different than humans. We are just harder to write off. There are few males in our history. They who do carry the gift, yet they seem to not be as strong in life as Sirens are…. I do not know why this is. Males, Urchins, have a genetic defect, if you will. Although, an old Urchin does make for a very mighty opponent." Rowan's eyes darkened at an unspoken memory.

"So the old gal seeks some fun once and awhile?" Christian joked.

Rowan sat back, staring at her brother's matching features. "She has found love, true love, and real love, to last the ages. The oldest Siren has finally found her mate...." Rowan shrugged. "Isn't that what we all search for in the end?"

Christian nodded, understanding a more complex side of his sister's life he would have never gotten the chance to know. "Thank you for sharing this with me, sister. I feel honored at the privilege of this knowledge."

Rowan's expression changed as she regarded Christian. Her eyes held his in a demanding manner. "Brother, by our blood bonds you are privy to this information. I am trusting you. Let it be known that if you try and speak the gifts and secrets of The Lady you will not find your tongue." His face creased with misunderstanding. "Our bond is stronger than any other form of loyalty. If you speak of our nature with cruel intentions to outsiders, we will know and we will come for you."

Christian looked concerned. "Alright... Is it the same amongst the crew as well?"

Rowan nodded. "The crew's loyalty runs deeper than the mere surface bond of captain and crew. All the men aboard this vessel have a degree of myth running through their veins. Those greater gifts lead them to Dorian. She is their protector, and they hers. In one way or another, we have all saved each other's life upon The Lady." She watched him. "The crew trusts Dorian's motives. She is their captain and therefore, when decisions need to be made, we await her final verdict."

"What of free will!?" Christian's voice heightened as tension grew in his body.

"Have you never been aboard ship before?" Rowan smiled at him. He had never been aboard such a free yet hidden vessel. Many secrets lay seated deep within The Lady's planks. "We have free will at all times, but trust the word of our captain. If a man ever wishes to leave the ranks of The Lady, Dorian will allow him to go, or come back, freely."

"It is trust, then, and devotion that grows between The Lady's wards." There was no question in Christian's words. He understood.

Night had begun to befall their world. The moonlight clouded in mist. Rowan moved to crack a window of her cabin, inhaling deeply the smell of her earthen home. "We near the port."

Christian rose to stand beside her. He could see nothing but waves. "I comprehend now, sister, the intricacy of this matriarchal vessel, and the beings who sail upon her. I will do my best to hold close the secrets entrusted in me, and to serve The Lady without restraint." He placed a hand on her shoulder, pulling Rowan close.

Rowan smiled up at him and nestled into Christian's embrace. "Thank you. I am sorry to appear harsh, but you need to have knowledge of the order of things.

Our secret has been a tightly held one. This ship is shrouded in mystery, which is how we keep our reputation. Although, it was rightly earned, to betray us and our secret of life is fatal." She straightened quickly. "I must go." She met his eyes, "Are you alright, brother, with my leaving?"

Rowan's movements were sudden but he knew their meaning. "Yes, sister. I am fine. Go." Christian lingered in Rowan's cabin for a while after she had gone. All the myth and lore he had heard since birth now seemed startlingly real. Christian had entered a world thought only true in stories written by people filled with imagination for such things. "I will accept this, for Rowan's sake and for my own sanity. My world's view has been altered and is no longer what it once seemed." He closed his eyes and leaned his head back. "Surrender." *I always knew greater things existed in this world beyond the realm of black and white. I have seen and felt them, but chose not to acknowledge them in reality. Now's the time.*

On Christian's way out of Rowan's room, he ran into Rahn in the hallway. She gave him a scathing look and continued on. "Rahn Masago." He pronounced it with accuracy. She had not heard her last name in years, *"Mah-sah-go"*. She felt Christian's eyes on her back as she abruptly stopped. "So it is you, Water Lily of the Sand." Rahn's back tightened at the English translation of her name. "I had suspicions it was you. Your physical form has changed over the years. I barely recognize you."

"Nor do you any longer know me!" He could feel her fury. Rahn spoke with her back to him, still frozen.

"I can distinguish that temper from miles away. During our years of separation you did not gain composure, or the ability to process your thoughts before you send them into speech, I see." Christian grew on edge.

Rahn turned on him. A violet blaze burned into his body. "Do not think I owe you any special treatment! You may share a blood bond with one lady aboard this ship, and for the time being it shall keep you safe, but you share nothing with me! Do not forget it." Her words came crisp and punctuated.

"What haste. I share nothing with you!? Truly, this is the route you wish to take?" Christian baited her, and hated himself for it.

"Yes. You are nothing more than a parasite beneath my shoe, an ant to be squashed. And believe me, when the time is right, I will do what your sister could not! I will take the opportunity for revenge." Rahn was livid.

"Well, there goes the element of surprise." Christian's words threw her back. "If revenge is what you wish, I grant you free reign to take it. I do not fear you or what lies hereafter." Rahn had been moving closer to him in her rage, Christian simply matched her step. "To know you still live assures me of a peaceful after-life. There is no more pain that you can inflict upon me that I have not already inflicted upon myself! Release your venom, Rahn! I await it with open arms." He spoke forcefully into her face, missing her nose by less than an inch. Her hate turned to lust. Christian could feel the shift in her body. "Perhaps you will finally be able to move on after you have defeated your demons. You hold too tightly to the past, Rahn, not even acknowledging your present."

Rahn slapped him harshly across the face. "I do not forget injustice easily. You mock me to your own demise." She turned and stomped off to the far end of the hall, slamming the door behind her.

Christian rubbed his assaulted cheek. "First contact went well, I think." He meandered back towards the deck, laughing to himself. She had always been a wild fire.

Behind the closed door of her chamber, Rahn's face flooded with tears she could no longer hold back. "I love you and hate you still. I cannot forget my injury!" She threw her vanity chair to the floor and collapsed into a huddled ball. "Christian laughs as though nothing has happened! I was not born into this life to be docile and timid. I will seek thee." Heaving tears raked through her body. She feared for many things, Dorian's life and her own pursuit of love were at the top of her list.

• • •

Sebastian stood at the helm of The Lady gripping the wheel with all his might. The battle with the ship had subsided as it grew accustomed to his human grasp. The Lady was not one to take the caress of an unknown lightly. Three-quarters through the voyage they had finally reached an accord. Sebastian spoke sweetly to the ship and reassured her that her captain would be returning soon. Smooth sailing with little resistance ensued after that. As they began to reach home port, Victor's constant pacing behind him was scraping his nerves raw.

"For loathing someone as much as you do, you are showing an ardent remorse at the fair lady's injury." Sebastian was tiring of the continuous angst encroaching on him from behind.

Finally, the disconcerted man stood still catching his breath. The image of Dorian's lifeless form intruded on his mind. The replay of her crashing into the deck, the red liquid escaping her body, taunted Victor.

"I hate her." His words were loaded with an immense fire of anger. He replayed the memory of Dorian's head as it crashed into the deck. All life leaked straight out of her eyes as a dull finish covered them. Her chest no longer rose with breath. Victor was at war. He thought this was what the man inside wanted, but all he felt from Jason was consuming anguish. Victor's brain did not feel sorry for her pain. Dorian Lily deserved every devastating injury. She was ruthless in her cause, whatever that may be. The man inside was raging at this thought. Victor should have been there to stop the bullet from entering her smooth iridescent skin. Jason had wanted their shared body to take the shot.

Ludicrous, Victor surmised.

You should have saved her, Victor. Jason stated before reflecting in silence about his wife. *She cannot die! Her destiny is yet to be fulfilled...* He was as concerned and confused as any aboard The Lady.

How could I despise her so much and still want to comfort and protect her? A Siren, or whatever it is Dorian truly is, must be a witch of some sort. She has to be. No woman... Victor thought of Rowan and Rahn. *No group of women could hold so much mystery and beauty about themselves without being cursed and damned to a life of eternal servitude to the devil himself!* Not that Victor believed in such things.

"Victor. Victor!" Sebastian was sick of these games.

Victor crashed into the present, delaying the inner fight for now. "WHAT!?" he yelled at his friend.

"Get out of my sight before I throw you overboard." Sebastian spoke with steeled words. "Do not speak ill of my Captain."

"*Your* captain? *Your* captain!? Oh, excuse my insubordination towards *your* captain. A captain you claim so earnestly and without question. A captain you have sailed under for less than five minutes! YOU used to be captain of your own ship! Remember that, Sebastian?"

"I was a captain, one of many, but I was not free. I am free aboard this vessel. Yes, I serve a captain, one I have taken without qualm. One who instills a greater sense of loyalty and trust within me than any word from a superior commanding officer ever did. This choice runs fire through my veins and fuels me with life! I have never had need for such a structured existence as was bestowed upon me in the Queen's Navy. I was a servant of will. Here, I am a player in the game. Stand down in your accusations of my motives, Victor. I require life without behavioral limitations. You may not, as is your choice. You always blended well within the restrictions of society. I always felt my back against the wall, itching to run."

That hit home for Victor. As much as he liked chasing the women of society he felt the same way about it as Sebastian did. *Trapped.* "You feel I was reformed to society!? Quite the contrary. However, I do not agree with you taking orders from this pirate!"

Sebastian let go of the wheel and affronted Victor. "And why not, Vic!? Is it because you lack the courage to do so? Is it because this woman, my captain, inspires within you a fight you never knew existed? Emotions you fear to let surface!?"

Victor's throat went dry. His eyes held Sebastian's with bitter resentment. "Your captain! The satanic-witch has enchanted you as well."

A voice of reason called to him. *Your fight is not with him,* Jason soothingly spoke to Victor.

Victor's chest began to calm from its heaving wrath. "You're right."

"What?" Sebastian was astonished. *Did Victor just resign from an argument before he won his way? Impossible!*

"What?" Victor's eyes focused on Sebastian. "Oh. You're right." He fumbled over his words. "I am sorry, friend. You bring a new light to my eyes. I released my inner torment onto you when it was meant for another. Forgive me."

Is this a trick? This was a new tactic Sebastian had not seen before from him. Victor held out his hand, he took it. "Who was it meant for?" Sebastian asked, not letting go of Victor's hand.

"Myself," he spoke softly.

Sebastian did not understand what was unfolding before him. Victor almost appeared broken, tired and saddened. It was a look he had never seen across the Lord's face.

Sebastian shook Victor's hand with gusto, "Yes, forgiven." Sebastian paused, searching his face and, again, not yet releasing Victor's hand. "This is not like you..."

Victor smiled slightly. "I have been brought to new light. That is all. You and I are more alike than we may think. I long for the life you were brave enough to grab hold of."

With hesitance, Sebastian nodded and released Victor. "We approach land. Go and help the crew prepare for docking."

"Okay, Captain." Victor hurried down to the main deck and held tight to the riggings as he was instructed.

Grasping the wheel again, Sebastian watched. *I will keep a close eye upon you, Victor. I do not trust this side of you... What dark desolate place have you entered within yourself?*

• • •

The day had grown into a dark night with ominous waves breaking through the air. The Lady pulled into port and its passengers quickly moved into action. Grim held Dorian in his arms as he slowly descended to the dock. A small girl with hair the color of a raven and green eyes to match her father's approached him.

"Daddy!" She charged towards him and slowed at the sight of what he carried. "Is D alright, Daddy?" Her wide eyes looked up to him. "Daddy?"

Grim nodded. "Yes, Ezzi. She is fine, tired from the journey. I will take her home."

A tall woman with light brown hair falling down her back arrived in the girl's wake. "Grim...." She looked from his arms up into his face.

"Take Ezmerelda home will you, Lidi?" Grim requested of her. "I will be home once the captain is settled."

The warm liquid honey of his wife's eyes comforted him. She moved to place a hand on Grim's upper arm. Lidi leaned up to kiss his cheek and gently whispered in his ear. "Is she alright, my love?"

Her touch gave Grim console. "I have prayed that it will be so. Do not worry Ezzi with this, Lidi. I will be home soon to your comfort."

Lidi nodded, her hand sliding from her husband's large arm as he walked away. The moonlight accentuated Lidi's fine features. She was beautiful with her rose colored cheeks and soft face. She knew Grim loved her deeply, but his heart also rested with the frail woman he held close to his chest. *Dorian, I hope you fair well, for all our sakes.* Lidi gathered up their daughter and hurried home to make supper for the defeated heart of her husband.

Grim stared down at the pale bandaged woman in his arms. He should have taken the bullet for her. A stream of moonlight broke through the clouds and landed on Dorian's cheek illuminating her skin. His lips took on a solemn smile. *She will heal,* he thought. *Once she loses her light I will worry.*

A large hand clapped over his shoulder. "Do not allow your conscious to be so hard on you. I can hear your thoughts friend."

Grim laughed, dissipating the inadequacy in his heart. "You and the women," Grim spoke as he glanced at the pale blue eyes staring back at him. "She will live, Aldus." He stopped his steps and looked at the tall Viking next to him.

"My heart beats anew at the sentiment." Aldus tightened the grip on his shoulder. "Wait." He turned back and called orders to the crew to finish unloading and return home with haste to rest. "I will accompany you. Have we notified the Shee?"

"Yes, Canon ran ahead with word." Grim was at ease knowing Canon was light footed and could relay the message to the medicine woman adequately.

"Good," Aldus said hating himself. The pair continued on in silence. "I should have been there, you know, Grim. I should have been the one to take that injury, not her. Not Dorian. It shouldn't have been Dorian."

"We all thought the same thing, mate. There is nothing either of us could have done, Aldus. Dorian has a fate to fulfill just like the rest of us." Grim's speech was full of hope, hope for Dorian's destiny.

Aldus glanced over Dorian in Grim's arms. "She's too stubborn to die, and when she wakes up she'll let us know that, too." He tried laughing.

• • •

Christian and Rowan followed a distance behind the lumbering forms of Aldus and Grim. Christian looked at the Viking, a terrifying looking man.

Christian placed his coat over his sister's shoulders to ward off her chill. They walked together in silence down the long dock and up the sandy beach to the green glade. Their steps echoed up the stone pathway towards the towering castle which appeared impressive and daunting atop the hill. Christian paused at the entrance to the draw bridge, taking in the full effect of the castle. The large stone structure was alight with servants readying for the return of their masters. Rahn had apparently rushed ahead of them to open the gates and awaken the staff. Christian could not find her anywhere.

The towering wood doors stood open to a courtyard. Stone pathways led strategically to various entrances with cool grass and flowers dispersed throughout the enchanted place. Entering into the walls of the fortress, it felt as though one transitioned into another world. Magic could be felt within the tingle of one's skin. A large willow tree stood near the double doors at the end of the courtyard. Its branches floated on the breeze with soft pink flowers fluttering gently overhead. Christian and Rowan walked straight for it. Water flowed under the bridge as the willow's leaves tickled the tops of their heads. Looking up, he noticed three towers. *Three towers for three Sirens,* he thought. Everything around Christian connected to a common path before they entered the main entrance of the castle. Enchantment floated on the air around him.

They entered into the grand hall bustling with servants rushing to and fro. A collection of pirates were dispersed into small groups, speaking in hushed tones. Everyone appeared so at home here, even amongst the mix of some of the most lethal men in the world. Conversations ensued between old friends. There was common ground amongst them. Far to the left, down the darkening hall, Christian watched as Grim carted Dorian towards the winding staircase. A tall white haired man followed close at his heels. Christian found Sebastian with food and drink in his hand as they passed by the dining hall. Rowan pushed Christian on towards Grim's path. He followed her up the long staircase wishing it were lighter so he could see the vast land that surrounded him. He could hear the crash of waves on a far-off beach.

Where is Victor? Christian wondered. *I have not seen him since before port.*

As Rowan and Christian entered the oak double doors, Dorian already lay atop a white fluffy bed. She looked as though she belonged amongst the angels. Her blonde hair lay around her body in wisps. A plump woman worked over her wound.

Christian took a quick moment to admire the room. *The uncluttered space fits her as a glove,* Christian thought. *That's how Dorian is, straight forward and clear.*

"Mmmmm…muck nick. She trattle mmnnnew say hacka laou." The rough, hoarse voice of the small woman startled Christian.

Rowan stood next to her, hanging on her nonsensical words. "Yes." She looked up and sought Grim. He was looking sorrowfully down at the inanimate form of his captain.

"Grim." His sad eyes met hers. "Please, go, rest your mind. The healer needs calm to do her work." He nodded at Rowan and hesitantly took his leave.

"Aldus?" The Viking man now turned to Rowan. He knelt at the bedside gently holding Dorian's hand. "I need Rahn if you can find her. She does not answer my call… Wait. You can go to the hothouse and bring me the Shee's batch of herbs."

"Rowan… I," Aldus tried to protest, failing miserably against the Siren's commands of him.

Rowan held up her hand, "No. You are best at finding. If you cannot find Rahn, seek the healing herbs. The Shee needs them for Dorian's wound. The bullet still rests within her. The herbs will help to bring it out."

"I do not wish to leave her. You already know this." Aldus' glare was ice. Christian moved beside his sister, ready to fight.

Rowan put a hand against her brother's chest. "Aldus is Dorian's brother-in-law. Aldus, this is my brother Christian. He means her no harm. Go get some sleep, brother. Nina will show you to your quarters."

"I will go." Aldus stealth-fully exited the room, glaring at Christian, untrusting of the man they had ventured to kill.

"He is her brother-in-law?" Christian asked, hoping the giant was out of ear shot.

"Yes. They have a long-term devotion of each other. He is ill at ease with her injury. Aldus is a good man, nay a great man. Since his brother's death, he and Dorian have grown even closer. He vows to protect her at all costs. The resemblance to his brother is uncanny. If you had ever met them in another life, you would scarcely have been able to tell the difference between Aldus and Jason, though they are not twins. Aldus is the younger."

Rahn entered, but stood still in the doorway.

Rowan looked to her. "Why did you not answer the call?"

"I cannot be summoned as your dog, Rowan. I had other things to attend too. I assisted Aldus. He brings the remaining herbs." She slinked past them to the Shee's side and began pulling off the blood stained wrap as the Shee had instructed.

Christian looked after them. "What language does she speak?"

Rowan stared at them. She pulled her brother closer to the door and whispered. "We do not fully know. It is a mix of the old word and the language of a dead culture. It is easiest to try and understand her gestures, for the language is so old, few can learn it. She was cursed many years back and her words cannot find a way of communicating in the current age, for otherwise, she could. We are all adaptable within the world's change. In truth, the Shee speaks utter gibberish and only speaks aloud to get our attention. Dorian is the only one who can fully communicate with her in tongues. Aldus does his best to answer back, but even he cannot fully understand the Shee."

Aldus pushed past them without a word and knelt beside the Shee, awaiting instruction.

"Go sleep brother, you will be better for it," Rowan suggested to Christian.

"Ye...." Sebastian stumbled into the room, disconcerting everyone. He walked sideways to the bedside, Christian and Rowan at his back. He stared down in wonder. The liquor made within the castle walls was distilled for the tolerance of immortals – a tolerance which far outreached that of humans. Sebastian appeared to have had more than his fair share with the dinner provided for the weary travelers upon arrival. The crew always enjoyed drinking with mortals.

A green salve had been placed around Dorian's bullet wound. The Shee looked up at Sebastian's drunken intrusion. She had one eye stitched shut and deep lines of age crossed her face. Her hair was frizzed around her head in white and gray tufts. Her clothing hung about her in dark rags. Dorian's body buckled up from the bed, regaining the Shee's attention. She hit Aldus on the arm motioning for him to hold Dorian down. Concern crossed Aldus's face as he held down Dorian's upper arms.

"What?" Sebastian was in shock. The bullet began forcing its way out of Dorian's body. Smoke emanated from its path. He couldn't wrap his drunken mind around it. *Dorian should be dead, or at least fast on her way. How could this be?* His face spoke volumes.

Dorian's body raged again and Aldus had trouble holding her violent thrashing. She writhed from the bullet's burn. Her eyes suddenly opened, black within their depths. The toss and turn of her head was violent.

Sebastian jumped back. "What is going on!?" He tripped over himself, falling backwards.

"Christian!" Rowan's warning brought the urgency to light.

Christian gripped Sebastian's upper arm, pulling him to his feet. "Come on, Seb." Christian forced him out of the room. Dorian's scream followed them. Their blood ran cold as they stood on the landing just outside. Sebastian pushed against him trying to see the action behind them. Aldus was bleeding from the lip and the tracks of Dorian's nails across his arms brought forth more multiple paths of blood. Aldus's pain-filled eyes were the last thing Sebastian saw before Christian slammed the door.

"But...." Sebastian jumped to get past Christian's shoulder, as if he could see straight through the wood to the other side. "I have never seen anything like it..." His voice was filled with wonder. "Did you see what Dorian did to that Viking man? Don't mess with her, eh..." he began laughing to himself.

Christian turned and shoved Sebastian down the stairwell. "No, I imagine you haven't seen anything like that. There is much neither of us understands. Let them be in peace and do what they need to save that girl's life. One of them will explain the occurrences to us when the time is right." Christian already knew. His sister's voice pounded in his head. Although Rowan thanked him, she also gave forth more information.

"Hah, girl? She is older than both you and I." Finally Sebastian turned his back to the door and stomped down the stairs ahead of Christian. "Where's Victor!?" he demanded in his drunken stupor.

Christian shook his head. He was amazed at Sebastian's sense of adaptability. His friend had no problem believing that these women were supernatural, nor did he have any trouble accepting it. He simply rolled with the punches. Christian wished he could be more like that, but with the reappearance of Rahn into his life he was scared past the point of clear logic and acceptance. She was his holy grail.

He watched as his friend stumbled down the last remaining stairs. Sebastian very seldom partook in the pleasure of wine, but when he did, he lost all logic.

On his way out of the stairwell, Christian spoke with one of the men waiting there, "Do not allow any others to enter this night, for it shall be long and gruesome."

"Aye," the guard answered.

As Christian walked away, he heard a bang and turned to see the double doors to the stairs being locked behind him.

• • •

"It will be a hellish night until that bullet makes its way out of Dorian's skin," Aldus commented.

Dorian's black eyes stared up at him devilishly. Her pallor had become ghost white and tension stiffened her body. Deep within himself, Aldus was petrified.

"It was laced! The continual burn within her tells of it. Who would have given Blue a laced bullet? Surely he did not acquire it on his own," Rahn added.

"Nay, Blue is neither that smart nor that devious," Aldus spoke between thrashes. "No doubt he was merely a decoy to distract us from a bigger plot that is coming our way."

Rowan paced the floor behind Rahn's chair. "That bastard!"

Rahn stared up at her. Rarely a foul word was heard from Rowan's lips. It sounded so wrong.

"He's gotten more cunning with age. I wish he would give up this vendetta. He killed her husband for goodness sake!" Rowan found Aldus's eyes upon her. "And your brother, what more does that insane lunatic want?" Rowan never stopped in her stride, nor did she notice Rahn's mouth agape at her cursing.

Rahn gazed out to sea. She wished she could kill the bastard herself. His lust had carried on long enough, bringing agony to them all. "He won't stop until either he or Dorian is dead. You know that, Rowan. Or until Dorian finally consents to love him as he so ardently loves her." She snickered under her breath. "I doubt he knows of Blue's actions. He was never clear of vision. He sees only himself, which is why he still thinks Dorian is his maker. He has not taken the time to really *look* at her. Impossible man!"

"The bullet was intended for her. I have no doubt that whoever hired Blue to carry out this plot, had not instructed him to kill, least of all Dorian. This has his name written all over it. However, the plan did not factor in Blue's hatred of the women of The Lady. He most likely assumed that Blue would obey any order given. Now we are living with his error," Aldus spoke the truth they were all thinking. "As usual," he added in his last breath.

"Yes," Rahn's voice was soft and dreamlike as she spoke the simple word. Her mind was lost within the racing thoughts of her brain. She needed to slow her mind so she could target them, work them out.

"We need to find him." Rowan stared at the surprised expressions on Aldus and Rahn's faces. "Blue knew what he was doing. He probably leapt at the contract to find The Lady. Blue has held a grudge against us, against Dorian, for years. He has always hated that women could survive in his world, a world in which he barely stood out. He was slight and ignorant."

"Well it turns out he couldn't survive in his world," Rahn remarked snidely. "Putrid excuse of a man. Little and insignificant Blue was. A bumbling idiot," she included under her breath. "You truly want to find him?" She stared at the smile upon her sister's face. The fire-haired, tall reed of a girl wanted to fight. Nah, she wanted to bring the fight to his door.

"Her breathing has slowed. Her heart's barely beating," Aldus spoke with terror. Rowan raced to Dorian's bedside. She stared down at her limp, lifeless body.

Dorian's eyes flew open, shocking them all, and her hands reached up to grip Aldus's forearms. His body jolted in shock. Rahn sprinted to Rowan's side as she jumped back in fear, hugging her close. Dorian looked like a woman possessed. Her body once again writhed in torture, contorting under Aldus's firm grip. His arms had been scraped raw but he bit back the pain of her lashes.

Dorian screamed the wail of a Siren's warning to the sky, awakening the Shee from her slumber. She swiftly shuffled to Dorian's side, protecting her head against the backlash from the echo beating against the walls. All but Aldus covered their ears to the screeching sound of fury. Blood poured forth from Dorian's chest as the bullet forced its way out of her skin.

The Shee instructed Aldus not to let go, regardless of Dorian's truculent protests.

Hold fast, she spoke to Aldus. *It's almost over.* While her hands held tight to her ears, the Shee yelled her gibberish over the wail. The Siren's call emanating from Dorian's throat could kill. Any mortal, and immortal, who could not protect against its call, lay near peril.

By the time the last of the bullet ejected from Dorian's skin and rattled against the stone floor, she was gone. Her body grew cold and winter white in color. The black of her eyes lay open and unblinking. The light of her life-force disappeared from her skin, the glow of her gifts gone. Dorian's arms that had once held tight to Aldus fell flat to the bed. He stared down at her, shock written across his face.

"En siaga neit cator nishka. Met vedir sa quishe gigo." The Shee spoke gesturing with her hands. *Gather the bullet, but do not touch. I need to examine the poison.*

A tear streaked Aldus' face as he moved to close the lids of Dorian's eyes. "That cannot be it... her life cannot..." he could not finish.

"Hhmmm," The Shee grunted. She bent to the table behind her, rummaging through her herbs and potions. She quickly mixed a concoction in a bowl with a vile smell. "Pusha kale." *Place this on the wound.* She shoved a small bowl into Rowan's hands. After bending to gather the bullet in cloth she hobbled out of the room. The group stared after her in bewilderment. They knew not what to do next. Dorian looked every inch a corpse.

"She's leaving? Just like that..." Rowan started after the round, tiny woman.

Rahn hastily grabbed the bowl out of Rowan's hands and smeared the mud colored paste over Dorian's wound. The blood flow stopped immediately. As her skin repaired beneath the paste, the inhalation of Dorian's raspy breath made the company jump. Aldus, still kneeling behind her, glided a gentle hand through her hair and rested it on her clammy scalp.

"Her skin begins to glow," Rowan noticed.

"She is healing!" Aldus felt joy growing within him.

"It will take time. But, I wager that before she has fully recovered, Dorian will be back behind the helm. Plus, within a week she will be heading straight for James." Rahn couldn't help but smile. She knew she would be right there alongside Dorian when it happened. "Stubborn wench," she said under her breath. Rowan and Aldus met Rahn's eyes and laughed. She was right. Dorian was as stubborn as they come.

"I heard that..." A meek voice spoke to them, barely audible above a whisper. Dorian had a small smile spreading across her face. As her eyes fluttered open, she took in the sight of the three. Gray swirled back into her eyes as her body recovered from the poison.

Rowan and Rahn sunk onto the bed to either side of her. Dorian winced at their touch. "Oh!! Sorry D. Sorry." They spoke in unison.

Rahn draped an arm around Dorian's neck and hugged her head to hers, kissing her cheek. "I am glad you live."

"Barely," Dorian joked.

Rowan gripped Dorian's hand. "How do you feel?" She stroked her arm tenderly.

"I hurt like the devil in heaven, but I'll live." Her voice was not her own, hoarse and dry from torment, Dorian did not recognize it.

Rahn laughed against Dorian's skin. "You will live to best the old goat, yet." She rose to look down at Dorian. The paleness of her skin remained. "Shall we leave you and come back to check in a few hours?" Rahn's hand smoothed the hair around Dorian's face. "You need to sleep, sister."

"I will come back with water." Rowan moved smoothly from the room.

"Dorian," Aldus gazed down at her.

She lifted a weak hand to his face. "Yes, you may stay longer if it is your wish," Dorian answered the Viking.

"It is." Love poured from his body, glowing to warm hers.

Rowan returned silently. "Drink this, sister." She lifted the clear, cool liquid to Dorian's lips. "Shall we leave?" Rahn gave a short nod in answer. Rowan skimmed a kiss across her forehead. "We will be back, love. Rest easy."

Thank you, Dorian wordlessly replied.

"Aldus take good care of her," Rahn called over her shoulder.

As the women exited the room, Aldus came around to lie next to Dorian on the bed. "Take my will and heal your own."

Dorian tried to protest but he wrapped her body within his and held her close.

"I will keep you safe." Aldus stated. Dorian's hand rested atop his arm and gently squeezed as she drifted back into the land between the living and the dead. As gently as he could, Aldus hugged her close. "I cannot forgive myself for not accompanying you." His eyes stared out the window as the moonlight broke through the clouds over the ocean, illuminating the blue waters beneath it. "I shall make amends." He clutched Dorian's body closer, encasing her within his own.

Rowan shut the door quietly behind her as Aldus lay down. She made her way down the stairs behind Rahn. *He will keep her safe,* she thought. A gentle smile filled her face.

"Mighty!! I could kill the man myself! With my bare hands!" Rahn stomped down the stairs raising her hands to the air in fists. Her tantrum filled the hollow space between the walls.

"Lower your voice and contain your rage." Rowan slowed behind her to widen the distance between them.

"She has crossed over into the land of the dead," Rahn declared. "An encroaching tidal wave couldn't wake her." Rahn turned back to look at her sister as she reached the arch of the double doors. "He should die slowly and painfully, as Jason did. The righteous, cock-sucking…" Her voice trailed off as Rowan hushed her with her hand.

"Look," Rowan whispered as she pointed down the hallway.

"What!?" Rahn whirled around. "What am I looking at!? I don't see anything."

"Well you wouldn't, would you? There's nothing to see." Rowan's laughter echoed down the hall reaching the ears of the looming force hiding in the shadows.

"You bitch," Rahn laughed slightly. "If you are done making fun I am going in search of a distraction." She pounded down the hallway with determination. Wrath still filled her mind. She truly sought solitude within her chamber.

Rowan stood in the doorway. "Go, eat, and be merry." She spoke to both guards. "Lock this door before your departure. Seal it and go, men."

"Yes mistress, Rowan." She waited until they had left and slowly walked down the darkened hall, her thoughts consuming her.

· · ·

Rahn thundered through the long halls, her mind one-tracked. Christian could feel the intensity of someone's mood radiating from the hall. The menacing air hit him like a tidal wave. He turned to see Rahn stalk past the open door. Swiftly deserting the map he huddled over, Christian moved to follow her.

"What is it you seek, pirate?" Rahn's voice floated back to him.

Christian thought he was being ever so silent in his pursuit of her. "I am not in search, my lady, but in quest of you." He should have known better than to quietly follow a Siren. He laughed at himself. *Ignorant man, catch up with the game.*

Rahn's hips deliberately swayed in front of him, as she slowed her steps ever so slightly. The scent of her came back intoxicating, ensnaring him. "I am here, but you should not seek me in my current state. I wish revenge on you. However, I wish it on another with a deeper hatred and urgency of the moment." Christian couldn't take his eyes from her. Glancing over her shoulder, Rahn gazed at him. His white tailored shirt was open deeply to his chest revealing well-formed muscles. His skin was tanned to a golden hue. The shirt was tucked into a pair of fitted tan trousers, and he wore black boots upon his feet. *Every inch the pirate,* she thought.

"You haven't changed from battle, my lady. May I ask why?" Christian asked, still slightly behind her.

Rahn still wore the same frock from earlier, yet much harder of wear. Soiled with blood, not all her own.

"You know very well why few of us have changed from battle. We care for our captain. Dorian's health and recovery are our primary concern," Rahn sighed deeply as she spoke. "Since you are so adamant in your pursuit of me, I'll allow you to follow me to my door, and that is all." She spoke with sarcasm upon her lips, but, truly, Rahn was too drained to fight Christian this night. She was not ready for the conversation that was beckoning them both.

Rahn slowed to allow Christian to walk closer to her. He grabbed his sword from its sheath and held it lightly to his side. She stopped, her violet eyes sneering from his sword to his face.

"In case I break through your resolve, I'll have to defend myself. I want to be prepared." Christian held out his arm for Rahn to take, but she brushed it off smugly and continued in her step. "Perhaps I will need this sword after all," Christian spoke under his breath as he gripped the sword tighter in his hand, following her.

After seeing the fragility of life pass before her eyes in Dorian's collapse, Rahn was having a change of heart. She did not want to be alone forever. *Why not be with the man who you once gave your heart to? Surely he would accept it again...* Rahn fought with herself over the good and bad reasons for allowing Christian back into her life. *I just can't forget... or forgive?* All the questions Rahn despised asking herself were creeping back into the light, waiting for acknowledgment. Generally, forgiving and forgetting were not in her vocabulary – vengeance, grudges and torture were.

Christian followed behind Rahn up the winding staircase to the far right of the castle. He could barely make out her form in the dark light of the narrow shadows. The moon still played hide and seek behind the clouds. As they reached the landing a cool breeze sailed through the windows to sway their senses. Rahn halted in front of the sturdy, wood door. Her body pressed into its frame for strength. The mistress of Rahn's life was calling to her within the sweet words of her salty smell. As the ocean's waves broke against the beach, Rahn could taste their wishes and desires.

"Thank you. That will be all." Rahn's tone was cold, masking the beating of her heart.

Christian approached quickly behind her as Rahn reached out to open her door. He swung her to face him pressing his body against hers into the door. "After weeks of tormenting me with your mood of ice, you think I'm going to let you leave that easily?" Passion burned dark in his eyes.

"Leave what?" Rahn scoffed, pushing him away. "A sniveling man who cannot forget the past?"

"You cannot forget it either, Rahn. I can see it in your eyes. I can feel it in your mood when you are around me. You are angry and have not forgiven me. But, for what, Rahn? Tell me of my injustice to you so that I can make it right." Christian pleaded.

Tears threatened to fill Rahn's eyes as she looked at him. "You…" she spoke with a broken heart, but could not continue. "No. If you do not know what you have done, then I will not enlighten you. You should know what you did, Christian, to evoke my anger."

One broken heart stared at another, in silence.

Christian was the first to break it. "You are angry with me, but it is not because of me. You made yourself feel this way, Rahn, not me." He paused, gauging Rahn's reaction. "You allowed anger to be the only thing you wanted to see, regardless of the truth." He moved closer, not yet denied for his actions.

Christian slowly raised his right hand up to cup Rahn's jaw. Cautiously he brought his lips down to hers. She held her breath pushing her body deeper into the door, wishing to break through it. Christian had not yet met her lips. As he pushed his hips into her, Rahn released her held breath, and deeply inhaled. Her head dizzied within Christian's scent, as it always had.

"Let us forget the past. Let us forget the pain. Let us both forgive the injustices we have placed onto one another, Rahn, and start anew." Christian ran his eyes up and down her face. He recognized every inch of that face, all the hidden beauty that lay just behind the shield of anger. Christian could see it trying to break free from its master's hold. Too long had this woman been hidden from the world, from herself.

Rahn opened her mouth to protest, but her cry was lost within Christian's kiss. It was a kiss every inch of her being remembered.

Rahn brought her knee up to his groin, but Christian had already anticipated her reaction and blocked it with his legs. He grabbed her face in both hands and deepened the kiss. His tongue roved her mouth, tasting her familiar warmth. She brought her fists up to his chest, but before she could use them for beating, he rapidly took a wrist in each hand and firmly held them to her sides, forcing her head back into the door.

"You have always liked a good fight, Rahn." Christian's voice was deep and husky. He knew she fought him because she desperately fought the demons deep within herself. He knew she still loved him, Christian could see it circling the anger of her eyes.

"Of course, and, as you know, I never pick a fight I can't win." Rahn's words came out in gasps as his lips moved down, nipping at her neck. Her hands weaved into his short sandy hair seizing it tightly. "Stop. This. Now." She demanded. Christian looked up into her eyes and they scalded him.

"That is all we are, a game?" Christian disputed her with his tone. He could not believe what he was hearing from her lips.

Rahn said nothing. She simply held his gaze.

"There is to be no love shared between us?" Pain seared across Christian's heart. "Loving one another was something we were once very good at together." Christian rose to his full height. "I thought you denied me out of punishment and would soon regain your senses. I thought your anger could be reasoned, as it once was." Pain tainted his last words. "Why do you do this, Rahn?" His emotions were palpable. "Lover's words used to cross the threshold of your lips with my name!"

"Yes, words of folly cross everyone's lips at one point or another. You should know we all have taken courses on acting, my lord." Rahn's voice was pointed. "I shall never love you, but I am pleased to find you thought I once did." Christian's eyes came to focus on hers. Black caverns of loathing reflected back at her. Rahn could feel the fury leaking from his pores.

"Is this truly how you wish to play!?" Christian's tone was thick with anger. She nodded. "Very well," his lips came close to her ear. She could feel his breath soft and warm against her. "I remember," he whispered as Rahn's eyes grew wide. "I remember the young girl begging me to take her virtue. I remember the same girl advancing on me for what she wanted, something I would not willingly give without her full consent and knowledge."

Christian slammed her against the door kissing her softly. "Do my actions fuel your lust or hatred for me?" he asked as he pushed away from her.

A smile curled Rahn's features as she stared up into Christian's face. Swiftly, she threaded her fingers through his hair, yanking his head down, pulling him back to her lips. She kissed him roughly before releasing him.

Rahn next pulled his left ear to her mouth so that he wouldn't miss a word of what she had to say. "I will never again love you," she stated before shoving Christian backwards, into the balcony railing.

Christian laughed as he regained his upright stance, leaning back against the railing to look at her. "Thank you for at least admitting you had loved me, once. It makes all your words henceforth unreliable." He paused briefly, noticing how Rahn was squirming. "All those years ago, that was not merely for jest, you playing with my heart. I have loved you since you were a young child, but as you grew into a woman, my adoration changed into one of a lover. I see now that yours changed alongside mine. Thank you, for you make it quite clear, you will no longer love me again, and that I can believe." Christian stood still in front of her, his arms crossed protectively over his chest.

Rahn shook her head. "You were simply an adolescent whim of my young heart, easily overcome with age."

"You know, Rahn, you forget that I know you better than anyone." Christian declared. "For example, in this moment, I would accuse you of being a liar. You are portraying all the classic signs of your deception – tense shoulders, erratic movements and verbal abuse. But, if I thought there was hope of the two of us once again falling in love, I would ask that you, please, tell me of the injustices that I have so wrongly laid upon you and how I can amend them." He was sincere. "I would then say, I am not one to plead, but here I am begging in front of you!" Christian bent to both knees on the cold stone floor. "Whether we are together again, or not, let us at least have this void between us mended."

Rahn gawked at the giant of a man on his knees before her. But, pride would not allow her to back down from her stance. Christian was correct. He knew her, far too well, but, regardless, she would not succumb to even a reconciliation of friendship so easily.

"The injustice, good sir, is working itself out. You need not make amends for they will do you no good." Rahn yelled at him. "I also have no great need for anymore friends," she pushed past him, heading back toward to the stairs in an attempt to make an exit.

"What has become of your heart that it is now as cold as the stone I kneel on?" Christian asked of her.

He did not recognize her. What had happened in her young life to make her so full of contempt as a woman? Where had the love that filled her very bones fled to? Where was the woman who he loved? What had become of the woman who had loved him? Where was the woman who he had wanted to spend the rest of his life loving and fighting for?

Who was this broken, haunted creature that walked away from him?

• • •

"Sebastian?" He turned to see the beckoner of his name.

"My lady?" Sebastian bowed his head slightly from his position. The effects of the alcohol had cleared from his system and his mind had found clarity.

Rahn's fingers called to him from the darkened hallway, "Will you accompany me?"

"Would be an honor, milady. How shall I assist you?" Sebastian rose and walked from the men at the card game.

"We are glad to see him go," Canon spoke.

"Aye, he takes too much of our money!" Laughter followed Sebastian out of the library.

Sebastian turned, "You will do well with the practice in my absence. I look forward to your heightened skills when I return gentlemen." He laughed and turned to his companion. "Wonderful men. What can I do for you, Rahn?"

"Yes, they are great men," Rahn's laugh was soft. "Shall we further our engagements of The Lady?" She ran a mild finger down the center of his chest.

Sebastian's gaze enticed her. "Are you sure you are ready for more?"

"I am ready," Rahn's smile was bright and consuming. She was ready to feel something other than the dismal hole within herself. Sebastian was the perfect distraction.

"Mischief plays within your eyes," Sebastian broadly smiled down at her, the rays of which warmed her. "I hope you aren't thinking of cheating... again..."

"Cheating! What? How dare you accuse me of such things," Rahn was lightening now with mirth.

Sebastian and Rahn had formed a bond upon The Lady. He had become a safe place for her. They could verbally battle wit for wit. Rahn appreciated the camaraderie of a like mind. Their friendship grew, but, because of the other inhabitants aboard, they kept their relationship a secret. The pair would sneak off and play games or challenge the competitor's fast wit. The companionship morphed quickly and with the frenzy of battle, turned into one of greater support. Rahn needed his silent shoulder to run to when all else was cascading around her, and Sebastian loved to hear the grandeur within her stories, so he would gladly accept her company.

"Aye!" Sebastian looked down at her. "How could I say such things about you?" He tapped his fingers to his chin quizzically. "Perhaps, I have witnessed their truth!"

"*Nancy*...you just can't stand being beaten by a girl," Rahn taunted him. This man, the man joking with her in camaraderie, was safe and warm and dry. Sebastian was the best sort of companion because he wanted nothing from her. He was not attracted to her. Sex was where Rahn found most of her trouble lurked anyway. A relationship without it was a godsend.

"Tell me of your wishes this night, lady. Where shall we start?" Sebastian was eager to play with Rahn some more. She had the humor of a man, which made her all the more funny as a woman.

"Hhmmm… How about fencing?" Rahn suggested.

"Lady, I am too tired for that at this late hour and I fear you would use it as an excuse to vent your day's frustrations on a poor mortal such as myself." Sebastian held a hand over his heart and bowed slightly. "What else did you have in mind?"

"I truly just wish for company. I do not really have a game in mind." Rahn felt vulnerable at her request. Sebastian smiled. She loved his smile. It was completely open and without obligation.

"Company, you say? Alright, I can do that. Actually, I was perusing the study across the hall and I came across a book of mythical heritages." Rahn was wondering about Sebastian's motives. "I would love to have a read. You?" Rahn stared at him perplexed. "I know it is not a game of wit, or a rush to win my money at cards, or a lesson in swordsmanship, but you will have your company and I, my expansion of knowledge of the world I am now subject to," Sebastian finished waiting for Rahn's answer.

"You are a strange one, Sebastian. I know not many men who actually *like* reading." Rahn looped an arm within his and lead him across the hall. "Very well, I just ask for the occasional funny retort or ridiculous antidote from what you read."

The banter between Rahn and Sebastian was more like a set between friendly opponents. The pair got along famously, but had no interest, what so ever, in anything more than friendship. Rahn liked Sebastian because he was a male she could talk to for more than five minutes without getting bored. Sebastian had a wealth of knowledge that Rahn could learn from, or add more too. Sebastian was teaching Rahn some rules of engagement with the sword and she was teaching him some samurai movements with a long blade. They pushed each other.

In the wee hours of the morning, Sebastian asked to take his leave of Rahn's company.

"You wish to rid yourself of me?" Rahn responded. "The book is not interesting enough for you?"

"Well, yes," Sebastian laughed. "It is only growing late, or early, depending on how you look at it. Our day has been long. I wish to clear my thoughts in the night air and then return in search of my chamber and the deep sleep that will ensue." He smiled. "I will pick up the book again tomorrow," Sebastian's eyes found an abandoned chess set in the corner beside the fireplace, "and, perhaps, a game of chess?"

"Your smile is devilish," Rahn noted. "Very well, be off with you. I will see you in the morrow. I accept your challenge of the game. It is yet another game in which you will lose."

"Ha, ha, my lady, we shall see." Sebastian turned to her before he exited through the door. "Rahn, you never told me what was bothering you."

Rahn's laugh sounded more like a soft exhale of air. "I did not think we had that kind of relationship, Sebastian. I thought we were just in it for the manly bonding," she mused. "Besides, isn't that what women are for, to listen to my problems?"

Sebastian laughed at her description. "Aye, the manly bonding is grand. We are both learning how to cheat at various card games in different languages." He searched for Rahn's eyes and held them. "I'll bank that you did not tell your women friends, either." Her stunned expression said it all. "I thought not. Very well, goodnight, Rahn. Keep your woes within you for one more night."

"Be gone, you cad!" Rahn laughed at Sebastian's back. "Goodnight, friend." She whispered at his departure. She admired him. When he said something, he meant it. He was straightforward. With Sebastian, you knew where you stood. He was gracious, and ardent in learning everything he could. His passions were knowledge and learning, no matter where the lesson came from.

Rahn had wanted to speak with him, to release the misguided monsters that resided within her, but she couldn't. The support of his company was enough to calm her. She would speak with him tomorrow. He could give her insight into the man she once loved.

The smooth air of the night did Sebastian's conscious well. As he approached the sandy beach, he saw a lone figure staring out to sea. Remembering a face he had not seen since landing, he changed course to approach the person.

"Victor? Victor!? Is that you? What are you doing out here?" The night had become cold and dark, with clouds hanging low over head. The moon barely lit a path along the dark waters.

"Answer me." He stood a few feet back from the man as his feet pounded against the dock. Excitement hung in the air, although it was not his own. "We have been looking all over for you, mate." Something wasn't right and Sebastian felt it seconds too late.

The man turned on him, the sharp end of his blade angled right at Sebastian's chest. "Hello, Sebastian." Sebastian's heart froze at the ice ridden tone. His body quit responding to his brain. "Reach for your sword and I will have to kill you, and I was so hoping you would join our side."

"Nicholas?" The tip of the sword scratched against Sebastian's coat. "What are you doing here? Where is Victor!?" Sebastian demanded. Two men crawled up from beneath the deck and flanked him. Sebastian looked past the thin man towards the end of the dock. "Who does your man carry!? If 'tis one of the women your head will be had!"

"He's assisting me, of course." Sebastian heard the voice at his back. "I have no need of your little fair weather prince. He merely stands in my way." Captain Forte came into view on Sebastian's right side, his eyes bearing down on him. "Inside that castle is something I want. Now, I must take something I don't want in order to draw out the thing I want. Do you see?"

Confusion creased Sebastian's face. He took a step forward and was immediately stopped by the guns that now faced him. "What do you want? Who is that, there?" He motioned with his head down the dock.

Forte turned and looked behind him. "No one to worry over. I 'spose I have you to thank for leading me to this island. Did you know that it cannot be found? Well, save for those who know where it is... It is a very well-kept secret, 'til now of course." Forte walked back and forth across the deck, "I am of Urchin blood you know, and even I didn't know where it was! Those women, they hid it from me," he mumbled to himself, anger within his every step. "I want Dorian. She is my love and maker. She gave me birth into this form, creating what I am…. I want her returned to me post haste!" Now Forte was yelling.

Sebastian had always known there was a different aspect of Forte that he kept hidden. No one who was a captain could truly be that inadequate at sailing the open waters. He finally saw the mad man peeking out. Forte had no reality save for what he created. Sebastian had to think fast.

"Dorian? Why do you seek a corpse?" Sebastian scolded him, his voice remaining calm. *Distraction is one of the best rules of the game.*

"You lie!" Forte was enraged. He stopped directly in front of him and his figure grew as his coat rose towards his ears and his fists clenched tight.

"Nay. I saw her death with my own eyes. Blue shot her with a laced bullet. Once she made the journey home, Dorian died upon the bullet's departure of her body," Sebastian held Forte's gaze. "I watched the whole thing." His mind cringed at the hazy memory. Such pain, such sorrow, everyone could feel it.

"Lies! All lies!" Forte's eyes swirled with rage. "I do not believe you. She lives."

"NO!!" Sebastian shouted. "She does not!"

"LIES! Nicholas!" Before Sebastian could react he was unconscious falling to the floor. "Allow him to gain composure and see the light of joining my league. Drag him off the dock and make sure to hide his body beneath it," Forte instructed. He was hoping that in the light of day Sebastian would join his crew. Sebastian had fantastic nautical abilities and he could read the sea. Forte needed more men like that. Sometimes, he felt he was surrounded by imbeciles.

Chapter

9

———————◆———————

FORTE AND NICHOLAS WATCHED behind darkened shadows as the exchange between Rowan and Rahn passed at the entrance to Dorian's chambers. He did not know that his prize possibly lay dying above him because of his ill conceived plan of misdirection, and slighted distraction. Forte could feel Rahn's anger. She stomped off down the hall to the right leaving Rowan, alone.

"Follow that one then," Forte gave instruction to his liege. "I am glad the other one turned away. She would be too angry to deal with, put up too much of a fight." Forte and Nicholas waited till the drifting of footsteps down the opposite hall faded. Off they moved through the shadows after Rowan. "Wait till she is indisposed. We want capture to be at the most vulnerable moment."

Nicholas nodded to his Captain. Forte smiled widely and thought back to his newly acquired leverage if his plan to capture a Siren of The Lady didn't quite pan out in his favor. Forte always thought having a back-up plan was an utter necessity and his last bargain had been greater than he could have ever bartered for. They waited until silence filled the hall.

Forte had been questioning Seth's loyalty for some time and when Seth took up a relationship with Ziah, Forte thought it cute but passing. He could not have been more wrong. Forte's second nature fell in love with the Siren in spite of Forte's dismissal of the union. Ziah had become a weak link in the bond between them. Every step Seth took towards Ziah was a step away from Forte and his plan. Forte needed Seth on his side. He needed their will to be a united front to best execute his plan of recapturing their lost love.

Being an Urchin meant, that in all probable respects, they should not exist
in the first place. But thanks to Sirens in lust, mortal males made their way into a
history dominated by women. Further, a genetic defect occurred with the Urchins
arrival into the Elemental realm, the Two-Natured. The soul of a male splits in
two upon the male's transition into his Urchin life. At this transition, another life
form, a whole other body, is created to house the second half of the man's soul.
A freak of nature is created. The two forms are neither better than the other nor
the same. The Two-Natured share the same soul and every other aspect of their
physical form, mental state, spiritual inclination, and emotional balance can be
exactly the same or drastically different from one another.

Yet, another barnacle on the side of Sirens, not only were men leaking into
their lineage but now they could double. Only Urchins could be of the Two-Natured life, but not all of the men's souls split. The Two-Natured is not gifted
immortality as the other Elementals are. The soul must reunite at some point
before death, in order to have a full immortal life. Otherwise both forms will
perish from existence. One body is gifted from the womb to house the first half of
the soul, while the other form is born of the sea, containing the second half of the
incomplete soul. The soul must unite in one body, one form, to gain immortality
and the full rights their life has to offer.

Forte thought Seth was every bit what he, Forte, had embodied in his younger
form. Seth wore the same coal eyes as Forte did. His features were handsomely
hard and his hair was full in its brown thickness. Seth was also surprisingly strong
and able bodied at any task. The two shared a soul and appearance, but little else.
Forte felt pleased with his decision, almost gloating. He had decided that Seth's
body would not be the one to continue with their immortal life. To take on the
same body, you also took on the same mind. Forte could not have Seth overpower
him with his warped sense of time and reality. In Forte's mind, Seth was weak and
needed to be controlled – his death was certain.

Weeks earlier, Forte pondered what his next step of action would be in
reclaiming his maker. He decided he would need greater leverage in negotiating
than he thought previously. *I know just the person,* Forte thought. *And then, I will
have Seth's undivided attention, too.*

Forte had taken a boat out to the Isle of Ore just past the pirate town of
St. Saul. Very few souls ever purposefully went to the Isle of Ore. They did not
want to encounter what lurked there. The small island could be seen from miles
around with its jagged rock cliffs and barren landscape. The sailors in St. Saul
would wager over cards and drinks that the loser had to swim out to the island

and return unscathed. Everyone cringed at this bet. Instead the loser would buy the men at the table another woman for company in hopes that the true nature of the wager would quickly be forgotten.

Forte tied his boat at the end of the dilapidated dock and steadily made his way over the broken boards and missing planks to the mountain side. He looked up at the tiny beaten trail that lay ahead of him and cursed. Forte hated the unknown. With thoughts of his creator filling his brain, Forte steadied himself as he climbed the hillside, tumbling rocks in his wake. As the trail of serrated earth finally began to level, the ground beneath him evened out and Forte walked into the mist and moss-filled opening at the trails end.

He looked around at the unsettling silence. The setting was too serene. "Give me strength, Dee, to bring you back to me," Forte spoke a soft prayer.

Dee was Forte's creator, his maker, his lover and his guide. She gave him the bite that transformed his life of sanity into chaos. She enticed him with immortality, and with the sweet whisperings of gifts thought only attainable by the God's themselves. Dee gave him life within the realm of Sirens. Forte took a deep breath and a slow step forward.

"Whoooooo are youuuu?" A shrill voice called to him from a place Forte couldn't see. "If you continue walking, we will have to kill you and we do sooo love the taste of fresh flesh in the morning." The voice had a childlike air to its sharpness. "Take another step," the phantom beckoned Forte.

"I wish to speak to an Ore," Forte demanded. "I am Captain James Forte and I would like to make a request of your people." He stood frozen in the clearing listening for movement. He did not want to agitate his new friends, or enemies.

"Niiccccccce save, Forte," the Ore goaded him. "We do not like demanding people around here." Forte was staring at the rock face in front of him as a set of light green glowing eyes began to appear. He jumped back. The body of a child followed the head that emerged from the cliff. "You are flighty for someone who carries an Elementals blood, Forte." The Ore stalked around Forte's frozen body. She was elfin-like with pointed ears and long slender fingers. Her head was round with a square jaw, and her skin was the color of wet earth. The Ore's body was no taller than a child of four or five. "Pleasssse, Forte, tell ussss what it is you would like from usssss." Her voice was liquid evil. "But," her eyes taunted him, "be aware that we do not take requests. All exchanges come with a price."

Forte nodded, his mouth beginning to dry. "Of course, there will be two sides to this negotiation. You will get what you want, and I will get what I want."

The Ore smiled slightly, without opening her mouth. "Continue," she waved her arm around the opening. "We are listening."

Forte cleared his throat before he could continue, "Can you not transform yourself into anything, any person?" Forte was growing comfortable in his surroundings of glowing eyes and small venomous people. He almost felt at home in their lair of hostility.

A high-pitched laughter echoed from all around him. The Ore who had been speaking to him bore into his eyes of coal. In a second's transformation, Forte was looking at an identical version of himself.

"What is it you want with our skillssss, Jamessssss?" The Ore asked of him as Forte watched a forked tongue hiss out of his twin's mouth.

Forte described to his listeners a tale of love, betrayal, deceit and revenge. He was animated and alive with his words. "I need your help in deceiving appearances so I can regain the love of my lost creator and unite my soul as one, and all the power that comes with it." Forte's smile was wicked.

The Ore liked him. He was stupid, and crazy, power-hungry. Those kinds of people were always the best ones to strike deals with – for they usually fell quickly in their quest, making the price all the more rewarding to claim.

The Ore looked around to all of her comrades and eventually her glowing eyes transferred back to Forte. Her body contorted, and broke, as she transferred back into her small form, discarding that of Forte's. "We will agree with your tassssk, but all of our work comesss with a pricce." An Ore's grin was terrifying because they had three rows of sharply pointed teeth.

Forte crouched close to the Ore's face to make his point known and to show that he did not fear them. "Name it."

The Ores screamed with glee all around him, causing Forte to cover his ears. "We will meet you in three days time with our price," said the one who had been speaking for all of them.

"What!?" Forte yelled over the screeches from the Ores.

"Three days." The Ore held up three long fingers with sharply pointed nails.

"Oh, alright, three days," Forte yelled over the screeching. The Ore nodded her head and smiled, jumping up to kick Forte in the chest. He went flying backwards off the cliff into the ocean below.

Damn tarts, Forte thought as he sunk below the water's surface. *I might as well take a walk.* As Forte's feet touched the ocean floor he began gliding over it. He so missed being able to reside here as he used to. Water was the birth of Sirens, the women's lineage, and, thus, the Urchins origin as well. The water was their source of solace and power.

A dark cloud of sand and ocean rock began to swirl around Forte's body. He could do nothing to stop it.

"I hear you have just come from the Ores. What would you want with them, James?" A voice spoke to him through the dark waters.

The swirl's walls kept Forte trapped. "What concern is that of yours?" Forte shouted. *How do such things travel so fast?*

As the water's shift subsided, Forte was joined by the ethereal form of a man in black garments. "I want in so I too can be free!"

"Poseidon, you are free…." The other's man's wail of rage cut off Forte.

"I am NOT free. I am still under the thumb of my father," Poseidon exclaimed. His eyes glowed aqua in the dim light beneath the sea.

Forte laughed at the craziness of the man. "You wish to overthrow Zeus, the God of Gods?" His laughter only irritated Poseidon more. "It cannot be done!"

"Yes, it can. If we release Calypso." Poseidon's eyes grew large with the images of taking down his father. "She is not governed by anyone once she is free. I, we, can use Calypso to over throw the Gods of Heaven."

Forte saw the advantage of this union. He could later use Poseidon for his bidding. Forte smirked in the darkness. He sidled up beside the angered man and sang the sweet words of his plan into Poseidon's awaiting ears.

Satisfied that he had told him just enough, Forte glided away, leaving the man with his qualms. *Silly man, you are soon to be mine! I will rule the sea and overthrow the land.* Thoughts of power flooded his greedy mind.

Poseidon watched him, laughing softly to himself, as Forte disappeared.

You have no idea WHO Calypso is. Poseidon smiled wickedly. *She will kill you upon her freedom.*

The Sea God let Forte go. Never reveal more than is needed. Poseidon knew the man had lied to him and withheld large pieces of the plan, but he didn't care. If Forte could help him release the Water's Goddess he could play along for as long as it took.

• • •

Rowan finally left the arch of Dorian's stairwell. She stared long after Rahn. Her mood still lingered in the air. Rowan made her way down the opposite corridor. It was dark and desolate as she stepped further down the hall. The sounds of the night's folly began to fade into the distance. She followed the passage as it curved its way around to the left, climbing the stairs that awaited her there.

Rowan entered her chamber. The ease of being there, in her own place, rushed through her veins.

Home, such a sweet word, she thought. The classic English furniture filled the room in dark woods and delicate pieces. Every time she entered her room, the sight of it sent her far away into happy thoughts of Ireland. It took her home, to a place before capture, transformation, and piracy, a place where the smell of her mother's cooking wafted to her nose in the wee hours of the morning. Rowan lingered on the threshold before entering, recalling her mother's sweet voice. She smiled. *Someday soon, I will see both of you again.* Happy memories of her parents filled her.

Rowan was drained and far too tired to concern herself with possible impending doom waiting behind her door. She washed quickly and changed from her day of battle. She nestled beneath the covers of her fluffy sage comforter. It was not long before she was lost deep in sleep. If she hadn't been so tired from battle and the stress of tending to the fallen of the day, she would have sensed them. Their movements and presence were a threatening dark cloud just off the horizon. Rowan would have heard the muffled voices or smelled the scent of their warning on the wind.

Awake my child... Quickly!!

A beautiful angel called to Rowan within her dream. As the being came closer, she saw it was the angelic face of her matriarch. The woman had long flowing golden-red locks that floated around her face in tendrils. Her gown was white with reflections of gold as the light streamed across her body. She had the rosy cheeks of a cherub below her high cheek bones. The blue of her eyes matched the calm waters of the sea's magnificence on a bright sunny day. Her age was indeterminable. She was simply immortal.

Be aware... she spoke again, the words entering directly into Rowan's mind.

Be aware of what, Ziah? Rowan responded as her dream began to spin towards darkness.

Forte held an arm across Nicholas's chest. "Ziah is calling to her." He closed his eyes. "Devil woman," he spoke under a coarse breath.

Forte took a deep, steadying breath and grasped the amulet that always hung around his neck. He closed his eyes tightly and willed himself to enter Rowan's dream world, pulling Ziah out of Rowan's realm from behind. It simply appeared as if Ziah had faded into the distance. Rowan's mind jumped, between dreaming and sleep, before she fell deeply into slumber once more.

Forte then appeared in the center of a circular cell, lined with stone from floor to ceiling. There existed no door. Darkness filled it save for the moonlight over head.

"You have no part in this, Ziah! Stay out." Forte yelled as he stared down at the slender woman in irons chained to the wall.

Despite Ziah's sorrow, the bronze color of her skin still glowed slightly in the moon's praise. Soot smeared Ziah's cheeks and dirt soiled her once white dress.

"I have every right! You are mad with jealousy, James. Leave my children alone! You have no place in our world. You should have been disposed of the moment you were created." Ziah spoke with conviction.

Forte dove towards her. On bended knee he smacked her head against the wall behind her. Ziah briefly lost consciousness as Forte pulled her head around. He closed off her breath beneath his hand.

"Harsh! Do not forget that at one point you did love me…passionately, if I may remind you." Ziah gasped for breath and clawed at his arm holding her down. Forte put his lips to her ear. "How else would I have lured the oldest Siren in existence into an antechamber designed to make her powerless?" Forte's smile caused the woman's skin to crawl.

"I have never loved you," Ziah spoke with calm, clenched words, as his hand released her mouth.

"Oh, that's right," Forte said, smacking his forehead with his free hand. "You love my counterpart, Seth. How stupid of you to get involved with him. He too will be dead soon." Forte's words were wicked. "Nonetheless, you are in no place to do anything about my actions, are you, Ziah?"

It was true. The man had locked her far away from salvation.

"I forgot you could send messages through a dream, little wench." Forte smacked her cruelly across the face and watched as blood fell from the corner of her lip. "When I return home with my love, you will pay for this insubordination. But first, allow me to remove the last vestige of your powers. We mustn't have any more slip-ups now, shall we?" He placed both hands around her skull and with a deep inhalation sucked the last of Ziah's will from her.

The chamber was forged to make all those held captive within it weak, and those who held their prisoners there stronger. The chamber allowed the assailant to gain the powers of those trapped within its walls.

Ziah screamed wretchedly to no avail. She did it simply to prove to herself that she still could. Forte grabbed her face so the aqua of Ziah's eyes had to look at the blackness of Forte's soul.

"So young in body and wise in mind," Forte said as he yanked her to her feet.

"You should have known better, Ziah." He pushed her hard against the wall. "I will always find out, no matter what you do, especially if your motives are against me!" His face was inches from hers, his stench of evil filling her nostrils.

"What are you snickering at?" Ziah could feel Forte's appraisal of himself. She remained calm. This man only thrived off of anger. She was not about to aid him in becoming stronger.

"The oldest Siren in existence is now powerless! I feel rather proud of myself actually." Forte laughed. "You fell for the oldest tricks in the book!" He laughed. "What an idiot," he declared. "You are held captive by a lesser Urchin!" His smugness was sickening. "How does that feel, Ziah?"

"You are the idiot, Forte." Ziah stated, his glare disturbing her. "Somewhere along the way you have made a mistake. Ore's are known for turning on their employers to start an all-out war, just for entertainment. They hold no allegiance to you or anyone, not even their own kind! Poseidon is rash and hateful, but smart. He can catch on to a ruse quick enough. He knows already that you plot against him. And the women..."

"Stop it!" Forte yelled at her.

Ziah's smile was seditious. "And the women," she continued. "The women are the ones you have most underestimated. That foul step will be your downfall, James, and I will be there to watch." Ziah's eyes now controlled him. "You pay no respect to the bloodline that created you. Sirens are not quick to forgive, and vengeful cruelty is our favorite retribution. You will suffer, James." Her voice remained smooth.

His snicker echoed in the small chamber. "For portraying such an angelic persona you favor the rougher side of life, don't you?" Forte moved forward to trace the edge of her jaw. "Then again, that is a trait predetermined within Sirens and Urchins alike. Perhaps it is merely because you still hold the body of a teenager, Ziah, that you think you are invincible." His eyes mocked her. "You like to see people in pain."

"No, Forte, it is inevitable. What you sow, therefore you shall reap. You will not get away with your plan. If you truly do release Calypso, you will not want to stand in the way of her wrath." Ziah held his dark gaze. "Calypso is not controllable, as you may think. You cannot lobby her to do your dirty-work, Forte."

"Quiet! You do not know the full extent of our plan. It will work, and Calypso will be controlled!" Forte grew in his outrage.

"I know your plan! I have seen inside your mind, Forte, a very scary place to navigate. It will not work!" Ziah shouted back at him.

"It will not work!? It will not work!? HA!" Forte paced the circular cell. "I have you, don't I, Ziah? When everyone said it was impossible, I got you."

"You got me through no skill of your own! You used the resources of other people," Ziah yanked against the chains that held her to the wall. "Without these, you would have never succeeded Forte."

"Awww, do not be sad because I beat you at a game you didn't even know you were playing." Forte stopped in front of her. "But, since I now have your gifts at my disposal, why not use them?"

Damnit, Ziah thought to herself. *First thing I do when I am freed is destroy the last of these bloody chambers!*

"No matter your place, your power, or your will, you can always fall! We are not infallible, nor are we unbeatable. Merely because we are gifted with this fate, do not forget we are still of human design, Forte, and held under soul law. The Siren who holds Calypso at her heart will decimate everything that stands in her path."

"Aaagggghhhhh!" Forte pouted. "You infuriate me so! I do not see how Seth could love such an overbearing woman!" His eyes met hers with violence. "Siren? A Siren contains the form of Calypso?"

Ziah did not foresee the consequences of her words. She thought Forte knew a Siren possessed the goddess. What a dire mistake….

His black eyes raked through her calm. "Nothing! You give me a nibble and not the whole carrot!?" Forte's breath was hot on Ziah's face as he approached her. Venom oozed from his core and threatened her silently. She would not break. She could not deny the safety of a Siren child.

"I have tired of this. You shall not weaken me! Sleeeeppp…." Forte's voice wooed her melodically into slumber. Ziah's body immediately grew slack as her own gifts were being used against her. Forte caught Ziah's limp form in his arms before she crashed to the ground. "I will be back, my pet." Forte stared down at her. "I prefer you like this, Ziah – quiet, agreeable. Can't you be like this all the time? " Gently, Forte lowered her body to the cool ground. "I will be back. More of your strength is still hiding within you, Ziah, and I want it, all." His sadistic laugh echoed in the winds of the chamber as the air swirled around him and he dissipated before her motionless body.

Poor Seth. Forte wondered what his second nature was up to. *First you lose your love, then you lose your life. Vicious cycle, is it not?* Forte smiled at his own cunning.

Forte reappeared in a mist at his servants side. "Has she gone to sleep once more?" he whispered.

"Aye, I believe so, sir." Nicholas silently cracked the door and peered in through the gap. "Did you deal with the redhead?"

Forte nodded. "Ziah's will has weakened, as the walls were designed to do. She is under my reign now!" His smile was malicious. The thought of all the power he was about to control made him dizzy. Ziah had more to give him and this Calypso…she was the wild card of aces. He could not wait for her will of fire to be at his fingertips.

"She sleeps, sir. She sleeps," Nicholas grinned back at his master. His beady eyes sparkled in the dim light of the moon.

"Silently, let's move." Crouching they crawled through the door. "Do you have the salts?" Nicholas nodded. "Good, move." Forte ordered the other man.

The pair rose slowly from the ground as they came alongside Rowan's bed. She faced them on her side, the covers pulled up to her neck. Forte gestured with his hand that he would push Rowan to her back and that Nicholas should cover her mouth. Forte shoved at her limp body. Rowan's face creased with shock as she landed on her back, her eyes still closed. Nicholas slammed the handkerchief down on her mouth and her squirming body went dead-still as the sleeping salts took their effect.

"Hand me the rope." Forte gestured toward Nicholas. The men made quick work of binding Rowan's hands and feet. They placed a black sack over her head as a final touch. Forte lugged Rowan's body over his shoulder and moved towards the door. "Check the corridor."

Nicholas moved from his sight with stealth. "Coast is clear, boss." Forte jumped at Nicholas' silent return. The boy's large smile spanned his thin face.

Chapter

10

---◆---

BAREFOOT AND CONFLICTED, Victor paced the long, deserted beach far behind the castle. The embankment created seclusion and quiet, exactly what he searched for. The peaks of the towers could be seen faraway and remote in the distance. Illuminating lights warmed the dark stone of the outside walls. After Victor had left The Lady and the torrents that surrounded her, he sought peace to be alone with his thoughts. Screams that stopped his heart still reached his ears. Even at this distance, Dorian's screams from her chamber still searched for him. Victor felt the terror of the man within him. Finally he sat, allowing the cool sand to ease his overstressed senses. The moon shone down in a thin strip over the black waters of the sea, landing directly at his feet. Victor stretched out on the sand permitting his whole body to melt into the cool earth.

"Why does she sink so deeply beneath my skin that I feel her within my veins?" Victor spoke to the stars, the moon that sought his skin, to anything that would listen. "I thought this was what you wanted, Jason, Dorian's death so you could be free of the entrapment within my body. Your love and my hate shred our shared mind to pieces." He shut his eyes to the world. Drifting between sleep and waking, the euphoric lapping of the waves to the shore line lulled Victor into submission. Dorian's moonlit eyes became his focus as his dreams strayed of their own volition.

Victor's eyes opened blue and clear, with focus. The moon still lit a path over the ocean and that was where she stood. As her clothing clung to her wet body, the silver gown she wore floated atop the water surrounding her. The golden hue of her skin had returned as her body healed, and she radiated light beneath the moons attentions of her.

Dorian, Victor thought as he stared at her.

"I do not understand the nature of your gift for it has not been revealed to me, but it is ready to seek its way out of your skin." The melody of Dorian's voice entranced Victor as she spoke. "Do you not feel you have fought it too long?" He nodded. "Embrace your life as it was meant for you, Victor." The clarity of the energy filling Dorian flooded him with its essence, invading Victor to his core.

"Why do you stand in the water?" Victor felt Jason's trepidation about getting closer to her.

Dorian lifted her head to fully bask in the moon's vivid luminescence. "I am a being of the water's currents. The source of it shall heal me fully as it wants to see its child well." Lowering her head, she focused on the deep sapphire of his gaze. He saw a flash of lightening surge across her eyes as it was immediately mirrored behind her, striking the sky.

"You grow in strength. Is that why you feel you know of my nature?" Victor asked.

As Dorian pondered his query, it wrote its way across her face. She shook her head no. "True, I grow in strength. I heal. However, if you deny the dragon within you, you will find only madness. I know not the man who hides beneath your skin, but he resembles someone I knew long ago. Why he has captured your body I do not know."

"You know this man?" Victor touched a hand against his chest. "He knows you, too." Dorian's gray eyes just looked at him, filling his soul. "He wants… I don't know what he wants from you."

"Come to me, Victor." Dorian reached out to him. Extending her calm, smooth flesh, her fingers twined with the air, inclining him forward.

As if possessed, Victor rose from his seat upon the sand and stood, locking his eyes on the pools of silver that swirled in Dorian's face. For the second time, Victor felt unease from the man within. Jason did not trust her motives. Victor felt the tightness in his chest, Jason trying to warn him. Yet, Victor's body responded on its own. No one could have stopped him at this moment. Graciously, he walked into the warm waters to meet her. He extended his hand to Dorian's. Just as their fingertips met she grabbed hold of his wrist pinching the skin in her grasp.

"Let's bring out your inner devil." Dorian's words startled him.

The ground beneath them fell as Dorian pulled him under the truculent sea.

Victor's lungs stung as the salty waters flooded his body. She pulled him further, deeper into the abyss. His body began gasping for air as he fought against her. Dorian floated before him ethereally. She looked like an angel, but Victor's mind fought in opposition. With every inch of encroaching darkness, she brought him closer to death. Dorian became the only light beneath the clouded sea. Victor tried to break her iron hold with all the strength he had left. His body weakened as he looked to the smile upon her face.

You have a strong fight within you yet. His head grew dizzy as Dorian's voice consumed it. *Would be a pity if you gave up and allowed me to drown you so easily,* she taunted him.

Victor inwardly screamed with agony against Dorian's cruelty, forcing her from him.

Thank you, Dorian. Victor's inner enigma spoke to her. Victor saw the physical reaction of her shock.

What? Dorian heaved with breath. Slowly she disappeared above them, taking all light from his eyes. Victor lost consciousness as the last of her aura left.

Relax, Victor. He heard crystal clear now the man within him. *Let us be one finally, and end the suffering we have caused ourselves and the others surrounding us.* Victor's mind was aware as his body contorted and rolled against the oceans current. *Let us reawaken and fully reclaim our life!*

A jolt, like lightening, collided with his heart, electrifying Victor's body. Air and water swirled around him as the man inside overlaid him. The alignment of hearts caused a shock that spread across the entire ocean in its wake.

Victor bolted awake with the ringing of gunshots through the air. A debilitating pain grasped his brain, and, as he opened his eyes, it dissipated into the night. Victor's vision aligned with precision. A sense of oneness filled him. Looking at his surroundings, he had awoken on a different area of the beach. The hateful screams of a woman assaulted his ears. Victor's heart felt as though it would pound its way out of his chest. Finding his footing, he tore off down the beach to the dock just in time to see a lone vessel breaking the moonlit horizon. Victor's eyes focused perfectly on the vessel at its distance, and he recognized it as the Black Stallion. He felt his vision rush back to him. Looking again at the black spot, he thought, *How did I do that?* A blaze of cannon fire shattered the clouded night around the departing vessel.

"GOD DAMN IT!! God damn it!" Rahn was screaming out to sea. She fired three more rounds aimed at the distant ship. "I'll kill you, James! With my bare hands, you BASTARD!" She yelled as if he was listening to her threats.

In his hasty arrival, Victor nearly collided with Christian as he stood a few feet behind the raging woman. Christian's knuckles were white as they gripped the hilt of his sword.

"What the hell is going on?" Victor commanded.

"They've taken her."

Victor's mind immediately went to Dorian and he felt helpless.

"They've taken Rowan." Christian's words were filled with hatred.

"Oh," Victor sighed.

"You sound relieved…" Christian leered at him.

"No, no, Christian. I thought you were going to say Dorian's name, for, if they took her instead, she would surely be at death's door sooner." He looked after the ship. "I meant no offence."

"None taken," Christian's voice was stern. "Forte and his leech have taken my sister!" He lost the words in his throat. Both men turned to Rahn as she approached them with thundering steps.

"What has become of Sebastian!? Have they taken him as well?" Concern spread through Rahn. Her world was falling apart rapidly. No captain, no sister, no friend…

"Sebastian? I have not seen him since last night," Christian answered.

"Aye, I have not seen him since port," Victor chimed in.

"Damn it!" Rahn's fury paced in front of them. "We must ready the ship. Action! We must take action!" No one moved to carry out her demands. Each face simply stared at her, immobile. "Impotent men!" She yelled at them.

"We should seek the captain's words before we take venture, madam." Nate, the young crewman, spoke timidly. His auburn hair and freckled face were infused with innocence.

"Aye, lady. Dorian cannot make the journey, but she will give her guidance. Captain has dealt with this James for centuries. She will know his weakness." Grim spoke at Rahn's side.

"Jesus, man! For your bulk, you are the air of silence." Rahn scanned the faces around her. "Fine! To Dorian." Rahn began to walk up the hill to the castle. "Not all of us. Grim, Christian, and Victor, follow me." The mass of men stilled behind her. "Begin preparing for departure. I am sure that Dorian will request we leave with haste upon our sails. Gooo!"

The remaining group steadied their feet upon the sand as the pirates dispersed into the night. "You are right, Rahn. We must make haste. James does not know of Dorian's condition, I am sure, or he would have taken different measures. When he does..." Grim was interrupted.

"I'll throttle the man." A hunched figure stumbled towards them. Sebastian came into the light of their torches with dried blood streaking down his face.

"Sebastian!" Rahn rushed to him stopping herself just short of hugging him. Displays of affection were not high on her priority list. "I am so glad you are alright." She knocked some of the dirt and sand from his clothes.

"Aye. A little worse for wear, but I will live." Sebastian placed an arm around Rahn's shoulders for support. His legs felt wobbly and he was worried he might topple over. He felt Rahn tense at the gesture, but he didn't care. It was his turn for support in their friendship. A choke grew in Christian's throat as he watched it. He did not understand their relationship. Christian watched Rahn's reaction.

"What happened to you, man?" Victor brought light over to his head assessing the damage.

"I came in search of you outdoors," Sebastian pointed at Victor. "Thinking you were the man at the end of the dock, I approached without hesitancy. Nicholas turned to face me. Forte's men grabbed me. He does not know of Dorian's condition. You arc right, Grim. I tried to mislead him saying she was dead, but he could not be dissuaded. Forte was persistent that Dorian was still alive, that I was lying. One of his men held a limp body at the end of the dock. It must have been Rowan." His eyes focused unseeingly at the ground. "WE must return her!" His eyes glazed over and his body slumped forward slightly. Rahn put a hand to his chest, righting him before he fell. "If I had known that was Rowan, I would have fought harder." His voice was soft and distant as he stared at the ground. "No one knew they approached?" Sebastian's eyes searched the crowd as silence answered him.

No one had seen this intrusion coming.

Rahn shook her head and patted his chest where she steadied him. "There was nothing you could do. They would have killed you, had you tried to defend her."

Victor reached up to touch the gash in Sebastian's head and a small spark ignited against the wound. "Whoa," Victor shook his hand off and looked at the healing that began taking place. The skin reformed together and stitched itself up within seconds.

"What?" Sebastian questioned him. He no longer felt a pain in his head or a gaping hole where the gash had torn the skin open. It felt tight again, like newly healed skin.

Victor stared at Sebastian's head. "Nothing...nothing, mate," Victor stammered as Rahn eyed him with disdain, aware of what had just taken place. She had witnessed the healing at Victor's hand and he could feel Rahn's distaste.

"Yes," Christian's voice was menacing as he stared at the three of them. "We must get Rowan back." He had not noticed anything. Jealousy filled his vision and he saw nothing but red.

Sebastian was not fazed by Christian's tone. His mind was filled with a fading mist. "What is this about!? Forte was a good if not misguided Captain. Why does he have a vendetta against you three?" Sebastian spoke directly to Rahn, ignoring everyone else. "He was employed to rescue Victor, and yet here Victor stands." Sebastian smacked Victor hard in the chest, having not regained his full sense of depth perception.

"Ah, easy, mate," Victor rubbed at his winded frame.

"Sorry," Sebastian pleaded, "Rahn?"

Rahn laughed. "Forte's constant bumbling persona for miscalculating directions is a deliberate façade. He knows the waters as well as I." She shrugged at the expressions that faced her. "Forte is an Urchin, far from a sane one." Glazed eyes met her stare. "Urchins are the male-counterparts of Sirens. They are in existence because of our Siren lust. Forte seeks Dorian with an intensity I have never seen matched. He is crazed and sees not logic. For centuries Forte has sought the company of Dorian. He thinks her his maker, Dee, the one who transitioned him into the Urchin way of life. He clung to Dorian because she embodies his creator in form, but nothing else. Forte is the cause of all Dorian's upset and unhappiness from years past. He is a parasite."

"As far as Victor goes, Forte knew that once Rowan joined The Lady's league that she would eventually come looking for her brother. So if he hung close enough to Christian, Forte knew that he could one day nab what he wanted and make Dorian submit to his will. Victor is just a pawn who was in the wrong place at the wrong time." Rahn's violet eyes held Victor's and a chill ran down his spine.

Waving his hands towards the heavens, Victor sighed greatly. "So 'tis true, my presence is of no importance."

Rahn bore into him deeply. "You have portrayed yourself of great importance, but we do not know what 'tis the cause... You hold something Victor...." Her voice trailed off as she really looked at him. "You have blended!"

"What?" Victor's stare was empty.

"Inside there is no more turmoil. You have tamed and accepted your demons. You have gained rule over them." Violet eyes poured into him. "The change has already begun." A voice, loud and clear, hit Rahn's mind.

STOP! It is my story to tell, allow me the freedom to make peace before you speak boldly, out of turn. Victor's eyes sent shivers of ice down Rahn's spine.

Rahn nodded once in understanding.

"What are you two speaking of?" Sebastian was still lost to a dream like world.

"Nothing," Rahn spoke as she rubbed the back of her neck, easing the pressure from Sebastian's arm. "You need to see the Shee." Sebastian nodded running a hand over his head. "I must find who will stay home with Dorian in case the devil's pariah comes back for her."

Sebastian's startled expression as he ran his hand over a smooth forehead was perfect. He was shocked to not find an open wound there anymore. Victor tried to hold back his laughter.

Christian could not listen to the conversation unfolding in front of him. Hatred boiled within him. His inner self rolled over and over in anguish as he watched what he thought was the budding romance between his ex-lover and best friend. He began walking back to the castle before he did things he would later regret.

"Who is this James you tell of?" Victor's curiosity got the better of him. "Is it not Forte we seek?"

"Yes. James is Forte's first name, Victor."

"I thought it John," Sebastian added, his brain coming back into balance. His fingers still rubbed the healed flesh and no one missed the gesture.

"Aye," Victor agreed.

"Incredible. For so long you trust a man who has played the part of fumbling idiot so well. Now it is he has betrayed all our confidences." Rahn was annoyed with her company. "James Forte, John Forte, they are one and the same. He gets no points for a creative name change."

Both men nodded and agreed with her.

"I am not staying behind," Sebastian added.

"Very well, Christian," Rahn called to him. "I assume you don't wish to be left behind either?"

"Absolutely NOT!" Christian roared over his shoulder.

Rahn rolled her eyes at his childish antics. *Christian could be so possessive. I've made myself perfectly clear. I want nothing to do with him anymore.* She stared at his back. *Oh well, let him jump to hasty conclusions.*

As they approached the entrance of the courtyard, Aldus spoke his peace. "Milady, I'll stay with the captain."

"Blimey, you're big." Victor stared up at the man who towered next to him, for not many men did so. "No, no, I'll stay behind," Victor stated, puffing his chest and facing the rest of the party. "Then I will be rid of this place and have my own ship to escort me home." Victor walked through the castle gates considering the conversation decided.

"Well, there you have it." Rahn waved an arm at Victor's back. Sebastian laughed at her lavish gesture. She next looked to Aldus. His face was a puzzle of bewilderment. "Aldus," she found his eyes. "Do you still wish to stay behind as well?" Her voice was sweet and calming.

Aldus nodded in accord. "Aye, I can't leave Dorian guarded by that man…a man who can't decide if he wants to love her or slit her throat." He turned and began to walk up the stairs. "His mind is a scary place. He has blended with his power, but not mastered it." He wondered who Victor was and why he had come to them. Be it for salvation, vengeance or truth?

As the party disappeared to their different directions, Sebastian asked, "Your men are loyal, aren't they?"

Rahn smiled up at him. "'Til death do us part we shall defend each other. Let's get you to the Shee," she guided him into the castle, "and then to Dorian."

"That wee, little, grunty woman that no one can understand, save for crazy people?" Sebastian inquired.

Rahn laughed. "Yes. Terrifying, isn't she?"

Sebastian thought back to the woman with skin the color of russet potatoes. He felt chills as he remembered her golden, glowing eye peeking out from her crazed hair. It felt like she could look right through you to the world beyond the space of your body. She spoke words rarely anyone could understand. The Shee was most definitely terrifying, but she could heal better than any soul in existence, and she would gladly accept any challenger.

• • •

Rowan stood leaning against the bars of her enclosure. She searched the vessel from inside out. *I will discern its weakness.* Listening to the main deck, she counted the steps of the men above her. Quiet as a swift wind, Forte was in front of her. Rowan jumped in her skin at the sight of him. The man was the devil himself.

"I hope you are finding your accommodations acceptable." Forte's sly voice made her cringe. If Rowan did not know his nature better it would have entranced her.

Forte wore his traditional black from head to toe. His salt and pepper hair hung down to his collar and in wisps around his face. If Rowan did not despise him so much, she would have found him handsome. Forte had a strong chin with new stubble growing there. His cheek bones were accentuated by the hollows beneath them. The tint to the glow of his skin was dark and eerie. His eyes were dark, yet intriguing. One wanted to know what happened behind them. A classic handsome face stared at her. He reeked of smug sophistication. She wanted to vomit.

Rowan felt the air shift as he became impatient under her scrutiny. "What a pity Dorian won't live to see your fine outer wear. Did you have your man friend pick out your attire for you?" Rowan teased.

"No, Nicholas did not…" Forte's voice trailed off as Rowan's words sunk in. "What did you say? About Dorian…"

"Oh, yes. Well, I suppose you wouldn't know would you, being so caught up in your voyage for lust." Rowan's eyes were like emerald daggers cutting into him. "And being there were no survivors, there was no one to report to you what happened."

"What do you speak of, whore?" Forte ordered.

"Blue put a bullet into your fantasized lady's heart." Rowan paused to let the emotions ride. "Right after Dorian stabbed him through the heart."

"Noo… It cannot be. That bastard!" Forte banged his fist against the metal bars. He began pacing in front of Rowan speaking solely to himself. "Blue was supposed to distract her and have her flee back to land, *not* murder her! Putrid decoy." As he became more enraged his foot falls became harsher and louder against the wood. "I would kill the man myself if he wasn't already dead! But, I could go to the land of souls and retrieve him for torture. I did not believe that bumbling sailor." His voice held question within the statement. "Sebastian was right?" Forte shook the thought off. "I have no time. My poor, sweet angel dying without her love by her side. I could go to the land of souls and retrieve her!" His movements slowed.

Rowan watched him guardedly, waiting for him to snap. *This will be fun,* she thought. She could feel Dorian's health returning. She knew Dorian would live, and more than likely kill this lunatic herself. She chuckled, catching Forte's attention.

"Why do you laugh?" Forte's eyes twinkled with insanity. He reached through the bars, grabbing Rowan's throat and pulling her towards him, hard against the metal. Her face came through to the other side in agony. "You mock my pain! He assessed her face. "Nooo, no. You can feel her, can't you!?"

Rowan coughed in his face. "I laugh because you are so deluded in your pursuit of Dorian that you had to kill her husband in order to draw the life out of her! The one man she *has ever* and *will ever* love with that intensity. The day you killed him you might as well have killed her too. She will not live again until you lie with Davey Jones! Listen...." Forte cocked his head to the right. "Do you hear Davy's call? He wants your devilish soul! You inconsiderate, spineless, hollowed-out, shell-of-a-man, pathetic, limp rogue!" Rowan's breathing was heaving from her body with revulsion. "You are too pathetic a man to ever have had the honor of calling Dorian yours. The gods should smite you down with lightning!" Rowan's eyes held Forte's as his filled with horror. "The woman you claim to love has been tortured and killed by you!"

Forte didn't know what to say, so he tightened his hold round her neck. "You do not know what you're saying! I *love* Dorian! She is my match in every way. I will find her body and bring her soul back to me!" His coal eyes met hers and the wickedness that leaked from them terrified Rowan. "She will love me again, you will see." Rowan gasped for air as her body fought against his physical attack. "I will bring her back! She will come back to me and love me as she always has!" The rage of his shouting beat Rowan's body. Forte had practiced, and built his will, and its powers, strong. His eyes bore into her, melting all the strength she carried. Without releasing his grip Forte shoved Rowan backwards, as far as the bars would allow him, and brought her forward slamming her into the bars. He released her throat and Rowan's body fell to the floor, blood dripping from her head. "Bitch," he sneered. "Do not test me again." He watched her body. No activity could be found anywhere. Her brain had been shut down. "Alas, you stupid girl you reveal everything I want to know. Dorian lives!" He raised his fist to the air in triumph. "Aye, a victory is in order!"

• • •

Air swirled around him as Forte materialized in front of his last sleeping girl. "Ziah..." Forte spoke to the chamber walls.

Her body lay where he had left her. He bent and took her face in his hands wiping off the grime from her cheek. Forte gazed down at her.

"Seth seeks you. Poor sod, I can feel him searching for you." Forte brushed a stray hair behind Ziah's ear. "It is our little secret where you are hiding." His laugh was maniacal.

"It has been too long since passion has filled you, Ziah." Forte stared down at her. "What kind of life did you lead in that haven of perfection? Nothing could sound sooo boring! What of the freedom of the ocean, the surprising swell of the waves as they build with storm?"

Forte gazed down at Ziah's unresponsive body. The only tell that she was still living was the slow rise of her breath within her lungs. "Very well. I just popped by to see if you were still here, powerless – and you are." Forte smiled like a serpent, slimy and devious.

• • •

Seth stood confidently at the helm of The Stallion. The night air was calming in its wake. Seth felt Forte's approach far before he ever reached him. Seth steeled himself. *You will not leech my secrets tonight, dear brother.*

"Good evening, Seth," Forte's voice always sounded cold and cruel to Seth's ears.

"Evening, James, what a fine night it is. Did you see?" Seth pointed his muscled arm over the helm, past the bow of the ship and towards the moonlit waters. "Luna calls to us. How shall we answer her?"

Forte laughed at his second nature's antics. "Always the dreamer, aren't you, Seth?" He stared at the freshness of what his complexion used to be in Seth's profile. "What of Ziah, brother? I have not heard word of you going to visit her lately."

Seth regained his composure after Forte's startling words. *Why does he care about my relationship? How does he know? James has never asked about her before, save for telling me to leave her...*

"Ziah? She refused to see me at my last visit and has refused contact with me since. I do not know what has come over her. Every time I see her, she grows more aggravated and shrill. It is like she is not the same. She has put distance between us, and now, I hear nothing."

"I am sorry, Seth. To lose love is an awful thing." *Perfect,* Forte thought. *Seth is breaking and will soon be back under my control. He will listen and obey soon enough.*

"I will accept what is meant to be. There is nothing more I can do. If Ziah does not want to see me, I shall respect her wishes." Seth had resigned himself.

James smiled warmly. "I am glad you got to feel what my heart once did. There is no greater thing. Love is worth fighting for. Now you know why I seek it once again so ferociously."

Seth watched his second-half with fear.

"My love is once again close at hand. Just wait, Seth. Soon we shall both have the women of our desires. Do not look so desolate, brother. We are the only Two-Natured in existence with both our forms living side-by-side. We can do this together. We can continue to live together, in both our forms." Forte stated, and then added, "If you want her back that is…"

"What are you saying, James?" Seth grew in confusion the more Forte talked.

Seth wasn't like him. His body that contained the half of their soul could think out a situation as opposed to simply reacting to it.

Forte smiled, always a scary thing. "I am saying that you have chosen the correct match, Seth. Together you and Ziah could rule the Siren and Urchin realm! If you choose to fight for her, of course."

"I thought it would be more difficult to love her. I thought Ziah would present a challenge and once I surpassed it I would move on but I have come to love her. She is my match, Forte." Seth felt his open honesty and immediately regretted sharing it with this man.

Forte's entire body cringed at Seth's words. "Your match, very well. Then you must fight for her. Join me in my fight for Dee and I will help you win the heart of your lady love back. Soon we will both be able to live freely. Praise your salvation."

"Join you, James? I am already with you in whatever task you undertake." Seth was honest. He did not understand why his second nature thought he was always against him.

"Yes, but I have felt you flailing lately. Now that I know of Ziah's treatment of you, I can understand why." Forte's gaze was sharp, questioning.

"I am back, Forte. I am sorry that I lost heart in our mission. I was lost for a time. I now see that you are right, and I will help you in any way that I can." Seth now turned to him and smiled.

Forte used all of his new will to feel if Seth was telling the truth or not. The boy was utterly sincere. A huge weight lifted off of Forte's shoulders. "I am glad to have you fully back, brother. Please forgive my doubt."

"Consider it forgotten," Seth submitted.

"It is time," Forte clasped a hand over Seth's right shoulder and Seth recoiled at the touch. He felt something Forte was unaware he was transmitting. "Are you alright?"

"Yes, yes. Sorry, James. I was lost in thought and you startled me," Seth coughed into the air. "What is next?"

"It is now our time, Seth. We shall execute this mission together!" Forte was so proud of himself.

"Finally you give me my reign, brother?" Seth locked eyes with his second half.

"Yes, I give us our reign." Forte nodded. "I will leave you now. I have had a long day and my bed is calling to me. I trust you will take good care of everything in my stead?"

"Of course, brother," Seth smiled at him and bowed his head. Forte waved as he descended the stairs.

Seth watched him. He mirrored Forte in his younger years. Seth's features were not as hardened above his strong jaw. Coal black eyes stared out from his chiseled face. He had a full head of dark, chestnut hair. His body was strong and muscled. His mind was his own and centered in a way Forte's could never be. Seth could never understand how half of his soul could be so wretched within Forte's body and so peaceful within his own.

I hate him, Seth thought. *Thank you, Ziah, for teaching me how to block Forte out of my mind and will without his awareness, so he can no longer control me so.* Seth righted the path of The Stallion as his course coordinates changed. *Ziah, what of you?* He thought back to the spark from Forte's touch. *James has sent you away, hasn't he, Ziah?*

Yes. Ziah answered him.

His body shaken, he called to her. *Where!? Where has he hidden you?* Seth's mind was urgently seeking her. But she was lost to his vision.

Can you not feel me within you? I am within you both now. When James touched you he transferred everything he has ever taken from me into you as well. He, of course, is too stupid to know what he has done. Forte has weakened my will and stolen it from me. Seth felt how livid Ziah was. Seth felt her urge to want to kill his second half, and he matched it.

Seth reassessed his body. He felt stronger and full of more power, of a will not his own. *I can feel you, my love.*

Let's keep it that way. Forte underestimates the bonds of love. Most of my will has transferred to you because you are where I feel safe. I am content with you holding onto my gifts, for now. They will keep you safe. Ziah sounded desperate and alone.

Where are you, Ziah? How can I help you? How can I get you out of your imprisonment? Seth pleaded with her.

Ziah's eyes fluttered open as she looked into her lover's face, a face she could not touch, a face that could not see her.

I can see you, my love. That is all that matters. Your face will help give me strength and guide me through this. I have missed you. Ziah rose from the stone floor to sit and stare at the wall across from her. Seth's frantic expression was searching over the wheel of his ship. He was searching for her. *You will not find me, Seth. Do not waste your energy. The walls are designed that way, to keep prying eyes out and to keep help from reaching the imprisoned.*

If I cannot find you, how can I help you, Ziah? Seth asked anxiously. When he did not hear her answer he went on. *I love you, Ziah. Soon I will rid you of the awful place James has stuck you. Then, together, we will rid the world of my brother. I am here because of his transference into the Urchin life, but I hate him! I hate him for doing this to you. I loathe him more with every breath and for taking your will. It goes against all order of the Sirens law!* Seth's voice calmed as he thought of her. *I knew deep within me that you did not desert our love.*

No, I did not. An alignment of such purity and truth cannot be broken when shared as we do. Tears poured forth from Ziah's eyes as she hugged her legs to her chest. *Your maker's maliciousness is classic of Forte's birth. I should have dispatched all transformed under such circumstances!* Ziah clung to herself trying to find peace in Seth's face. *When I am rid of this place I will seek Forte in the open air on my terms.* Ziah hugged her arms around her body trying to protect herself. *My gifts shall return. Do not worry about that, my darling. And as for you, you make me stronger. Your love is what has kept James from ruling me completely. I will release you from his nature upon our freedom.*

I know, my love. Seth was devastated he could do nothing for her.

Because of you, I cannot hate Forte, fully, or your maker Dee. Without them, I would not have met my match. We will get through this. You need to seek the help of the Sirens. Dorian will know how to find me. Ziah was direct and Seth felt nothing but fear settle within his chest.

But, I thought you could not be found? Seth was confused and aggravated that he couldn't rescue Ziah himself.

I cannot. But Dorian is a special kind of Siren and she can help you. Approach her with ease and caution. She will not trust you, Ziah warned him.

I will, my love. Thank you. Seth was terrified at the mention of Dorian's name. She had every right not to trust him, not to want to be near him, and not to help him. She would mistrust him immediately simply for being a part of Forte. Seth inwardly cursed himself. He could not let these obstacles stop him from saving Ziah. He would seek out this Dorian with Forte and hope that he would find her first.

I love you. Ziah's last words to him before she tired and could not carry on the conversation. The Hidden Walls sucked the life out of you.

• • •

Victor was the first to arrive in Dorian's quarters. He burst through the double doors and a jealous lust filled his veins. He felt Jason rejoice as he saw the large white haired man sitting in a chair beside Dorian's bedside, making her smile. Victor didn't understand Jason by any means, but at least now they had a clear communication. Dorian's complexion was still pale but the energy in the room was far better than it once was. It had lightened, as life breathed within it again. Dorian's hair fell loose behind her in golden tendrils. She had been aided in changing out of her clothing from battle. The pale blue of her garment matched the Viking's eyes, as Aldus held her attention. Gauze sleeves hung lightly down from her shoulder as she moved to brush a strand of hair from her face. The thin straps holding the dress to her shoulders plunged down around her breasts in a deep V with a gold accent around the edges. The bullet wound's bandage could be seen beside her heart. The pendant she always wore was displayed against her warming skin catching Victor's attention. The pendant was important to Jason, but Victor did not know why.

Sebastian ran into Victor from behind, not seeing his steady stance in the doorway. "Oh, sorry, mate." He moved around Victor and took a seat in a chair to the left of the bed.

Dorian's silver pools captured him. "You can come in, Victor. I know we never settled on the terms of your freedom, but none of us will bite, I can assure you." Victor made a gruff cough rise from his lungs as he moved inside the chamber to sit by Sebastian. She watched his every move with interest. The Viking moved his chair closer to the bed taking Dorian's hand and whispering something into her ear.

I hate him. Victor thought.

No, we cannot hate him, Victor. Jason reasoned within him. *Aldus will be a great ally, if you can get past your arrogance. He is just doing what I requested of him if I were to die before...*

Aldus is bedding our wife! Is that what you requested of him, to take your place? Victor was furious.

You jump to hasty conclusions, Victor. Jason could feel he was not going to get anywhere with Victor in this mood. *Open your eyes and see truth through your veil of jealousy.*

"Are you alright, Vic?" Sebastian inquired, whispering. Victor's eyebrows pinched together and he shook his head. Sebastian laughed at him. "I know that look. Trouble has just spelled its way across your face." Sebastian returned to study the map he had brought in with him.

"The place you search for cannot be found by such a common map, Sebastian. You will need my map and compass for the unchartered waters you seek." A symphony played within the men's ears as Dorian spoke to them. Few were immune to the charms of a Siren's voice.

Outside, Rahn approached from the stairs. Christian saw her walking ahead of him and rushed to catch her. She was fiddling with something in her hand and did not feel him 'til he was upon her.

"Damn it." Rahn blurted out. Christian grabbed her arm, pulling her down to him so they would not be heard by the ears above. He held her body tight against the wall.

"What is this?" Christian's anger penetrated the air around them. "When did you start sleeping with lowly humans again!?" He demanded harshly shaking her beneath his grasp.

"Why are you talking crazy? Who am I sharing company with?" The violet that stared at Christian was challenging but sincere. She did not know what he was saying. "Because I'd like to know so I can find him and bed him this very evening. I deserve a good romp," Rahn joked.

"Shut up, woman! I do not wish to hear this." Christian's hair had grown long and fell about his face. Eyes like emerald daggers pierced her sharply. "Why do you punish me so? Why do you lie!?"

"Lying, what am I lying about, Christian?" Rahn stared at him tentatively. "You are mad."

"You are sleeping with Sebastian. Admit it!" Christian demanded. "That is why you have been so cruel, and unforgiving of me. You wish to spite me more!"

"Have you had too much drink at dinner? Did you nip off and down an entire bottle of whiskey in the short time we've been apart since the beach? I am not sleeping with Sebastian, Christian." Rahn's eyes locked with his.

"Why are you lying? I can see the way you two look at each other. You could at least have had the decency to tell me straight, Rahn." Christian's mind began to calm as Rahn fed him soothing vibes, filling him completely. "I love you, Rahn. Look at me. I love you."

Rahn had trouble meeting his face now. Her confidence was shaken. "You know not of love." She turned on him, releasing the full blunt of her memory's vengeance. "If you truly had knowledge of such things you would not have deserted the young girl whose virtue you took. You would not have left in fancy of lying between other women's thighs. You would not have promised sweet little nothings, whispered as lovers do, and then not upheld them. You are a robber of heart, body, and soul! Does it pain you to see that I have reclaimed mine!?" Venom spewed from Rahn's lips with every word. "Believe if you want that I am bedding your friend, but try and see it for what it is. We share a friendship, just as he and you. Nothing else!"

"If you truly believe that this is what I have done to you, then Sebastian can have you, whatever the circumstance of your relationship. You reject my love. And trust me, my lady, for it is as pure as the sea after the storm has washed away its sin. I want nothing but happiness for the long, long life you have ahead of you."

A tear streaked Rahn's face. "You know nothing of love."

Their gazes met as they once did. Love was once again in the air between them, but it was tainted. One had hurt the other and vice versa in retaliation, or so it was thought. The truth still lies somewhere in the middle of both their tales.

"Neither do you, my dear." Christian's voice was soft and resigned. "There is nothing more to be said. I withdraw all advances towards you in surrender of my fate." Christian stepped away from her. "I am sure that we can still work together on The Lady amicably, for I am not going anywhere."

Christian moved farther away from Rahn as she spoke to him, "Wait…."

"What more could you possibly want of me? It seems your path of revenge has been successful." Christian stood still in front of her once more and pressed her into the cold wall behind them. Longingly he took Rahn's face and gently stroked the skin along her cheek. His soft full lips grazed hers tenderly. As he moved back Rahn moved slightly towards him in silent anticipation. Christian's lips returned with passion. Reclaiming the small, pert lips beneath his, he savored the touch, the feeling of Rahn's tongue against his own.

Christian wrapped himself around Rahn's body thinking, *that's enough. If she is so adamant, then that is enough.* Rahn's lips fed his in response.

"No more." Christian rested his forehead against hers. "You have fully and utterly broken my heart. I wish you well, Rahn." He walked away without looking back and entered Dorian's room at the top of the stair, closing off the light that fell down the steps.

Rahn stared after him, the clap of his footsteps echoing in her mind. *Good.* She silently sneered after him. *I have wanted Christian's pain painted across his face. I have wanted his pain handed to me on a platter since… since…what has felt like an eternity.* Rahn climbed the steps in an air of smugness and entered through the doors. Christian stood by Aldus and would not look at her as she entered.

"Forte will seek my love until death claims him…or me. I do not know the mind of his counterpart, Seth, but we should approach him with caution and kill them both if we can." Dorian was speaking to the group. "We want to leave no loose ends behind that could later lead to retaliation."

Rahn placed a hand on Sebastian's chair, fueling Christian's paranoia. She watched Christian and assessed that the gesture no longer bothered him. *You let go so quickly.* Rahn put her anger on simmer in order to attend to the more pressing matter.

"What do you suggest we do, Dorian? I know you wish to kill Forte yourself, but that is absolutely not an option." Rahn spoke. She refused to acknowledge the swallowing hole she felt consuming her chest. Pain was something she did not like to bear.

Dorian smiled. "You read my mind, sister. I wish to…." She wrung her hands in demonstration.

"No, my dear." Aldus grasped them both and laid his own hand atop them, securing them to the bed. "I will sedate you if I must to prevent you leaving and healing fully. I could never forgive myself a second time."

Dorian laughed. "You are too much a mother bear, Aldus. Very well. I have enough sense to know I am not ready. I just wish the time was not so near for this journey. Yet, I tire already with this conference. But I so long to be by your sides in battle, my heart aches at the thought of not partaking in the voyage." Dorian paused as her eyes focused on something no one else could see. "I wish to see the final demise of Forte's creation."

"It is unlike you to speak in such terms, Dorian. You must be ill." Rahn's eyes sparkled as Dorian looked at her. "I do hope some of this new wickedness stays. We need another in the group with a mindset closer to mine. All this rational thinking simply gets in the way."

"Yes…." Dorian and Rahn laughed together. "Over thinking is the greatest sabotage a person can possess. The balance must come from knowing when to stop." The captain continued.

Rahn nodded. *A bit of your wisdom stretches farther than any bullet or sword.*

"Where is the best place to attack? Is Forte as lethal on open water as The Lady, or shall dry land be his down fall?" Sebastian inquired.

"Forte holds many mysteries. Perhaps the greatest one is why he is still living. He shall be formidable in any direction you choose because he is mad. No boundaries exist within his mind. Forte feels no fear in his actions because logic does not prevail in his brain." Dorian relayed.

"That's comforting," Christian sighed.

"However," Dorian began.

"Oh, thank God," Sebastian and Christian spoke in unison. They smiled at each other.

Rahn smirked and softly shook her head. *Sebastian had no idea you recently despised his very being, Christian. Now look at the two of you! Men.* She sighed. *Give them adventure, whiskey or sport and all is forgiven and forgotten. Fickle people.*

Dorian did not skip a beat. She was healing and accessing with a crystal clarity all of her gifts like she had never before. She waved the turmoil in Rahn's head. She knew Rahn would soon be forced to break down her barriers or hide deeper behind them.

"However, Forte is not equipped to handle an attack from The Lady. Although, you do not match him in years, Rahn, we are at the advantage. A Siren waits aboard The Stallion. Rowan's capture is an asset to Forte's demise. Rahn, trust your instincts, and those of the people around you. Sebastian will be a good captain, The Lady likes him. Christian," she looked to hold him with her gaze. "Release your dormant fury and bring forth the pirate that hides behind your new manner."

Christian nodded at her smiling.

Smart little wench, she knows all, doesn't she? Christian smiled softly.

Not all, but I'm getting there. I instruct you to unleash the demons of torment and relish in the demise of those who would stand in your way. It will be therapeutic for you, Dorian comforted him.

Devilish little smile of yours. If I did not already love another, I would have passions after you, Captain. Christian looked at her with admiration in his eyes. He knew he had chosen the right ship and the right captain. No matter what became of Rahn he was going to enjoy every minute aboard The Lady.

Honored, my lord, truly. Now, keep your head above ground, trust yourself and let go of what is rendering your heart immobile. It will be very liberating. Dorian spoke with certainty.

Thank you. You are very wise, Dorian. Do you know that? Dorian smiled at him.

"My lady," Christian addressed Dorian out loud and bowed slightly in his review of her. Dorian was something else entirely. *Dorian holds more cards than she will ever let on.*

The entire party was staring at them. Rahn grew frustrated that she did not hear their exchange. No one had.

"I believe this voyage is in capable hands. Attack on the seas if you can, but if Forte is not caught 'til land you must attack swiftly or death will befall you. You will be at the disadvantage, because wherever he leads you, he will know the area well. Forte does not delay with pleasantries. He will attack at the first sign of pressure. In doing so, he will expose his weakness through panic. Use it against him." Dorian looked around her. "Do not be afraid to exploit any fault you find, for Forte will search for them in each of you."

"Will you make sure he does not sense us?" Rahn stipulated more than questioned.

"Of course," Dorian's smile was broad. Energy tingled in her fingertips with every breath of life through her body. She felt brand new. "What of you, Victor? I am hardly in a state to spar with you now. What do you wish?" Dorian asked the seething, quiet man in the corner.

Victor glared at Aldus with disgust. The man had the audacity to sit so near her and display such free emotions of admiration. "I will stay at your need, Lady. I do not wish to venture out into the seas if you are to remain here inadequately protected." As he spoke, his stare was directed at Aldus, disgust hanging from his words.

What a pompous idiot you are, Victor. Jason was annoyed. The two had blended but not fully taken on one form, one mind. Victor was in the dark as to the true nature of Aldus, Dorian and Jason's relationship before his death.

"What a streak of heroism you have had." Dorian mocked Victor as she gauged Aldus' body. He did not take a liking to Victor staying. He did not trust him. "Rahn, be off with speed in your sails."

"Thank you, sister." Rahn held Sebastian's hand as he rose to help steady him. His head was still not right since the knock it had taken. However, the gesture could be easily misconstrued. "I love you, dear girl," Rahn said, and they were gone, pounding down the darkened stairwell.

"I will be of service to them, and then back to your side." Victor left Dorian and Aldus to help in loading the ship. Truly, Victor couldn't stand the sight of the smitten Viking any longer. He loathed the man as jealousy clawed beneath his skin.

"I hope to do The Lady an honor, Captain." Christian added on his departure.

"Keep your head above ground, Christian. 'Tis not the end." Dorian spoke to his back as he stood under the arch of her door.

Christian nodded. "Thank you. I will heed your words with great care and hope for survival." Dorian knew he meant of more than just battle. He was a broken man ready within himself to be whole.

"Shall I lock the door so Victor does not come storming in to interfere with your healing?" Aldus broke his silence after the group left. His thoughts went to the man. Aldus could not place why Victor agitated him so.

"Thank you, Aldus. He infuriates me so... I do not understand why... He...." Dorian was trying to gather the words.

"...Carries the scent of my brother," Aldus' face was almost irate as he finished her sentence.

"Yes, yes, Victor does. You noticed. How naive of me to think you wouldn't. Do you know why?" Dorian respected his opinions.

Aldus sighed. "I feel at a loss. No, I do not know why. Jason has been dead for centuries. Why, now, has a glimpse of him resurfaced?" The inner pain he carried was written across his strong face.

"Was Jason of the Two-Natured? That is the only clue I have assembled. There is an Urchin force that lies dormant within Victor. I see now that he has melded with his other half, but that he has not fully awakened to it yet. Victor does not understand what he is." Dorian was tired and confused.

"Jason could have been of the Two-Natured. There are so many rules to the Urchin form and an exception to all of them. Males of the Two-Natured are born from the coupling of Sirens with mortals. The Two-Natured can also be created by the bite of a Siren with the intention of transforming the mortal. But if that happens, you get crazies like Forte running around. The bite creates the master-servant relationship." Aldus stopped.

"Jason and I were born of a Siren and Urchin match. This is why we do not have a second nature. Our souls cannot split from being of the Elemental birth, as far as I know." Aldus has growing confusion, as well. "Although, somewhere along the line a Siren had to breed with a mortal to create our father."

"I understood that if a Siren breeds with a Two-Natured Urchin, who has joined his soul, the child of their union, if it were male, would not have a predisposition of the Two-Natured," Dorian added.

Aldus looked at her, exasperated. "Jason and our father did not share the knowledge with me if it was so. But, if Jason was Two-Natured why has this form come to life now, in Victor? Why wasn't he born when Jason was?"

"There are many facets to the form. A Two-Natured can be born of different life times, and because we are immortal they will meet at some point of destiny and forge their future together. If the first half of the soul-bearing person has died by the time the other is born the second form gets very lucky. They get the whole soul without all the complicated mess. Usually, anyway. Victor holds no knowledge of who he was, or who he truly is. He has no direction of where he's going." Dorian slouched in the bed, sinking into its comfort.

"As Victor has chosen to stay behind, perhaps I can help to bring out the Urchin in him and see if he hides Jason under his folds." Aldus spoke, standing up in his excitement. "I so miss the companionship of my brother."

"You would be the only man I know to do it, Aldus." Dorian stated, laughing at him as he approached the bed. Aldus held his arms out and knelt beside her.

"Though, he won't entirely be the same man. You must be prepared for that, Aldus."

Aldus nodded. "I will accept your warning, Dorian. But I do hope to gain a little of the brotherly bond I lost, if he does indeed hold Jason's half of a soul within him. Otherwise, we still need to discover who Victor is, regardless of who he was."

"I feel that he would remember you. Your affection for each other was too strong a bond to break that easily."

"Aye." Aldus stared down at his brother's wife, a woman he had sworn to protect. She looked like a child in a sea of white blankets. "Are you ready for sleep? You look like you need a rest, Dorian."

"Such sweet words you bestow upon me, brother. It's a wonder you don't have a lady friend to call your own." Dorian's tone teased him.

Aldus laughed for the first time all night. "I have many lady friends, Dorian. They leave me no choice other than not to choose between them."

"Be careful with that. They might wind up choosing for you and you might be left alone." Dorian pulled the covers up to her neck.

"I am sorry, Dorian. I realize the stupidity of our fight. Harsh words were said to rashly." Aldus gazed down at her. Dorian looked so small and fragile in the fluffy folds of her bed's covers, so angelic. This did not look like a woman who struck fear through your bones at the sound of her name. "I should have been there for you, when you were shot. It would have been better if I could have taken the bullet for you, but..."

"Sssssssshhhhhh," Dorian sighed. "'Twas mine to take and I am stronger for it."

Aldus rolled his big blue eyes thinking, *that's exactly what she needs, more strength.*

Dorian sighed, hearing his thought. "I am sorry as well. We must remember to think first before we allow the wild blood that floods our veins to speak for us, for it only wishes to win and is provoked when cornered." Dorian looked into the man's loving eyes. "We must also remember that we fight like crazy brother and sister, and we need to keep our cool in such a situation."

"Aye," as Aldus fluidly bent down to kiss the top of Dorian's head. "You remain fairly calm until the very end when I am almost all run out of steam and can no longer yell back. Your serenity in the delivery of your threats is most aggravating." With a brotherly love and devotion he stared into her eyes.

"You know that Victor thinks we are sleeping together, don't you?" Dorian teased him.

"He does, truly?" Aldus was shocked.

Dorian nodded.

"How could he think such a thing? I find you utterly repulsive." Aldus said matter of factly.

"I know, I know! But Victor is still on a different thought pattern than whoever resides within him. If it is Jason, he knows we would never do such a thing. Jason knows of our protection for each other, our adoration. It is what he would have wanted after his death, for us to look out for each other." Dorian stated. "Besides, he would slaughter us both if we slept together," Dorian added.

Aldus reclaimed his seat in the chair. They both sat in silence for a bit, drifting off in the calmness that was now overtaking the night. However, thoughts of his brother filled Aldus and a smile spread his face. He had missed Jason.

"Do you hear that?" Dorian inquired.

"Hear wha... Oh, yes." Aldus hung off the end of his seat. "The Shee wants me to change your bandage."

"*Ugghhhh.* Is it that time again already?" Dorian sounded like a child pleading not to have her evening spoonful of vial tasting medicine.

Aldus gave her a reproving look and walked to the back table to grab the supplies. "Are you going to be a good girl?" Dorian huffed and pushed the covers down from her chin. Aldus first removed Dorian's soiled bandage as carefully as his large fingers would allow. Wiping the area clean, he then re-applied the paste and placed a new bandage over it to seal in the healing effects once more.

"Ugh, that is wretched." Dorian looked down at her chest. "I fear the Shee wishes to play a cruel joke on me with the smell of that muck," she winced. "And it stings!"

Aldus laughed deeply at her remark. "I smell nothing but the scent of you." He batted his long blonde eyelashes at Dorian, "and you smell awful." His large muscular arm reached down to pull the covers back up around Dorian's neck. "Sleep now. I will settle in on the couch just in case you need anything."

Just in case some psychopath comes in the night to kill me? I am so grateful for you, Aldus. Always my safe place. Dorian stared at him with fondness. "I love you, Aldus." He kissed the top of her head as she snuggled into her bed's warmth and drifted off to sleep.

"And I, you." Aldus blew out the last of the candles as he sat on the sofa, hearing it lurch beneath his weight.

Victor, I hope you are Jason's second-half. With one soul, the two of you will truly be a force of nature. How I have missed you.... Thoughts of Jason filled Aldus' mind as he drifted into slumber, a brother in hope of a second chance at life with his dearly departed – a feat that did not come around often.

• • •

Seth loved the smell of the ocean's waves as they broke around The Stallion. The twilight hours were lifting as the approach of dawn began to lighten the sky. He held the helm tightly in his hands, reveling in the freedom.

Soon, he thought, *The Lady will come to meet us and I will be free of form once and for all. No need to quicken our pace.* Seth felt that Forte had long been at rest so, at his ease, he allowed his mind to drift back to Ziah.

Ziah no longer responded to his calls. The Hidden Walls is a devilish place. Seth figured that their communications would be few and far between, but he was glad he did at least speak with her once, so he knew that she lived and was alright. Seth thought of what he would do when he got to see his beloved's face again.

• • •

Warmth near her ear stirred her body, but Ziah's mind did not yet follow. "I could not stand to leave you just yet." The voice was strong but soft. "I had to make sure you were completely incapacitated before I went forward with this journey."

Ziah rolled up from the floor and leaned against the back wall for support. She rested her head against the stone and slowly opened her eyes. Her body felt drugged. As Ziah's eyes focused on the evil inches from her a terrified scream was muffled as Forte covered her mouth firmly with his hand. The chains around her wrists pulled her arms taunt, so she could not fight. Her legs began to squirm as Forte bent nearer.

"Hello, pet. There is no sense fighting me, I now fully own you." Forte ran a single finger down the length of her arm chained straight at her side. Helpless, Ziah whimpered against his touch. "Do you not feel it?" He whispered to her in a lover's voice. "'Tis the full moon, always a crucial time for our kind. Sirens love the power of the full moon against their skin. It amplifies every action they take." Ziah's eyes went dull as she felt the full moon breaking the horizon.

Ziah nodded, defeated.

"Together, we shall rule my second form, especially now that I own you so completely. Seth will soon do anything I ask." Forte was as giddy as a school boy. "Together we will rule the waters. Once Dorian joins us, we will live in shared bliss." Forte looked into Ziah's eyes like a slithering snake. "Well, except for you, of course, and Seth. I will dispose of each of you when the proper time comes. Once I hold your power within me, I will no longer have need of you."

Ziah hated his smile, hated to see it directed towards her. *I will let you think whatever you wish in your maddened craze. You know no realm of reality.*

"You want to know the best part!?" Forte's hand against her mouth tightened and her cheeks puffed out under the pressure. "No one will ever be able to find you here. This is the last of the Hidden Walls left standing, the rest have all been destroyed. The beauty of this one is that it can be moved, masked, hidden." Ziah's eyes teared with Forte's words. "Oh, don't look so sad. As long as you are here, you are mortal. How shaming. I might as well hide you away, so no one knows what you have done to yourself." Forte pressed his forehead into hers. "I am so happy that you have shared your gifts with me, giving me all of them. What a pity you swayed Seth into thinking for himself, so that I am not able to share this accomplishment with him. Before you, he would have been so proud to hear that I had taken someone's will. He would have wanted me to show him how."

Forte felt the strength of the moon at the back of his neck. "It is time for me to go. Many things to do. Oh, Seth is coming back to my way of viewing things, just thought you should know that, princess." Forte's body evaporated before Ziah in a cloud of mist.

Ziah screamed for all she was worth, just to hear for herself that she still had some fight left in her. "What you don't know, Forte, will be your damnation."

• • •

The Lady set sail with dawn's breaking light. Rahn stood solemn at the helm, her countenance unwavering. She searched the horizon for air, for any message it may carry of the new day. Sebastian's mind, while he leaned over the map behind her, was beginning to agitate her nerves.

"'Tis fantastic!" Sebastian spoke in marvel.

"'Tis barely a new day Sebastian! Don't you have something else to busy yourself with, elsewhere?" Rahn was getting aggravated.

Sebastian focused on Rahn's solid back. "Grouchy in the mornings, aren't we?"

"YES! I hate mornings," Rahn reminded him.

"Yes, but with these two instruments, man can find anything! We could sail the uncharted reaches of the earth and reap the benefits of the glory awaiting us at its end." Sebastian was like a child fascinated with a new toy. He completely ignored Rahn's dismissal of him.

"What do you think that map is... honestly?" Rahn asked him shortly.

"It is the key to unlocking the hidden treasures of the world! Why do you grow more and more and more irate with me, Rahn? Do you not marvel at this phenomenon?" Sebastian was surprised at her reaction to him.

"If you had found that map alone in some desolate place, you would not have known how to handle the power that comes with it." Rahn spoke quickly.

"What do you mean?" Sebastian asked.

"What the map gives, it also takes away." Rahn stated. "The map has a personality all its own, and it loves to fool the minds of mortals the most. The map and compass work separately, but together they are accurate. Individually, they cannot always be trusted."

Sebastian stared at the side of her face before speaking again. "One would not know of the treasured places it possesses if one did not already have knowledge of what this map could do?" Sebastian asked. Rahn nodded. "Well, aren't I lucky that I was gifted the good fortune of not just a Siren's goodwill to inform me of such things, but also both pieces of the map needed to make it work?" Sebastian smiled at her.

"That map and compass was created to keep mortal men out of our havens and for us, the Elementals, to know extensively what our world holds within it. However, of course, we have to deal with curses and hexes and shields and fields of shock to get to a destination, just to list a few. Simply because a place can be found does not mean it shall be easy to get too. Witches and warlocks are an awful lot when it comes to hiding and protecting a place they view as important. That map and compass will show you all the world's secrets if you linger over it long enough. Alas, it will slowly suck your soul for doing so, for it thrives off of a greedy nature. The map will place you in the Dead Sea, along with the rest of the sorry men who have fallen prey to its promise. Now please do not badger me with more questions, Squirt, I am trying to listen," Rahn scolded him as she turned an ear to the wind.

Christian moved to stare over Sebastian's shoulder. "New nick name for you is it, Squirt?" Sebastian just laughed. He had no rebuttal. Christian saw the constant movement springing forth from the map. Ships moved en route to their destinations. Bodies of land he had never seen before sprang to life. Hidden valleys, sunken caves, and howling whirlpools moved across his vision. "What does the compass do, then, if the map will show you the destination?"

"Once you have decided on your course, it points you in the right direction," Grim answered from across the bridge deck. He too stared out over the horizon, searching for answers to questions he didn't have. "Those trinkets are like a succubus. The map wants your soul and the compass will gladly show you the quickest way to death for your body." Rahn smiled at the crewmen. "Do not simply fall for the dimples before you have seen the whole woman. Those items only want your defeat."

The air around them grew quiet as the mortals assessed the whims of their immortal counterparts. Deceit always appeared to be the goal. Softly, the current rose, whispering news to awaiting ears.

"Rowan told him Dorian's dead, but he uncovered the truth from her mind's eye. We need to work on her control of that!" Rahn allowed the light of the waking sun to caress her face. "Forte has injured her."

"She lays unconscious," Grim added.

"Forte is much stronger than we would have anticipated," Rahn added as the three men huddled around her. "He draws strength from another Siren source, his second nature maybe?" Grim shook his head no. "No. Who then?"

"I do not know, Rahn. We must catch Forte before he does more harm to Rowan, or to anyone else, for that matter." Grim could feel the tension in Rowan's body before she collapsed. Rowan was scared.

Christian and Sebastian stood side-by-side, slightly behind Rahn and Grim at the helm. Their bodies were hard lines of stress.

Rahn threw her head back embracing the sun's break from slumber. "The Stallion has been steadily slowing its pace. We will approach them sooner than we think. Grim, take the wheel. I've got work to do."

Chapter

11

———◆———

VICTOR'S FEET DROPPED from the stool they had been resting on as he bolted awake to the ear-shattering scream from behind him. His eyes flew open and landed on the thrashing body amidst the white sheets. Dorian was writhing in pain, her back arching at the torment. Victor rushed to her and landed at the side of her bed on his knees.

"Dorian! DORIAN!!" Victor grabbed her face in his hands but Dorian's eyes would not focus. "Dorian, look at me."

"Let go of her!" Aldus rushed up behind him. He grabbed Victor by the shoulders and yanked him away from the bed.

"What are you doing!? Unhand me!" Abruptly Victor was let go. His back crashed into the stone floor.

"The remaining poison is forcing its way out of Dorian's system. She must do it on her own." Aldus towered over Victor, not because his height was that much more, but because of his muscle bulk and the intense gleam in his eye. His voice was as calm as the day outside. "You, as well as I, know that that bullet should have been the death of her. As the rest of the poison works its way out of her body, her skin, Dorian will be living through the death the poison had intended for her." Aldus spoke calmly through Dorian's screams. "Once it breaks the skin and is out of her body, she can fully heal." The men stared back at the agonized woman. "It is a quick process once it has begun, but painful for all involved." Aldus rarely felt helpless, but the feeling now consumed him as he stared down at Dorian. "What would Jason think?" Aldus spoke under his breath.

"What?" Victor had heard his mumble. Aldus shook his head dismissing Victor's question.

I would say you have done better than I ever thought you could in caring for my wife, Aldus. Jason's Urchin ears inside Victor did not miss what his lost brother had said.

"I had hoped the Shee's potions would have pulled all the poison out to avoid this, but.… This is the last step of the process, and it is the most final. If the bullet does not kill Dorian, the poison spreading and searching for a way out might. She is not in the clear, as I would have hoped." Aldus stood motionless.

"Did the Shee discover the poison's origin?" Victor asked aloud for Jason.

"Aye," Aldus stared at Dorian intensely. "'Tis venom."

"Venom from what!?" Victor demanded.

"Narrah's snakes." Aldus had become so cool, resolved. Victor didn't understand it.

"Narrah's snakes...of course." Victor was beginning to wonder if anyone was safe to walk with in this world.

Jason blended fully with Victor, and their speech was one for a moment. "Narrah's venom is the most deadly in all of creation. The slitherers dwell beneath Narrah's very skin and are easily summoned. A bite from Narrah's snakes can kill humans before the fangs have even penetrated. One drop of poison is all it would take. Where could Blue have gotten such a trinket?" Jason stared at Aldus through Victor's eyes, "…without being killed himself for even asking of it?" He added under his breath.

"Aye. Have you heard of such things on the banks of St. Winnifred?" Aldus inquired as to Victor's sudden spurt of knowledge. The Viking knew it came from within him, from another source. A source that had been around longer than Victor had been in existence. Only the souls of old knew the truth of Narrah's snakes, the souls from centuries past.

Victor stared at him, shaken. He felt for the first time what it would be like to have Jason merged within him. One brain to access both men's set of memories and pull on the information at will. Victor just shook his head under Aldus' stare. "No, not St. Winnifred. Fables and that sort of thing, you know."

Nice recovery, Jason filled Victor's mind with his sarcasm.

"Fables, like bedtime stories?" Aldus inquired.

Victor nodded.

"Narrah has reached into the fables of sleeping babes?" Aldus stared at Victor amazed. "What kind of fables were you read as a boy?"

Victor felt it was a rhetorical question and chose not to answer the Viking. He merely shrugged it off.

"The only way to obtain the venom of one of Narrah's snakes is to kill it. The only way to do that is to enter Narrah's chamber and live. We are dealing with a very brave, but undoubtedly stupid, soul." Aldus spoke without seeing, his mind preoccupied.

The men turned to watch as convulsions raked through Dorian's body. White foam dripped from the corners of her mouth. Focusing on the pain her body took, Victor tuned out the screams of her lips. Aldus shuddered with every quake of his captain's screams. The sound seared his body through. Dorian's body began to seizure rapidly. Victor turned away and shut his eyes. Jason did not want to watch this suffering. As the last scream left Dorian's lips, the rocks outside her window could be heard cracking and bursting at the shrillness of her voice. A reverberating clap palpated the room. Aldus stared in shock, as Victor turned back. All was silent. Dorian's body lay in a distorted pose, her skin as white as a mother's milk. The silver of her eyes had glossed over as she stared at the ceiling. Her chest did not rise with breath.

Victor took a step forward and rammed into Aldus' arm against his chest. "Is she dead?" he whispered. His throat began to dry and his mind raced.

"I don't...." Aldus' voice caught in his throat. A ray of sunlight lit a trail across Dorian's face and her skin embraced it. Aldus ran to the window and ripped open the drapes. He came back and knelt beside the bed taking her hand in his.

Victor felt a rush of possessiveness strangle his body as he watched Aldus caress her face.

Do not feel threatened, Victor. Aldus became Dorian's protector after I was killed. There is a deep love shared between them. A love of protection and adoration as siblings would share. A love as I have shared with Aldus and you will share with him again, nothing more... Jason tried to reason with Victor but it was too little avail.

"Her skin's beginning to glow," Aldus remarked. The men couldn't take their eyes from her as she came back to life before them. "Nothing comes without a price."

Aldus' last words resounded deep within Victor. He felt he knew that better than anyone.

As the sun fully filled the windows in the east it showered Dorian's body with its beams. The bronze of her skin spread from the wound in her chest, covering her entire form once more. The men heard the beating of Dorian's heart as it pounded again beneath her ribs, echoing from wall to wall. Her body flushed as new blood coursed its way throughout her veins. The gasping of her breath made Victor and Aldus jump as the sound reached their ears. Dorian's lungs filled with air and rose high in her chest. Her eyes opened un-theatrically. Aldus and Victor almost didn't notice because their eyes were focused on the slow movements of her limbs. Dorian blinked as the sunlight hit her face, regaining the men's lost attention. The silver of her eyes sparkled at the sun's embrace. She took deep breaths, inhaling her new world.

"Are you alright?" Aldus held Dorian's hand to his face so he could feel the reactions of her body more accurately. Her eyes met his lazily, not quite ready to focus on the world. She appeared years younger in his eyes. The air that floated around her felt lighter. It felt as though a deep-seated burden had been lifted and she was born anew.

Victor's conflicted voice cut in. "Of course she's not alright!" His eyes searched over her. Dorian's movements echoed a far off serene dream. Aldus stared blankly at Victor's face.

"What do you mean she's not alright?" Aldus gazed at him.

Dorian's face creased with a sharp pain. She brought her free hand up to rub over the site of the bullets entry. "Ouch..." her hand ripped off the remaining bandage revealing smooth, blemish-free skin beneath it. Her eyes examined it, a sigh of relief escaping her. "I'm fine." The words were soft and sweet, laced with caramel.

Aldus brought his attention back to her face, catching her eyes.

"Will you take me to the water?" Dorian's voice was a sweet melody.

The men would have granted Dorian anything, her voice enthralled them.

"Of course I will, my lady," Aldus ran his free hand affectionately down the side of her face as she turned to him. "I will grant you anything."

Hatred reformed within Victor. "Do you not think it improper to take her to the water after what she has just been through?"

Aldus gathered Dorian up in his arms, ignoring Victor's protests. Dorian's head fell to the left, flopping in Victor's direction. Victor's heart stopped as his eyes locked onto hers. A spark passed between them, paralyzing every system in his body. Aldus headed straight out the door. As they passed out of sight, Victor fell to his knees, frozen.

My God! I thought I was the jealous type, Jason spoke to Victor. *I've got nothing on you, mate.*

Victor sighed, fed up with himself. *What now?*

Go after her and watch. There is more we need to know. Aldus will be our greatest confidant if you will let him, Victor. Jason was ready to blend with Victor so their soul could be at peace as one, but he was willing to allow Victor the time to catch up on the Urchin life he knew nothing about.

Just as Dorian touched into the ocean's currents, Victor burst through the trees behind them. He admired how fluidly she moved. Catching sight of Aldus sitting far to the left, his pants rolled up to his knees in contentment. Victor joined him.

"Enchanting, isn't she?" Aldus gazed up at Victor's face, searching his expression. He could feel the menace coming from the man. He was glad he hadn't left Dorian alone in Victor's protection. Aldus turned back to watch her. The soles of her feet rested on the edge of the sand where earth met sea. "Even after escaping the threat of death Dorian arises more beautiful than before its coming, as they all do."

"What?" Victor's voice brought back unanswered questions to his mind.

Aldus realized, once he spoke the words, that he had said too much. He had forgotten to approach Victor with caution. Staring at Victor's face in the sun, he saw the profile of his brother as a passing reflection. Aldus' heartbeat rocketed.

"Dorian was brazen enough to kidnap me and make me bleed. She bested me in swordsmanship and turned my best mates to her will," Victor paused as Dorian's head sunk below the cerulean waters. Aldus continued to stare at his face. "I don't know whether I want to kill her or make her mine forever." His face was mirrored back at him through the calm of Aldus' eyes. "Nor do I believe my own words."

The Viking laughed. "Do not be so hard on yourself, Victor. Most men feel that way about any woman who carries mysticism about her. 'Tis of no real consequence anyway, your feelings." Aldus did not understand the contempt they held for one another. He had debated telling Dorian of what he knew, but had bitten back his tongue many times. *I might as well tell Victor, and my brother, first.* "Besides, mate, forever is an awfully long time." Aldus liked making the man next to him squirm. "As a promise to my brother, I swear to you, if you do decide to kill Dorian, your death will be soon to follow." Scorn laced his words and held Victor's eyes. "Plus, you are not Dorian's type." Aldus smiled. He had gotten another jab in.

Victor's chest felt as though he had taken a dozen daggers to it. He couldn't breathe. His eyes searched the water for any sign of Dorian but could find nothing. She was gone beneath its depth. "Better that way. I could never love a woman such as her."

"Why are you here, Victor?" Aldus stared at him once more, the amusement gone from his eyes.

Victor looked at him, enraged. "Because..."

Aldus cut him off. "No, no. I know of the circumstances that brought you here. But, what of the fates? What do they hold for you?" His eyes questioned him, along with his words. "It is not merely bad fortune that landed you where you are."

"You said it yourself. Circumstance brought me here. I believe there is nothing more than that." Victor was smug. Jason did a mental head-slap at the arrogance of his second form.

Aldus laughed at him. "What lies you tell yourself." Aldus again stared into his eyes, unnerving Victor. "You have the eyes of my brother. Did you know that?"

Victor held his gaze, but it shifted in its malice to curiosity. *Could this man hold secrets of my past?* He assessed him. *Noo...*

Yes, his second form answered.

Victor could not respond for their conversation became quickly interrupted.

"Aldie! Aldie! Aldie!" A small boy, possibly around the age of two or three collided into Aldus' open embrace. Child's laughter filled the air around them as the boy looked up at Victor. "Who's that, Aldie?" The boy had the same golden blonde hair as the vixen that haunted his dreams and the same cool blue eyes of the man who held him.

Who is this boy? Victor wondered. *Is he the love child of these two? That would explain his affection towards her... He resembles them both.*

STOP it, Victor!! Aldus and Dorian are NOT lovers! Jason was becoming sickened with Victor's jealousy and accusations.

"This is Victor, Jax. He's a... friend of mine and your mother's." Aldus stumbled over the words. He held the boy in his lap comfortably, as if he did it every day.

Mother!? This was Dorian's son...must be true. Victor's heart stopped and clenched in his chest.

You do so delight in drama, Jason chided Victor. He took the boy in. Jason felt every inch of him and the invasion did not go unnoticed by the boy. Jax squinted hard at Victor trying to force Jason out of his thoughts. *He is strong.*

The boy's liquid gaze stared up at him. "Nice to meet you, Victor," Jax beamed. His angelic hair fell round his face in soft curls. He had a broad, bright smile with straight, shining teeth. He wore brown trousers rolled up to his knees and cinched at the waist with a leather belt. The gold buckle glimmered in the sunlight.

Victor took note that Jax's skin glowed as well. He also carried the same tanned skin as his mother and father. Victor's mind lapsed. *Does she bring the boy with her to sea!? Does she put him in peril's way with her gallivanting around?* The boy's face creased as he tried to understand Victor's expression. Jax looked as though he had never had a care in the world or never a burden lay on his small shoulders.

"Mama hasn't taken me to sea in… a long time." The boy answered Victor absent-mindedly. Victor bore into him.

"JAX!! My love," Dorian called to the boy and he tore off barefoot and shirtless, shouting to his mother.

Victor couldn't help himself from wanting to protect the cherub babe. He took a step forward. "Wait!" He spoke a warning in his voice.

Aldus placed a firm hand on his ankle. "Victor, he'll be fine." He pulled Victor down beside him. "He's grown up in these waters. The creatures below fear him more than he fears them." He laughed heartily. "He is a terror amongst them, but they tolerate him, nonetheless. I'll wager Jax can even swim better than you." His deep laugh echoed off the breaking waves. The men watched as the boy leapt into the waiting arms of his mother. Dorian hugged him tight and showered him with kisses. They fell together into the water's embrace.

"Are you his father?" Victor felt panged at speaking the words.

Stunned, Aldus turned to him. "Me?" he pointed a finger at his chest. "You know the answer to that question already." He waited, but Victor said nothing. "I can only dream of someday having such things. But not with Dorian, she is my brother's wife. I only think of, or see her, as my sister." He stared affectionately after the two playing and laughing in the water. "I was in a bad way long before my brother's death. Dorian never judged me nor did she criticize my state. She and my brother were always there to support me, mainly to their detriment. After my brother's death, Dorian ensured my redemption from my own drowning pool."

"I am sorry for your loss. It's always hard losing someone you cherish. And I'm sorry to hear Jax is not your son, for he is your spitting image." Victor observed.

"Aye, thank you, Victor. My brother and I are the spitting image of each other, actually." Aldus added.

"The boy is your brother's?" Victor asked.

"Nay, 'tis your child," Aldus watched Victor's stunned expression, as the words slipped coolly from his lips.

Victor gasped for breath after being hit in the chest with the knowledge. "*What…*"

What!? Jason spoke seconds after Victor. *This is remarkable! Wonderful! A son.* Victor could feel Jason's contentment in their shared body, but Victor was terrified. *I knew he shared our marking. He is a full blooded Elemental! Another male Urchin. Oh, the Sirens are going to love that,* Jason laughed. He was utterly delighted at what Victor had unconsciously created.

"Jackson was conceived from the coupling of your life as plain Victor, before the change within you took place. That is why Dorian does not recognize you nor the scent you carry, for 'tis not the same. Plain Victor smells nothing like Urchin Victor. You and Dorian met nearly five years ago. I think it was at a masked ball that Rahn dragged both girls to at St. Winnifred. Dorian never saw your face, but the passion between you remained to grow within her womb."

"How do you know this!?" Victor demanded answers. That night had been the catalyst for altering the rest of his life.

The ice of Aldus' eyes came round to hold him and Victor felt his composure shrinking beneath their chill. "The morning after, as you departed into the hall, you removed your mask and I was waiting there to escort Rahn and Dorian home." The Viking paused, remembering Victor's expression. "You removed your mask with such arrogance. I wanted to kill you!" Aldus' face bore into his soul as he stared straight into Victor. "My thoughts went to my brother that day, when I saw your face and how you betrayed him."

"How *I* betrayed him! Aldus, I've never met him!" Victor fought back.

"I know. Once I saw the spark of your evening growing within Dorian, I decided I could not feel such hate towards someone who could grant such a wonderful gift. She was made to be a mother." Aldus smiled. "I also realized that I should not feel contempt for a man who was doing what I would have done when placed in the same situation, with a different girl of course. My brother had been dead for near…oh, three centuries. I could not hold Dorian accountable. We all have desires. I should have known there was something special about you. The seed of life took in one go."

Actually we had several goes… Victor calmed and gathered his thoughts. "Why was I not found and informed about all this? I have the right to know I fathered a child."

"Dorian had no need for a husband or support so she never sought the boy's father. I have kept your identity a secret these past years, but now that fate has delivered you here, a nightmare brought to life to ruin all that has been built up in your absence." Aldus tried to joke with Victor, but it was like poking at a stone wall.

"Then why now do you tell me the truth?" Victor searched for a glimpse of Dorian or Jax, but found none.

"I have carried the information long enough. And, you are right. A man deserves to know that he has fathered a child. What you choose to do with the information is up to you." Aldus looked back to sea. "But know that if you try to take Dorian away from the sea it won't release her without a fight, nor will it easily relinquish her child. Death is certain to claim one of you." He rose, walking the short distance to shore. Jackson rammed into his legs and they toppled backward together.

Victor felt cold despite the heat of the midday sun on his skin. His body sat frozen on the sand. *Death is certain to claim one of us...* Victor knew that Aldus spoke of himself and Dorian. He wished he could push the knowledge from his mind and bury it far away. He remembered that night more prominently than anything else.

Three women had been the bells of the ball in their becoming and lavish attire. But that was not all. Their physical appearances were breathtaking, and something lingered about them and shone bright through their eyes, mystery perhaps. Victor had not had the chance to behold the other women's beauty for he had landed his sights on one, and once he saw her, his world contained nothing else. She wore a black velvet dress that draped off her smooth shoulders. A large diamond broach lay in the center of her breast. Her thin waist fell into a full skirt that swept around her. One blonde tendril curled long down her back. The rest of her hair fashioned atop her head with pins. Another teardrop diamond hung in the center of her forehead over her black satin and lace mask. The lace wrapped around her head to a bow in the back with ties that cascaded teasingly over her shoulders. All that could be seen of the woman's face was a silken jaw line and the fullness of her heart shaped lips. Gray pools taunted the room from the depth of her mysterious mask. Her smell was intoxicating, ensnaring Victor more as he approached her and it swarmed around him.

They danced long into the night within a world of their own. No man could vie for a dance after Victor had claimed her. He would not let her leave him. Under the full moon's mischief she bewitched him. As the night's dance went on far after midnight, she beckoned Victor to follow her. They found refuge in the castle's far and winding stairs. The enigma enticed him to her chamber door. Inside the hidden room, she seduced him and he willingly allowed her to do so.

Victor wanted to see more of her so he reached up to remove her mask. "No." her hand stopped him. "Does it not fuel your desire to know that my face shall remain a mystery?"

I shall marry this woman tomorrow if she'll have me... I will play along with her charade for now. Victor was enchanted.

"Does it awaken yours to not know mine?" Victor asked.

The woman nodded, running her tongue out over her bottom lip.

"Very well," Victor kissed her softly, lingering before pulling away from her lips. "We shall remain two strangers in the night's game of deception." He pulled her face towards his. His hands wound their way into her hair releasing it from its binds. It fell lush in his grasp as pins dropped to the floor. He took her mouth possessively. Victor wanted to own every inch of this woman, to know what it felt like beneath her skin. "What shall I call you, my lady? You have given me no name."

"Nor will I," her voice was sweet. "My lady suits me for our purpose." Her hands gripped the jacket Victor wore, pushing it from his shoulders.

"And what is our purpose?" Victor teased her. His mouth kissed along her revealed jaw line and nipped down her neck and chest to the swell of her bosom.

"This…" her hand ran across the bulge in his trousers, "is our purpose. Allow me to bring to life your deepest desires." The woman's eyes twinkled in the moonlight. "Shall we see if they can match mine?"

Victor moaned, pushing her backwards. His hands tore at the fabric of her dress 'til it lay at her feet in a shredded mess. The moonlight glided across her naked body, illuminating her beauty. "You are beautiful," His voice was in awe of her. "What a pity I cannot see your face, lady."

She walked towards him. Their eyes met through their masked faces. One hand slid up into his buttoned shirt and ripped it down the center. Both of her warm, soft hands now caressed his smooth flesh, stopping at his shoulders to remove his shirt fully. "What a pity I cannot see the full effect of your body against my touch." Victor inhaled a harsh breath as she ripped at the confines of his pants. He stepped out of them and lifted her into his arms. They stumbled backwards, colliding with the bedpost. He held her firmly against it, lavishing in her ardent kiss.

"After this, my lady, you will have to marry me, for you will be utterly ruined in society." Victor reasoned with her sweetly as his kisses glided across her neck.

She laughed softly. "You think I conform to English societal restrictions? Noo…" she whispered in his ear as her nails dug into his back. "You also assume that I am of a virtuous nature. My husband has long since passed. I am no novice to the pleasures of a lover's touch." Her hips pushed against him, turning him around as they landed on the bed.

"You truly are the greatest riddle," Victor gazed up at her. She pushed against his chest as he tried to rise. Moving down his body she placed herself between his legs.

"I have chosen a better bedmate than I would have anticipated." Her eyes roamed his essence with pleasure.

"I am pleased you approve of my endowment. Aaahhhhh..." Victor moaned his head jerking backwards. Her tongue licked across the sensitive flesh tasting his juices before taking him fully within her mouth. She tasted the length of his shaft, nipping it gently. In and out, she took him. His body shivered with pleasure. She reached a hand up to massage and pull at the flesh between his legs, bringing his release closer with every touch. He moaned and quivered beneath her. She took his orgasm within her. He tasted sweet and warm.

She rose and crawled atop him. His breath was still heavy. "I hope you are not done, my lord, or I shall have to find another fellow to satisfy me." Her smile was beautiful and bewitching below her mask.

"Nay," Victor rose to his elbows. "I am not done."

"Good," her voice was husky with lust. Her legs widened around him and she pushed him further up on the bed. On all fours, she crawled up to him. "Fulfill me..." It was not a request but a demand, and he knew it. His manhood jumped between her thighs as her hard nipples grazed his chest.

"May I not see your beauty?" Victor was pleading now.

Her hand gripped him between her legs. "Nay, my body shall be enough to fill your dreams without the addition of the sight of my face." Her hips rose and came down to take him into her ready warmth. She moaned as he came to a stop deep within her. Her body began moving over his. Victor's hands traced the curves of her sides up to cup her breasts, moving quickly down to her waist, once more. He pulled her body to his and rolled on top of her.

"'Tis my turn, my lady, to elicit the pleasure," Victor moved tauntingly slow within her. He took her moan within his mouth and quickened his thrust. Having his first orgasm over with, he focused on hers. He made love to her for what felt like hours beneath the moon's illumination of their coupling. He moved her to varying positions, filling her body with pleasure.

"Ooh, my lord." She quaked beneath him. He could hold back no longer. His second release was coming fast.

"Are you ready once more, my lady?" Victor's voice was hot with desire. She nodded, moaning softly beneath him. He gathered her in his arms and pushed them both to the brink of insanity. Neither could refrain any longer and they came together on waves of satiating pleasure. As their bodies clung to the aftershocks, Victor pulled from inside her and held her close, kissing tenderly her lower neck. "I do not know how to leave you..." His voice was sincere and slightly grave at the thought of never seeing her again, never holding her, never touching her, nor ever hearing her laugh as it sweetly tickled his ears.

She grasped his hand and held it tight within her own. "Do not worry your mind with thoughts of our departure. Morning shall come and take us both from this place, leaving our paths to be forged separately or together." She snuggled closer against his chest and his arms tightened around her.

"Aye." Victor kissed her shoulder.

Together, Victor thought as he watched their son Jackson. *Together is how it was always supposed to be.* He remembered that night. He remembered that he had never wanted to be without that woman for the rest of his life. Yet she had left, and he had been awakened, awakened to Jason.

"In another time and place..." She hadn't needed to finish for he had known what she meant. Come morning his mystery woman would leave him, just as she had promised.

The woman in black's silken body had occupied Victor's dreams every night hence. Her cries of pleasure as her body writhed beneath him had tormented him. Passions were not the only thing that had run deep that night. The words of their conversations constantly played within his head. She was wit, and beauty, and grace. No woman had been able to match his knowledge or challenge him, as she had, since.

I now have a name to put with the mysterious woman, Victor thought, *Dorian... And a face,* Jason added.

Are you always there, always listening? Is no thought sacred or private anymore? Victor yelled at Jason within him.

Truly, Victor, you ask these questions... We share the same soul! You should thank Dorian. She reawakened you to your true form that night. She helped us come together so we could live as one, be one. Although, with your obstinacy it may take us longer than I would have hoped. Jason grew taxed.

"Victor. Vic-Tor!" The boy was calling to him.

Victor's mind rattled to grasp hold of the present. Dorian had approached Aldus. She looked as she had in Victor's dream, yet she did not hold the same menacing emotions around her. Nor did she seek to take his life beneath the water's rage. *How could this be the woman of my past? When I returned to her chamber the morning after the ball to find her mask pinned to my jacket... How could this be the same sweet creature that made love to me? How!?* A smile lit Dorian's face as she gathered her son into her arms. *Their son...* A chill ran through Victor's body at the thought.

"Night is coming fast," Aldus spoke to her. "You are near fully mended. Let us go." Dorian glanced back over the water's changing colors. The sea swirled with vibrant yellows and oranges. The deep blue of the sea melded at its meeting place with the sky and mixed into a dark violet of the rising night. You could not tell where the sky ended and the sea began.

As Dorian turned back to Aldus, Victor gasped at her beauty. He had never seen a woman glow so brightly, nor had he felt the vibrancy of the energy surrounding her so pure. This was where Dorian's heart was, here on this island, with her son and family. This was the essence of her strength. It was as much a part of her as she of it. However, there was still an element Victor could not fathom. He couldn't put his mind to it. It was as though it had been blocked from his consciousness for later acknowledgment. He struggled with the concept of being left in the dark for so long. A life had come into existence and grown without Victor knowing about it. He should have known that a child had come of their coupling. Since that night, he had never been the same. Something always festered beneath the surface of Victor's skin. His whole world had begun to transform, succeeding their one night of pure passion.

Victor was having trouble adjusting to the light.

And love, Victor remembered utterly and devotedly loving the woman whom he had never before had a name.

Do you still not understand!? The long silent voice of the other man within him came to life. *We are one, Victor. You and I both love and hate the same woman with a passion that cannot be extinguished by any means. Death does not stop the fire burning within us.*

"Vicccccccctoooorrrrrr!" the boy called to him once more. The mist of Victor's mind jostled as he looked up to see Aldus and Dorian walking away from him. Jackson peered over his mother's shoulder.

Aldus paused and turned to him. "Are you alright?"

"Aye," Victor called to them. "I shall tarry here until the sun sets."

"Indeed." Aldus turned back and pulled Jax from Dorian's arms. She scolded him. Then Victor heard their laughter as they disappeared in the dusk of the day towards the castle, Jackson reprimanding his mother for harming his uncle.

Victor faced the sea. "Alright, show me! Show me, Jason! Show me who we are!"

Victor heard the laughter of the other man. *Finally! You are ready. I thought this day was far from coming.*

A life streamed before Victor's eyes as the blanks of his birth were answered, and the gaps of his memory filled over centuries.

● ● ●

Morning light was encompassing the world before Nicholas. He had always loved the dawn of a new day, it always brought with it new feats and conquests. He looked over the starboard side of his captain's vessel, The Stallion, to find the same island level with his eyes. Nicholas checked the compass. It hadn't moved in its course of direction either.

How odd. Nicholas could feel the wind gently assaulting him from behind. *That should not be the problem,* he thought. He glanced around the ship. It made no motion over the ocean's waves.

"Captain," Nicholas called to the distance. "Captain FORTE!!" The man was panicking at the helm.

"Yes!" Forte yelled up to him from the main deck. "What the devil do you want!?" He stood, regally facing Nicholas, hands on his hips and chin held high.

"The boat…the ship's stopped its advance in the water." Nicholas gripped the wheel, turning his knuckles white. Having his captain mad was a terrifying sight. He held his ground. His dish water blonde hair blew faintly in the breeze, his clothing rustling in its winds.

"What do you mean we've stopped our advance!?" Forte rushed to the side of the ship, the water stood still all around it. "What the…." He slammed his fist down upon the railing, causing all the men around him to jump several feet back. "Are we stuck on a hidden reef? Is that it?" Forte stared up at Nicholas. Looking all around him, Forte couldn't find the cause of the stop. Forte used his will to try to get the waters moving beneath them. The Stallion lurched forward, rocking everyone aboard it, but it did not, could not, go further. Forte's Urchin gifts failed him.

"No, sir." Nicholas' voice regained Forte's attention and he lost his concentration. "We would have felt it if we'd hit a reef. The water is dark here and very deep, and the wind does blow. I do not understand it." Nicholas was scared as he looked over the ship then back down to Forte. He didn't want to admit what he was thinking. He didn't want to verbalize the fear he felt.

"Excellent!" Forte glanced over the faces of his shocked men hanging on to anything they could find, and then up to Nicholas. "The women are coming to us, lads!" A meager roar went up throughout the crew as they released the holds they held on the ship. They all reveled in a good battle. "However, I do not see how they caught us so fast!?" Forte was stunned.

Nicholas was at his side in seconds. "Perhaps 'twas Seth, sir. He did not sail with the heftiest of speeds while he was at the helm the other night." He was a weasel at Forte's side. "I watched him closely, I did."

Forte laughed and patted the man on his shoulder. "This is why you are my second in command. You are as faithful as the day is long." Forte searched the horizon. "However, I feel you are wrong in this accusation, Nicholas. Seth has rejoined my cause. He would not do anything to betray me now. He would only act to better our chances…" Forte pondered over his brother. "Seth loves the salt air as much as any of us. Perhaps he was simply enjoying it." Forte thought for a moment. "Nah!" he yelled. "Seth has a great plan up his sleeve. Brilliant that boy is, dedicated to my cause." He looked around briefly. "*Our* cause." He winked at his crewmen.

Nicholas leered at him. He hated Seth. He despised his relationship with his captain. "Perhaps, Captain." Nicholas began mumbling to himself. "Would you have me kill him?"

"What!" Forte called up to the man at the helm. "No, that will not be necessary. Besides I need Seth living for now. He spurs the queen to life. If he meets death, Ziah will soon follow. Seth just needed reigning." Looking east to the sun's rise, Forte felt The Lady's sails approaching him. "Seth is on our side, Nicholas, never forget that. The ladies near us because of Seth! Go and see to Rowan."

"Aye, Captain." Nicholas scurried off towards the lower deck. *I'll kill that mangy traitor when I have the chance, I will. Seth may have fooled the Captain, but he hasn't fooled me.* As he came close to Rowan's cell, Nicholas found her waiting for him. He peered in to see her. A weighted energy could be felt in Rowan's air. Nicholas could see the dried blood at the base of her hairline as Rowan turned to look beyond him. He laughed cruelly at her. "You should not have tousled with my Captain. He does not take obstruction kindly. You should find comfort in knowing that your sisters come for you. Alas, they shall meet only death." His smile was wicked.

Rowan's eyes bore into him. Jagged emerald knives pierced Nicholas' heart. He fell forward, finding support on the cell bars. Rowan came close to his face. "Your captain is formidable, a fault I will not overlook again. But you," her fingers traced Nicholas' throat, "are nothing more than an insignificant leech attached to the side of this ship." His air passages began to tighten as she stroked his throat.

"I know the wrath of a woman, but I have never felt one like this before." Nicholas coughed as his air passages shrank.

"Rowan!" Her eyes darted to Forte's. "Release him and I will grant you clemency."

"I would sooner trust the words of the devil. At least he is swayed by the pleasures of the flesh where you are controlled by them." The palm of her hand pushed into Nicholas' forehead shoving him backwards against the wall.

Nicholas gulped in the air once taken from him. "Thank you, Captain."

"Be gone, pest." The servant rose to his feet and fled the cabin. "I see you regain your strength, Lady Rowan." Silence answered Forte. "A mistake I shall not replicate in the future." He brought a hand to lightly rest on the bars. Rowan moved far away from it. "Do you fear my touch?"

Rowan laughed softly. "Nay, I would sooner fear a fly buzzing around my head."

"You compare me to an insect!?" Forte's temper raged.

"Aye," Rowan swiftly grasped Forte's wrist and pulled it towards her twisting it. "They are coming for you and they have strong allies on their side. What do you have?" Taking his wrist in both hands she snapped it. Forte winced in pain. "You are legendary in your underestimation of an opponent."

Forte whimpered, pulling his arm from Rowan. "Thank you for that observation of my faults. I will remedy the error." He filled with loathing.

"Are you sure?" Rowan held the coal in Forte's eyes, played with it. Forte felt his world shrinking as the wooden walls surrounding him closed him in. His vision began going blurry as Rowan would not release him. Forte's breath was leaving him. He forced the waters outside to lash out against his ship, throwing Rowan's gift off as her body thumped into the bars of her cell, catching her.

Forte hissed at her as he ran away, rubbing his throat and breathing in more deeply than he had ever known.

Rowan laughed in his wake. "I have done what you asked, sister. A chink in his armor is forming."

Forte mumbled to himself as he reached the top deck. "Sirens! I have forgotten their strength and bitterness. A woman scorned is one thing, easily handled. A raging Siren is far more treacherous than I recalled." He rubbed his throat. "Tread lightly, they will fold." He smiled broadly as he looked out to sea. His wrist throbbed. With a deep breath he steadied his eyes and looked out to sea, popping the bone back into place. Forte grunted as his energy tingled beneath his skin, mending him.

They will not beat me. I will have her back soon enough and the life force that comes with her! My powers will be great and I will defeat them all! Forte tried to intimidate the sea beneath him, but it merely mocked his hollow words.

The sea held a great many secrets and it knew greater things than it cared to tell.

Chapter

12

———————◆———————

RAHN STOOD AT THE BOW of The Lady, the opposing vessel in her sight. Her men were ready. She could feel their emotions fueling them for battle. Rahn didn't know if she could defeat Forte for he carried the blood of an infected Urchin and the gifts of another whom she could not place, but she would die trying.

"Why do we sail to meet them when your gifts could have had us reaching them instantaneously!?" Rahn hadn't noticed Christian's advance to her side.

Rahn exhaled, releasing her surprise. "It's true there is no distance within our world. We take the long way about things because what else are we to do with our immortality?" Rahn turned to Christian mildly. "You overestimate some of our abilities. And we cannot take ship and crew with us for battle if we travel our way, for not all aboard this vessel can travel with us in such a way."

Christian stared at Rahn, unseeing. His body anticipated battle and the reclaiming of his sister was close in his heart. He longed to know of Rowan's safety. As the woman beside him spoke, the words fell on unhearing ears.

• • •

Forte was older than two of The Lady's Sirens by centuries. He was turned Urchin on a day when no squall was predicted for the sea, near where he resided. He was a young, strapping man who could have lured many a woman from her betrothed's bed. He had inherited the title of great lover throughout the social ranks of London. Every woman wanted a piece of him and every man wanted the pleasure of tearing him to shreds. Forte's hard, handsome features paired with his black hair and coal eyes made him dark and mysterious, enticing to any eye.

Forte set sail off his coast to bring in the night's bounty. Born into a wealthy fisherman's family, he picked up the trade for fun. His mother and father were the Count and Countess of Sherry and he always shared his father's longing for the sea and its plentiful waters. He joined the Queen's navy at a young age and wasted no time making a grand name for himself. Forte was Captain of his own ship at the age of one and twenty. His popularity and skill only grew from there.

One night, Forte ventured out alone in a small boat of his father's just to smell the night air on the sea and to see the magnificence of the new moon. A soft voice was carried to his ears, pleading for help. Forte stared out over the dark waters, searching for a person in the moonlit crescents of the waves. His sight landed on a figure cloaked in white, gripping a piece of driftwood, floating miles out to sea.

"I come to help you, my lady," Forte called to her, rowing forward with all his might.

"Please hurry, I am terrified of the creatures nearing me below surface." Her voice melted his heart. Forte had never wanted to take a wife before this moment. Something in the girl called to him. She spoke to his soul.

Forte approached her quickly. "Here, reach to me," as he met her eyes, Forte's heart was stolen. "I've got you, my lady." The moon's silver light was reflected back to him, her golden hair shone in the night's touch. Forte pulled the stranded maiden onto his boat and covered her with a thick wool blanket. "Here, drink this. It will warm your spirits." Forte could not conceive how the lovely drenched woman beside him had been left to the sea this night. She drank deeply of the warm elixir he gave to her, the heat making her skin glow in a beautiful way. He couldn't remove his eyes from her. "What is your name, my lady?"

She coyly reached up to his eyes. "My name is Deirdra, but you may call me Dee. And you are?"

"I am James Forte, madam. How did a creature as lovely as you become trapped upon the ocean this night?"

Dee eyed him, moving her head from side to side like a snake nearing strike. "A *creature* such as me? What beautiful wording, James," Forte felt she mocked him. "For I am just that, a creature."

"What?" Forte pushed himself into the corner of his boat. "I fear you are going mad with exhaustion, madam. I must get you ashore and to the town doctor. What is your last..." He never got to finish his sentence before Dee shoved herself across the small boat pouncing on his chest. Forte could feel the water brush the top of his hair as he bent backwards over the edge.

The blanket fell from her, the dress Dee wore was water logged and clinging to the curves of her body. Forte couldn't help but notice she was enchantingly beautiful. Her breasts heaved with each breath as if it were a hard task for her lungs. The gold of her hair fell around her body, curling in wet tendrils. Forte's eyes made their way up to her light face. The features there were exquisite. Dee was smiling at him with teeth sharp and gleaming.

"Have you no shame!?" Forte questioned her. "I am here to help you and you jump me out of nowhere! Cover yourself, madam." He began to struggle under her. Trying to regain his freedom and rid himself of this creature. Usually his strength had no trouble removing people from him, but Dee wouldn't budge. She just laughed at him and smiled. "What are you!?" he spoke frantically, startled as he noticed the sharpness of her teeth grow more pronounced.

"Don't worry, James Forte," Dee giggled like a young school girl. "I am sick with fever, as you say, but it is far better than you could ever imagine. My fever will make you invincible!" Dee's voice boomed over him. "This won't hurt…me at all." Her laughter echoed through the dark night. Pinning Forte's arms at his side Dee bent her head to his neck. They were so far off the land that no one heard the screams of a tortured man but the ocean, who kept his secrets quiet as the pair toppled over the side of the boat landing beneath the water's currents.

The steady lapping of the water against the boat's side awoke the sleeping man. Forte turned his head slowly from side to side, gently opening his eyes. He reached up and felt the dried blood on his neck, the wound almost nonexistent. He flashed back to a violent fight between him and his captor, the woman Dee. He could still taste the blood in his mouth after he bit her in an effort to stop her torment. Forte felt the cracks of the dried sun as he ran his tongue over his parched lips. Slowly he rose and looked out over the boat's side. He was miles out to sea yet he could still see his dock far in the distance.

How long have I been asleep? How long have I been out to sea? Forte wondered. The moonlit eyes flashed into his head, causing Forte pain. He could feel her upon him once more, her teeth tearing into his flesh. *Has she left me for dead?*

"You wake, my love." Forte jumped, almost capsizing the boat. "Don't be so testy, love," Dee's arms hung over the side of the boat, the rest of her submerged below the water's surface. "You know I had a mind to let you die last night." She laughed.

Upon seeing Dee's face, Forte abandoned all sense. "I feel not quite myself."

He spoke absent mindedly swaying with the breeze. Dee was now the beat in his heart.

"You are quiet the fighter." Dee's tanned skin radiated with the suns stroke while her grin warmed him. The pointed teeth of the previous night were gone. *Had I dreamt it all? Had we been attacked on the sea and we both escaped?* Forte looked around him. His boat drifted towards an abandoned island not far from the banks of his home. He saw a man standing on the beach waiting there.

The melody of Dee's voice drew him back to his tired body. "Your will is strong and useful. I could not have asked for a better mortal. You have the disposition I seek. Plus," she reached out to stroke his face and he knelt into her touch instinctively. "…you are wickedly handsome." She lifted her naked body from the water and moved to sit in front of him, wrapping herself in the woolen blanket. Her movements were fluid and other-worldly. Dee had a grace Forte had never seen before. "Do you wish to meet him?" Dee's head pointed towards the shoreline they now approached.

Forte's eyes roamed Dee's face. He had lost his voice at the smell of her sun kissed skin. His eyes lingered over her full lips. All he could do was nod.

"Good. I will explain everything to you." Dee sat up and pushed the ores in Forte's direction. He stared at them before grasping them awkwardly in his hands. His rowing was clumsy and uneven. Cocking her head to one side and coyly allowing Forte a full view of her glorious form, she floored him. "I knew letting you live would be worthwhile." Forte saw the mark he had left on her shoulder.

"What? I did not dream it. I bit you, I see the mark now." Forte met her eyes.

"No, it was no dream, pet. You've shared my blood as I have taken yours from you. Don't worry," Dee said. "No one will ever hurt you," she looked towards the man at shore. "Or Seth, again, while we stand side-by-side."

Forte stared at the man on shore wondering who or what he was. He felt a connection with him, even at their physical distance that he could not explain. Forte's eyes fell to the water, catching his waiting reflection. His encounter with Dee had aged him by years. Forte's once black hair was now spread with gray and his face had lines of wear. Forte almost didn't recognize himself, save for his smile. He was more handsome than in his youth.

Seth was born of Forte's transformation into the Urchin life. Forte had been given the gift of the Two-Natured in his new life. Their mistress, Dee, loved them both and controlled them endlessly. The beginning of Forte and Seth's new life was filled with carnal desires that Dee was always happy to fulfill, for either one of them. Eventually, Seth tired of their maker and Dee gladly let him seek his bedding elsewhere. Forte, however, claimed Dee all for himself, lost to the powers of her seduction.

Until her disappearance from their life, she was there morning, noon and night. Dee always had an answer for everything, and anything she asked of Forte and Seth they *had* to do. A detriment of their transition into the Urchin life, they had to obey their Siren maker. The two were at the disposal of her constant bidding.

At Dee's departure, Seth grew independent and matched Forte in his will. Having a second form is always tricky and comes with consequence.

Urchins of the Two-Natured can be identical in their physical build and share the same mental mind, or they can be opposite in all ways from appearance, to action, to thought processes. The variations of the Two-Natured are endless and confusing with complexity.

Although Seth grew in will, Forte thought he shared his thoughts and actions, but he found out the hard way that Seth did not and needed to be controlled.

Ever since their mistress, Dee, had been murdered, Forte had sought her relentlessly. He needed Seth's joined mind and cooperation in finding her. When Dorian entered his life he knew his Dee had returned to him. Because of Dee's infected Siren blood she passed the madness onto Forte and in his blinded world, he could not accept that Dee was dead and forever gone from his and Seth's life.

• • •

As The Lady approached The Stallion, the waters began to quake beneath them, fear shredding the waves apart. The bright, sunny day was a contrast to the dismal faces of either crew. Both crews held weapons at the ready, both longed for the others' blood. The only cards Rahn held were that Dorian still lived and her protection would shower The Lady's ship and crew, and that Rowan was aboard The Stallion patiently waiting to wreak her revenge upon its inhabitants.

"Good afternoon, Lady Rahn. You are looking well, I see." Forte stood at his ship's plank awaiting The Lady's arrival. Attired in the sharpest of gray suits he looked like a king. His silver buttons shown in the day's light. He was handsome, only to the easily deceived eye.

"The centuries have been kind to you as well, Forte. Save for the graying of your hair that comes with old age." Rahn smiled at her adversary. "Please save your pleasantries. I have no use for them."

"I am in no way old!" Forte exploded. He looked Rahn over from head to toe. She wore her favored color of blood red in a silky blouse covered by a long black vest and matching skin-tight pants hidden in knee-high black boots. Her hand rested on the hilt of her long blade at her waist. "If you make a jest on my failing abilities because of age, my dear, I fear you will be sorely mistaken, for I have centuries on you. Now to the business at hand. I want my creator's body and I shall be on my way."

"Your creator perished long ago. Dee has not stood by your side, nor in this world, for many, many centuries, Forte." Rahn paused to feel his expression. "She died at the tip of my blade. Do you not remember?"

"Lies!! All lies!" Forte shouted across to The Lady. "She walks with you and speaks with you. Dee lives and breathes the same air as I! Bring her to ME!!" Forte stood heaving with frustration.

"NO!! Dee was an evil abomination to the name Siren! She killed for pleasure and pain. Why she ever let you live is beyond my comprehension!!" Rahn was gripping the railing of The Lady yelling over the torrents of the water's rage. "She was sick with fever and imparted it onto you!"

"Have it your way." Forte spun on his heel as the first round of cannon fire sounded from the guns of his men. Forte ran to his quarters to riffle through his trunk in search of the box. He pulled the box carved of driftwood out from beneath piles of books and clothes. He held it longingly in his hands as he ran his fingers over the inscription. *"For my ever and only love"* it read. He pulled out the picture painted of Dee and him.

"We will be together again, my love. You have only forgotten me, in your new form. You will remember. I will make you remember." Gently, Forte ran his fingers over the face of the woman in the picture. She was small in stature and build. Her flowing blonde hair curled around her slim body as the intense silver of her eyes stared out to him. "You have merely forgotten..." He tucked the picture in his front pocket and grabbed his pistols from the bed stand. Where Dorian had soft welcoming, features to her face, Dee had sharp angular ones. Dee's face had grown hollow with rage and insanity. Evil stared out from the strokes of the painting.

Forte burst through his double doors, a war cry on his lips. Guns drawn, he began to fire off rounds at all who opposed him. A soft rain began to pelt the decks of both ships, the winds bringing darker clouds rolling in on their wisps.

• • •

Christian worked his way through the raging men of The Stallion. Sword hit sword as Christian hustled towards the stairs leading to the lower deck. The men challenged Christian and cursed him. A sailor cut into his arm. Christian held in the pain and sliced the ruffian through the heart, as his body fell out of Christian's way. Another man shoved Christian's body, and as he turned to see his adversary he was flung backwards into the stairwell, colliding with the wall.

The toothless pirate laughed at him. "Is that all the once great Roberts can do...."

His rough taunting voice did nothing but give Christian fuel. He charged back up the stairs and grabbed the man's sword-wielding hand pulling it beneath his arm. "Nay," as he forced his sword through the man's chest "'tis not." He let the body fall and headed back down the stairs in search of Rowan.

Sebastian was close on his heels, trying to guard Christian's back as they made their way beneath the main deck. Sebastian had wounds of his own. A cut had been made along his left side, running parallel with the length of his neck. Sebastian did not feel it, nor did the man who harmed him, for his head lay somewhere amongst the rubble. The light grew dim the farther he followed Christian under the deck. He could barely make out the length of the hall to its end. A cannon ball thundered through the side of The Stallion, startling Sebastian in its wake.

"Shit..." Sebastian heard Christian say though he could barely see him.

"Chris!" Sebastian called to him.

Christian had collided with another human and they both fell to the ground. Christian tried to pull his gun out but was flattened to the floor in seconds. "I'll kill you, you mangy bastard!" He squirmed under the other person's weight. The frame was thin but sturdy.

"Christian?" A woman's voice called his name, a voice he loved.

"Rowan! How... What the hell are you doing out of your cell?" Rowan grabbed Christian's hand as she stood up, hoisting him up with her.

"You sound dismayed that I'm not where I was supposed to be for a proper, gallant rescue," Rowan teased.

Christian could hear the laughter in his sister's voice.

"I am remembering who and what I am. A Siren does not falter. A Siren does not fear. A Siren does not wait to be rescued." Her confidence was palpable. Rowan finally felt something that she hadn't in a long time. "Never underestimate a Siren, brother." A smile, foreign and cruel, crossed Rowan's lips.

"Will you ever need my help again?" Christian felt defeated already, his shoulders slumped slightly in his strong frame.

"Yes." Rowan grabbed his sword from its sheath and raised it to the oncoming intruders. "Sebastian can't keep all the men at bay." Rowan charged the dirty pirate, forcing him back up the stairs.

Christian laughed at the poor man's stunned expression. *Did he know nothing of these women?* He thought. Following close behind Rowan, armed with his pistol in one hand and a pirate's stray sword in the other, Christian charged back up the stairs intent on more blood.

The air topside was thick with the haze of smoke as Christian, Sebastian and Rowan burst through to the main deck. A mist seemed to linger around the fallen bodies. For a moment Christian could not see. The fog had enveloped him, blocking his vision. He was right behind Rowan when they arrived, but now, she had moved one step out of his mist and disappeared. It appeared as though a wall had built around him. Christian could hear the clash of swords and gunfire raging all too close. The hit of steel crashed just out of sight. Christian could hear the final cries of men and the thud as the bodies dropped, but he could not see them. The fog moved in around them all. Rowan burst into his field, a smile on her face and blood sprayed across her chest. She grabbed Christian's arm and tugged him through the invisible door to freedom.

"Come on! We must make haste," Rowan yelled over the fire of guns. Christian took one step behind Rowan and was submersed in the full-out battle waging around him. He looked back to stare at the fog that had been his shell. Its thickness dissipated and floated up into the air hovering overhead just out of reach.

Someone was shaking his arm. "Christian, Christian! Make way to The Lady there." Rowan pointed inches away to the plank. He nodded. "I have to get Sebastian. GO!"

Rain began to pound on the decks causing fatal slips for the men caught at the wrong time. Christian did not understand Rowan's urgency but he trusted that she knew what he did not. He clanged sword against sword as he made his way back towards The Lady. Many a man lay fallen behind him with death upon his face. The shouts that once seemed so loud were drowned out within the building storm.

Sebastian was locked in combat with Nicholas. Scrawny in stature, but imposing by nature, he wielded the sword as if it was an extension of his life, his body. Both men bore cuts and had gaping wounds dripping with blood. The dark fog swirled around their bodies enticing them to follow it.

Sebastian sliced into his upper thigh. "You bastard!" Nicholas lunged for his heart.

Sebastian side-stepped Nicholas and was wrapped in fog. "Bloody Hell!! Nicholas, you sniveling excuse of a man, come out! Come out and fight me!"

Sebastian yelled into the fog. The world around him echoed its calls back to his ears, but he couldn't see. Sebastian tried to move out of the cloud but it moved with him. He could not escape it. "Fuck, my aunt," Sebastian began a stream of curses to the walls guarding him. He was livid inside their sanctuary. His mind cleared as he saw a hand reaching through to him. *Have I died*, he thought. *Is this purgatory?* Sebastian snapped to attention as Rowan's full figure entered his enclosure.

"You're not dead." Rowan grabbed his arm. "Ready your sword, we..." She gasped as he pulled her to him.

Sebastian ran his hand across her blood-stained cheek and the cut that lay there. He spoke to her, his breath inches from her cheek. "Who did this to you?" Rowan looked down, embarrassed at his attention. She shrugged her body, closing herself. "Rowan…" Sebastian's voice was sweetly demanding of an answer from her.

Focusing at a point on the wooden deck, "It is of no consequence," Rowan squealed as Nicholas cut between them.

"Thought your little mist of protection could keep me out? Ha!" Nicholas screamed. "I know better the will of a Siren than any, and I know how to best it!"

Rowan stared at him, astonished. *What an imbecile.*

Sebastian parried his attack and shoved Nicholas away. Rowan shook her head. Christian yanked Rowan's arm, pulling backward. In reaction, she grabbed onto Sebastian, dragging him with her. The fog was thick around both ships. It encased them from the world.

Sebastian's life came back to light. Bodies fell at his feet as he quickly moved to jump over them. Blood stained the deck of The Stallion and all its passengers. Rowan had released him, moving a few feet ahead of him. Christian had a foothold on the plank. He was ready to jump when Rowan's arm was snagged and she was pulled abreast Forte.

"Hello, my dear, have you come to let me finish the job?" Forte ran his knife over the cut on her face. Sebastian froze, anger flooding his body.

Rahn stood still in the place where she had first witnessed Sebastian's closeness with Rowan. *Why had I not seen it before, of course!* The battle raged around her, but it did not matter. Rahn felt a waterfall of emotions for Rowan. She so desperately wanted her sister to be happy and to know what real, true love was like.

Nicholas brought Rahn's attention back to the present. He slashed into her body cutting deeply along her side. She gripped the wound in surprise. The hellfire of her wrath turned on him and Nicholas whimpered in the heat of her eyes.

The force of Rahn hit against his body. "Do me no harm, lady. I am no one of importance," Nicholas coward on the floor, his back against the sideboard. "I meant no offense."

"You meant no offense, Nicholas, really?" Rahn's voice was oozing with revulsion. "Your childish antics work not on me!" Her sword pierced his flesh. "No," Rahn stopped her blade from killing Nicholas. "That is far too easy a death for the likes of you." Rahn summoned her creatures from the deep. "How would you like to meet my friends?"

"What?" Rahn motioned over the edge of The Stallion. "No, no, no… Please!" Nicholas whined for his life.

"I'm sorry. I don't negotiate with vermin." Rahn marched the few paces to Nicholas and grabbed him by the belt of his pants. She lugged him over the side of The Stallion into the awaiting mouth of a serpent from the deep. It lurched out of the dark waters to grab Nicholas in its fangs, towing him deep into the black depths. Rahn watched as the creature's massive tail rose up out of the water, splashing a tidal wave against the ship and disappearing. Rahn turned to search the deck and ran to Christian's side at the plank. Forte held Rowan to his body, a knife against her throat.

"Approach me and I shall kill her!" Forte was scraping for more seconds to his life. The threat of defeat lingered around him as his men lay fallen at his feet.

All eyes turned upward and the whole world stopped as an imposing thunderous clap broke the sky to pieces.

• • •

Victor watched as Dorian tossed and turned in her bed. It was afternoon, but she had taken a nap after her morning of play with Jackson. Sweat dripped off her face. Her clothing clung to her body as she fought an unseen force. Dorian's whole body stilled in one fluid sweep, and Victor felt the urgency of her dream beating into him.

Victor moved to perch on the side of Dorian's bed. Staring down at her angelic face, he loathed her with every inch of his being.… Or was it love? *You are sleeping with my kin! I could kill you right now and rid myself and the world of this she-devil.* The anger built inside him as the thought of all her betrayals. Victor raised one hand to her throat and rested it there for several paces. He began gently squeezing it closed. All the injustices Dorian had caused him were brought to light before his eyes.

I could kill her now and be rid of her… Victor's hold tightened around her neck. Dorian's hand came to rest on top of his. She didn't wake. A thunder clap illuminated the black sky outside and drew him back to what he was doing.

"What are you doing!?" Victor spoke to himself. "She is a woman nonetheless. You do not harm women, Victor!" Victor glanced out her bedroom windows to the sea. *When did it get so dark?* Returning to look at Dorian's face he released her neck and gently pushed a stray hair out of her face. All the injustices he, and Jason, had placed upon her came back with an aching clarity.

And she still stood by me... Victor's mind paused. *She still stood by you, Jason. All those years...after everything you put her through, everything we put her through....* Victor's heart clenched within him.

Dorian stood by us, Victor. She still stands by us. She deserves the chance to love us as one whole being. Just as we deserve to love her with our whole heart. Jason reaffirmed for Victor what he had been feeling. *Love, Victor. Remember love? You love Dorian, or you would not be here. If you truly felt nothing for her I would not be able to do anything about it and my love would fade into the background as you sought the company of someone else.* Jason spoke within Victor. *If you did not love Dorian, if you were not destined to love her, she would not have been the pawn to reawaken you to your Urchin life. Without your love for her, we could never be fully joined into one soul, one being. If it was not your destiny to love her, another circumstance would have been predetermined to reawaken your urchin blood instead. Love, Victor. Love...* Jason's voice faded. *I have faith she will, and can, forgive us.*

Dorian's eyes flashed open, the silver pools swirled to black as she focused on Victor's face. "Dorian...I...." She placed both hands on Victor's chest and pushed him with a force that sent him flying across the room, crashing into a chair behind him and toppling over with it. She rose from the bed and stormed down the stairs, her white gown trailing on the wind behind her.

It took Victor a few minutes to regain his senses. Rising, he gripped the ribs of his left side. "Dorian. Dorian!!" Victor called after her and hurried in her wake. He could follow her by the frenzy of energy she left behind. "Love, Victor. Remember what that feels like..." He hobbled out of the room gripping his side.

Victor made his way through the double doors of the castle's entrance and stumbled over the bridge to the beach. He could see Dorian walking briskly towards the water. She looked as though she were gliding atop the earth. Her white night gown was a stark contrast to the black and gray gloom that lurked around her. The high wind trailed through her hair. Dorian paused just at the entrance to the sea's current. She waited. Victor ambled up behind her, breathless. Dorian took her first step into the irate waters.

"Dorian," Victor tried to reason with her. "What are you doing!?" he hollered after her.

Dorian's body was deeply submerged with the incoming waves as they crashed against her waist. She raised her arms out straight to her sides, her head fell back to meet the sky with closed eyes. Victor watched in awed horror as Dorian's eyes flew open and in their depths was the swirling of the black, raging sky. She raised her head and brought her arms together, slamming her hands into one another. Victor gawked as the sky rippled with her movement, a surging storm heading off into the sea. Electricity flew from her fingertips as lightning filled the sky. Victor felt the shocks of her energy running through his body.

Dorian's voice boomed around him as she spoke to a far distant menace. "My love is stronger than your hate."

Dorian's face swirled in the clouds above the warring vessels of her ship and The Stallion. Victor followed the path of her storm and saw the two ships paused in battle.

Rain pelted down on their decks. Rowan took the opportunity to smash her foot down, and Forte yipped as he released her. Sebastian moved in close to her. Rowan grabbed his arm with force and urgency, her strength making him wince. "We must get back to The Lady now!!" There was no fight as Rowan and Sebastian made their way back to the plank. All the sailors stared transfixed at the woman in the sky swirling above them. Rowan was first to run the distance and leap onto The Lady's safe harbor.

Sebastian stared after her, "He did this to you?" He held his hand out for her to see. It was dripping with blood. He turned in search of Captain Forte.

"Sebastian NO!!" Rowan called to him. "No, come back. NO!!" It took both Christian and Rahn to drag Rowan back over the railing of The Lady.

Rowan and Rahn both shot their eyes upward as they heard the residual clap of thunder coming their way. "Sebastian!! Get back on the ship!! Get back on the SHIP NOW!!!" Rowan screamed her heart to him.

The thunder hit over the warring vessels, causing all eyes to watch as the lightning flashed through the sky. The ocean's waters began to tremble and rock with anger. The currents forced The Lady further and further away from Forte's ship. A distressed Rowan clung to its railing and searched The Stallion's deck for a lone man.

The crew of The Lady watched as Sebastian cornered Forte, and they lunged back and forth at each other. Rahn cringed as he took hit after hit. Christian was by her side holding tight to his sister's waist.

The ocean built within its fury, producing a wave bent on swallowing Forte's ship whole and dragging it under to its deepest, darkest depths. The crew of The Lady watched in horror as the wave took the ship in its fist and snapped it in two. The terrified calls of the men aboard were drowned in its crash.

Rowan fell back onto the deck and stared up into the face of the wave, Rahn by her side. "He stabbed him," her voice trailed off with laughter. "Sebastian may have rid us all of that horrible man."

"Look, look Rowan." Rahn was hitting her to get her attention. They watched as a body was flung out of the wave's peak and propelled toward their ship.

Cries went up aboard The Lady. "Look Out!!" "Watch ye head!!" All went silent as the body floated just above deck and then crashed to its surface unconscious but unharmed.

Rowan ran to the body and turned it on its side. Sebastian's unconscious face peered up at her. She hugged him to her.

Rahn turned to see the whirlpool that sucked the whole of The Stallion down. Crushing wave upon crushing wave came down upon it.

"Couldn't stay out of it, could you, Dorian?" Rahn smiled to herself as she spoke to the sky. A laugh echoed over their world. She turned back to Rowan, who held Sebastian protectively within her arms. Rahn smiled. *Give him comfort, sister.*

"Go. We must move back home before the reverberations of the swell reach The Lady." Rahn yelled over the pounding waters.

Grim nodded at Rahn's side and made way for the helm. "I'm glad you are OK, Lady Rowan." He smiled at Rowan's frail figure. She nodded, smiling lightly up at him as she stroked Sebastian's hair.

"Can we get some men to help move Sebastian out of this wretched rain?" Rahn called to the hands upon deck, as her eyes lovingly held Rowan's.

Chapter

13

————◆————

THE AIR AROUND DORIAN began to still as she lowered her arms to her side. The sky began to clear of darkness, allowing the light blue of the afternoon to peek through. Dorian stood a few moments longer as she calmed the breath within her. A gentle breeze floated around the air as Dorian turned to face the mesmerized man behind her. She faced Victor, the sun pouring over her silhouette, exhibiting her as an angel in its glow. The column of the storm gently rushed off towards sea, thick clouds following in its wake, running to rain havoc elsewhere.

Dorian took one foot after the other out of the clear blue of the ocean as she exited it in her stride. The sand didn't shift under the presence of her weight. Victor stared intently into the space her body once occupied. He couldn't remove his gaze from the ever calming waters appearing in front of him. Victor felt the brush of contact to his shoulder. He turned his head to the left to meet Dorian's calm, moonlit eyes. She stood alongside him, never breaking contact with his body.

Dorian made him keep her gaze. "You thought of strangling me?" Her eyes roamed his face, a beacon of light in Victor's darkness. He could no longer meet her face. "I can feel the imprint of your hand on my neck." Simple electric shocks zapped Victor's body as she continued to touch him.

Victor still clutched his injured side as if his arm would shelter him from further harm. His eyes reached Dorian's neck and the fading bruise there. It had already begun to fade to yellow around the edges. Under the scrutiny of his gaze, it faded completely. *What is she?* The question disturbing Victor's dreams had finally been answered. "I..."

"Sssshh," Dorian's finger brushed his lips, charging him with electricity.

"No." Victor hovered over her hand taking it within his. "Did Aldus speak to you?"

Dorian's eyes questioned him.

"I am your son's father. How could you not have sought me out to tell me of his existence?" Victor got straight to the point. His time could no longer be wasted, nor did he want it to be. His new life beckoned. His voice was calm, trying not to release his inner torment.

"What?" Dorian's features crinkled with doubt as she looked at him. "You are not his father." Her entire body filled with shock, but her voice remained calm and soothing. "You are of no resemblance to his father." Victor held onto her wrist as she tried to pull away.

"Really? Save for my build and the utter sameness of my appearance! You never saw Jax's father's face. How can you doubt my words?" Victor forced her to remember, to think of the night of Jackson's conception. "I do not fear your wrath, for I can bring forth my own. It is you who should fear me, for the dishonor you have bestowed."

"Dishonor? I know not of what you speak. Aldus would have said word if..." Dorian was interrupted.

Victor cut her off, shaking her body in his grasp. "Aldus would have said nothing because of his affections for you and the spark of a babe that would grow in your belly. But the words I speak are true. Aldus told me himself it was me he saw leaving your chamber the morning after the ball." Victor paused, thinking about Aldus and his loyalty. "He is truly the most honest man. He was protecting you."

Dorian's eyes grew wide with the recollection of that night. "But it was not you. The man was not of Urchin descent nor was your scent the same." Victor still held her hand close to his face and her fingers moved against the air to stroke it absentmindedly.

Victor did not miss the action. "Does your whole world revolve around smell?"

Dorian stared into Victor's eyes and the memory flashed between them. She gasped and tried to move backwards away from him. "But how... how are you one and the same?"

"Since that night my mind and soul have not been at rest. I have longingly searched for the woman who tainted my dreams, and here she is." Victor forced her closer to him. "You awakened my dragon for the first time that night, but in our lustful passions neither of us heeded the sign. You have brought me back to life! Do you not see?" Victor's voice was loud and forceful in his excitement. "If you do not see who it is that I am, then you are the one at fault."

She looked into the depths of Victor's eyes, searching his soul. A husband long-dead stared back at Dorian. She saw the joining of a Two-Natured soul that had long been at unrest. "Jason." The realization of who stood before Dorian hit hard her body and mind.

"That name from your lip rips my heart. You should no longer be of privilege to use it," Victor's voice stung.

Will you shut up with that nonsense, Victor! We love this woman, you idiot. Jason was tired of hearing his second nature's voice.

"You are of the Two-Natured. Why did you never tell me?" Dorian's mood gave nothing away. Any feelings she had, she kept well hidden. "You love me, remember? Such things would normally be shared with your wife." Her smile was mocking.

She can hear me!? Jason was astonished. Dorian's eyes still held the man in front of her and her subtle nod let Jason know he was right.

"I had no need. My gift was not of the same life. This form, Victor, was born of this life, and my love for you guided you back to me so you alone could revive me to my nature. You alone could awaken Victor's Urchin blood." Victor's mind began to mix with Jason's as his voice took on Jason's words. It was beginning to be hard to tell where one life ended and the other began.

Betrayal filled Dorian's core as hate crept in behind it. "You have lied to me, Jason. I loathe thee." Her free hand slammed into the side of Victor's face knocking him sideways. She finally understood and guarded her smile. *This is what I have been waiting for.*

"I see you still pack your punch," Victor had not released her hand, so he yanked her towards him and held her fast to his body. "Although, you have become stronger in my centuries' absence of you." Dorian could no longer tell who spoke with her. Victor and Jason were interlacing their comments as one being.

"Release me," Dorian's voice was demanding as her body stilled against him.

"I recognize your defense pattern, Dorian. A praying mantis will use a similar response. They still their bodies in prayer before they attack their opponent." Victor allowed her to step a few feet away, for his own safety mainly. "What a pity you loathe the man who saved your life as you died trying to deliver our first child."

"Our son saved me, not you!" Dorian's eyes were alight with lightning flashes. She was furious.

"Nooo," Victor's voice grew calm beneath her rage. "Our son was long dead as the labor persisted. Jason's form had to die, his love gifting you immortality, so you could live for me to find again. The theory has proven true. We have another son who lives and breathes amongst us."

Dorian pushed hard into Victor's chest and he fell backwards. "You will never be Jackson's father. Nor will I accept your love. Your deceit runs far too deep to find redemption within my harbor."

"Do not deny the giver of your gift, my dear." Victor called after her.

Dorian turned back to face him. "I do not, nor will I ever. Look behind you to see the giver of *my* gift. The ocean's waters have given me far more than the wish of a dying man." Victor felt Jason spasm in pain at Dorian's words. "The ocean gifted me something that once released, will relish in a terrifying wrath. Beware where you stand when that day comes." Her smile had turned cruel and pointed.

Victor did not understand. "What do you speak of?" He had a growing feeling within him that Dorian's transition was not because of Jason's gift after his death, that is was something much, much more.

"I see now that you are right. I am a Siren because of you, but it was already predetermined that my destiny would be so. I have seen the records. Anger fills me at your words because it brings everything I endured to life once more. Death is inevitable, rebirth is certain, and the journey is never one of expected turns. It saddens me that my husband had to die in order for me to cross over. But look into my eyes." Victor did. Smooth silver lights guided him. "Do you not see what your life has given me?"

Victor nodded, unable to speak. Dorian had far surpassed any ability he knew of the Siren and Urchin realms. She was something more, something different and terrifying. *How did you become this? What lurks within you that far surpasses our lineage?*

"We will take you home." Dorian turned and was gone as silently as the wind. Victor saw her white gown trailing on the air. Large hands gripped him from behind, hauling him to the waiting vessel. The Alastar was to take him home.

Aldus perched on the hill overlooking Dorian and Victor's tiff. He laughed deeply and fully. "You finally return to us, brother. Beware, for Dorian is merely toying with you. She plays her part well and in truth needs something from you to release her hidden passenger. That much I know, but I do not know what inner gifts she possesses. Your paths are not finished intertwining. If she sends you away, she has a purpose for it." Aldus watched as the men dragged Victor off, willingly, to the ship.

"I can take your wrath. There is no other way to unleash your full will without a threat of some sort. A little brotherly competition is just what you need." Aldus laughed, shaking his head as he walked away from their scene. He saw that his brother still existed and that his fight, Victor and Jason's fight, was far from over. Jason was ready to play catch up and Victor was ready to be full. "I have missed you, brother."

• • •

Sebastian was livid, storming up and down The Lady's main deck. *I almost had him. Damnit! I almost had him.* He almost got his full revenge on Forte. He felt slightly incomplete, that he hadn't gotten to rein havoc on those around him. *That damn fog!* He kept thinking to himself. He didn't know if the mist had saved his life at the moment he was to lose it, or if he had missed out on the mayhem of murder that surrounded him because of it. There was still a gap in his memory. But Sebastian had gotten in a wounding blow to Forte, before he lost consciousness. His mouth curved in an attractive smile his pride swelling.

The last thing Sebastian could recall before waking up in bed was Forte's body pressed to the helm of The Stallion. *The man spoke nonsense, utter incoherent nonsense.* Sebastian waved his arms in the air, startling the few onlookers he had. *He must have gotten the fever, he was a raging lunatic.*

"Seb… Seb!" Sebastian turned to the speaker of his name. "I've been calling you for ages, mate." Christian slapped him on the shoulder making him jump. "What's the matter with you? Have you gone mad?"

"I'm struggling to remember!" Sebastian held his hand up to his chin. "Nothing. How did I get on this ship!? The last vision that keeps replaying in my head is of the building wave. The swell must have been hundreds of feet high…" He was pacing again, gesturing to Christian. "I felt the impact collapse my lungs as the water sucked me under." He gripped the railing, staring out over the serene waters. "I had him Chris. He was in my hands."

"So this is really what your insanity is about? You almost had Forte. We all saw it, mate. He is long water-logged by now. Forget about him. Be grateful you're here, man," Christian tried to rationalize with his friend.

"I am, Chris, I am grateful to be here. It's just…I don't know," Sebastian pushed away his thoughts. "I don't know who to thank for my good fortune. Should it be the Valley of Angels who watch over my path in this world," Sebastian spun around to look up at the helm, "Or the mysterious women who man this vessel?" He caught Christian's eye. "Those three women possess more power than our mortal minds can comprehend. And you know what?"

"What?" Christian played along with his ongoing antics.

"I'm jealous. They are something supernatural, terrifying, and beautiful! They can do things our pitiful little minds can't comprehend. They don't need us, really. The Sirens of this ship are strong, independent, willful, and brave creatures that even in a mortal human form would be feared and respected." Sebastian felt alive aboard The Lady. He felt as though magic was seeping into his veins as well, at least the thrill of it.

"I know not what to tell you my friend," Christian agreed with him, but wouldn't say it aloud. "Be grateful you still breathe in this world. Not every man can be that lucky." Christian moved away from his friend. "Count your new friends as blessings and continue to stay in their good graces so you can be grand allies." He walked briskly below deck with his parting words. Christian could not bear to hear anymore about the wonderful women aboard The Lady. His stomach rolled as his thoughts always fled to Rahn.

Sebastian followed Christian's abrupt movements. "You poor sod. Lovesickness is a terrible emotion to waste time upon." Laughing, he turned back to the ocean's lulling currents. "I hope that man is fighting with Davey Jones. These women are special, I believe, even amongst their breed. I hope Forte is not as strong as they are."

• • •

"God damn it! Goddamnit!!" Christian pounded through the doors of Rahn's room.

She jumped and began to rise from her vanity chair.

"SIT!" He stalked over to her and began pacing in front of her. "What kind of woman are you that I can't shake you from my mind? I can't speak to my best friend of you because he knows nothing of our past affair. If you do not love me then why can I not rid you from my blood?" Christian crouched in front of Rahn. "I am with your sickness! I will ask you once more and depending upon your answer, I will never seek you again."

A fear built deep within Rahn as she watched his erratic behavior. She had never lost something she hadn't set loose in the first place. She was used to being in control. The emotions Rahn felt now were ruling her head, her heart, and she continually pushed them away. She hadn't believed she could ever again fully love or trust any man.

But him... But Christian.

And now Rahn would not allow herself to let him back in. She felt he didn't deserve that sort of pain, or pleasure. Deep within her, in a space she would not acknowledge, Rahn felt that she truly didn't deserve him and all his goodness.

"Speak one more word and I shall banish you from this ship!" Rahn's molten eyes locked on Christian's as the words crippled the beat within his chest.

"That is your rebuttal, to banish me before you have even heard my case?" Christian's eyes fed her with a hunger Rahn didn't remember she had. "Well, I fear, beautiful lady, that you cannot make that decision. I shall no longer seek you, but my allegiance does lie with my sister, as well as this ship. I am not leaving because of the uneasiness between us. My heart calls to this way of life whether you are in it or not. Good day." He rose and left the room, venom poisoning the air around him.

Rahn knew that within the tension in Christian's back that he would no longer come for her, and she hated it. She truly wanted him to do the opposite of what she spoke, but was too stubborn to admit it. Rahn was stunned with her own brainlessness. She rarely trusted anyone, most of all herself.

Rowan called to Christian from the helm as she saw him emerge from below. "Dear brother," she spoke as he approached her. "Are you well?" Concern wrinkled her face.

"I am better than I've felt in months." Christian pulled his coat closer as the breeze hit him off the sea.

"Liar." Rowan explored the side of his face. "You can be honest with me, you know. That's what sisters are for, confidants who can't get out of the job." Her smiled warmed the recesses of his heart.

"You three are enough to drive any and all men mad. You know that, right?" Christian's eyes never left the horizon line. "My heart is now able to mend from a breaking that happened long ago, Rowan. It will take time, but I assure you that I will be back to my happy self soon enough. Just let me be with the current unfolding of events, to sort them out. This has been a long time in the making and I have finally been set free. I have carried this pain for so long that it felt like a part of me when truly it was a menace. I myself am to blame for holding on to it. Now that you are back in my life I can let go, move on from my past, and stop looking behind me."

Rowan knew that her brother spoke not just of her. Christian also spoke of a broken heart. She wanted to kill the woman who broke it. Rowan wanted to protect her brother and take away his pain. *You should have not been made to feel like this. It is a cheap manipulation from a petty girl. She would not let you go... and you have suffered greatly for it, because of this girl's selfishness. And now you blame yourself...* Rowan could feel that Christian would not share any more with her tonight. He was done.

"Alright, brother. You will be fine in no time." Rowan turned back to her task. She desperately wanted to know the name of the woman who had used her brother up. But she could wait. Revenge was sweeter when the person never saw it coming. The ache her brother held onto had been long and painful.

"When will we reach port?" Christian thought back to the pelting rain that flooded the battlefield. His countenance became clouded and a dark veil surrounded him. He didn't hear Rowan's words, if she spoke them.

• • •

A calm and comforting sea welcomed The Lady into port. The sky was a pure blue that radiated its warmth down to each crewman aboard the ship.

Cheers rang out as the men saw Dorian standing at the water line, her empire-waist white gown flowing lightly behind her in the breeze. She held onto Jackson's hand as The Lady approached the dock. Aldus stood a few paces behind them, watching and guarding the pair. As The Lady's anchor dropped, and the crew began busying themselves with securing the ship, Jax ripped out of Dorian's grasp and stormed up the dock to the ship's bridge. He leapt into Rowan's arms as her foot hit the dry wood.

Pulling Jax close to her body, Rowan breathed in his smell of playful innocence. Burying her face in his soft curls, "I've missed you," she whispered to him.

Sebastian laid his hand on her shoulder. Rowan turned to look up at him. He gestured with his hand and mouthed the words, "Is this your child?"

Jax sensed he was being discussed and glanced up to look at Sebastian. "Who is this, Aunt Rowan?" The relief flooded Sebastian's face as the eyes of the cherub looked him up and down.

"This is Sebastian. He's a friend of the family, Jax. Sebastian, this is Jackson or Jax as we all call him." Rowan met Sebastian's eyes. Liquid pools of honey peered back at her. She could feel his happiness. He wouldn't have cared if it was her child. Christian was wrong about Sebastian being driven mad as well. He was thoroughly intrigued with all the women and wanted to learn more, everything he could. His mannerisms were easy to read. The energy vibrating off of him was pure and content.

"Nice to make your acquaintance, little man," Sebastian reached down to take the toddler's hand.

Jax pushed out of Rowan's arms and placed his hands on his hips. His features suggested he was trying to look menacing. "I am not little!" his voice roared.

Rowan rose and whispered into Sebastian's ear, "Oh dear, you've offended him."

Sebastian searched back and forth between the faces. He didn't know what to do. "Please forgive my offense of your stature, my lord," Sebastian pleaded playfully.

Jax puffed up his chest and straightened his spine. "Off with his head!!" He yelled and then he doubled over in laughter, music to all who surrounded them.

Rahn caught wind of her nephew's giggle and immediately her emotional tidal wave lifted slightly. She could not give into Christian. He had left her all those years ago. She was scared of having to relive the heartache again. Yet, was it utter betrayal now... to refuse him? To refuse the life and love she had hunted the waters for? Was she mad...or just being logical, finally, for once in her life? Yes, that was it. She could never be satisfied with one man. She would continue her ways, the ways she adopted during her stint as a courtesan. Hearing Jax's laugh brought Rahn back to the present once more. The boy was standing right in front of her.

"Auntie!! Where are you lost to?" Jax had a grimace on his face.

"Nowhere I can't be found." Rahn laughed and lifted him into her arms. She wasn't much for children, but every time she looked into his full blue eyes she longed for something more.

No! No, I don't want more. I want the life I've lead for years. A life without Christian, without restraints... without love? Rahn now questioned herself.

"Aunt Rahn, let me down, please." Jax was squirming in her arms. Dorian approached her and searched Rahn's face. Jax stretched his arms out to his mother and leaned out of Rahn's embrace.

Cradling her son, Dorian made Rahn hold her eyes. *Are you alright?* The words popped into her head.

No. Yes. No. Rahn shook her head back and forth. *He's in my heart, always, but I've pushed him away... again and again. I don't know what I seek.*

I think you know all too well... You can't have both the worlds you long for. You can either have a world half-fulfilled, with all your plundering of beds...or you can have the life you've wanted since he walked out of your family's door all those years ago. He still does not know the truth of your rescue? Dorian paused and saw her words take light in Rahn's eyes. *You can't keep running scared. If you don't take the time to see if the love is real, you will live on for centuries and he will parish in this lifetime. Your heart will remain half-full for the rest of your life if he is your true mate and you let him go.*

Christian and Sebastian stared up at the two women still on deck. They looked as though they were communicating something urgent but no words escaped their lips. The women's expressions simply changed.

Rahn looked out over the ship's rail and met Christian's eyes. She was surprised they did not drift away from her. Christian nodded to her, but did not turn away. She turned back to Dorian. *You're right. If he is my mate and I let him die in this life, I will forever regret it. He does not know what my mother did to save us that night. I do not know how to tell him… But, Dorian,* her eyes were pleading, *how can I forgive such things?*

My darling, I am sorry for your conflict, but you cannot continue to think you don't deserve the best that life has in store for you. Settling is never an option, Dorian reminded her. *You think too little of yourself and forget that you are the only one holding you back from getting exactly what you want. Another saying is life is always destined to be far greater than you could have ever thought if you let it. I can see in your eyes that you don't feel worthy of Christian's love. You are scared, but what of?*

Rahn sighed. Dorian had a way about her that made you see the truth of your actions. She could give you a heck of a reality slap without being harsh or demanding, just honest and blunt. Dorian made you see the fears you would have rather remained hidden. *I am scared that I am not good enough for him, and that he will see that. I am scared that he will leave again and that my heart will once again be broken. I am scared that he will see how hollow and lost I have become, and forget about me entirely. I am scared to want and deserve something so good…*

You are forgetting that he may also see how wonderful you are. That you are full of fire and will not take no for an answer, even if your life depends on it. You are forgetting that he already loves you and that you are the one pushing him away. Dorian and Jax both stared at Rahn, intimidating the incorrigible Siren.

What I am hearing is that you don't think it's worth the risk. Allow me to remind you, Rahn, that not everything in life is worth fighting for, but the only way to get what you want is to risk it. Risk the chance of failure, risk the chance of refusal, and risk everything you've got. Risk it so that in the end, whether it does or doesn't work out, you can walk away and say you gave it your all. And that, right there, is the best feeling in the world, because you didn't give up until you dove in and found out for yourself if the journey was worth it. Too many broken hearts are because of one person being too scared to risk themselves for the other. Too many disappointments are because of an individual being too scared to chance the risk of success.

Rahn watched both sets of clear, calm eyes that looked at her. *Damnit.* Rahn just shook her head and laughed at Dorian as she laughed back. *What a tight spot fear puts you in…*

Fear can be the greatest motivator, if you do not succumb to it. The only way to surpass fear is to defeat it. Meet the challenge and win. Even through failure can come your greatest success. Dorian held her sister's eyes. *I know that a place dwells within you that will not allow fear to overtake your will and conquer it. Everyone reaches the brink of no return, the point of winning or accepting defeat. We sometimes forget WE are the choice… Choose wisely, sister. Choose for yourself.*

Rahn could do nothing more than stare at her captain. Dorian held truth at each syllable of her words. The choice was hers…everyone had a choice. The question was who would make it? Rahn decided no one could decide for her, but her.

Jax cut off Rahn's thoughts by pulling at Dorian's top. "Momma, sshhh. They can hear you." The women followed his tiny hand in the direction of Sebastian and Christian.

Dorian and Rahn laughed again, as the men gazed up at them. "No, that's only you who eavesdrop on Mommy and Auntie's conversations." She tickled Jax's ribs making him squeal.

"There is more of you in him than we thought." Rahn ran her hand over Jax's head, smoothing his hair. "He is developing many of your devious traits." Rahn wrapped her arm around Dorian's petite waist.

"He has traits of his fathers, too." Dorian buffered her son's mind and spoke to Rahn. *He is Victor's child. Victor is of the Two-Natured.* Dorian held back her laughter as Rahn's eyes grew large with surprise. *Victor's second-half is Jason. The two are reuniting into one body, one soul.*

What!? Rahn's eyes grew to saucers. *Really?*

Yes, Aldus knows the truth and he showed me himself. Victor and Jason have bonded into one body. I often felt Jason's soul wandering and now it has found its way back home.

Infuriating! Rahn was disgusted.

Is it? I just never understood how Jason could have never told me that he was of the Two-Natured, nor how I missed the signs. He hid so much of his life from me, I can now see. I do not know how to trust him, this Victor. I suppose in the end it will all unfold. I need something from Victor and he needs time to rediscover his nature, independent of Jason. The only way he can do that is with my help. Dorian watched over her men as they busied themselves with unloading and taking down of the ship. *Victor will not stray far, although I will push him too.* Rahn's expression questioned her. *I want to see what he's made of in this form.*

Rahn nodded. *Your anger for him grows?* Rahn stared at her wild eyed.

Dorian laughed. *I feel no anger towards Victor. There is no use in it. I need him to help me when the time is right, but he is of no further consequence until then. I have Jax, you and Rowan, Aldus, the crew... What more do I need?*

Rahn felt compassion. *What of companionship? Everyone needs that, Dorian. What do you mean you need him for something?* She did not miss the comment.

It is of no importance now, my love. Later, when the time comes, you will know it, Dorian stated.

Always so secretive...fine. Wasn't Jason your match? What will become of that now? Eventually Jason and Victor will become one and your match will be staring you in the face once more. Rahn wanted answers so she was going to ask lots of questions. *Or does it not work in that way?*

Dorian had thought about this many times since Jason re-entered her life with Victor. *I do not know. To deny your life-mate is to live a sort of half-life because you are always searching for something to fill the hole. If you have already had your mate and lost them, you know what you are missing, but can also get past it. I have Jax. I do not know what will become of his father and me.* Her eyes twinkled. *Time will tell if our match is one to last the ages.* The captain's eyes drifted into the mist. *He is not Jason...*

Rahn understood her meaning. Jason was her life-mate, and Victor was someone else entirely. Dorian could not foresee the outcome. Rahn bore into Dorian, thinking of herself. *You already know of mine and Christian's match, don't you!?*

Dorian nodded.

You're not going to tell me, are you? Rahn questioned her captain.

Dorian smiled at Rahn and shook her head.

Jax reached over to caress Rahn's face. He now had both women's attention with a gentle hand upon their cheeks. "I don't like when you do that." Jackson did not like being left out of any conversation.

"You are too nosey, nephew!" Rahn tickled his side.

Chapter

14

———◆———

"ROWAN, WHERE IS VICTOR?" Christian pulled her back, as the crowd went into the castle's fortress.

"He is awaiting departure aboard The Alastar, I believe. Dorian is sending him home." Rowan responded.

Christian glanced back to the docks. "I wish to captain it home."

"Really?" Rowan searched her brother's face. *What is he hiding from me?* "I'll ask Dorian, but I'm sure if that is your will, she will approve it." She made him hold her eyes. "Why do you wish to leave, brother?"

Christian averted his eyes. "I wish to sail again. My life has been so stagnant, for so long… I simply wish to keep moving forward, now that my momentum is gaining." Rowan could feel the full warmth of her brother's smile as he held her eyes. "My allegiance lies with you, and The Lady, of course." He kissed her hand. "Come with us."

Rowan's mind was reeling. "Of course, brother, I will speak with Dorian." She paused. "I will think about your offer." Christian nodded and headed back towards the docks. Rowan watched him. *You carry burdens of little importance far too heavily for their worth.* She knew that a part of him was fleeing, *but from what?*

Christian paused and looked back at her. "How is it you fight, sister? I know your heart does not lie with the sword."

Rowan stared at him. "I enter a world of my own, a place where no one can shatter my resolve. I bring forth the fear that Jester instilled in me and I avenge myself through it."

"That makes sound reason. But how do you do it?" Christian urged.

"I sense your meaning brother and I cannot say. I dislike conflict, but when I absolutely must take part in it I call on my Siren-will to carry me through. Once I regain my mind afterwards I never feel right for it. I feel as though I live two lives sometimes. They get hard to differentiate."

Christian saw the sorrow in his sister's eyes. He promised himself he would someday soon make it so she no longer had to fight. "I will fix that pain in your eyes, sister. Does not Dorian know of your sentiments?"

Rowan laughed. "She knows, of course. The damn sprite knows everything! You can't hide things from her. However, fighting is unavoidable with the company I keep. I was tending Jax before rumor of your whereabouts came out. Revenge drove me to get back on The Lady." Her emerald eyes stared longingly out over the sea. "After a battle several years back, I was injured, for I was never aggressive enough with weapons. I fled for cover from the world, and, in my distress, Dorian gave me another task."

"You seem more than capable now." Christian looked at her with a worried expression upon his face.

Again, Rowan's soft laughter floated to him. "Dorian made sure that I was well trained before my debut this time around. I fared better because I had reason burning my veins. In truth, I never wanted a violent revenge upon you. Somewhere deep within me I knew that the lies embedded beneath my skin were false. I wanted my family back." A smile lit the sun's gaze against her face. "I wanted closure for my past and a new beginning within my future."

Christian came back to her and hugged her lovingly to him. "I find we have both gotten a renewed life, together." He kissed the top of her head bringing her closer.

When they released, Rowan stared up into her brother's face caressing the side of it with her hand. "Tell me what bothers you? Siblings should confide in each other."

Christian laughed softly, taking her hand in his. "You are right, sister. But I thought I had already told you my troubles."

"You did, but if they are still within you so strongly, I wish to help you release them." Rowan was adamant. "Christian you gave me no real depth. You skimmed the surface with your words."

Christian exhaled deeply. "I wish not to burden you with this, or alter your opinion in any form…" Rowan's eyes simply challenged him. She had come so far from the days aboard Jester's ship just by being amongst her kin in the passing weeks. Christian was her rebirth, and he knew it, so he continued on. "I love

Rahn. I have been in love with her for years. I rescued her and her mother many years past and continued to visit them. With every year that she grew closer to womanhood she stole a piece of my heart until she owned it completely. Rahn's defiance and stubbornness constantly challenged me. The willfulness within her I tested persistently, and she would fly into a rage for it." He smiled. "Now I have found her again after all these years and she wants nothing to do with me. In truth, that is what disturbs me most. We were so in love and now there is nothing but ice running through her veins."

"You saved her, but…" Rowan stopped. Her mind spun. "Rahn… What was her age when you saved her, do you remember?"

"Thinking back I cannot fully remember. I would say eleven or twelve." Christian thought. It seemed so long ago that it had happened.

"Really?" Rowan was in shock as things came to light within her mind. She knew that Rahn was at least a century into life before Christian's birth.

"Yes. Why do you ask?" Christian was worried about her.

"No reason, brother. When was this?"

Sorrow filled his eyes. "The rescue was what delayed my venture home to escort you to school. I saved Rahn, and you disappeared from my life." A tear ran down Christian's cheek.

Compassion replaced her betrayal as Rowan wiped it away. "Nay brother, I never disappeared. I simply transformed." Her smile was half-hearted. Her sibling smiled and righted a stray crimson strand of soft hair behind her ear.

She now understood. Rahn was fully grown when Rowan was captured at sea. A portal had been created and Christian had been drug through it to save the Siren woman and her daughter. Time was always a loose concept in the world of Elementals. It could be manipulated, changed, and warped to fit a need. Christian and Rowan had both become a victim of a Siren's time.

"I am sorry, Rowan. I should have been there."

"If you had, I would not be who I am today, with the blood of a vicious, ancient bloodline coursing through my veins." Her smile was whole now, and sincere. "I truly would not have it any other way."

Christian embraced her, and Rowan filled him with a calming light. Healing would take place on a level deeper than his physical form. He was ready to release the hold of an inconsistent woman and his sister was more than happy to help. He released her slightly staring at her physique. She had subtly morphed from the girl he knew to the woman who stood before him.

"I like your hair." They both laughed. In Rowan's transition of life to life, physically, her hair had changed the most. Her subtle crimson streaks now took over her head defeating any blonde that tried to remain. She had a mane of fire.

"Thank you, brother. I will take my leave of you. The chills of hunger are filling me." Rowan tried to hurry past him. "Are you alright, or better, for now?"

"Oh, yes. Head back to the castle. Goodnight, Rowan, if I do not see you." Christian waved to her as she rushed past him. "A calm has filled me like I have never known. I believe I have you to thank for it, sister." Christian spoke to her back as clarity entered his mind.

Rowan waved to him as she stalked through the twilight passage way. She had to get away, but instead of retreating to the sanctuary of her quarters, Rowan's anger called to her, and she intended to see it through. "Rahn!!!" She bellowed to the walls.

I'm in my rooms, she answered her. Rahn stuck her head out of her room and yelled against the stone walls. "What on earth could be so important, Rowan!?"

Rowan came up and blocked her door. She dug her finger into Rahn's chest. "You! You conniving snake!"

"What on earth, Rowan?" Rahn shot up in defense.

"I should have known that the only reason you agreed to this venture was because you sought my brother! How could I have been so stupid?" Rowan began to pace the entryway. "You wanted to continue making him miserable!"

"Rowan...I..." Rahn stopped as a hand was waved violently in front of her face.

"Don't!" Rowan's eyes were fierce upon her.

Sebastian came up behind Rahn. "I shall take my leave. We can play chess any ole time." He shuffled by them. "Rowan," he acknowledged her.

Rowan's mouth was agape behind him. "Of course," she stared after him. "Don't try and convince me that you didn't have anything to gain from this! I should have known... Only after you learned my brother's name, did you insist on capturing him and helping me seek my revenge. Do you only think of yourself, Rahn?" Rowan paused to stare at the woman clinging to her door frame. Rahn's face was awash with guilt and self-loathing.

"Oh, right. Stupid question. Of course that's all you think about." Rowan commenced pacing again. "I should have been suspicious the moment you agreed so heartily. You never wanted to help me. You wanted to gain another bed fellow! Well you have gained two at others' expense. And now, Christian's leaving because of you!!"

Rahn grabbed Rowan's arm. She saw the fury in her eyes. Rahn thought she was going to be struck. "Calm down," she demanded. Rowan's breathing slowed and she began to regain her composure. "I…. Will you listen?" Rowan nodded in answer. "Come inside and sit with me, Rowan."

Rowan allowed herself to be ushered into the room and settled in a chair by the window.

"Tea?"

"No. What is this about, Rahn? Tell me the truth!" Rowan was tired of the world being hidden from her.

"Alright, alright…. I never believed you would actually injure Christian in your quest for revenge. I just never thought you truly had it in you. No offense. And if you had tried I would have found reason to stop you, or helped alongside you," Rahn explained. "I still could not decide…" She spoke to herself now in a soft whisper.

"Wha…" Rowan was sitting on the edge of her chair.

Rahn held up her hand to halt her. "Let me finish." Rahn took the seat opposite Rowan and stared out the window. "He saved my life, you know…many years ago. You remember the story?" Rowan nodded, easing back into the chair. "Christian saved me from the barbarian that killed my father and wanted nothing more than to ruin my mother. For a long time, I felt indebted to him. He would stop in from time to time to check on me and see that I was doing alright. I grew attached over the years. My change came late and once it hit, the few people I associated with didn't recognize me anymore. I felt proud to have inherited my mother's Siren nature and the change of my Siren roots had taken shape upon my features. But then Christian stopped coming. What he never knew was that my mother pulled him from the future to aid in the past. Every time he came to our Inn, a time warp took place."

Rowan saw the heartbreak on her face. "Rahn, I'm sorry. But I don't understand…" She thought for a moment. "That explains why he rescued you when you were eleven, and he wasn't even born yet!"

"I was twelve, and you already knew this," Rahn raised her voice slightly. "You've spoken with him about it already."

Rowan threw her hands in the air. "Is nothing sacred? No secret can stay hidden within these walls!" She gestured to her head, her mind. "I must have Dorian teach me more about guarding my kingdom. It is unfair how the two of you manipulate it so."

"It is a learned gift, Rowan. One you also possess. It is hard to keep out, once you have learned it." Rahn paused. "I am done defending myself. May I continue?"

Rowan nodded, mad at herself for not having wanted to know more of her

Siren legacy, she was ready now. "Christian would not speak your name until now, but I have heard of the heartbreak again and again." Her words were fire struck with daggers of ice.

Rahn nodded. "He was my first." Her eyes finally held Rowan's. "Did you know that? After him, I went in search of a man who could make me feel as whole as he had, and as satisfied. I know you disapproved of my life choices, but I kept clinging to the memory of your brother. Dorian believes him to be my mate. She says I should feel lucky to have found him."

Rowan finally understood the dark shadow that hung around Rahn, one that had kept the two of them at arm's length. "Do not raise your voice at me. He is MY brother! It is an enticing fairy tale, is it not? Find your mate and live in love for eternity, or deny your love and live a life of half-contentment in every way." She saw that her words pained Rahn. Rowan knelt on the floor taking Rahn's hands. She could never stay mad for long.

"My mother, in her infinite wisdom, knew that Christian was the only man who could redeem us from the barbarian. My mother's mind raced that night searching for a savior. She pulled him to us because he was the man in my dream. He felt safe and secure within a spinning world of darkness. Christian has no idea that all our exchanges happened more than a century ago…before his birth." She held Rowan's face with her eyes. "He has no idea that we changed the course of his life by doing so. You were captured because of my family. When my mother pulled him back she stopped him from moving forward with plans he had already set in motion."

Rowan sat stunned in silence. "When Christian was to return home to me, he was fixed in time with you…"

Rahn nodded.

"Then it was already predetermined that I embrace the Siren form?" Many of these conclusions Rowan had already reached from speaking with her brother. Now she was bringing them to light, recommitting them to her memory.

"I am sorry for what you suffered. My mother knew a great many things she still has yet to share." Rahn felt guilty because of her actions. She was selfish and she knew it.

"How does this work?" Rowan demanded.

"It is the same as time travel. All time exists around us, within us. Whenever Christian's current mind thought to come visit us he was transported back through a gap in time my mother created when she first called to him. We met for the first time in this life and he is none the wiser for it. In his conscious, it all happened a few years back, not a century. Our souls have caught up with each other, so to speak."

"And your love for him... Did you carry it through the centuries?" Rowan was furious that Rahn was the woman who had caused her brother so much unneeded grief, but she also knew that Rahn was the woman to bring an end to it.

"I thought your brother was dead...for many years. I could not find him, or any trace of him, anywhere." Tears began rolling down Rahn's cheeks. "I thought I was foolish to have fallen in love with a pirate and one many years my senior. I figured I was just being young and naïve to have thought I found a man to withstand time alongside me." Rahn tried to hold herself together as sobs beckoned from behind her eyes. "I was young and did not fully understand all the nuances of the Siren form, as I do now." She was sarcastic. There was still much she did not understand and could not understand because her character was not stable. She had shut much of her world out because of her changing mood and inconsistency. "I was too young to realize that the portal created in time cannot withstand in time forever. The gap eventually disappears, but the memories remain...forever."

Rowan hugged her close, stroking Rahn's hair gently. "A love bond is too great for anyone to overcome, even you. And a bond between lovers is one that should not be denied."

Rahn's tear drenched face stared back at Rowan's. "I'm so sorry I didn't tell you. I wanted you to work out whatever issues you had with him."

Rowan laughed. "What lies you tell, Rahn. You were in war with yourself and were weighing your feelings for him. I see you have still not found an answer...." Rowan's words stung in their truth. "Well, I did work out the, nonexistent, issues with my brother and we have reunited. What are you running from, Rahn?" She sifted through Rahn's emotional energy. "I know you, Rahn. And I also know that you are usually the first for a fight, and that your anger dangles on a string. You are the breath of fire. When you do love, you love more fiercely than anyone I know. What scares you?"

Rahn was still offended by Rowan's words, but she continued in truth. "I am scared." She clutched Rowan's hands to her stomach. "I never thought I would find him. That eternal love seemed too farfetched for me to be able to attain."

Rowan held Rahn's face in her hands. "Well you have. Are you going to let love get away because you're scared? Life will be far worse if you do, I'm afraid."

"You are right." Rahn peered down at her through glassy eyes. "You are not upset with me?"

"Of course I am. You have the love of two honorable men. You are the reason

I am of this life. However, I cannot fully fault you for that. I would not choose any other. I still love you, dear sister, but we do not see eye to eye on this, as is normal. You will give me space and time to reason through this." Rowan rose and turned her back to Rahn.

"Sebastian and I are not lovers as you and your brother think. We merely found companionship in our friendship, nothing more. You misread our close-ness." Rahn spoke to Rowan's tight back. "We enjoy each other's company. There is no intimate love between us."

"Again, Rahn, you think only of yourself. You have let us all believe that you and Sebastian are lovers. You have only corrected people in private. You like the attention of the façade Sebastian offers you. I still love you, my sister. And I will forgive you, but you need to give me time. I not only feel for what you have hidden from me, but for what you have also hidden from my brother." Rowan stared at Rahn's shrinking form. "I will not let you hurt him again." Her words were final as she walked out of the room.

Rahn stared after Rowan as the thick door closed, sighing deeply. "Sebastian fancies *you*, Rowan. He has for some time. I wish you could see it, and hear the way he speaks of you." Rahn broke behind the closed door. She felt the full weight of her decisions, now, and she was more conflicted than ever. She was brash, quick to act, and always hiding from the backlash. Rahn did not like to think she had any fault. "Time offers forgiveness. I must not forget myself…. My crossroads have come up all too soon." Again, sobs overtook her.

• • •

Dawn filtered through the cloud-covered night sky. The sun's rays broke the blackness of the morning cutting over the rough rocks at the beach's end. The renewed life of day gave fresh hope to the failing souls. As the sun rose higher, its light gave warmth to the deadened paces of haunted men.

Christian stood at the bow of The Alastar breathing in the new day. *Look where life has taken me, straight back to adventure… How will I continue to sail amongst these women?* His thoughts drifted to his sister and all the years they needed to make amends for. Thoughts of Rahn swiftly chased her away. *How will I face you continually without the warmth of your touch, Rahn?* Her violet eyes held him at the edge of sanity. *Am I able to do it?* He asked himself. Christian sought The Lady with his eyes. She floated proud and strong upon the morning's low tide. The stain of her wood glowed in the sun's early light, as a soft wind blew through her sails. *Who am I kidding,* he thought, *only myself. I cannot be far from this call of life now that it has lured me back. I will ride upon The Lady until I am no longer able.* Christian smiled as he stared at the woman at The Lady's bow. *Nor can I leave my sister, now that I have found her.*

Victor sidled up to him. He felt at peace beside Christian. "I can't wait to be far from this demonic place and the devils that reside here," he lied. He had no intention of leaving.

"You sure know how to hold a grudge, do you not?" Christian laughed at him.

"These women are not of this earth. You cannot survive the feats they get themselves into, being merely human. Their skin holds no story of their accounts." Victor gazed out over the glass-like waters. "Their skin is flawless," he spoke softly to himself.

Christian patted his friend's shoulder. "They aren't human, mate, as we all know well. You'll do good to remember that."

"Aye." Victor searched his face. "What's gotten into you, Christian?"

"The promise of adventure." Christian's smile was devious and ready for play.

"Are you ready, mates?" Sebastian had approached them from behind, startling them both.

Christian turned back to the castle's towers once more. "Yes, Seb. Take us out to sea."

"I will have that honor." All three men jumped as her voice touched their ears. They spun to see her.

"Dorian?" Christian was confused and intrigued.

"Dorian!" Victor was fuming. Then he saw the little boy by her side. "You can't mean to take him with us!?"

Dorian just looked him over as if he wasn't worth her time. "Seb, ready the crew. It's time to leave." She stared out over the horizon.

"Aye, aye, Captain," Sebastian saluted her before he dashed off. He loved this woman, especially for all the power she held over his dear friend Victor's mood. Victor had become testy and irritable. Sebastian loved it. He had never seen Victor squirm so.

"I wan' to help, I wan' to help!!" Jax reached up to be lifted into his mother's arms.

There was something about the boy that Victor envied. Perhaps it was the vicinity to his mother's heart. *She truly does hate me. Someday she will understand that we are a match. I will make her see.*

"As you wish, my love, you shall assist Sebastian and me at the helm." Dorian cooed into her son's face. "We are aboard Sebastian's vessel and he will man it."

The lilt in Dorian's voice was strangely familiar in a far and distant memory that Victor contained. *Why can't I grasp it!?* He stomped off to the galley, realizing it was Jason's memory he had been accessing.

Christian matched Dorian's stride as she headed towards the stern. "What of this new development, Dorian?" He looked her over. Jax had wanted to follow after Sebastian, and he had succeeded. "Why do you make sail with us? Not to say I am bothered by the event…." His eyes twinkled. Christian was ready for the pirating life once again. His veins pounded within him.

"I have been away from the ocean's air too long. My heart aches for the rocking of its currents." Dorian's gaze didn't falter from her mark on the upper stair. "Do you not approve of this?" She could feel the stunned tension in his body.

"No… I just thought that… no. I have no problem with your accompanying us to the harbor." Christian's eyes had fixed on Rahn as she gripped the top deck's railing, her eyes already locked upon him, causing him to halt his paces. "Is everyone coming?"

Dorian stopped a few feet ahead of him, watching. "Yes, I thought you wanted adventure?"

Christian's smile quickly mirrored the captain's as she fully turned towards him.

"Will you do me a favor, Christian?" She followed his eyes up to the top deck. "Fetch me the compass from my quarters."

Dorian was staring at him. Christian could feel her eyes on the side of his face. He tore his eyes away from the angel in red and the way her garments floated on the air around her.

"Yes," Christian turned to face Dorian again. "Of course, Captain. I do hope we are are intended to go further than St. Winifred's in search of the open air." His smile was sweet and genuine as he walked away from her.

"Good man." Dorian spoke to his back as he made his way towards the double doors. She looked up and Rahn nodded down to her. Rahn moved swiftly and with angelic force as she made her way down the steps. Placing her hand on the door, she turned to wink at Dorian and slid silently into the corridor. Only the careful observer could hear the clank as the lock was set behind her.

Chapter

15

———◆———

SEBASTIAN SEARCHED THE MAIN DECK for something to do. His eyes wandered to the woman at the bow. His body felt drawn to her, perhaps simply because of the gifts she possessed. He didn't know, but he wanted to know more.

Her back was to him as he approached her. Her silhouette was long and lean as she propped herself against the railing. The midmorning's sun outlined every inch of her slim form. Sebastian had either found heaven, or was searching for hell. His mind raced back and forth between the present and the fantasies his mind rapidly created. Sebastian cursed both brains who did his thinking and the newest organ to vie for a right of speech, his heart.

"I am glad you are safe, Lady Rowan." Sebastian's voice carried to her over the breaking of the waves in the ship's forward glint. Sebastian stood almost touching her, his gaze far out to sea. Nervousness was a new emotion for him. The smell of her hair wafted to him sweet and gentle.

Rowan glanced over the side of his face. Strong features outlined his profile. Sebastian's long black hair fell across his face shielding it from her gaze. His eyes were warm honey when they looked upon her. Rowan could understand why Rahn had taken to him. He probably challenged Rahn in all the games she liked to play and beat her at them. Rowan laughed to herself.

"Thank you, Seb. It is nice to know that my safety rates in your concern." Her eyes examined him. He was every bit the gentlemen pirate. Dressed in the finest brown pants that formed to all the right places, his white tunic complimented his darkened tan. He wore a dagger at his belted waist to the right, and a pistol and sword on the left. Armed, yet regal in his stance and walk. Rowan loathed Rahn at the moment for first attaining this man's attentions, even if it wasn't in anything more than friendship. Rowan envied their bond, a bond she was too shy to pursue.

Sebastian's face looked almost appalled at her comment. "Of course, your well-being ranks!" The Irish accent he had trained into the background came to life in his voice the more he worked himself up. It reminded Rowan of home. "You are a lady, and should be tended to in your hour of need. I wish I could have throttled that man myself for..." His eyes focused on the cheek that had been bleeding in battle. His hazel eyes swirled, trying to comprehend why that cut was no longer visible on Rowan's angular planes. "...harming your person." Sebastian's hand reached up to stroke over where the scar should be. "Extraordinary." His eyes gleamed like a school boy's as he analyzed her skin.

"I've always been a fast healer." Rowan pulled away slightly from Sebastian's grasp, distancing herself. "Comes with our Elemental traits. And what of Rahn, did she attain any injury during battle?" Rowan was feeling him out to see if he truly did hold a torch for Rahn, even if it would never amount to anything. Rahn loved her brother too deeply to share her heart with anyone else. Rowan had at least assessed that.

"Nay, I believe our friend Rahn inflicted injury mostly. Extraordinary creatures, your lot. You are all quite the mystery." Sebastian's hand still wished to caress her face. He reached towards her again. "It's a Siren gift, is it not, the healing nature?"

Rowan nodded, apprehension gripping her gut. "What are you doing?" Her eyes met Sebastian's. Her cheek slid against his hand once more as she bent into the embrace. She could drown in his pools of warmth.

"It's incredible how you heal. I must admit I am envious." Sebastian smiled brightly down at her. She was near his height so he needn't look far. "Beautiful." His voice was a dream. The world stopped as his face moved closer to hers. Just as his lips were about to lay on hers, her sweet breath warmed his face.

"What are you doing?" Rowan's voice was filled with worry.

Sebastian's eyes opened abruptly, the air of the moment gone. "I was bending to see your cheek better." He bit back the words. His fingers rubbed a smooth piece of her hair to the side of her face. Their closeness did not change.

Rowan chilled him with her gaze. "We cannot do this." Her words were short as she backed away from him. Rowan's eyes became glossy as tears built within them. "I cannot do this. I cannot do this to Rahn, or myself, not right now." Conviction backed her words.

"What are you talking about, Rowan?" Sebastian knew the remark was not aimed at him. He felt that Rowan spoke mainly to herself. *I do not know what Rahn and Rowan are at war about, but it does not involve me.* "I am sorry, Rowan," he apologized. Her body went rigid and she moved farther away from him. "Please forgive the audacity of my actions. I know not from whence they came. I meant no offense, Rowan. I just thought..."

Rowan cut him off. "Of course, of course, the fault was mine."

"No, Rowan. No it wasn't. I am sorry." She stormed away from Sebastian not wanting to hear the rest of his words.

Rowan was terrified. *I have never been kissed before and he... he... he had wanted to kiss me!?* She thundered off to anywhere that would be far from him. Rowan did not believe in the sincerity of Sebastian's affections, nor did she know if she wanted them.

"Will not happen again," Sebastian spoke after her softly. "Usually I'm on my best game. Rowan must need much gentler persuading." *I must find Rahn. This has gone on long enough!* He stared after Rowan hopelessly. "Until later, my lady, when I can fully claim your heart as you have invaded mine." As he turned back to the sea, a glimmering streak of sun raced in front of him across the serene waters. Inwardly he cursed the wild antics of Rahn.

From the first moment that Sebastian had seen Rowan standing across from The Alastar on The Lady's rail she had intrigued him. The other two women aboard The Lady did nothing for him. They held no secret he wished to uncover. As he watched Rowan and learned about her from Rahn he became enthralled. So much so that Rahn would no longer talk about her sister in his presence. Rowan would claim their conversations every time.

Sebastian thought Rowan was statuesque in her beauty. She had a long, lean build that he loved. Her face was beautiful and sharp, her smile all encompassing with its welcome. He wanted to unearth the trepidation and hesitancy that lurked in her green eyes and erase it. Sebastian wanted to find all the curves of her body and memorize them for they hid beneath the confines of her clothes. As he stared over the smooth waters beneath him, he wondered if he could ever pull Rowan from her sheltered world and love her completely, if she would even let him.

· · ·

Rahn quietly turned the lock and placed the key back within the folds of her dress. She tip-toed down the corridor 'til she came upon Dorian's chamber door left slightly ajar. She entered silently and locked it upon entry. She spun around softly and searched the room. She saw Christian's back enter the far door into Dorian's study. She took a deep breath to settle her churning stomach and floated toward the open door.

• • •

Victor watched as another friend became enchanted by a lady of the ship. He would have no mates left after this. He felt the bulky presence of another being. Victor turned to find Grim standing beside him.

"Lost to the world are ye? I've been standing here for near five minutes," Grim announced.

Victor looked up to the helm. "No, I'm lost to right here." Grim followed his eyes to Dorian.

"Statuesque, is she not?" Grim's eyes roamed over the side of Victor's face. "Almost as if her skin is an illusion not to be used in reality..."

Is he reading my mind!? The bastard! Wouldn't put anyone past it after this... Victor thought.

You aren't plain Victor anymore. Elemental blood flows through your veins as well. You are no longer simply human, Jason reminded him.

"...because it couldn't possibly be so supple and such perfection." Grim saw the muscle in Victor's jaw twitch. He was getting somewhere now.

"You taught me, Grim. She is no such perfection. Dorian embodies all that is opposing to such a phrase in this world. She has lain with the devil, I am sure of it." Grim noted that Victor's eyes never faltered from their mark upon Dorian as he spoke to him. "Only one to match his wit and cunning could have risen unscathed from such an encounter. Nay, they would have to surpass it." Victor tore his gaze from Dorian's perfect form to make sure his last words would resonate with the man. "She shall be your death, sailor. Escape this haunted path while you still have breath." With a heavy heart, Victor turned his back on Dorian and Rowan, heading back for the sanctuary of the lower deck.

"Aye, good sir, aye." Grim smiled broadly to Victor's back. "She is your personal Calypso. Every man has at least one."

"What has he been saying?" Aldus emerged from shadow to Grim's side.

"Victor? Oh, not much of anything. He will soon remember all that he lost." Grim met Aldus' eyes and the pair shared a silent smile.

"I fear he already has. He is none too happy with me," Aldus added.

"Well, Victor thinks you have been bedding his wife while Jason tries to convince him that you have not. Jason knows better of you." Grim's sly smile mocked him. "I'd throttle the man who even thought of doing such things with my Lidi."

Aldus laughed at the older man. "Aye, I would do the same if I had a wife of my own. The war within Victor is very prominent. He hasn't fully melded with Jason. He's fighting it. He swings wildly between emotions." Victor stomped by them and was mumbling to himself. The pair jumped slightly at his sudden, hasty reappearance.

"I think the re-bonding will drive him mad." They looked after his path. It was straight in its destination. "Should we stop him?" Grim inquired.

"No, this needs to be done. Victor needs to see." Aldus patted his friend on the shoulder for reassurance. "There needs to be a point of total collapse for the two of them to reconnect. Jason has been wandering many life times waiting for Victor to be born. The spirit, body, mind, and soul need to align, perfectly, into one." They watched as Victor approached the steps leading up to the bridge. "Dorian brings out the fuel needed to make the connection blaze. I just hope he doesn't do anything drastic."

Grim patted his back. "No need to worry there. If Victor gets out of line... well, I'd hate to think what *she* would do to him..."

Aldus laughed softly as he watched Victor. "Aye, till my dying day, I will never tire of seeing that woman's wrath." Aldus nudged his mate's arm and whispered, "I'm glad she's on our side."

• • •

Rahn propped herself against the doorjamb as she watched Christian fumble about the room looking for the compass.

"Looking for this?"

Christian froze with his hands on the desk. His body spread with tension. He very stiffly straightened his spine, and slowly turned to face her. "Yes, that would be the object I seek. Thank you for finding it so...nimbly, my lady." His body remained stiff and uninviting. His presence did not welcome her.

Exasperated with his air, Rahn flung the compass, smashing it into the nearest wall. The glass shattering broke his mood, for the moment.

"Why have you done that!?" Christian rushed to the wreckage to see if the device was salvageable. "Now we have less a sense of direction and in these waters that ensures defeat, you crazy cow."

Rahn glared down at him, the violet of her eyes edging into blackness. "*WE* don't need the damn device anyway, you bastard!" Her hands settled heavy on her hips. "And cow, did you say cow!? Is that in reference to my large hips?" Her cheeks began to flush crimson in her rage.

As Christian fiddled with the pieces of the compass, it took on a life of its own and swiftly reassembled itself into working order. He moved to touch it and it disappeared from beneath his out stretched fingers.

"You have nothing to say?" Rahn would not let him rest.

"NOO!! You ninny." Christian rose to his feet, confronting Rahn, their bodies inches from one another as each grew with their own wrath. "It was in reference to mad cow. A fever, I am sure you must be sick with for all the indignity and insolence you've shown me, you petulant child. You are no longer the girl I recognize from days past. The world has changed you into a damnable woman."

"How would you know what type of woman I was to become, you left right after you made me one!" Rahn's finger dug into his chest, deeper with every word. She followed his retreat, backing him against the table.

"What lies you tell yourself, Rahn! I did not leave after making you a woman. I came back time and time again, and you now refuse me." Christian stared into her. "This is your doing."

Rahn heaved in anger. "I have spent a lifetime trying to forget you, trying to find someone who could satisfy the hunger in my belly. Every man just made the ache expand."

Christian's eyes bore down on her and his spine straightened.

"Oh," she ran her eyes up and down the length of him. "Does it pang you to hear that there have been others?" Rahn could no longer determine the color of his eyes, they had turned black. With a smile on her lips, she spoke. "There have been many others." Rahn touched her hip to him and ran her fingers up and down his chest.

Christian grabbed her hand tightly. Rahn opened her mouth to scold him, but his expression stopped her. "I knew there had been others. I have spies from one coast to the next. You should not have been so careless in your exploits if you had not wanted me to know. There is a little thing called discretion, which you still have need of learning its proper meaning." He yanked her hand tightly across his chest. "Answer me this, for I have no time for patience." Calm had leaked back into Rahn's resolve, her purple eyes locked on his. "Why, if you say all these past men were so minuscule, do you refuse me? I assume you mean to clump Sebastian in with them."

Rahn dropped her eyes and her body sagged slightly in his grasp. "I am a daft, fearful woman!" she yelled to his chest. "The last time you left my bed I was thrown into a deep seated depression without salvation. I fear a life without you, but am terrified of a life alongside you. Sebastian made me trust again. He was kind and will not leave me!" Rahn's anger was inches from his face. "I have never slept with Sebastian, nor will I ever. He does not excite me. We are simply companions of convenience. We laugh together and play games."

Christian finally saw the little girl from all those years ago, the scared, insecure, daring little girl who warmed his heart and later stole it away from him. "My love," his hand cupped her chin, pulling Rahn's face towards him. "I am here. I have always been here, waiting for you." He put her hand to his heart. "I came back for you, did you know that?"

Her eyes creased in disbelief. She had no idea.

"I came to ask your hand, but your aunt told me you had left long ago. She returned these to me." Christian moved and pulled envelopes out of his back pocket.

Rahn ran her hands over the age-worn letters inside. "You wrote to me…" her voice became very small. "I thought you didn't love me. I thought…"

"You thought wrong. I wrote to tell you of my sister's death and my resignation from the pirating world. I wrote to say I would come visit you one last time before returning home to my family to assist my father in his blacksmithing business…"

Rahn's rage cut Christian off. "You wrote to say you were coming to say… goodbye!?" Rahn's voice was a mix of hate and tears.

Christian took the letters from her and rifled through them, finding the perfect one. "Here," he stretched his arm out to her. "Read this one."

Rahn slowly slid the envelope from his long fingers and backed away to sit in the nearest chair. She placed the note in her lap and shyly looked up at him. "No, I will not read it. There is nothing in here that I do not already know." She rose to her feet. "You are a coward!"

"Read it, Rahn." Christian calmly ordered. He took the chair opposite her and rested his elbows on its arms.

Rahn looked once more into his eyes and ripped open the envelope. "Before I read this you need to know that our love will never be again. I will read it out of courtesy to you, a privilege you have never bestowed upon me."

Christian's eyes halted her. He had regained his composure. "Why did you come here, Rahn? Why did you follow me? Don't give me that look. I know you did." He stared at her. "I think it is because you are still interested in what I could offer you. I think it is because the day I stole your virtue, you also gave me your heart. Your anger has nothing to do with me and everything to do with your nature." His words battered her in their calm resolve.

"How dare you make such assumptions!" The letter crinkled in Rahn's grasp. "You were nothing more than the boy my mother called upon to save our lives. If your life just so happened to be lost in the process, then so be it. You were expendable, Christian. You were of very little importance. I can see now that nothing has changed."

"You really have become a stubborn, hateful woman. You still do not answer my questions. If I am so expendable and unworthy of your affections, as you claim, then what, pray tell, are you doing here!?" Christian knocked the chair over in his fury of rising from it. He kicked it away behind him. Rahn raised her hand to her lips with a soft gasp. She watched as the letter fluttered to land on the floor. He approached her. "It's always been you, Rahn. I have loved you from the day I first met you. You stole my heart when you were just a teen playing board games against me. You challenged me as you do now. I know that you still love me!" His fist crashed against the wooden desk. "Deny it!"

Rahn's fist slamming down next to his on the table cut his words short. "I do not love you any longer." Each word was thoroughly punctuated.

"Do you mean to say you no longer passionately love me?" His smile was treacherous, "I do not believe it." The kiss that followed crushed her lips and restarted her once-useless heart. Christian's tongue delved deep within her, warming her soul. Slowly, his arms drew her body up, enveloping her. Rahn's arms took over for her and reached down for his trouser buttons. Passion clouded her thoughts. Christian's long fingers stroked her luscious thigh, slowly lifting her dress as he sat her atop the table. He circled the curve of her hip, slowly pulling the strings of her under-garment resting there.

"No. I will not allow you the power of overwhelming me with your senses. We must stop." Christian moved swiftly away from her.

"We must stop?" Rahn pulled him back for more fevered kisses. Finally, she broke through the confines of his pants and pushed her way in. She felt him pulse in her grasp. "Truly, you wish to stop?" Her voice lulled him and he began to fold.

"No, no!" Christian shouted. "If you are so done with me, I will not allow you the pleasure of my company ever again. It is not worth it, if it is not forever." His eyes held hers in a violent rage. "If you do not love me, I see no further use in such exploits. I shall not surpass the boundaries of friendship any longer." Christian tried to pull out of Rahn's embrace, but she would not release him.

Rahn screamed at him, throwing her arms in the air. "You bastard! What position are you in that you can deny me? It is ludicrous."

"Thank you, Rahn." Christian's voice was soothing against her heated skin.

"For what?" Rahn hissed.

Christian bent forward and kissed the side of Rahn's neck. He could feel the fury of her pulse. "For allowing me to have this last memory. I shall no longer need you in my life. I shall remember your anger forever and know that some-where within your cold heart, it beats for only me." He pushed himself away from her, trying to leave, but Rahn gripped his arm, digging her nails into his skin. She would not allow him to move.

"Rahn!" He shouted at her in pain as the pin pricks broke the skin beneath his shirt.

Rahn pulled him firmer against her. "You shall think of me every day, and the happiness someone else will bring me. Our meeting has just reminded me of what I have not missed."

"What harsh and cruel things you are capable of saying, Rahn." Christian could not remove himself from Rahn's grasp. "I wish you and this new man the best of luck. He, I know, will need it. I am glad, however, that I will not need to run out and warn Sebastian of your wickedness. I would hate for a good friend to fall prey to your shallow antics. "

"I…." Rahn stuttered.

"You came to me willingly. Remember that, Rahn. You need to think about why that is, and why you now deny me. Your plans were not well-executed, nor were your words well chosen." Christian had contempt in his words. "Release me."

Rahn rose up, pushing him further away from her. She righted her skirt as he pulled up his trousers. "You were nothing more than…"

"Someone who was expendable, I understand. No need to keep reiterating it." Christian gathered the letter from the floor and ripped it to pieces throwing it in the fireplace. Grabbing the stack of remaining letters he threw them on top and lit the pile. "You have released me, lady. I no longer want anything to do with you." He stormed to the door, kicking it through when it wouldn't open. He lingered in the doorway. "When I came to your family's inn they told me you had left and disappeared long ago, never receiving my letters…. They handed them all back to me. I suppose my next journey will be to your aunt's inn to thank them."

Rahn's eyes bore into him in disbelief. *She kept them from me…* Her eyes roamed the floor in front of her. *She kept me from loving you…* She twisted her hands in her lap. Her eyes searched for Christian's, but met his stern back as he turned from her.

"I am sorry that I allowed the brotherly affection I first had for you to change into something else." Christian met Rahn's black stare over his shoulder.

"You will always…" Rahn's voice was trying to fill him with pain.

"Rahn," Christian's stern tone stopped her, breathless. "I would rather be alone – than with someone who makes me feel as alone as you do."

The scene came before Rahn's eyes, vivid with life and color.

Christian came to his knees in front of her and lightly held her hands. "I shall only ask this once more of you, your answer will seal both our fates. If I am refused once more I will not be able to go on living in joy and I shall take you with me to the depths of Davey Jones' Locker to drown for an eternity. If you so cordially accept, I shall be deemed the wealthiest bastard to walk this earth until my dying day."

Rahn's body toyed with him, her movements' fluid. "Wealthiest?" She questioned him.

"Aye, wealthiest." She still did not understand Christian's meaning. "…wealthiest of sea, land, and heart. No man shall surpass my grace as long as I draw breath."

Rahn made a grand show of gestures. "Oh, I see," she said allowing the words to roll off her tongue. Christian tightened the grip he held on her hands, drawing her eyes there.

"So you see, I will only ask this once more with my life in your hands. Be my wife, Rahn. Make me wealthy beyond my wildest dreams and farthest forbidden desires."

Rahn ran her eyes slowly up his chest, around the curve of his face to his steadfast eyes. They held the heart of the first man she ever loved and housed the temple of the last man she would ever bed. She locked her eyes with his, bending forward, she brought her lips to his ear. "I take thee and give thee my whole heart."

Christian's head dropped to his chest, a spreading smile on his lips. He rose to look at her and took her face in his hands. "My beautiful wife," he spoke softly, the melody of his voice wrapping around her body. His lips met hers in mutual love and adoration, an introduction of a new life… together. Christian rested his forehead on hers, "I will always love you." His eyes sparkled adoringly down at her. "My lovely wife," he spoke gently.

Rahn reached down to cup his face with her hand. "My lovely husband," she answered back. "Shall we go relay the merry news?" A smile just for him spread her lips.

Looking up, he knew their love wouldn't be all clear water, but he knew every squall would be worth it.

Rahn opened her eyes to an empty room. "That's what he would have said, that's what he had wanted to say." *That he loved me and still loved me.* Tears rolled down her cheeks at the illusion. "What a daft, petty girl you are, Rahn." *The man loves you and you let him go...* She thought of Christian. Staring at the fire she willed the pieces of the torn letter to rise to her. They came upon beckoning, drifting from the ash and soot. Slowly they reassembled in the form they once held. She waved her hand over the parched paper and it came back to life, the letters jumping from the page…

My Dearest Love,

Your face has guided me through my darkest hour. Your love has pushed me onward when I would have liked to lie dying. I can feel your body flushing from here and it feels like the sun's glorious rays are shining into me, giving me hope for a new life, a new start.

You would be proud to know that my voyages, which have taken me from your loving company, have not been in vain. I have finally found word of my sister's whereabouts. However, it is laden with sadness. She has been dead for near a year, killed by a pirate.

I am cutting all ties to the pirating world and hope that you will support me in my decision to right my wrongs. I know that is the way Rowan would have wanted it. I am also going to settle back home with my father and join him in blacksmithing. Another wish I'm sure my sister would have wanted fulfilled.

I hope this letter reaches you in good health and stable mind. My next visit to you will be one of abrupt endings or ripening beginnings.

I leave you with this to ponder…

Make a new beginning with me far from this land and the past it holds for us…

I ask in every sense of the word, be my wife?

Your Forever & Devoted Love,

Christian.

Rahn's dark clouded resolve slid off and melted into the sea below. She knew what she wanted.

• • •

Sebastian couldn't help himself. He simply wanted to be near her. This justification he thought was enough. He walked back towards Rowan at the bow. He would tell her everything she wanted to know and ask for nothing in return.

Rahn darted out from under the bridge and grabbed him by the arm. "Elllllo poppet."

Sebastian rested an arm around her shoulders. "Hello. What is that smile? It looks devious."

"Only the best of kinds." Rahn spoke in lightness. "I have a great many plans for us." She held his eyes, speaking her secrets to him.

Startled, Rahn and Sebastian turned their attention to the helm as Dorian's heightened voice drifted over the open air. Victor stood inches away from her, confronting her with rage. Jax was nowhere in sight. Rahn looked back to Sebastian and almost smacked her face into his. Her face crinkled at the near contact and he focused back on her. They laughed at each other. Lightness surrounded them as a new plan molded between them.

• • •

Dorian saw him coming.

"How could you do this to me!?" Victor's voice boomed before him as thunderous footfalls beat into the worn deck.

"DO what to you exactly? You seem to be doing it all yourself." Dorian's voice was calm as she held the wheel.

"I want to be a part of my son's life. It's my right! And you, you should be hung for the deeds you did with my brother!"

"I have done nothing wrong with your brother. We love each other and protect each other. A task you, Jason, left him to, I might add, upon your death. Part of you has been dead and out of our lives for centuries, I may remind you." Dorian was growing tired of fighting a double-sided battle with Victor. She felt she could not win for no reason existed. Accusations flooded Victor's mind with no real hold on the world.

"Do not taunt me woman!" Victor's blood boiled with anger. "True love never dies and death only lengthens its parting until reunion. You are not as virtuous as I thought all those centuries ago!"

Ah, you are fighting Jason's battles now. Dorian spun her body on him and her hand grasped his skull. "Do not question my love for I could do the same of yours." Victor's head felt as though her hand was ripping into it. She pulled her arm away gripping the air's essence. "I no longer wish to speak to you." Jason's ethereal form crept out of Victor's. His face floated outside of Victor, transparent.

"I never stopped in my love for you," the ghost spoke.

Dorian stared at him. His clear pale blue eyes sparkled beneath the soft blonde curls around his face. His neck was bronzed and muscular. "You look as you did the day you left me, save for the true colors of your form."

"Do not try and dissuade me with your smooth speech. You have betrayed everything we had!" Jason was finally getting to vent without interference.

Aldus was stunned. Victor truly was the second-nature of his brother. Grim's hand clasped down on his shoulder as Aldus took a step forward.

"Your time for reconciliation will come." Grim spoke as he tried to hold Aldus back.

Aldus nodded, blankly staring at the ghostly face of his brother he had loved and lost so long ago. He barely acknowledged Grim's words.

"You wish to speak of betrayal? Fine." Dorian had not yet lost her temper, but blood pulsed within her head. "Why did you not tell me you were Two-Natured? I have found, throughout my years in this form, that you withheld many secrets from me. It was you who desired such honesty between us. Yet, it was you who denied ever having to own to it. You knew everything of me and I find that I knew very little of you."

Victor's body had backed away during Dorian's heated speech. He bumped the starboard rail, but Jason's form did not miss a beat at his retreating.

"I hid very little from you. I did not think it best to lay bare every detail of my Urchin form, because I did not know if you would be there to welcome my second coming into existence. I loved you with all my heart and soul. It was my life that saved yours during childbirth, not our son's. And now we share another son. Do not deny me this!"

"You have denied me centuries of love while I walked this world alone with thoughts of my dead husband." Dorian left him, heading down the steps. "A husband I thought to never see again!" She yelled over her shoulder. "A husband who did not give me a chance to prove that I would be there, no matter what."

"Do not walk away from me, Dorian!" Jason smashed back into Victor and again they were one. Heavy footsteps followed in her wake.

"I have every right to walk away, for that is exactly what you did! I owe you nothing in this life, in this form. It was I who had to scrape against the earth's dirt before I was able to claim my full life in this body." She spun on him, nearly colliding. "I am not yours anymore, Jason."

"What are you saying!?" Victor's eyes were awash with a sorrowful rage as the weight of her words sunk in. "You wish to separate our bond?" His body steeled in front of her. "Do you have any idea how hard the task you wish to undertake is or how...."

"Yes." Dorian's voice was cool. "I have made my decision. I cannot be with a man who wishes to shield his nature from me, nor can I be with one who is split in two, nor will I stand by and watch as you rip yourself apart bit by bit. Jason. Victor." She acknowledged both men in front of her. Her eyes tightened in anger as she watched the expressions race across their face. She felt the change in Victor's body, in his mind. She was standing by the plank. "You grimy, yellow-bellied, lizard skull, coward, smug, aristocratic, pathetic excuse for a man! Have you gotten so accustomed to servants waiting on your every whim, you pungent excuse for last night's laundry. Forget your vows to me. Do you no longer remember the vows and loyalties you once held as a pirate?"

Victor's worlds collided. "As I recall, no such thing exists. It is merely word of mouth and understandings." He examined her. "I see that you have done very well in forgetting all your loyalties and vows! This," he gestured to all of her form, "is not the woman I once married." *That's it, the fierceness in her eyes, bring it forward.* Victor thought. He could feel himself respond to her muse. Dorian's emotions were what caused Victor and Jason to join, to see and see as one.

Dorian's body cooled and a resolved calm filled her mind completely. "You are right. I am no longer the woman you married, and, let it be known, that you are not the same man either." Victor did not realize where she was guiding him in her words. "I once thought you the king of my world, and now look at you, a new face and you think you can get everything you want. Forget about me. Forget about Jackson. Neither one of us will be a part of your life, and vice versa. You no longer are allowed the privilege. Remember that. Once I break what binds us you will have no memory of me, Jax, or what we were."

Victor didn't have time to gather the logic out of his thought pattern before Dorian was stepping to him. He stumbled backwards feeling the bob of the plank beneath his feet. The force of her will pushed him harder and closer to the edge.

"Don't set foot in the water." The air drifted around Dorian, the garments she wore floated on its breeze. "I will find you, and you won't get a second chance such as this." She boarded the plank as well and brought her arms to his chest with a strength that sent him flying off over the sea.

Victor focused on the look in her eye right before she pushed him. He recognized that look.

Victor prepared his body for the enveloping splash of the sea when his back collided with the hard deck at St. Winifred's. He sat up quickly and searched the horizon line for The Lady. No ship could be seen for miles. The clear calm of the sea settled all around him as heaven met earth at the horizon's line.

Victor slammed his fist into the wood's planks and stilled his body as he watched the reverberations make a wave out to sea. He sat shocked as the current rolled out from under his landing point on the dock. He lifted his fist and examined it with scrutinizing eyes. Not a mark was left on it, but the indent of his hand was left in the wood.

"Do you feel me, Jason?" Victor's words came in hot breaths. "I feel you, I feel who I was, and what I am to become." He laughed deeply as he looked to the sky. A bright clear sky shone down on him and the crisp ocean breeze filled his lungs. "Let us be one in this new form. We need one another to regain our life!" He searched the sea once more. "I seek you, lady. Feel my breath, hot against your sails."

Chapter

16

————◆————

EVERYONE ON DECK WATCHED as Victor's body fell towards the water and disappeared in a flash of light landing in the place of Dorian's choosing. She had sent him home. Let him sort his mind in a place far removed from her and her son.

Rahn and Sebastian stood nearest Dorian. "Good riddance, sister." A broad smile spanned her face.

Aldus and Grim stood gaping at her from across the deck near the galley's entrance. "What has she done?" Aldus asked astonished.

"She has done what's right by her. Victor's neither your brother, nor he her husband, anymore. 'Twas not meant to be I guess." Grim departed from his side.

Aldus just stared. "But, how..."

Grim turned and laughed at him. "Don't try and figure it out, dear boy," Grim called back to him.

Aldus glared at Grim. "You lie when you say it was not meant to be. Dorian needs him just as Jason needs her to reawaken him to his Urchin form." There was conviction in his voice.

Grim came back to speak with him. "Ah, I see where your confusion lays my friend. He is not Jason anymore. He is now becoming one with Victor, and Jason is becoming one with him. They will create an entirely new being with their combined mind and actions recognizable only by those who knew them in their separate forms."

"Yes, I just do not understand why Dorian sent him away. She needs him."

Aldus's voice drifted off as he stared down at the water.

Jax bumped into him from behind, dislodging his thoughts for now. The boy was sword fighting with Canon. The pair pushed past him and Jackson's little voice grunted and ha-ed with his movements. Grim laughed and walked away from the scene, going back to his duties.

"Don't be too hard on the boy." Aldus called.

"Nay, Aldus, I won't. He's a little pistol." Jackson lunged, smacking his wooden stick into Canon's leg. "Oouch!"

"No prisoners. No survivors!" The little boy shouted.

Aldus laughed. "I was talking to Jackson." He charged his nephew and gathered him up in his arms kicking and screaming in merriment. "Now, let's really get him, lad." He took Jackson's hand in his own and guided his sword in battle with Canon.

"I fear I am at a slight disadvantage." Canon jumped to the side avoiding a blow.

"Was it you who has kept him distracted all this time?" Aldus inquired.

"Aye, I had a premonition about what would happen and I didn't want him to see the exchange between them just yet. He is sharp enough, though, for his age. You can't keep much from him." Dorian, even at a distance, did not miss Canon's words from across the ship.

"Aye," Aldus laughed. "Smart enough thoughts... You and your bloody premonitions, man!" He mocked him, disabling his shoulder in play.

"Ayyeee, young sir, you got me, you got me!" Canon gripped his shoulder in faked pain. He looked to Aldus, smiling wickedly. "Premonitions just like this one." He lunged hitting the final blow of battle. Jackson giggled as he and Aldus fell to the deck in defeat. They let their bodies grow slack as if they had died a warrior's death. "Oh no! Has the little squire fallen in battle?" Canon stared down at them. Jackson was trying so hard not to laugh his eyes squeezed tight. Aldus lay limp beneath him.

"Are we alive yet?" Aldus whispered to Jax's ear.

The men were met with a fit of laughter. Jackson could no longer contain himself. "Uncle Aldie!!" He giggled. "Get up, get up. We regroup tomorrow." His little fists pounded on his uncle's chest. Aldus opened one eye in a slit and glanced at the boy. "Aldie, wake up!" Aldus wrapped both arms around Jax and dragged him up tickling his sides until he couldn't stand it anymore. "Momma! Momma! HELP!!" His words came through between laughter.

Dorian was at his side. "Hhmmm, should I help you my darling?" Jackson just laughed more. She took him from Aldus and they turned on him, forcing him back down to the deck, winning the tickle war.

"White flag, white flag. I surrender." Aldus laughed at the pair now lying on his chest.

"Momma, I'm hungry." And Jax was gone rushing towards Snow in the galley to plead for his favorite snack.

"Off he goes, just like that." Dorian watched after her son.

"It's the whims of a child." Dorian helped Aldus up. "You know he's going to beg Snow for sweet bread and chocolate." Aldus glanced after his nephew as he disappeared below deck. He brought his hand up to caress the side of Dorian's face. The motion caught her off guard and her body tensed. "What are we going to do about this?"

Dorian smiled at him. "We need do nothing. Victor is gone and will not return. We are free to do as we please."

"Is that really how you feel, or are you hiding something?"

She just stared at Aldus.

"I know how you felt about his first form. Jason was your match. You cannot deny that." He stared at the side of her face. "You cannot believe your own words. You know he will be back."

"Nay," Dorian shook her head. "I do not believe them, but I can out run them for a little while." Her eyes were lost, Aldus recognized the distance. "He is no longer...Jason. Within Victor they are becoming one and something, someone, entirely new."

"You cannot hide forever, Dorian." Aldus cautioned her. "Even if you never love Jason, or Victor, again, you will need him for your release."

"Ssssshhhh," Dorian's gray eyes warned him. "You speak true, but only when the time is right. Victor needs to fully claim his new life. I want to push him to see how far he can go. I believe he will surprise us all."

Aldus nodded. *All but you,* he thought. He was the only one who knew of what hid deep beneath Dorian's skin. The force was clawing to get out. Not even Jason in his first form knew what his wife would someday be capable of. Aldus had become Dorian's confidant through the centuries and they relied on, and trusted, one another implicitly. "Something must be done if you truly wish to relinquish your match. 'Tis hard, but possible." He stared at her through his pale eyes. "Do you truly wish to end your love match? It's very final."

"Right," Dorian laughed. "I believe my threat of cutting the ties that bind us for eternity is mainly a hollow one. I must see first what Victor is to become. A great love that lasts forever is incredibly tempting, and the threat of losing it is simply devastating."

Aldus watched as Dorian lapsed into an unknown emotion, sadness. He had not seen it take shape across her features for many, many years. "It is a big risk you take. Are..."

"I am aware of the many consequences. I am not sure if that is what I wish. Jason's new form infuriates me inside and out. I never knew.... I never knew so many things about the man I loved. It pains me to now find out so much about Jason, so much that he hid from me."

"He hid them from me as well, his own blood." Aldus could feel the betrayal of his brother and father as it now beat against him.

"I know." Longingly, Dorian held his eyes. "I do love you, Aldus." She hugged him to her. "I am so grateful to have a brother-in-law such as you. I could not have asked for a better sibling in all my life. Sometime I feel I ask too much of you, that you should have to carry my burdens as well."

"Nah, Dorian. I could not have asked for a better sister. Your burdens are not hard to bear for they are few and far between. We are destined to be eternal survivors side by side, protecting and guiding each other." Aldus brought his forehead against hers. "We are destined to be alongside each other. Fate would not have it any other way."

"Aye, the fates. What a tricky thing they are." Dorian stated.

Aldus smiled. "We will get through this together, as we always have." He kissed her forehead. "You are more a sibling to me than Jason ever was. This Victor better hope he can stand within your light long enough to win you, and keep you. I have high standards for my sister's lovers. I hope Victor can withstand the test."

Dorian laughed, pushing at his chest. "Always the protector, Aldus, even though it is nonsense that you speak. I see it in your eyes that you long for your brother."

A hearty laugh filled Aldus' chest. "Well, someone must look out for you as you look out for everyone else. You can't always have your own back covered, Dorian." He ignored her for a moment, whispering, "You are right. I miss the companionship my brother and I had. Very little is stronger than that."

Solemnly Dorian held his eyes. "Thank you." She laughed at herself. "It will return. Jason and Victor are alike. A partner for eternity," her gaze shifted. "Look at all the trouble they get one in. Let's hope you find yours soon, Aldus, so you too can enjoy all the persuasions that come along with it."

"Aye," Aldus pulled her in close, enveloping her. "Eternity... That is an awfully long time." He spoke airily. "I'm not sure if I'm ready for that just yet." Dorian turned in his grasp and they both looked over the smooth waters as the day began its stalk into the night. "What shall we do about Forte?"

"You can feel him too?" Dorian searched the horizon. "Forte's imprisonment either did not work or it did not hold. Either way, we must go to the Water Dragon." She sighed. "I think they will help us finally defeat him."

"Truly?" Aldus' voice was filled with anticipation. "I have so longed for this day." Dorian smiled at his childish enthusiasm. "Yes! I'll take the helm." He turned back to her. "What of Jax?"

"I think I will send him home with Rowan." *Her heart needs mending from what it has already overcome and what it chooses that it cannot take.* Aldus nodded in understanding and headed toward the bridge, abuzz with the new course of the journey.

• • •

Christian steered the helm beneath his death grip. He strove to keep his eyes on the horizon and not the scene below him. The Alastar was smooth under his command.

"I shall take over, mate. We are changing course." Christian didn't budge. Aldus looked at the expression across his face. "What do you stare so ardently at? The horizon must be telling you all its secrets."

Christian snapped back to the present. "I am sorry. I only wish to steer with the best of my abilities and thus stare straight."

"Very well." Aldus pushed his body sideways and slowly Christian released his grip on the wheel, stumbling slightly, his eyes unfocused.

"What kind of devil does she think she is?" Christian's eyes were clouded. "She treats people as her play things and disposes of them accordingly." His body stood slack, and his shoulders slumped as he swayed with the winds. Aldus simply glanced at the man who stood too near him, brushing his arm as he rocked. Christian vigorously shook his head. "I am sorry." He felt himself again. "I do not know the emotions that just came over me."

"It's alright, lad. You have been too long away from the magic. You will soon regain your bearings and not be so affected by its gifts. Allow the sea and her mysteries to reintroduce themselves to you, my friend, slowly." Aldus suggested to the crazed man.

"You are right. I will leave you." Christian was drunk with emotion. He could not steer his body straight.

"Christian," Aldus called to him, "rest." It was a gentle command. "You will need your strength for where we are heading." The man nodded and continued down the stairs to his quarters not meeting the eye of any sailor.

Aldus watched as he made his way below deck. "If that is the reaction to finding ones true match then I wish never to find mine. Who would want that swinging thrill of emotion coursing through your veins?"

Aldus preferred order and sanity. As he stared at Christian's back, he couldn't help but wonder what the man was truly feeling, within his heart. He was sure Christian knew, but that Rahn, the counterpart to his emotions, was ignoring it.

A person truly can think themselves in, or out, of anything – disregarding the only thing that mattered in the first place – the way it made them feel. Aldus heard Dorian's voice coursing through his mind. He had spent enough time with her to know that 'feeling' life was the only way Dorian lived it. Her first instincts were never wrong.

Where one found trouble was when they pushed the feeling away – no matter how good or bad it may have been. To truly overlook such things was futile, Aldus thought. He felt sorry for anyone who disconnected from what they were feeling. In the end, the punishment would only be greater.

• • •

"My darling, will you ease your body and return home with Jax?" Dorian had finally found Rowan buried deep within the ship. She brought her topside into the day's fading light.

Rowan's eyes questioned her motives. "But, you go to the Dragon. I could not let you venture alone."

"My dear, I will not be alone. I have an entire ship full of crew to assist me. You need distance from this place." Dorian could feel the angst that surrounded Rowan. She had found out that the girl who held her brother's heart was Rahn, and it devastated her, as did the betrayal of how she became a Siren.

Relief filled Rowan. "It has been much anticipated. I will tell my brother of my departure, and then Jax and I will be off." Her smile was energetic. She was ready to leave.

Dorian nodded as Rowan rushed off to find her brother. She had a feeling the space would do them all good. The tension between Rahn, Christian, Sebastian, and Rowan could be cut with a knife. Dorian did not need it aboard her vessel when she undertook the Dragon. She wished she could send Christian or Sebastian off with her, but it couldn't be so. The call of adventure rang truer to them, at this moment, than the call of any woman. Dorian laughed as she waltzed out of the corridor into the open air. She knew that Rowan did not need this adventure in her experience.

The sun was beginning its descent from the sky. Clouds hung low, forming ridges of pink against the suns last rays. Far to the west the last of the days light spread across the clear aquiline of the water. Rich, warm colors seeped across the sky in a vibrancy of yellows, oranges, pinks and purples. The sun brought all the colors with it as it sunk below the ocean's depths.

Rowan found her brother pressed against the glass, taking relief in its support. "Christian," she called to him, her voice gentle and sweet.

She watched as the muscles of his back moved and his torso turned towards her. "Dear sister." Christian looked her over. "By the gleam of your eyes, I gather you have brought me news." He had rested as Aldus instructed, and his mind felt clearer and less focused on the mud he was trudging through within it.

"Yes. I am going home with Jax while the rest of you continue on…to…to the Dragon." Rowan swallowed hard, her last words. "I am eager to return to my life with Jackson as my charge. I will look forward to your safe return and the stories you shall bring." She smiled weakly.

Christian moved towards her. "What is the matter, Rowan?"

Rowan shook her head. "Nothing is the matter." Inwardly, she cursed her sense of hearing. Far off in the distance, she heard the laughter and heightened voices of Rahn and Sebastian.

"Will you be alright to travel alone? Are you certain of safety once you return to the island? Perhaps I should go with you…" Christian was worried about her. She looked so frail in front of him.

His concern warmed Rowan's heart. "No, Chris. There will be no lapse of time in our travel." His face was puzzled. "We only use human ways of transportation because we have all the time in the world to get there. Anyway, not all can travel as we do. And what would fearsome pirates be without a ship, eh?" She smiled meekly. "Jax and I will be quite safe once we return home and enter into our routine. I shall revel, for the time being, in not having to wield a sword."

Christian's face lightened as he smiled broadly down at her. "I trust this to be true. A part of me wishes to accompany you, but I feel a greater calling aboard this vessel at present. Rowan, this shall be my last voyage aboard Sebastian's vessel. I cannot wait to sail under The Lady's colors fully. My soul feels at peace upon her."

Rowan understood him. She had almost completely forgotten they sailed upon The Alastar. "I could have guessed as much. As much as the pirating life isn't for me, it is everything to you. I am proud that you will sail with Dorian. She is a fine captain and will protect you like no other could."

"Aye." Christian wrapped Rowan up in his arms. "I am sailing again, and I have my sister back. What greater joy could fill me?"

She hugged him tightly and began to speak.

"That was rhetorical." Christian added as Rowan sighed, laughing into his chest. "After we seek the Dragon, perhaps I shall visit with you on the island for a time. I do not wish to stray far from you, Rowan."

"I would love the company of my brother for as long as he can bear mine." Rowan smiled up at him. They mirrored each other in their tall slender builds. "Oh..." Her ears pricked as she listened to the silence of the waves. "Dorian is calling. It is time to make our journey home." She moved away from Christian towards the door. Rowan held his eyes as she turned back to him. "I love you, Christian."

Christian beamed at her. "And I love you, Rowan." He followed behind her as they came out to the twilight of the main deck. Dorian was holding Jax towards the bow, pointing out over the darkening sea, holding him close. Whatever Dorian had said caused the boy to laugh and hug her neck tightly.

"Jax's ready when you are," Rahn spoke blandly. "I shall miss you, Rowan."

Rowan finally looked at her. "Thank you, Rahn. I will await the safe return of The Alastar and all those who inhabit her." She strode off towards Dorian's place. Rahn could still feel her sister's chill. The distance would do them good.

Christian was a few paces behind her staring at the two. "Lady Rahn, you look well." Her skin was flushed as if she had been fighting. Christian couldn't imagine the trouble she got herself in. Then he reminded himself, he didn't have too. Rahn was none of his concern.

Rahn glared at him. *What game are you playing now?* She wondered. Her eyes roamed Christian for secrets, but found none. "Are you trying a new tactic for seduction?" Outrage built within her at his laughter.

"Nay, nay. I was just being cordial since we will *all* be aboard this ship for a time longer." Christian stared at her directly. Then, as her voice began to break from her lips in malice, he turned and walked away. "I no longer must listen to your diatribes, Rahn. Go corner someone else. Good day."

Rahn stomped her foot like a child against the wooden deck and huffed her frustration. "Fine!" she called, after he was long gone. She looked to the plank and met Rowan's glistening eyes before she and Jax stepped off its edge and disappeared, emerging at the shores of home. The emerald green of Rowan's eyes mocked her.

"Where is Rowan?" Sebastian had come beside her. Rahn remained silent. She pushed him to the sanctity of her closed quarters before answering.

The room was dark and the ornate furniture cast looming shadows against the lightless walls. Sebastian was too antsy to sit. He paced while Rahn went about the room lighting candles. Still, she remained quiet. The candles' glow brought light, but the air remained menacing. The wind grew outside and the splashing waves crashed against the window panes. Dark blue swirls of current began to build on the ocean's surface. Large swells would soon assault The Alastar. Rain trickled from the gray clouds forming a barrier against the night sky. Sebastian knew that with the company he kept, his vessel would fare well against the storm.

"Rowan is back home looking after Jax while we continue on with our journey," Rahn finally spoke, sitting across from Sebastian's striding form.

"What? Why did you not tell me before? Surely you knew... well, you must have known, she was leaving." Sebastian's voice was level, yet stern with anger.

"I knew what your reaction would be," Rahn stated.

"Petulant child, do not use such tones with me. I have not wronged you! I have done only what you asked." Sebastian glared at her. "I am your friend, Rahn. Why do you treat me as a pawn?"

"Child!? I am sick of the term being deemed upon me. I am not a child." Rahn pounded her fist against the desk.

"Do not act like a child and there will be no need to call you one. Did Rowan leave because of you?" Sebastian gauged her rage.

Rahn shook her head no. "She left because of the pair of us. Jax was her easy out."

"Rahn," Sebastian's arms rested against the desk's top and his eyes pleaded with her. "Let me be free. I feel the charge I held against Christian is gone. I no longer wish to bear the lies of our arrangement. I no longer wish to exact retribution upon him. Christian is one of my best friends. In the flurry of our new friendship I forgot that."

Throughout his speech, Rahn's eyes had widened with fury. She cut him off. "You wish to be free!? You say that you no longer hold your grudge, but you truly wish to walk out of here!?" She had risen and her eyes held his. "I cannot allow it."

Sebastian released his held breath. "I am sorry you feel that way. I can no longer do this. Christian is a good man. The grudge I held against him is nothing. We are even. Whether you allow it or not, it is no longer up to you to say." Coolly, Sebastian turned to leave the room. He flinched as he heard the desk slam against the nearest wall. *Keep walking. Get out of the door.*

He was rammed from behind as Rahn's body collided with his and they fell to the floor. Rahn rolled him over and sat atop his chest. "We are not finished."

Her knees dug painfully into his arms as she held them down. Sebastian's vision swirled as he tried to regain focus. "I know what you need to set your mind at ease. You need to remember how Christian wronged you. You need to remember why we joined ranks in the first place."

"Rahn." Sebastian's body was still trying to catch up with him after the hit.

"Ssshh. I thought you too could not forget indecencies when they were at your door. Christian is vial! Help me one last time and then we shall both be free." Rahn did not see her own actions. "Remember what he did to you? Christian lied and cheated you out of everything! He left you for dead, deserted on that island without hope or salvation."

Sebastian's hazel eyes clearly focused upon her. "I see there truly is only one man who can handle your insanity. Those are your feelings, Rahn. I see now how you used me. You led me to believe that those injustices had been Christian's doing, that he had somehow caused them to happen. I see now that he had no part in the actions of my past that left me stranded. Christian is a good man, an honest man, and he means no harm. You manipulated me with your gifts. I see now the illusion you created before my eyes." She loosened the pressure on his arms and he brought his hands up to rest on her hips, pushing her back.

"I am sorry. I cannot allow further revenge upon my friend. I will not take part in it. Your score cannot be settled through me, Rahn." He sat up, moving her off his body, and stood up. He bent down to her and gently patted the top of her head. "All I can offer you is friendship, Rahn, you knew that going into this, I truly believe." He rose and stared down at her.

"I did, but I so hoped I could have changed your mind. You are an admirable force, Sebastian." Rahn could barely look up at him. Her eyes filled with tears.

"You need to fight your own battles, Rahn, instead of running from them. Eventually they all catch up with you, and pray it's not at the same time." Rahn laughed at Sebastian's words. "You will be alright, Rahn." The hazel in his eyes held hers for a moment, and then he was gone.

Rahn stared after him in shock and disbelief. Never had a man been brave enough to speak such truth to her, save for Christian. Watching Sebastian disappear, she wished him and her sister well. Sebastian would still be there for her. That was all that mattered. Rahn had not lost a friend through her crazed actions. Yet, her mind raced with doubt. She stared after his path. It was hard for Rahn to believe in the friendship of a man for it usually came at a cost.

"You truly are a decent man, Seb. One that cannot even be seduced by my will to bring injury to a friend. There aren't enough men like you in this world."

I am sorry, but I must ensure you will be there... Rahn smacked herself in the forehead. *What am I saying!? Of course he will be there for me. We have a kinship, a bond. Sebastian understands my crazes and gives me berth to scream them out. He will be there... for the proper support I need. No more of this... I cannot keep puppeteering others to avoid the life lessons I wish not to face.*

• • •

Rowan and Jax touched down on land as the last of the sun set. They wiggled their toes in the last of the warmth from the day. She turned back one last time before they left the cool tide of the ocean. Rowan's heart cracked a little with the thought of what she had left upon The Alastar. Dorian had sent them home just in time. The waters were turning black, and, even at this distance, Rowan could tell Poseidon was awaking in fury. He was ready for a heart-wrenching, life-capturing storm. She felt his devilish smile as he dusted the sand from his slumber.

Beware Calypso, my dear Poseidon.

His laughter answered Rowan.

She could not be faulted for trying to warn him of the goddess's strength. Calypso was the Siren's silent protector, their eternal matriarch who always gained a silent prayer from the women's lips. She was always spoken of with great affection and admiration, a woman who could best the Gods and held no debt to anyone, a free servant. The goddess had fallen into legend, even amongst the Elemental realm. She was a legend of fury and untamed fire who held true to her own devices. No one could cross her. No one could contain her. No one could rule her power for their own, or so the stories went. Rowan had a long nagging urge to have met the goddess before Calypso had fallen victim to the pages of fairy tales. She believed no one embodied the Siren name more than the goddess Calypso.

One day she was there, the next she was gone. Something had happened to the goddess, but those who knew weren't telling.

Rowan tugged on little Jax's hand as it rested in hers. He tore his eyes from the sea and looked up at her.

"Shall we return to our castle?" Rowan asked.

Jax nodded. The poor boy was tired. She looked up one last time at the night's approaching sky and swore a silent oath.

Trust is too far a concept for me. Rowan sighed and began her movement forward.

Trust, believe, love, care for, and respect people until they show you otherwise

– it usually happens fairly quickly. Dorian entered Rowan's mind, bargaining with her. *They also just might surprise you.*

Rowan had heard this before, many times. Dorian let others show her what they were made of, instead of making assumptions about their character. Fear always seemed to hold Rowan back, she couldn't get past it.

Jax and Rowan walked hand in hand up the small embankment to the castle, back towards home. Their figures were black against the oncoming night. As they approached the sanctuary of their home, Rowan lifted Jax's tired body into her arms and nuzzled him close. She loved his smell and the essence he contained within his energy. The boy was pure life – unbridled, uninhibited, and unafraid of what lay ahead, come what may. He was so much like his mother. Rowan smiled.

Dorian watched as her sister and son made it safely within the castles walls. She spoke a silent prayer and their castle disappeared from the sight of those who would wish it harm. Dorian crashed back into her body as the ship rocked sideways with the waves' force. The helm spun beneath her fingers. On deck, Grim shouted orders to tighten rigging and hold fast. Sebastian and Christian worked side by side with gallantry. Rahn was nowhere to be found.

Lightning was the only illuminator in the blackened night as Zeus threw down his bolts. Poseidon had hidden the moon for his entertainment. Swells hundreds of feet in height thundered toward The Alastar. The waves attacked on all sides, flooding the deck in their wake. Lightning crashed into the water, electrifying the waves. Zeus was none too happy with his son as he berated him in his wrath. Poseidon shot back, bringing higher waves to crash down upon the sea, trying to drown the heavens, hoping with every swell that he would succeed. Thunder boomed across the sky as Zeus tried to make his voice heard. Winds grew harsher. The rain pelted heavily upon the deck. Lightning struck The Alastar with rage. Fires raced across the deck, but were extinguished by Poseidon's rage.

Dorian harnessed the volts within her as the lightning zinged across her skin. She would store them for later. Her heart beat quickened and electricity sparked within her veins. Grim fought his way across the deck to the loose rope. He anchored it finally, struggling with the wind. The waters swelled with Poseidon's laughter as The Alastar rose high on his breath. He nearly crushed the ship as it crashed between his enclosing waves. The Sea God did not care what causalities were lost this night. War struck the air with every strategy of battle between heaven and earth.

"Poseidon, calm your craze!" Dorian shouted with no one to hear.

Lightning pounded down all around them, bolt after bolt. The waters caved under its velocity. The light came faster and harder until the entire sea surrounding them glowed. The water's assault slowed and Dorian took the chance to invoke the water's currents to gain speed beneath the ship. The Alastar flew between lightning hits and spun its way around the waves to calmer waters. Looking back, she observed as a staff-like lightning bolt crashed into the waters. Dorian laughed. Zeus always won in games of war with his children.

Poseidon's tears of defeat fell gently all around them. He would regroup and try to convince the goddess Calypso to join him in the next round, if he could find the mythical beast. Zeus had never tamed her spirit, nor was she his child to be forced to obey. Poseidon slithered back into his cave to plot more dastardly ways of revenge. A smile lit Poseidon's haughty face as he thought of the gems held up his sleeve. He stared up through the waters black currents to the open air above him, searching for his father's face. Zeus' last mockery of his son's failed attempt was to allow the moon's glow to fill the evening.

"I will find her, you will see! You will no longer make a mockery out of me, Father." Poseidon spoke to the air as it carried his words to the heavens.

Zeus' laugh carried the last of the clouds from the sky. "You are searching for a ghost, ignorant child. Someday I hope to see an end to this false vendetta, but until then, keep on your toes."

His father's words always pained Poseidon. They cut like the chill of the arctic sea, a place Poseidon knew well from his youthful years of punishment. Zeus was neither a forgiving, nor a lenient God. Son smiled up to father as the truth never crossed his lips.

I know where she sleeps. Poseidon had discovered the secret which he would not share.

Dorian smiled as the light of the moon lit her skin and the crew heaved a sigh of relief under its touch. "Everyone alright!?" She called out.

They cheered and aye-ed up to her. She could also feel that all was well, save for a little electricity filling their veins from the storms intensity. Dorian felt sorry for the mortals aboard her vessel. They were the worse for wear, but they would be good enough.

Days and climates changed as they made their way to the realm of the Dragon. Squelching heat led into freezing winds as their bodies battled the element's force. Mountains of old grew to surround them with winter snow caps as they entered the Straight of Diah, a rare place on Earth where the ocean's salt water wound its way through heavily wooded forests, large open valleys, and rock faces of cliff to the blackened walls of Diah's cave. The water did not lead those upon it astray for only one path did it follow. Only one path did it know. Beware the light traveler for the water knew not the way out. The crisp green of the pines and cedars wafted around them as birds sung high overhead, imparting their mournful calls of warning. You could feel the chill of winter in the air.

"What kind of place is this?" Sebastian asked in wonder. He had never seen such beauty. The air was dry and sharp as it filled his lungs. It was neither the damp air of England nor the humid warmth of St. Winnifred. He reveled in the plentiful scenery around him. Such ruggedness he had never seen.

"It's the realm of the Water Dragon, Leon," Dorian answered him. "The only place on Earth where salt water combines with fresh to create a new order, a realm where nothing is as it seems, an empire of magic."

"Fascinating," Sebastian spoke as he looked out over the new water. "This Dragon is what we need to finally silence Forte?" He stared at the side of her face. "You do not think he was done in at battle then?"

"The Dragon is where our kind originated all those centuries ago. The Dragon's blood, bones, breath are what gave the Siren-kind life. We cannot live without them, nor they without us. Leon is the oldest of his kind. He has knowledge that far surpasses anything we comprehend. He has seen the rise and fall of all the great empires in our past. I fear he holds the help we seek."

Dorian turned to him. The silver light of her eyes drove into his being, slowing the blood in his veins. "I know Forte was not killed in battle. It takes much more than the wound of an instrument to kill us, especially that of a human sword. I also feel that Forte's imprisonment will not hold at the water's depths." Dorian turned back to the ship's course.

"He has help," Dorian added under her breath as she sifted through the emotions buried beneath her in the water's slow tide. "We need a force older and stronger than Forte to make his stay with death permanent," she spoke strongly over the bow of The Alastar.

Sebastian stared at her, trying to figure her out. "You fear this Dragon, this Leon?"

Dorian's body tensed as her eyelids fluttered with shock at his words. "Fear him?" She laughed, meeting his gaze once more. She became solemn. "Yes, I do. He who gives life can also take it away."

Sebastian nodded. He understood she not only feared for herself, but for those who came with her. Perhaps even more for those she felt responsible for.

"I do fear more for others than I do myself."

Sebastian laughed. "You must stop doing that. It is considered quite rude to eavesdrop on people."

Dorian's smile was enchanting. "I do not fear the Dragon. He is a kind and loving soul, who can be vicious when cornered." Dorian's eyes caught his mischievously, unnerving him. "But aren't we all?" Her eyes twinkled like a child's on the eve of summer. "He would not harm a Siren that comes to grant his freedom. Is it not always the journey in which the perils lie, not the destination?"

Sebastian's breath caught in his throat as he stopped in his answer. If Dorian feared this voyage, he was petrified. "Freedom..." His voice drifted as his eyes sought the jagged black cliffs ahead of them.

Dorian nodded. "Freedom," her body was fueled with life deep within her as she thought of the word. *One step closer.*

• • •

The Alastar dropped anchor in the pool of the valley. The ship floated in the center of the enclosure. Wide spread land with lush, tall, green grass flanked either side of the ship until it met its end at the mountain's base. In front of the crew was a daunting mountain, all by itself. It seemed to carry no life with its height reaching into the heavens. The energy that poured from it was pure malice. The mountain did not want anyone entering into its sanctioned territory. Death seemed to emanate from every crevice, from every break as rock crashed into the open water below. The mountain stemmed a life of its own as its gloom watched over the ship resting in the pool. No one was welcome. The mountain appeared to tighten its hold, closing all cracks to the inside of its walls.

Dorian would not allow anyone to explore the open lands around them so near night fall. She demanded no one take a foot off the ship, final orders would come in the morning. At the protests of her men, Dorian added that, "Any who wish to leave may do so, but take note that any soul who leaves The Alastar's protection will no longer have a soul to call their own. What lurks in the shadows of the alluring green, feasts on the downfalls of man."

They stared at her in trepidation and were quickly silenced by their captain's words. The crew drank rum to ease their tired bodies and sang of pirate lore to the star's anticipating ears. Songs of men faded as the sky's dark night settled over this foreign land.

Rahn watched. She waited until Sebastian retreated towards his chambers for the night, tired of his banter with the other men. She held her breath until the door closed on his cabin. Swiftly, she moved across the deck amongst the shadows, avoiding the last prying eyes of the crew as they slipped into their drunken slumber.

Intensely focused on her destination, Rahn jumped as a hand grasped her ankle. Christian lay sprawled across her path. Slatted eyes stared up at her as he mumbled drunken slurs. Rahn exhaled, relieved, and shook his hand from her leg. He rolled to his side speaking of fairies and night crawlers.

"Idiot," Rahn whispered. Staring down at Christian slowed her movement. She felt a change of heart as her eyes roamed him. *What are you thinking!?* She reprimanded herself. Physically, Rahn shook her body and moved quickly to the hallway.

He is not the one for barter. A cruel smile spread across Rahn's lips as she remembered.

Outside Sebastian's door, she paused and listened hard, her ear against his door. He was seated on his bed, his back to her, as she soundlessly opened the door and slid inside. His head rested in his hands. He didn't hear her approach until he looked up, shocked.

"What…" Sebastian tried to jump back, but Rahn grabbed his shoulders holding him in his place. Her eyes held a fierceness Sebastian recognized only in the glare of the damned.

"Sssssshhh…" Rahn's eyes began to glow as she stared him down. "I fear you will not uphold your end of the agreement," fear held him speechless. "…and I can't have that. I need you to obey."

Confusion raced across Sebastian's face as he fought for his freedom. "Rahn!" Urgency fueled his voice. Her head twisted as she looked at him. The grip of her left hand on his shoulder tightened and the form beneath it buckled. He collapsed backwards gasping in pain as the weight of her body covered him.

"Do you wish to see the true nature of a Siren?" Rahn's eyes blazed fiercely green and her teeth sharpened beneath his watery gaze as tears dripped down Sebastian's face.

"Rahn, you are not yourself." Sebastian pushed her off of him. "What have you become?"

Rahn pushed off the ground. Her movements were lurid, and contorted, as her body bent before him. "I have become greater than any Elemental!" Her voice dripped with acid. Rahn lunged towards him, tackling his body. Her hand covered his mouth as he screamed beneath the pierce of her teeth into his neck.

"Don't scream," Rahn taunted him. "You are mine. There is no sense in fighting it."

Sebastian struggled against her as his world slipped away from him.

Chapter

17

———◆———

FOR FOUR DAYS the crew stayed aboard the ship and waited. A stench began to invade the entire vessel as the bodies of the crew baked under the dry, hot sun and gasped into the windless air. They all stared at the sheer rock face at the end of the pool they resided in. It taunted them. It begged them to leave, for the battle of wits had just begun.

"I see no cave!" Came the resounding call from deck. "Why are we just sitting here!?" The crew grew anxious.

"Listen!" Dorian yelled to the men at dusk. Just as she spoke a lightning flash filled the sky and rain began to fall mercilessly upon them. A broad smile filled her face with the relief of its coming. She stood rooted in front of the wheel, her arms spread wide and head back, cascading the rains current over her body. On deck everyone fled to man their posts beneath the water's assault.

Finally, you have decided our wait will persist. We will not back down from your stance. The valley had grown impatient with its trespassers.

Lightning struck again. The rock face chipped and people sought cover from the boulders that flew from high above. A bright, illuminating bolt hit the cliffside, shattering its resolve. The water of the pool rushed towards the hole at the bottom of the mountain.

"Hold on!" Dorian screamed as she braced herself against the aft deck's railing. The Alastar was being sucked down, the currents spinning around her as lightning and thunder crashed in the night's velvet sky. The bow of the ship took a dive into utter blackness. The top rigging shattered as the ship followed the swirl of currents into the depths. The masts broke beneath the hard rock, smashing into the deck, and rolling forward into the abyss that awaited them. The Alastar landed crooked on something hard. Torches went up quickly, for there was no light.

"Get off the ship!! Grab what you need to fight and move!" Dorian commanded. The crew was shocked, frozen. The Alastar began to creak and moan beneath them. An eerie silence consumed them. Screeching filled the air as large tentacles landed on deck, crushing the ship to its hidden body. The men shot into action grabbing what they could and rushing away from the murderous arms that began crushing the ship to pieces.

"GET OFF! Get off the ship now!!" Grim yelled as he threw Dorian across the crevice to land, and quickly followed. The majority of the crew now stood beside them on the out stretch of sanctioned land staring in horror as The Alastar died before them.

As the last of the ship's colors slipped below the blackened surface with the final cries of the men aboard, the survivors bowed their heads in tandem.

"May your pirate souls be at rest as you find your final solace in the depths of the waters you loved so well. Awaiting to welcome you home are the open hands of Davey Jones. Do not fear him for you have done no wrong, dying a pirate's death." A Siren's mournful call went up as the last of the crew's joined words fell.

"Good men." Canon said as he turned with the rest of the crew away from the hole.

"Have any of you heard tale of the woman with venom in her veins?" Dorian still looked out over the calm pool. Its water's glassy finish hid anything that could have happened above it.

They looked at each other. "Nay, mistress."

Aldus' broad presence moved beside her. Dorian's eyes looked up to him. "You remember Narrah, don't you?" She whispered. He nodded, frowning. Dorian turned to the rest of her crew. Aldus couldn't move. "Her name is Narrah. Snakes crawl beneath her skin. She ensnares men with her beauty and grace and kills them with her venom." She looked at the faces. "The rain did more than one thing for us. Its wrath opened the cave that has no entrance and the water dissolved our scents. We smell of dampened earth rather than human."

"Why does that matter, my lady?" Sam asked.

"Narrah is blind and relies greatly on her other senses to find her prey when they will not willingly come to her." Dorian's eyes flashed in front of them.

"I have heard tales of her, but none that she is blind." Snow cautioned. Dorian stared at the large man who tended to fear his own shadow. His belly was large from testing his creations in the galley of The Lady. His beard was thick and patched with gray framing his strong face.

"She was not always blind. One of her last challengers deprived Narrah of her sight. In the end she deprived the man of his life. Narrah relies mainly on her senses of smell and hearing. It has been rumored that she can see body heat so beware your perspiration." The crew laughed mildly.

"Why do you tell us this now? Where is this Narrah?" Christian demanded, a lifeless Sebastian by his side. He had had to throw the man overboard to save him from death. Christian tried to raise Sebastian from his lethargy, but nothing worked. He had barely saved Sebastian's life.

"She lies through the tunnel, a path we must travel to reach our destination." Dorian stared long and hard at the man by Christian's side. Sebastian would not hold her gaze and his eyes were flighty. As he slowly turned away from her she saw it, the bite of a nymph. Grim and Aldus stood within ear shot. "Where is Rahn?" Her words hissed in their ears.

Both scanned the crowd quickly and spotted her near the entrance to the tunnel. "There," Grim spoke and they both pointed.

Dorian regarded her. Somewhere in time, Rahn had shifted into something, someone else. "Watch her." The men stared at her as she moved forward. "I shall go first. There is only room for one at a time to crawl through. We will make a line. If you can, rub against the inner walls so the dirt can mix with the smells of rain on your clothes to hide your scent further. Breathe silently." And she was off, disappearing in front of them.

Aldus and Grim stood back. "Do you see anything different concerning Rahn?"

"No, but..." Aldus trailed off as they watched her disappear. "You can feel it, can't you?"

"Aye. Menace is following her."

"Aye. Shall we?" They were the last two to enter the darkness. In their focus forward they did not notice that someone had followed behind them.

The group stood in light. Cobwebs and dirt clung to their bodies, as their eyes tried to adjust to their surroundings.

"Where are we?" was being murmured throughout the cave.

Light may not have been the proper term. The air was dense, a vapor mist floating around them, and the light seemed to simply reflect off the clouds. It was not light, nor was it dark. It was as though the world had been encased in the gray of an oncoming storm. The ceiling of the cave could be seen in spurts throughout the fog.

"Stay close and move with caution. Narrah's territory holds no truth." Dorian whispered to her men. They nodded in accord.

A shrill laugh echoed through the cave as they made it halfway through. They could see the door to escape.

"Did you really think I wouldn't find you?" She laughed again. Narrah emerged a distance away, facing them. Standing between their freedoms, Narrah froze like a Greek statue, tall and poised. Her head was bare and tribal markings inked her flesh, traveling down the sides of her neck to bare shoulders. Thick black lines ran from her elbows, transforming into dots as they laced down her fingers to black nails. She truly was a work of art. Her skin was pale, making her markings look all the more bold. A faint blue filled her eyes where sight had once been.

"There is no s-s-s-sense hiding from me, your smell is intoxicating." Narrah took a step forward. The short length of her black skirt split high revealing ancient scripts on her legs. Narrah hissed, slowly arching her back and lifting her arms above her head. Her stomach began to move and the coils of snakes appeared on her skin, winding their way up. Small black pieces of fabric covered her nipples and straps spread from them like a spider web. Snakes moved beneath her skin, creating ripples across her body. Two broke the confines of her skin and slithered up along the sides of her face resting their heads at her eyes, their tongues stuck out slightly. When she lowered her arms her entire body was filled with the markings of serpents.

Part, Dorian instructed her crew. They separated just as her body effortlessly walked between them. Narrah did not notice the beings smelling of dirt and rain. She walked right to Rahn staring her down with her glacial eyes.

Rahn, move slowly backwards and to the left. She attacks mainly from the right, Dorian warned.

Rahn stood still with fear, an attribute not her own. Narrah struck out and bit into Rahn's neck with one of her snakes that was once her hand. Rahn crumpled under the pain of the venom entering her system. Her body flashed between two people as the second bite smashed into her side. By the third, Rahn had transformed into someone else entirely. Her thin frame shook from the poison and her head sagged, swaying forward with her feet still planted on the ground.

"I could smell you a mile away, nymph. How dare you enter my realm and expect to go unnoticed!" Narrah's eyes were serpentine. Her forked tongue darted in and out of her mouth.

The crew held their breath's as they slowly inched away from the two women. Terror was awash on all their faces. They couldn't understand why Dorian was just standing by calmly watching her sister struggle.

Rahn looked up, haunted, and lunged at Narrah, knocking her off balance.

RUN for the passage!! Dorian screamed throughout her crews minds. And they did so without hesitation.

"You witch!" Rahn's weak body was yelling up at Narrah. "Only your curse is what makes you what you are! You are nothing and no one without it."

Narrah hissed and struck towards Rahn's moving body. "Do not insult me, woman of the Isle, you are on my land!" Rahn hit her hard across the face. Narrah just laughed.

The crew watched from the passage door. Narrah had slowly been changing into a serpent as her anger grew. Her body slid to and fro, missing Rahn's remaining attacks.

"I will not be defeated by a cursed woman!" Rahn screamed through Narrah's hissing. But she missed her footing and stumbled backwards. Narrah dove towards her and began coiling around her squirming body.

"Hus-s-s-s-sh now, child. The more you resist, the more pain," bones popped within her coil as Narrah spoke, "you feel." She laughed as the girl began to go limp.

Dorian's will had been holding all the men back but Aldus stood beside her, fighting it. "I must save her!"

"No Aldus." Dorian's arm held firm across his waist. "Did you not see the flashes of change? The body is not Rahn's!"

"Let me pass!"

"I cannot change her fate as you cannot change yours."

"You saw this?" Aldus' anger hit hard against her resolve. "You saw this coming and did nothing!?" He turned back in anguish to watch his friend die. He winced as the color of her legs changed, but then looked back as the color fled to a wet brown.

"What?" Aldus couldn't remove his eyes. Rahn's arm fell from between the coils and her nails were pointed and yellowed with cracks of age and dirt beneath them. Long, slender fingers grew lax in the snake woman's embrace. Narrah released the body and a petite girl, skin the color of dampened earth rolled forward lifeless. "She was an Ore, but..."

"Rahn will meet us at the end of our journey," Dorian abruptly reassured him.

"Is she alright!?" Aldus demanded.

"Captain, who is that?" Canon spoke for everyone.

"That is an Ore. Small in stature and vicious in nature. They are nymphs of the evil sort. Most entertain themselves through others' pain. She was helping someone. They can take on the forms of others to manipulate and deceive whomever they wish. We will see Rahn soon enough." Dorian lingered as she regarded the two people before her. Swiftly, she brought her pistol up and fired. The bullet landed right between the snake form of Narrah's eyes.

The animal screeched and fell to the ground convulsing as scales scattered across the floor. Blood poured from the wound as the last of the snakes withered at the pale woman's side. Her skin was smooth of markings, her body bare as the day she was born. Narrah's spirit rose and targeted Dorian.

"What was in that bullet?" Aldus questioned her. Mortals instruments could not kill the viper before them.

"Her own venom laced with my blood," Dorian spoke, not removing her eyes from the ghost before them. Aldus nodded his approval. Elementals had to be conniving when planning to kill one another; the task was not an easy one.

"You have freed me from my hell." Narrah's hands came together and her head lowered in gratitude. "Thank you." She was ethereal in beauty. "What is your request?"

"Free the souls you have taken so they too can move on from this earthly prison." Narrah's eyes sprung up in surprise.

A low hiss filled the air. "As you wish," Narrah spoke through gritted teeth. Her spirit evaporated and the thousands of snakes that had fled from her dying body burned as they released the souls trapped within them. The cave, now serene, was filled with a mist as the many victims finally got their peace in the next life.

Sebastian moved forward to look at the dead nymph. His body shook violently as his skin forced the poison from the bite out of its surface. Aldus ran to catch him as he fell towards the ground.

"Hold him tight." Dorian instructed. Aldus nodded, tightening his grip around Sebastian. She yanked the rest of the nymph's infectious pore from Sebastian's skin and threw it toward the body.

Sebastian's eyes glazed over as his body convulsed one last time. As his eyes focused on Aldus, the man helped him to his feet. "Thank you."

"You're welcome, Seb." Aldus spoke as he gently released Sebastian to stand alone.

Sebastian rubbed his neck and looked toward Dorian. "Thank you," he stated again.

Dorian held her hand over the wound and it sealed beneath her touch. "You must be more careful who you let into your bedchamber, Sebastian." The color had reentered his eyes.

"Why did she do that?"

"Many actions of the Ores are unexplainable. The bite, however, is how they control. Once their saliva is in your system, you are theirs to do their will. They control you." Dorian patted his shoulder. "Do not worry, you are free of her. With her death and the sight of her cold body you are released." Dorian looked around. Only the mud colored body of the nymph lay in the room. Unseen screams echoed throughout the cavern. "We must move forward." The crew hesitated, looking for the source of the screams and quickly followed their captain out of the territory. They did not want to find it.

● ● ●

During Poseidon's storm, Rahn was hit with lightning, a bolt that sent her flying overboard into the thrashing waves. Her body crashed into Poseidon's grasp and the tow of his under currents yanked her under. Rahn lashed out against his hold to no avail. He pulled her deeply into his night. Her body collided with the sea bottom and melded into the sand which held her captive.

"Hello, Rahn." His voice leeched out from the shadows, but she could not find his face. "How nice of you to join me." The words slithered to her ears.

"Forte, you are a fool!" Rahn detested him.

"Why is that? I rather think I am quite smart. I have struck a deal with Poseidon. He wants Zeus thrown out of power, and I want Dorian." Forte's smile disgusted her.

"And how do you think you are going to throw a God out of power? You are too simple an Urchin for the deed."

Forte laughed mockingly at her. "Calypso."

"Calypso? She is neither here nor there, an uncatchable force, nay a fabled force. No one has even seen the vixen in more than four centuries. She does not exist!" Rahn was seething beneath his gaze.

Again the laughter that made her grate her teeth. "Have you forgotten what you are? How can you, being of a mythical race, truly deny any being's existence?" Forte stared down at her. "You really never saw it?" He watched her face. "Fascinating! The Calypso lived and breathed right beneath your very nose and you never noticed." Rahn felt inadequate, like she had been overlooking a prize, key to the puzzle. "No? What a sorry use of the Elemental blood you are." She wanted to crush Forte's eyes within her grasp just so they would stop mocking her.

Rahn felt the moment her imposter nymph died at the hands of Narrah. With her death, a tiny ripple was created in time, and it loosened the grip of her captor's hold. She shot out of her enclosure leaving Forte behind in a whirl of sand. She had to escape this mad man's oncoming wrath. She had to warn the crew.

Forte cursed her escape. Rahn was the bargaining chip he needed. If Rahn had paid more attention, she would have noted that Poseidon did not fully trust Forte. Poseidon may have helped Forte escape imprisonment, but not fully. Forte's feet were secured to the bottom of the ocean as the sand clamped him in irons. He could not catch his fleeing prisoner.

Chapter

18

------◆------

DIM TORCHLIGHT GUIDED THE SAILORS FORWARD, deeper beneath the ground. Water dripped from the ceiling, dampening every crevice it could find. The decline was subtle, but with each step onward the walls shrank in around them. The crew was a brave one but with every inch of creeping darkness that gained on them, their resolve's began to quiver. They did not fear to be amongst the fallen of battle, for they knew all who had died had been sent to peace. No soul would wander lost while Dorian watched over them. She always made sure of it. Rumors spread of the protection The Lady offered, and therefore, once a man joined the crew, his loyalty was relentless and unfailing. The progressing line was a silent one. Barely a breath could be heard throughout the cavern. The plodding of feet echoed swiftly to their ears. The men all felt a fear but they knew not from where it came. The sailors upon The Lady never felt fear of the unknown. They embraced it. Nay, they sought it purposefully.

However, the encroaching eeriness of Diah's cave was consuming. An emotion of dread filled the air, penetrating all of their resolve's. Energy swirled around them, dark and menacing. The presence that lurked within the shadows of this cave was demanding everything from the trespassers. It would not stop until it claimed their lives.

"We will soon have to crawl." Dorian's voice bounced off the walls. "Then we will be at the center and, hopefully, quickly out of this dank darkness." She turned to face the men behind her. "Do not give into the cave's tricks. It will try to ensnare your mind and fill it with deception and weakness. Do not sell your soul to the dread of this place." As she turned, she stopped short, bunching up the men behind her.

"What is it, Cap'n?" Grim asked a short distance behind her.

Dorian brought a torch closer in front of her and stared at the thick-framed, solid wood door before her. "I do not recall this door." A murmur went up behind her. There was very little any lady of the ship missed, and if Dorian did not remember a door then the men had a slight cause to fear what lay beyond it.

"What do we do now?" Christian inquired behind her left shoulder. Dorian turned and eyed him up and down, lifted her leg and pounded it against the door which buckled under the impact. The old wood of the portal crumbled and splintered as it fell to the moist ground. A rumble was felt within each man's chest as the last of the door surrendered. The crew exhaled as one, mustering the nerve to move forward. A putrid stench clung to their nostrils. It had everyone moaning as it sought after their nostrils from the darkness.

Dorian's leg landed on the other side of the entrance. She barely regained her balance before she was yanked through the hole. The sound of her back hitting the dirt floor reverberated off the walls. The last sight of her disappeared into the blackness. The men stared in astonishment. Not a sound could be heard through the dimness of the tunnel. Not a one of them had heard or felt the approach of an unknown enemy.

Aldus screamed her name but got silence in response. *The cave will try and trick you, misleading you straight into its trap.*

"We must follow!" Sebastian was abreast Aldus as he glared at him with fire. The nymph bite was now barely visible upon the surface of his neck.

"We must find her," Grim spoke with clenched teeth.

Ear-deafening screeching drowned out anyone else's words. In the dim light, the men of The Lady met eyes and nodded in accordance. Christian and Sebastian stared at them in bewilderment. Their human brains could not grasp the telepathy of the supernatural.

Grim finally turned to them and spoke in a hushed whisper. "We must move, and it must be quickly. Follow our lead. Be prepared to fight." Between his muddled Scottish accent and the screeching from behind, they could just decipher what he wanted them to do. "We don't know what lies ahead but..." He was interrupted by the shrill cry of a woman. They all turned their heads toward the entrance and without a word stared into the blackness.

Aldus lead the way forward, stopping just past the shattered door. *Someone pass me a torch.* Snow handed him one from behind. He took it and while they both held it, he asked, *Will you be able to defend yourself?*

Snow's breathing skipped, but he answered him without fear. The chef heaved a sigh of unconvincing relief. *Yes. I can sling a skillet like no man you've ever seen.* Aldus laughed as he turned to look at him. Snow had various cooking utensils hanging from his waist and more hiding beneath his apron. Aldus' large shoulders faced him now and he released a silent sigh.

Always prepared.

Aye, for anything. Snow smiled. There was no turning back.

Aldus peered over the edge. There appeared to be no bottom to the black abyss. He dropped his light and watched as it fell, never lighting the floor. He assessed the depth. He couldn't find its bottom. It seemed endless. He looked upward finding no top. His brow furrowed in dismay as he sighed with aggravation. It was unusual that he knew not what to do. Another scream had all of them frozen on edge.

Where was it coming from? Above, below… they couldn't target its direction. The cavern echoed, displacing any sound from its origin. Let the illusions begin.

The cave appeared hollow and solid at the same time. The drip of water could be heard in the distance as it found its way to a pool, or was it just beside the entrance of the shattered door? The men were disoriented. Any way they looked led to a different deception. Bottom was top and top had no bottom. Screeching and calls of whining echoed to their awaiting ears. Not a breath was heard as they held their air safe within their lungs, waiting. Scurrying creatures could be heard just out of sight.

"Why have we stopped? We must help her!" Sebastian was right behind Aldus, breathing down his neck.

"There is a drop. And there appears to be no bottom to it. If you wish to plummet to your death, be my guest. You will be no help to her in the spirit world," Aldus' tone reprimanded him.

"Why is the lot of you worried about that?" Sebastian looked to the different faces. Some still had blood streaking them from Narrah. "Can't some of you fly or something?" He demanded.

"You assume that because we are not entirely human we have all the abilities you think we should have!?" Canon fumed. "Fairies can fly because they have bonded with the elements of earth. Everyone aboard The Lady has bonded with the water's elements. And no! We are not all Sirens or Urchins." With that, Canon shoved his way past Aldus and Sebastian and leapt off the cliff into the darkness disappearing completely. Aldus listened as Canon flung a suction pad from his palm and latched onto the opposite rock face that no one could see.

"Incredible." Sebastian spoke under his breath. At the last second, he had seen Canon's gift take life throughout his body.

"Canon has found solid ground in this land of trickery." Aldus called to the men behind him. "Can you see what we are up against?" He called to Canon from across the void.

Canon's eyes searched the night around them. Cautiously he scaled the wall. "No. I can neither see nor hear anything. No sight of Dorian either." Everyone waited with held breath. They could not move on an enemy they couldn't find. "There is a ledge just below you Aldus. It winds down to the bottom which is not as far as you may think."

"I see no ledge." Aldus called up to him. They all watched in a chilled silence as the glow of Canon's eyes disappeared above them in the torchlight. "Canon! Canoooooon!" Aldus yelled in frustration. "Where has he gone!?"

"How can he see in this void?" Christian spoke staring into the emptiness.

"Canon was born in the deepest, blackest ocean beneath the highest crevices. His eyes adjust to a blackness none of us can comprehend. His eyes glow white in the darkness," Aldus responded.

At the sound of rocks crumbling the crew looked several feet below them and Canon emerged from an unseen crevice. "This place is filled with illusion. Do not trust your eyes." He scaled to the outer wall and stuck there. "Behind this edifice there is an intricate world of burrows, shafts, and passageways that smell of hell." Canon pointed below them. "Slowly climb over the edge and your feet will find their resting place. The path will be revealed to you once you are on it."

Sebastian stared at him dumbfounded. "How do you see it?"

Canon laughed. "My angle is different than yours." The neon-white glow of his eyes startled them all. "Come on. You must make your way to the bottom and quickly. The creatures that lurk here are large and monstrous."

"They are coming back." Grim spoke while staring out past them both. Canon nodded in agreement. Aldus looked back towards the men behind him. None of them knew fully what the other was capable of. They only knew that they all possessed some gift in one way or another that bonded them. Their common threads were the water that each had a love, a longing for flowing through their veins, and the women who had brought them together.

Swiftly, Aldus slid his feet over the edge and brushed them against the hidden path. Once he placed both feet upon it, it sprung to life beneath him. "Hold tight to your torches and follow me." Everyone complied, following behind him. They had just rounded the curve of the trail when the slap of wings and a low screech echoed in their ears, far different than the noises of before. The crew stood frozen, waiting for movement. High above them, the batting of wings filled the air. The low light reflected diagonally up the rock, displaying hidden things. Creatures with black, fur-covered bodies darted in and out of the crevices. Hundreds of bats frantically swirled above them.

"The bats will do us no harm. It's the black shadows we have to look out for." Grim said, staring at the ceiling.

Slowly, they began their descent once more. Canon met them at the bottom of the cavern, retracting his sticky palms and morphing them back into hands.

"Where has she gone?" Snow murmured. No one dared answer his question. The crew did not want to acknowledge the state their captain may or may not be in.

They continued on down the path. Light began to creep in towards the end, yet they still held tight to their torches. Grunts and yowls now filled their ears with the incessant flapping of wings overhead. The noise became deafeningly amplified. More than once they had to plug their nostrils to keep out the vile stench from the Shadows above them.

It can't be that easy! Where is she? Aldus could see no entrance into the Shadows' world. The walls shifted, closing off any hope of entering to save Dorian. The cave was vengeful, resenting their presence.

As they approached the exit of the cavern, a figure stepped in front of them. Large and imposing, it gripped Dorian by the neck, making her look like a rag doll. It screeched at them and its breath nearly knocked all of them over. It held something in its left hand behind its back.

Aldus did a quick assessment of Dorian. Her lip was bleeding, blood dripped down her chin onto her blouse. Dirt and grime covered her body as though she had been dragged for many paces. Nothing appeared broken. Her right eye was swollen and bruised. Her sword was missing from its sheath. Blood stained much of her clothing.

"Dorian…" Aldus inched towards her and the thing gripped her neck cutting off her air and stepped backwards. They all watched as her lips turned blue but she did not scream, grab at his arm, or make any move to free herself. She was simply still.

"It is a being of the Shadow," Grim whispered. "I haven't seen one in centuries. They are brutal, incredibly strong and smell like the wrong end of a dog."

"What do we do? Dorian has stopped breathing. Can we kill them?" Canon inquired.

"She's fine. She is waiting for us. The Shadows communicate through a series of yowls and screeches and cannot understand us when we speak. It infuriates them to hear our voices. They only grow in hostility. Our very being here aggravates them into erratic behavior. They hate fire and sunlight. See how he is slowly inching towards the hole in the wall. If he takes Dorian into their lair, we won't find her." Aldus did his best to keep the terror out of his voice.

"Why has he not done so?" Christian whispered.

"A fight. They live for the thrill of death in their hands." Grim looked him over. "The Shadow knows that Dorian is of some importance to us."

"Vengeance is on his mind. He and his clan believe that we have wronged them in some way. Listen…" Aldus raised his ear. "They have long been imprisoned here."

Grim looked at him. "We must move quickly and aggressively if we want to make it out alive." The smell of acid grew stronger as the Shadows moved in around them.

Aldus nodded.

The Shadows inched towards the travelers from every angle. They were covered in mats of soiled hair with black leathery faces, hands and feet. Growling, they bore yellowing teeth, dripping with saliva. Beady black eyes challenged the crew with their glare. These creatures knew only hatred and defiance. They worked from the reactive brain. Everyone was a threat. Difference deserved to die, and animalistic craze solved everything.

The crew waited, protected for now by their fire light. The Shadows' breath grew nearer in its heat. The creatures surrounded them, just an arm's length away. No one moved in the stifling air.

Aldus held Dorian's eyes, waiting. The air was electrically charged as she nodded back.

"Everyone charge with your torches!" Aldus yelled surprising the creatures. In seconds, they were in an all out battle with every Shadow of the cave. The creatures crawled out of every crack and hole like ants. More of them appeared than any of the crew could have imagined. The Shadows screeched and clawed until they killed the humans in their grasp. The one that held Dorian had flung her into the side wall in his fear. Aldus rushed to her aid and she cursed the entire way to her feet.

"That bastard took my sword. Everyone make for the light! They won't follow us there!" Then Dorian disappeared in the rain of blood and bodies. Killing a Shadow only made the smell worse. Death provided no escape.

Snow flung knives and spatulas at their heads and hit a few square on. The rest of the crew were fighters, and decimated the putrid animals as their bodies flew towards them.

The Shadows' faces felt like leather and were wrinkled from decades of hatred. Warts covered their bodies and sprayed a yellow poison when sliced off. Their blood even stank when released from their bodies. Screeching echoed in the small space and crippled the men in pain that they had to fight through. Slowly, the crew of The Lady killed their way through the Shadows, towards the end of the tunnel where the light was blinding. A few Shadows followed them into the light. Most of them howled when they were dragged into the light, burning beneath its heat. The stench of rotting flesh and burnt hair filled the air. The men now stood bathed in light, and far from harm. Few had sustained injury, but nothing fatal. Even the poison from the warts was not life threatening. They stood in wait. The wounded Shadows yelled in protest as they fled to the sanctuary of their caves. Some, the resilient ones, stood just past the reach of day waiting in fury.

"Where's Dor..." Christian halted his words as a small figure emerged from the void of blackness behind them. She wiped her sword on her pants and sheathed it.

"What took you all so long? I thought I was going to be lunch for those creatures." Dorian's boots were drenched in a dark liquid the men could only assume was blood. Her pants were clawed and ripped to nearly nothing. A mud-stained hand print marked the ankle of her boot. "You did well, men. You saved my life, thank you."

Murmurs of "no" and "it was nothing" ran through the crowd as well as a blush growing upon the men's cheeks.

"Are ye alright?" Grim pulled her into the light and farther away from the Shadows that wanted to grab her back. Glowing eyes scolded him from the dark.

Dorian touched his face affectionately. "Yes, I am fine. The lot of you seems fine as well." She beamed at them. Even through her mud and blood-covered body, she glowed. "Turn, men, and see that we have reached our destination." Grim and Aldus rushed behind her to seal off the entrance with a boulder, smashing the giant leathered hand that crept out from behind it.

They all looked. Through the light reflecting off a thin veil the group could see down into a land of illumination and green bountiful grass. Waterfalls poured forth, refreshing the air. Sweet-smelling flowers warmed their senses. Dragons, young and old, flew below them.

"What is this place?" Christian and Sebastian said in tandem.

"The Cave of Diah." A sophisticated voice echoed around them. A polite little man with a royal blue jacket of velvet danced out in front of them. His movements were full of grace as his legs did a jig to silent music. He paused in front of the bedraggled crew. His white tights were spotless in the bright light as the puff of his shorts landed high above his knees, a fashion worn by jesters in the king's court. The man ran his eyes over the faces. His eyes sparkled, consuming Dorian within his gaze. "How do you fair?" The man posed with his hands on his hips, turning his profile to them to be admired.

Dorian examined his long, large nose, the sharp features of his face. Recognition dawned on her.

"Spiro?" The moons of Dorian's eyes raced across his perfect form. "Spiro, I would recognize your pompous, French voice anywhere. We all thought you long dead." Spiro lavished in the attention raining down upon him from his onlookers. It had been many years since he was the center of attention.

"Nah, mistress," Spiro sighed profusely. "I escaped the wretched clutches of that mad man as he came to take my life. I owe my presence to Diah, as she gave her life for mine. I have no greater calling than to protect the creatures she loved so well. Thus being, I cannot let you pass."

Dorian's brow furrowed and she began to question him. "But…"

"Who is this Diah everyone keeps speaking of?" Sebastian wondered out loud without realizing it. The small French man's eyes were swiftly upon him, squinting in their fury.

"Whoooo was she? Who was she!?" Spiro's voice rose in octaves with his wrath. "Diah was the guardian of all Two-Natured, supernatural, and gifted beings. She was the keeper of the Elemental race! Her love and sweet innocence charmed everyone who knew her. The only way to describe Diah is to say that she was a saint, a safe haven for anyone in trouble. She protected all creatures. The Shadows claimed to have loved her the most and vowed to protect her till the end. This is why they still haunt her now blackened halls." Spiro pointed behind them, his long delicate fingers mocking the crew. "Wretched creatures, but even they can love."

"What happened to her?" Sebastian wanted to know.

"My mistress was put on this Earth to guide and help. She was beautiful in her raven hair and fair skin with rosy cheeks. Her eyes were the color of a soft sea in shallow water." Spiro paused in remembrance. "Diah was murdered by the very kind she swore to protect! A man damaged by his transition into the life of the supernatural, a crazed abomination, fell in love with her. When she would not yield to him he made her life hell."

Spiro flashed upon the face of the man and shivered. The anger of his chiseled features still haunted him.

"Eventually, the man disappeared and Diah thought herself free to continue her duties in peace. This lunatic watched her from the shadows as she fell in love with another. The man was a good and honest soul who would truly love and serve her. His name was Eric…." Spiro could not shake the memory from his mind. "Such love…" his voice drifted, "should never be degraded so." A tear glistened down his cheek. The company was enthralled with his story. Spiro's hat bobbed to and fro with his movements. The feathers constantly swept across his thin face as the hat added another life to his story, another character.

Spiro nodded to Dorian as her eyes locked upon him.

"On the eve of Diah's nuptials, her stalker killed her husband-to-be, Eric, in cold blood. Eric was a good fighter, but no match for a stark-mad lunatic bent on retaliation. The men, who found Eric, shrank back in horror. Blood stained every wall. He had put up a good fight, but could not match the madness of this man… A tragic tale of love lost." Dorian continued where Spiro had left off.

Dorian's gaze held Spiro's as he silently remembered. She continued on with the tale Spiro could not stomach.

"Diah sought the man out. She had had enough of his constant torment. The man saw no logic save for what he found within his own head."

"Did she find him?" Sebastian breathed.

"Who was this man?" Christian asked disgustedly.

"James Forte." Dorian paused at the gasps behind her. "Forte has only gotten more cunning in his old age, and, I could say, even more irrational. He latched onto Diah right after his creator was murdered. And of course, she took him into her refuge, trying to help, and heal him. Diah did not realize the full extent of Forte's mind until it was too late." Dorian's thoughts raced to Rahn and the story she had relayed of Dee's death. "Forte had not been in this life long and has since adopted more skills. Diah did find him. However, she did not calculate the abilities he could draw from his second form. Her wounded wrath was no match for him. Diah went into battle with a muddled head and broken heart. She never stood a chance."

"No, my mistress didn't, she didn't…" Spiro silenced himself before he broke down completely. It had been a long, long time since he had held the company of others. He nearly forgot how to act in their presence.

"She was murdered then?" Christian stated more than he asked.

Dorian nodded. "Diah put up one hell of a fight, but her soul was defeated and she fell too easily within Forte's attack. Her will to live was diminished after the death of her mate. Not even the love she had for all creatures could lift her from the gloom that consumed her world."

"She misstepped as Forte threatened me. I was there," Spiro became a shell beneath their eyes. "Diah could not see another killed on her behalf. I would have died for her!" His voice was harsh and gripped with pain. "Instead, I get to protect the legacy she left behind. I tried to help her, but..." Spiro's words grew in softness, before they disappeared entirely.

"Diah was maven of the Dragons. Upon her death, Forte convinced a witch to enchant the creatures and lock them in this place forever. The Dragons were the first Elemental force of this world. All gifted life stemmed from their birth. With their powers locked behind a hardened cell, evil grows more powerful." Dorian's eyes focused on something unseen and her voice was hard, and blunt. "Forte has grown so great over the centuries that not many of us can compete with him for long. He has had the help of other supernaturals to increase his strength. If one knows the incantation, one can take the essence of an Elemental upon their death. One can also manipulate it while they still live." A vision of the release awaiting her flashed through Dorian's mind. She shivered. "Forte has decimated our world for his own gain."

"Yes, and I was banished here to protect the Dragons from further harm." Spiro was babbling now. Forte had used him to defeat Diah once and for all, imprisoning Spiro after Diah's death. He saw no use in killing Spiro, so he made him disappear. Spiro stilled blamed himself for a fate he could not change. Diah's death was no fault of his own. He had been captured to play out Forte's plan.

"Not even you can defeat him, Dorian?" Sebastian asked as he looked back and forth between Spiro and Dorian.

Dorian laughed. "I need the Dragons for another purpose. I will help them if they will help me. Having Forte gone makes the world a much better place for the rest of us. However, I must take into account his second life. I do not know what side Seth lies on. The Dragons do not forget injustice easily. They will be ready to seek vengeance upon those who have oppressed them."

"Second life?" Christian questioned.

"Aye. The Two-Natured Urchins have two separate bodies and lives, although in the end only one can survive. They can look identical, be a younger or older version of the person, or look completely different. Their personalities can be identical or opposite. They can hate each other or work together. One can have more control over the other or they can be equals. They can even be born in different eras, I have found recently, even after the other is long dead. Eventually only one survives to house the shared soul." Dorian answered him.

"So what you are really saying is that you can defeat Forte, but you wish to have a bigger, badder force backing you in his defeat?"

Dorian nodded.

"You have a greater need of the Dragons than simply taking out Forte?" Dorian smiled at Sebastian's quick wit. He grasped things quickly. Sebastian laughed. "Consider me answered for now." He smiled. Sebastian understood that Dorian had an agenda no one else knew. Releasing the Dragons was all a part of something bigger, a means to an end she saw fit to carry-out.

Christian stared, annoyed at Sebastian and continued. "How is that possible, that one be born after the other is dead?"

Although the crew was of the mythical kind they listened intently to Dorian's answers. Not much was known of Urchins and all their complexities. Some of this was news to them all.

"If an Urchin carries the Two-Natured gift, as Forte does, then they can call forth that gift whenever they wish. Subconsciously, they have control over it, and over time it becomes conscious. We have a predetermined set of genetics that we need to enter into our right form and one way or another we will get there. I had to be born of mortal parents, marry an immortal, and be gifted my immortality through my husband's death. There are rules, and then there are exceptions. Forte was bitten by a plague-infected Siren and it made him crazy after his transition, instead of killing him, as the plague would a normal person. His second nature emerged right after he healed from being bitten, and his creator guided the two together."

"But I don't understand how…if your husband was immortal, how did he die?" Christian was beyond confused. "*Immortal* means one can live forever, without the threat of death."

"I use the term immortal loosely because we do not age throughout our many, long years of life. Our immortality offers us a youthful forever." Dorian stated. "Most Elementals are of the human design. Therefore, we have similar weaknesses. However, a human illness affects immortals differently. We do not fall prey to nor contract its symptoms…"

"Then how do immortals take ill, or die?" Christian interrupted.

Dorian simply smiled. "You did not let me finish, dear boy. Your eagerness will blindside you when you least expect it." The captain paused, taking in her new charge. Christian would be a valuable ally.

Christian shrugged. "Of course, I am sorry. Please continue…."

"Forte is a perfect example of what the human plague can do to our kind. Immortals live with the effects of the disease for the rest of our lives. Yet, immortals can only contract such human diseases by way of a curse. Dee, Forte's maker, was in very few good-graces. Forte has her to thank for his health."

Christian nodded, beginning to understand. "And what of death?"

"Death can only be brought upon us by another supernatural, and by some humans who use *the crafts*. However, the feat is very hard." Dorian's eyes sparkled with mischief.

"Oh, I see. Your realm is also your greatest enemy." Christian was in awe and his head felt full of voices.

"Very astute, Christian," Dorian praised him. "I've had enough questions for now. We must get the Dragons out of here. Our safety here will only last so long." Dorian turned back to Spiro who was listening closely to the history lesson.

"You are right," Spiro answered her. "The talents of the cave are vast and hideous. It does not take kindly to intruders."

"What must we do to be enabled to pass through the veil?" Dorian asked with sugar on her lips.

"Allow my ears to hear the password," Spiro stated. His stance had become lively again.

Dorian smiled. "Allow my ears to hear the riddle."

Spiro smiled, his teeth aged and crooked. Delighted, he danced around them beginning with his clues. "I am swift and I am soft. I'll warm your bones or freeze your senses. I have many names, but I am looking for the force. I am the exhale of a gale. Do you know what I am?" His eyes sparkled with joy.

"Wind?" Canon mouthed.

"Air?" Grim added.

"I am in your body. I course through your lungs. You must embrace me and release me, or you will die. Do you know what I am?" Spiro's words were punctuated and spaced.

Dorian smiled, "The breath."

Spiro was surprised she answered so quickly. "Very good, lady, how did you know?"

"Spiro in French means 'to breathe'," Dorian spoke softly.

"Ahh, I see the mistress has refreshed her skills of language. Then what is the exact password?" Spiro asked.

Again, Dorian smiled, "Breathe."

Spiro waved his hand gallantly behind him and bowed. "You and your fellows may pass." The veil behind him drew apart, like curtains opening to the first act, revealing the vivid color of the land inside. "Remember to persuade the Dragons, mistress." Spiro smiled as Dorian paused beside him.

"You are free." Dorian whispered. "Feel your purpose served, and the end of your destiny fulfilled. The next step is up to you." Her words were soft.

"Gratitude, my lady." Spiro spoke softly from his bowed pose. He finally felt the peace he had lost all those years ago when Diah died before him. To his core he felt for the first time that her death was not his fault. As Spiro's eyes followed Dorian's steps, he could feel what lay within her and he knew that she would conquer anything. Spiro rose and turned to gaze at the passengers one last time. Dorian felt his calm eyes upon her and twisted to see his face.

"Adieu." His word was quiet as he waved goodbye. Spiro's apparition dissipated into the mist, released from the Dragon's land, he had gone to play with the Gods, his soul at peace.

None of the men had moved from the cliff overhanging the lair below them. Dorian watched them all as she stepped to the edge. From her lips came the most beautiful melody any of them had ever heard – a Siren's song to persuade the hearts of Dragons.

• • •

Sebastian and Christian stood at the back of the group. They were the only other two, besides Dorian, who had seen Spiro's release from the confines of his curse. In hushed tones they relayed their excitement. A larger understanding of these women and the world they dwelled in had been brought to light, and they reveled in it.

• • •

The Dragons below them landed to listen and swayed in the harmony of the Siren's voice. Another tone chimed in and could be heard through the crashing of the water over the rocks. Dorian's heart leapt when she heard Rahn's melody. She had escaped and awaited them outside. The two sang in blended unity, lulling and calming the hearts of the cave. As their song came to an end, a loud yawn resonated throughout the cave. All the Dragons turned to the waterfall with hopeful eyes. Thundering footsteps moved towards them, rattling the inside walls of the cave. A head broke through the waterfall, cascading water every which way. Iridescent, violet scales trailed down the long neck, to the clawed feet, over and around the smooth, dark violet skin at the stomach, further along the back to the tip of the swishing tale. Its wings shattered the waterfall as they rose up in a stretch. A low growl was wrenched from deep within the ancient Dragon's throat as it looked up towards Dorian.

"Lady, you have finally returned to me." The Dragon smiled broadly, baring all his sharp fangs.

The crew wondered what other secrets Dorian held hidden within her. This Dragon that approached them was ancient and it was Dorian he knew amongst them all.

"And you to me, Leon. I have missed you," Dorian answered the Dragon's call.

"The time has come." The Dragon stared up at her, waiting. Dorian nodded. Leon turned to acknowledge the rest of the Dragons. "My children, grandchildren, great grandchildren, great-great grandchildren, great-great-great grandchildren…" His speech went on for many more 'greats'. "It is time…. My dear friend has finally returned to set us free and bring us back to the air of the sea. She has brought with her, her crew. They will do you no harm. Do none unto them." The Dragons began to stir with excitement. An array of brilliant colors rustled below the pirates. "Be ready to see the world as was intended by the Gods." His voice was majestic.

"If you pick a Dragon, and they you, you are each other's for life." Dorian whispered as she spoke to the crew, looking directly at Sebastian and Christian. "Are you committed to this life, this crew, and your captain? If you aren't, safe passage awaits you, but do not choose." The intensity of her eyes frightened them.

"I have already openly given my vow to The Lady, her crew, and her captain. I am ready for the next adventure." Sebastian bowed.

Christian stared at him and looked back down. A green Dragon eyed him and wiggled his butt as a dog does when he is happy to see you. His heart warmed. "I am all in."

Dorian caught his gaze. She could feel that he was sincere and would not let matters of the heart interfere with his quest. She nodded as he also bowed to her. "Very well, men. Tread lightly, and pick your partner. They are our only way out of here. The trail is that way." She pointed down with her left hand and off they went. "Choose each other." She stood overlooking the decisions. Dragons instinctively knew who their person was and they sifted through the crew in search of the right one. She had long ago picked her match and he had picked her. Both she and Leon just watched. Nothing more needed to be done. Not everyone would get paired today. Not every person had the affinity for Dragons and vice versa.

Dorian was surprised to see that Snow had found a match. A plump white Dragon with cool, ice-colored features chose him. She couldn't have foreseen a better match. They could eat and fly together. She laughed. Christian had been chosen by a jade yearling. Although young, this Dragon could match him tit-for-tat and would push him, with his ecstatic disposition, into a new, adventure-filled life. Sebastian sat and watched from a boulder at a distance from the others. He did not hear the rustle behind him as he was stalked by a fire Dragon. The creature sat in poised wait just behind him. Swiftly he pounced, knocking Sebastian off balance. Sebastian rolled over ready to draw his sword and the thing licked his face from bottom to top as he lay over his body. Sebastian laughed at the assault. Aldus and Grim stood in search, side by side. They had been gifted Dragons before, but did not know if theirs had made it through the fight for freedom. Quickly their woes were put to ease as two shadows towered over them. Their beasts had grown.

"Everyone who will be joined has been. Everyone else gently persuade a Dragon or friend to grant you a ride upon their Dragon's back." Dorian spoke from atop Leon. A few pirates had not been joined by Dragons, but it did not bother them. They had gifts of their own that did not bond well with other creatures. Everyone had mounted up and was ready for the descent. "I will go first. The order does not matter, what does is that you follow quickly. The portal will only be open for a short time and if you do not get through, you will be stuck for another century." Dorian removed the amulet that hung round her neck, it radiated with life. She joined it with Leon's, completing the amulet once more. The noise could be palpated as it surged forth with a blinding light. The walls of the cave began to shake and shattered to the floor.

"Come, follow us now!" Dorian screamed over the internal earthquake.

Leon disappeared, diving straight down into the center of the waterfall. The well fluctuated in size, pulsating, as everyone followed as quickly as they could. The creatures allowed anyone carrying a human to make the venture first. The last of the Dragons soared into the water, barely making it before the water-passage closed and began to collapse above them. The current gripped them and pulled them deeper into the water ways.

Christian and Sebastian almost ran out of breath. Just as they thought they would drown, the shaft switched directions and sucked them upward. Dragons and pirates alike were shot out of a fissure. Some bounced off the jagged ceiling while others skidded across the wet rock floor of the cave. The mortals desperately gasped for air to refill their lungs in the mouth of the cave overlooking the crystal waters.

Rahn ran to Dorian and gripped her with an embrace of fire. "Forgive me, forgive me. My emotions overruled all other thoughts and actions. I was irrational and stupid."

"Yes. Love will do that to people." Dorian said, hugging her tighter, speaking softly. Turning to her men she ordered, "All those mounted, fly! I will see you at the haven. I will wait for the mortals to catch their breath." Her laugh was echoed by the rest of the immortals.

"Aye, Captain! We will see you at the shelter." And off they flew over the calm glowing waters of the day's end.

Step one had been completed. The Dragons were free. What would follow next was still hidden from view, but Dorian could feel it waiting. Leon took a deep breath of freedom beside her.

Christian lay closest to the mouth of the cave. Slowly he rose from his stomach to stand on wobbly legs. Sebastian hadn't quite made it up yet. Christian laughed down at his friend who gave him a warning look. As Sebastian's eyes turned to terror, Christian stepped back.

"What is…" Christian's words fell as he turned into the end of Forte's sword.

"Chhrisssstiannnn!" Sebastian yelled, climbing to his feet, spitting water from his mouth.

Christian wrenched his sword from his side and swung at Forte. His movement pulled at the gaping flesh at his side, pouring more blood forward. Forte laughed at him, slicing his sword through the air, and across his chest. Christian cried out in pain.

"Weakling. I do not see what an immortal would see in the weaknesses of such humans." Christian fell to his knees. Forte put his foot on him, stepping on his chest as he fell back.

"Forte!" Rahn's voice stopped him from pushing the tip of his sword into Christian's neck.

The remaining Dragons began to hiss and stalk around him. Forte dug in his coat and pulled out the shrunken head of the witch that had imprisoned them. Her spell still flowed through their veins, and they shrunk back seething. The creatures could do nothing.

"Move and I'll kill him." Forte threatened.

Christian looked around with glazed eyes. He could feel himself slipping, so could Rahn. Leon howled his disgust.

"You think yourself untouchable? Come fight a true competitor." Dorian challenged him.

Forte snickered. "I wish not to fight you, my love. I could not harm you. I..."

"What about me?" A voice harsh and determined called from behind him. The stranger had a firm grip on the neck of a man Forte had brought for back-up. In the stranger's arms, the boy whimpered like a babe.

Forte turned to acknowledge him. "You...." Every inch of him burned at the sight of this man. "I would gladly take pleasure in killing you twice." He grinned. "That sniveling rat you hold is of no importance to me."

"But, James, you said..." Forte advanced on the dirt ridden crewman and stabbed him through the gut. "You said..." Were the last words the man spoke before is captor released his lifeless form to the ground.

"I gladly accept." He bowed.

Everyone stood in awe. They couldn't move.

"Victor, don't!" Dorian scolded him, finally saying his name.

As Forte and Victor locked swords, Rahn rushed to Christian's side. "Christian, Christian! Can you hear me? Christian." Sebastian was by her side, tears streaming down her cheeks. "I'm so sorry." She stared into his eyes.

"Let it be forgotten." Sebastian placed a comforting arm around her shoulders.

"Sebastian, I..." Rahn's mind was racing with all the things she wanted to apologize to both men for.

He cut her off. "Christian." Sebastian nodded toward him.

"Yes," Rahn peered down at Christian through wet lashes. "I'm so sorry, my love."

Christian was turning pale and loosing blood by the second. She touched her hand to his heart.

"I love you." Rahn whispered. As she poured her life force into him she sought to stop the bleeding first and would heal the wounds later. She wanted to heal him from the inside out. Light expanded around her as she knelt by his side. Her eyes opened when a hand lay atop hers ever so gently.

Christian's eyes focused on her. *I love you, too.*

Rahn watched as his head dropped to the side in unconsciousness.

"Dorian, we need to get him out of here and home to heal. I can't do it all from here. I need peace." Rahn's voice was frantic.

Dorian nodded as she watched Forte and Victor battle for their lives. *Time to intervene and get this over with. Maybe I'll kill them both! Aggravating fools.* She took ten steps and was immediately in the midst of battle. She pulled out a long knife from the sheath at her side and fought them both.

"What are you doing!?" Victor demanded. "Get back." Dorian advanced on him. Her elbow collided with his chest, forcing him to fall on his back. "Dorian, he'll kill you!" Victor remained on the floor, watching. "Or maybe you will kill him," he whispered as he watched Dorian and Forte.

Forte lunged, knocking her off balance. Dorian's back slammed into the wall and he pinned her, his knife against her throat. "Drop your sword, or I'll cut off your hand." Dorian's eyes burned him as the sound of metal clattered to the floor. "Be a good little girl and come with me willingly. No one else will have to die at your feet." The sting of his blade dug into her throat. He watched her eyes. The cut had caused a rasp inside her. Her eyes never left him as he watched her and waited. There was a flicker. Forte moved forward and grabbed her neck in his hands to stare straight into her eyes. She felt the tip of a sword kiss her flesh just underneath her breast as it passed through his body. Forte gasped as he tightened his hold on her neck looking down at the blood pouring forth from his wound. "But I loovee yo…" his voice trailed off as his body hit the floor.

Dorian stood in silence for a moment still backed against the wall. "You idiot!" She screamed at Victor.

"I think a thank you is more in order. He was going to kill you." Victor's voice was harsh but calm. "Did you not feel him!?"

Dorian stared at him. In the time since she had removed him from her ship he had melded with his second nature and learned how to use it. "Now only you can kill his second form if need be, you bastard." Loathing crossed her lips.

Victor just smiled at her. "Why don't we go home and talk about it. I remember everything and we have much to discuss."

"Some things are better to let go, Victor." Sebastian spoke, only half listening, as he and Rahn gently lifted Christian towards Rahn's Dragon.

"We have nothing to discuss." Dorian added, not skipping a beat. "You should heed the advice of your friend, Victor. Let it go."

"Come on. By the looks of things you could use a hot bath and some healing. I can help with that." Victor was growing desperate.

"Dorian, I'm ready to fly with Christian." Rahn had determination in her eyes. Christian's Dragon paced and whined behind her. He was anxious for his rider.

"Go. Sebastian, follow behind, quickly!" The captain stared at the Dragon who had picked Christian. Von was pacing erratically. "Von will not be far from Christian. When you reach home, allow the Dragon to help heal him. It will go much quicker with the two of you working together. Get Rowan's help as well. I will follow you shortly." Dorian's eyes did not move from Victor.

Rahn nodded and her midnight-blue Dragon leapt into the air, followed by Sebastian and Von. They flew with fury on their wings.

Dorian stared Victor down. Without a word, she knelt by Forte's corpse and began rifling through his pockets.

"Are you a pick-pocket now? You have to steal the valuables of others?" Victor was curious as to her motives, and just angry.

Dorian pulled the articles from Forte's person and laid them on the floor in front of her. Closely, she stared at the photo of a youthful Forte and a blonde beauty. They sat together on a large beach rock, the ocean crashing behind them, the rays of sunset lighting their skin. The pair looked so serene and happy. Dee resembled Dorian so much it made her jump within her skin. Dorian held the picture flat in her hand and willed it to float just above her palm so she could see the couple within it. Her eyes blackened as a fire sparked the bottom of the photo, releasing the ties that bound the two as it burned its way to ash and disappeared on the wind's breath.

Next, Dorian examined the head of the witch. She had been the coven elder and her magic buzzed around Diah's Cave with menace. Dorian pulled a dagger from the side of her thigh and murmured an ancient tongue as she held the blade just overhead. "Say nah lemmik kasshna eborrow fortuo." Her hand came swiftly down, penetrating the witch's skull and deadening the scream of the witch as it tried to lace their ears with its poison.

"You have far surpassed my expectations of where your powers would be, my love." Victor was in awe of his wife. *I believe she far surpasses me as well.*

Dorian looked up at him. Her laugh was mocking. "You truly have no idea." She rose, melting Forte's sword in her grasp. As she flung it against the wall of the cave, it melted into the side reforming in perfect likeness. "So he can never use it again." Dorian walked back towards Forte, seeking the necklace around his neck. As she studied it within her hand, Victor's voice surprised her.

"You still need me, Dorian, I know you do."

Dorian's eyes slowly found him as she lingered over the pendant. "I need you less than you think I do." She placed Forte's necklace in the remaining pocket of her shredded pants. *I shall keep you for later, just in case Seth gives us any bother, or you bother him.*

Victor was aggravated. "What!" He motioned towards Leon. "You think this Dragon will help release what lies within you? Don't look at me so! I can see something is dormant, just as it was within me."

"Now that you are back among us with all of your knowledge, please enlighten me as to what is lurking beneath my skin. What do I need you to help awaken?" Dorian was toying with him and Victor could feel it.

Victor wouldn't be baited. "You mean to tell me that you do not know the force that lies within you?"

Dorian laughed heartily. "Nah, I know exactly what is within me. I will give you credit. I do need you to help fully release its constraints, but you must neither be here nor there." She turned and mounted Leon. Victor moved to catch her, but Leon blew fire in his face.

"Leon!" Victor coughed and hacked at the smoke. "You speak in riddles, Dorian! Why won't you let me back in!? Do you not remember?" His eyes held hers in the last of the day's light. "Of course you do." Victor felt the fight he held flee him as his eyes caressed her face.

"It would be wise to stay away from my mistress, sire. You are of no further use." Leon knew of Dorian's plan and he so enjoyed making this man suffer, for the time being. His death as Jason was another reason the witch's spell worked in constraining the Dragons. He no longer felt her menace. Dorian had killed the last of her powers over all Dragons.

Victor stared up at her in disbelief. "That is why you have sought to free the Dragons! You are going to diminish the force that binds us together. I won't let you do it!"

Dorian laughed at him. "What you do or do not want is of no concern to me. My decision to free the Dragons is one you know not of." Her tone was melodic.

"Do not ensnare me with your speech! I know your reasoning and I will not..." The anger that filled his words slipped from his being and his shoulders slumped to the floor as his mind raced. "If this is truly what you wish, then I will let you continue on with your course of action." He paused. "Whatever that may be." His eyes reached for hers. They were gray, calm.

"I dare say you have found reason in this form. What I said to you on The Lady still stands. But, if the time comes when we need to eradicate Seth you will be called upon."

"So that is it then, I am to be called like a dog?" Victor stared at her. "You are as stoic as ever, Dorian. Why do you hold so many secrets? You used to share them with me..." his plea was soft and unbridled.

"Secrets? I do not hold secrets. I simply wait for the perfect moment to allow my knowledge to be known. There's no use wasting it on unlistening ears." Dorian smiled. Her radiance warmed him and broke his heart all together. "You held so many secrets from me that mine should surely seem trivial. Goodbye, Victor." Leon moved to the entrance of the cave.

"What of our vows?" Victor called after her.

"My husband is dead, Victor. I know not who you are." Dorian's words hit him like cold daggers on the warm winds of the day.

"You are going to leave me here?" Victor yelled.

"You found your way here. Surely you can find your way back." Dorian spoke over her shoulder. "I would make haste, the moment the last of the Dragons leave this place it will crumble." Leon was gone, diving over the edge disappearing towards the horizon through the twilight's light. His clawed feet broke off the first of the decimation and the ground shook beneath Victor's feet.

Victor stared after her until she and Leon were nothing more than a speck on the horizon of the ending day. The walls cascaded around him. "I saw the light in your eyes, lady, the glow of your skin. Love still resides somewhere in your heart. It is simply harder to find than I thought." He searched the waters for nothing. "I am coming, for you. Be warned, my lady."

Victor stayed until the last of the pale light faded and the stars of the evening popped out to play. As the moon enveloped the world in her glow, her rays inched towards the fallen Urchin. Forte's body flushed with the color of the moon's light and evaporated into the night. Victor aimed his palm at Forte's remaining garments and filled them with fire. He waited until the last of Forte was gone.

"I needed your love, your taste in my mouth to remember who I am." Victor spoke to a long distant Dorian. "I can feel the crimson of your skin's blush against my fingertips." He smiled broadly as wondrous thoughts of Dorian invaded his mind. "I am coming for you. I give you my last warning, lady." He stepped off the cliff, free-falling into the water's open embrace. As his body collided with the element, the structure that once housed the captive Dragons crumbled in his wake.

Chapter

19

---◆---

AS VICTOR'S BODY WAS SUBMERGED in the water, he felt the place of his birth, recognizing it for the first time. He was Jason's second form, born of the sea. The liquid now flooded his veins and coursed through his body with each beat of his heart. The water was his power. Never before had he felt so whole, so alive. His world was no longer a series of gaps and disorder. The memories of Jason now converged with his own, making them one. Victor knew who he was and where he needed to be. In his heart, however, he knew that he needed to go home, back to his family. His mind wandered to the port at St. Winifred's and he felt raw feelings within himself. His parents had much to explain....

Victor swam beneath the currents, gliding through the water with a new sense of ease. St. Winifred's held the beginnings of secrets he needed uncovered. As he reached the cove of his home, Victor emerged from the water at the dock. He stood on the pier, immobile, contemplating his life.

Victor was amazed at where life had taken him. He looked back at what he had been, and looked forward at who he was becoming. His body tingled with a life-force of eternity at his fingertips. The will to command the ocean's elements now sprung to life within his veins. Even with his new-found wholeness, Victor questioned how he was to move forward in his united form and get where he was supposed to be. He knew his path was not one to be walked alone.

The woman Victor loved with passion and devotion had sentenced him to return to his home, the very place she had taken him from, a place he no longer wanted to be. Victor wanted to know the light in his son's eyes. Victor felt so lost.

He did not know which path of action was the right one. Jason reminded him of what he had lost, and Jax reminded him of what he was missing.

He felt like a man without a place to call home, a man without a name to his face. Victor did not recognize his reflection as it stared back at him, bright eyed, silently anticipating his next move. Victor didn't know what it was. The life he knew had been taken from him and altered completely when Dorian walked back into his life, awakening him from his human-slumber. The life that now stretched before him was a life Victor had not yet led. He was ready to grasp it, and never let it go.

Victor sat down on the dock at St. Winifred's and began hitting the deck with all his might. He watched as the water fled towards the open sea, the waves growing bigger with each hit. He could feel the man inside him, the counterpart of his soul. Jason was waning, not because he was growing weak, but because he and Victor were growing stronger together – as one.

He watched the sea, conflicted. Jason Lily was becoming more and more a part of him every day. Victor knew this is what he should have wanted. He just wished it was over. In his heart, Victor was not ready to venture after Dorian again. Victor knew he wasn't strong enough to stand beside her just yet. Dorian was fire and ice. He loved every second he spent in her presence, even the moments when he hated her. Even before Jason appeared to him, Victor knew that Dorian was the key to unlocking the piece of himself that had kept him from feeling whole all these years, or perhaps his entire life.

"Dorian…." His voice sounded strange from his clenched throat. Victor had been cast away from The Alastar and the people he knew, but did he ever really know them? Was this body, this form, real? Was Victor who he was supposed to be, or was Jason the man waiting to shine through?

You, Victor… You are the man to live through time. You are the man, the only man that Dorian will ever love, truly and completely. It was never me, but us – in you, as one. You will be stronger than I ever was, and will be able to do the things I would never be able to do. Your will, your life-force, Victor, is stronger than mine could ever be. You, Victor…

Victor listened as Jason's voice faded within his head. Jason was never meant to be, only Victor. Jason built the being that Victor was to break away from, and eclipse. Jason only made him whole, but Victor was the true immortal form.

"Son, what are you doing out here?" Victor turned towards his father's voice. "Your mother and I have been worried sick about you." Lord Athencourt stared at the son he knew, not recognizing him.

Victor shuddered, turning away as he thought of Jason. The man left behind a high-bar to surpass.

That was very rude.

Victor's eyes grew wide within his head. His father had just spoken to him without words. He turned slowly back to face him. "How did you do that?"

"You have much to learn Victor, about the ways of being an Urchin. Our bloodline is ancient and strong."

"You are an Urchin too?" Astonishment spread across Victor's face.

Lord Athencourt laughed. *Of course I am.*

"But…"

"You were born of the sea, and Jason the womb." Charles gazed at his son with compassion. *Victor, you have so much to learn.* "It's a predisposition that only occurs when a Two-Natured Urchin is being brought to life. Upon conception, the soul splits and the two halves must, eventually, become one, or die half-lived. Part of the Two-Natured being is brought to life through a woman, the other the sea. You will be Jason and Jason will be you, Victor. I can see that." He laughed again. "You will desperately love the same woman, to your own demise, I am afraid."

Victor could not recall a time when his father had spoken so candidly and with such joy about him before. It was unnerving.

I was waiting for you to wake up.

"Please stop doing that. It aggravates me." Victor's stare rattled his father as it turned upon him.

"Only because you are jealous." Charles ignored his son's pointed frustration as though he hadn't seen it. "Jason was very powerful in his half life. Once you fully tap into yourself you will revel in it!" He held his fist high.

"Are you of the Two-Natured?" Victor asked.

"I see you have learned some things from him." The old man paused. "No I am not, neither is your brother. For some reason you, my first born, were cursed, or blessed, with a split soul."

"Aldus?" Victor whispered as he thought of the Viking man.

"Have you seen him?" Lord Athencourt's glee was overwhelming, but he quickly kept it in check. Victor nodded, squinting at him slightly. "Yes, Aldus is your brother. Does he know who you are?"

His son nodded again, words escaping him.

"I am pleased to hear of his safety. After your first death as Jason, he…" Victor watched through his father's eyes as he relived all the horror of losing both sons to the sea. "Aldus was lost, however he quickly found a sense of duty. He sought

Dorian and she sheltered him. They leaned on each other. Aldus swore to me that he would protect her. In his doing so, we lost sight of him. Aldus would not leave her, out of duty to you, to Jason." His father's chuckle was snide. "Dorian can fend for herself, quite well in fact, but he could not distance himself from the last thing his brother loved. He had to shelter and protect her. In doing so, Aldus became the man I always knew he was capable of becoming. When I get the chance I shall thank my daughter-in-law."

"Aldus...." Victor's mind raced across everything he had seen between Dorian and his brother. It was nothing more than what his father had said. They protected each other. "I have seen Dorian's defense. You are right, she needs no help." Victor agreed. "She refuses me."

"Aldus needed her to find his way in the world, and he has." His father laughed. "Of course she refuses you. You, your mother, and I are the only three people who know of your trait. Well, were..." Charles looked at is oldest son. "We never shared the knowledge of your gift with your brother. We didn't want to get his hopes up, and then have you never come back to us." Charles paused in reflection. "Does Aldus also refuse you?"

"No," he shook his head and rubbed a rough hand against his chin. "He seems rather excited that his brother has come back to him. I must admit, I am glad as well. However, I do not yet know him in this form. How is mother?"

Lord Athencourt stared at his son. "You know him...." His words were calm. "You simply get to re-learn what it is to be a brother." Charles paused. "Your mother is well. She has waited long for this day, as have I. We have waited many years to have our son back, 'tis time for you to know your full potential, as a whole." The old man paced the short width of the dock not knowing what to say next. "You will know your brother again, Victor. Do not worry." Charles stated.

"Does Sophia know?" He spoke with a catch in his throat.

"Mmm, why do you call her that, son?" Lord Athencourt thought of his wife, his life-mate of perfection.

Victor looked at him, bewildered. "Sophia is everything I am not. She cannot be my mother. My mother must have died and you remarried..."

"Interesting," Charles looked down at his son. "Yet, she is everything you were." He let his words resonate within the thick skull he was trying to penetrate. "You resemble me, Victor. Jason and Aldus resemble the light hair and glacial eyes of your mother. She is as much a Siren as I am an Urchin. We shielded what we were from you until you were ready to see it."

Victor rose to his feet, towering slightly over the height of his father. "Show me." His father could feel that his son was livid within his skin for being hidden from the truth, but that Victor was pushing past it towards the future.

Victor got a crash course on the life he had missed out on, and it was just what he needed. His parents guided him and pushed the edges of his capabilities so he could surpass them. He watched as the woman who reared him, always appearing so timid and coy, transformed into a woman of the sea. His father left the cool reserve behind and unleashed his will against the elements, portraying a man of boldness and vigor.

It worked. Jason was Victor and Victor was Jason. Victor was Victor to the fullest potential he could be. The stories of his two lives now felt like one long tale embedded in his memory. He could recall his far past with his wife, as Jason, and his present with the deadly *Sirens of the Sea*. Memory gaps no longer plagued Victor as his story was now one he had lived, felt and would continue forward with.

His parents had completely morphed before his eyes. They told him they had aged to fit into society and the sea's gift of Jason's second life. They didn't mind, they were doing it together. Victor smiled when he looked upon them. His father and mother had been lucky enough to find their love match and stay with each other through the ages. The pair did promise, however, to reverse the signs of their aging when Victor brought his brother home and they could leave St. Winifred's for a place more fit for immortality.

It did not take long for Victor to become whole. He was already nearly there. He simply needed a push in all the right directions. His guard finally dropped, allowing the magic of life to thread through his body. Energy surged into his core and shot out his fingertips with purpose and determination. He was not going to take his second chance at life, a life led through one fulfilled soul, for granted. Victor was ready to reclaim what was his and strive for more, greater, and wondrous achievements in his years of immortality. At the very top of his list was learning the sound of his son's laughter.

Victor sat on the cold sand as he watched lightning strike the sky. Black, thunderous clouds edged towards him as the currents beneath them swirled into gray. He inhaled deeply the assault of the winds. A storm was brewing and his body ached to feel it.

"What are you waiting for?" The woman's voice behind him was startling. His mother sat down beside him, a shawl wrapping tightly around her shoulders. The rain began to drizzle softly overhead. "You are ready, Victor. No Siren will best you, you outrank them by centuries."

"Most, but not all," Victor's voice turned sentimental as he remembered his only death. "It must have been hard losing a son like that and then gaining him back in a different form... Am I worthy?" His voice was soft and contemplative.

Sophia felt the weight of her son's question. He wanted to know, to feel, that he was worthy of a whole life. "It would have been harder, knowing you were never coming back to us. You got a second chance, Victor. Don't waste it."

"Mmm..." Victor reached for his mother's hand and pulled her arm through his, holding her gently. "You don't..." He stopped short as his mother shot up and glared at the sky. Victor followed her gaze to the swirl of the clouds and the menacing eyes waiting there.

I'm coming for you.... All of you. The eyes were coal black and vicious. The words were that of a woman.

"Who was that!?" Victor demanded. "Who are you!?" he yelled to the unrelenting sky.

Rain began to pour down like heavy tears from a treasonous God. He swore an eye winked at him before disappearing. A block of ice settled down his spine and he shivered, although he didn't feel the cold. He tugged on his mother's arm, but she seemed paralyzed.

"You must go, Victor. You must go to your brother and save him," Sophia's eyes were desperate. "And your son..." her voice was nearly lost as the anger of the sky shattered across the beach of St. Winifred's. "Come, come." She pulled him up the embankment and they both tore towards the sanctuary of their house. "We have to tell your father!" Her voice was frantic.

"Tell him what? Who was that!?"

Fear stained eyes were his only answer.

Victor received no answers from his parents other than he had to depart immediately. The lives of all he loved were at stake and he needed to be there to do something, anything that could help. As he swam leagues below the surface of the sea he remembered the feeling of the eyes that watched him from the sky. Death seemed to call from within the black irises of a face he could not see.

Victor recalled the feeling as the last of the Dragon's jail collapsed. The destruction had pulled him from his memories of Dorian as she flew away, into a devastating landslide that rocked the entire ocean. He had killed the man who had slaughtered Jason out of jealousy and he felt at peace, but now the eyes of Forte haunted him. His ghost had unfinished business with Victor.

Who was she?

What did she want with him?

What did she want with his family?

How could he protect them?

As Victor tried to swim away from the fear of yet another dismissal of his wife's, he knew he had to get to her no matter what. Envisioning Dorian's face, he felt unprepared and inadequate. Were they ready for him? Were his son and wife ready for him to return?

It did not matter. Victor's life was becoming more complete within every new breath of the salty waters that he now called home. He knew that Dorian had known that distance would force him to grow stronger, and it had. Victor laughed as he thought of his wife's brilliance. Dorian always held more cards than the deck allowed.

As he raced through the ocean's breadth to his wife and son, one question plagued him that no one could answer, but his wife.

What does she need me for?

Chapter

20

————◆————

RAHN SHOWERED ALL HER LOVING ATTENTION on the man who lay asleep in her arms. The moment they touched down on the Isle of Oza, Von was under great distress. The hulking yearling would not let Christian be removed from the beach before he helped him. Rahn lay him down with his head in her lap and allowed Von to approach at his own pace. The Dragon was weary of her. He knew not whether to trust the woman who held his human so close to her breast, but he could not stall any longer. Von eyed Rahn in warning and slowly skulked forward.

"He will have a better chance of survival if we do this together," Rahn spoke calmly and subordinately to the massive creature.

Von looked at her and hissed lowly, "Life is the objective."

Wise, Rahn thought, *for such a young Dragon...*

Von spoke no more to her, but began calling on the force of his strength to begin helping Christian. Rahn watched in awe. She had not seen a Dragon work quite like this before. He dipped the very end of his tail into the cool currents behind him. The water began to draw towards him and he glowed with a white light as the water lapped around his body. He licked the gaping hole at Christian's side with a rosy tongue then moved on to the wound across his chest.

Christian lay motionless. His consciousness was no longer awake within his body. The wound had been too deep and he had lost too much blood. Death was waiting just outside the door, knocking softly.

Von sat back and looked at Rahn. Her eyes questioned him, but still he said nothing. The light around him only grew brighter as he studied her. Sparks began swirling and cascading over Christian's body, targeting his wounds. She stared at Von in surprise. He was drawing her will out and using it in tandem with his own to heal the broken body. For a moment, Rahn thought of protesting his invasion. She had no idea that another mystic could take her power, and yet, she felt no drain at all. Quickly she lost the thought from her mind as the crack and re-fusion of bones was heard. Von knew what he was doing.

The ribs that had broken during the impact of Forte's force mended, reforming perfectly. The water, Rahn noticed, was re-energizing Christian's blood supply, replenishing what had been lost. Light swirled around Christian's side as the lacerated skin moved and reformed. The sliced muscles of his chest filled with new blood and reconnected as the skin sealed to cover the wound.

A deep inhale of his chest startled the unbelieving Siren. Christian's breathing had turned from the wheezing in his chest to a powerful breath. Rahn could feel his heart beat pounding once more within him. She ran a light finger over his chest in the direction of the scar as it sailed straight across, sloping down to the right.

"Why the scarring?" Rahn looked at Von.

"To remember." Slowly Von stood from his crouched position and shook like a dog, lightly spraying the beach with droplets. "He is human and healing is not a perfect art. The scars will never fade. They will remain an everlasting reminder for Christian. They will act as a protection for him as well." Von smiled as only Dragons can. A big toothy grin that unsettles you more than it welcomes you.

Rahn laughed. "What now? He has still not regained consciousness."

"Patience." Von gazed at her with eyes far older than he looked. The silver pools calmed her. "He is not of mystic blood. Give him a few days for his mind to catch up with his body. After a healing from the brink of death, it takes one time to realize that they are no longer dead." Von looked over Rahn's left shoulder and bid a farewell. "Death, you have no soul to carry safely home. Find another."

Rahn shivered as fingers of ice passed through her body and gently blew her hair in wisps toward the sea.

"We must get him in a bed to rest. Have the Shee mix him some brews to keep his body in strength."

Rahn stared at him. "Why do you know so much? You have lived all your life in a cave without the direct light of day. You are younger than me by centuries."

Von laughed, throaty and deep. "I watch, listen and learn from the actions of others and myself." Again, he looked at her thoughtfully. "You would do good to learn from the mistakes of others as opposed to making them all yourself."

"Devil Dragon," Rahn smiled. "Leave it to Christian to get the wisest of them all."

"I am far from the wisest, but I am continually learning." Von lifted up in flight. "Perhaps it would do you good to go live in the Cave of Diah and watch the world through our looking glass." The wind of his wings blew her hair long behind her. Von smiled as the flight of his wings enveloped the open air. *If she does not yet know what my human is to become then let her wait.*

She shivered. "The solitude would drive me mad." Rahn glanced around her. "Aldus, Grim!" She called out over the beach. They were by her side within seconds. "We need to get him into bed, gently."

• • •

Days passed into nights, longing for respite from their silent vigil. Dorian had assisted where she could in aiding Christian's comfort. Soon there was nothing more to do than wait. She couldn't do that. Sitting idle had never been in her nature unless it was in wait of attack. Dorian was discharged willingly by the other two women of The Lady. They had no need for her at the time so she fled with Jackson on Leon's back in search of the wind's breath and the sea's kiss. Distance was the best thing. If anyone needed her, they knew all they had to do was call. She needed time to think. Victor had wormed his way back into the equation and Dorian needed to figure out how to extricate him from it.

The moment Christian was brought to the castle, Rowan was relayed the news of her brother's acquaintance with death. She stayed by her brother's bedside on the endless nights, Rahn watching from the corner. Neither would leave him.

"It has been nearly a week and he has not so much as fluttered an eyelash!" Rahn paced the floor, wearing it thin beneath her. "That damn Dragon," she muttered beneath her breath.

"He grows stronger every day. Do you not see his progress?" Rowan was growing tired of Rahn's outbursts for they were nowhere near constructive. "Von said it would take time, especially for a mortal being cut with an immortal's sword. They are not one and the same. You know this." She was exasperated.

Rowan knew that she had the blessings of the Siren lineage on her side, and therefore the bloodline would grant her brother at least a chance of recovery. For a mortal to be stabbed by an immortals sword is a sure way to death. The blade of an immortal is forged within the Elemental realm, granting the sword gifts only the bearer can bring forth. The weapon of an immortal is a mere extension of their being, and all the power they possess.

"Yes, I know they are not one and the same," Rahn spoke with a childishly mocking voice. "I…"

"RAHN!!" That got her attention. "If you continue on with this irate, immature behavior I will be forced to ask you to leave. And I assure you, you will do so. You are the superior Siren! You should have learned centuries ago the calm and tranquility that comes with the life of an immortal. You should have learned that throwing a tantrum never gets you your way. That pouting in a corner isn't constructive for getting things done. That running from your issues doesn't solve them, it only creates more. And that denial is a lonely, self loathing and pitiful place." Rowan's breath heaved in her chest. She felt great. "Behaving in this manner will not accomplish anything faster! It will inhibit it."

Rahn's mouth hung agape. Never had Rowan talked to her like that. "Wha…. I…" She couldn't form comprehensible sentences so she thought about what her sister had said in quiet.

Hours passed on the fifth day to the sixth hour of the night. Still nothing. Silence filled the room in leisure of the events to unfold. Rowan sat by her brother, having swapped places with a still silent Rahn. She had to know. Lightly Rowan placed a hand over his and gently held it with her palm. She searched his life, past, present and future. As she spoke to the "Beings of the Key," they comforted her. Why had she not sought them earlier to put her mind at ease?

If you do not ask, we cannot tell you. The Beings answered.

Rowan chuckled softly to herself and turned to Rahn. "He will live and heal to full health."

"What? How do you know that?"

"The Beings of…" Rowan wasn't allowed to finish her sentence. Rahn cut her off.

"The Key! Of course! You and Dorian and your damn talks with death."

"Jealous?"

Rahn looked at her seriously. "At this very moment in time I feel nothing but relief. I can't believe neither you nor I thought of you asking them sooner, Rowan."

"I was trying to wait and not intervene with Christian's destiny, but I could hold back no longer." Lovingly, Rowan touched his chest and felt his steady breath. "I need sleep. We have been at this for far too long."

"Aye, sister, go. I will stay by his side, I promise." Rahn beamed at her sister. The news was a welcome comfort, but she also felt alive with panic at what awaited her from Christian's lips when he awoke. *Would he remember what I said?* Her mind bounced back and forth. *Will he remember what he said?*

"I know." Rowan rose. On her way out the door, she spoke back to Rahn.

"What's your guess Dorian already spoke to the Beings of the Key?"

They both laughed as Rowan disappeared down the hall. Both women knew there was no way Dorian could have not spoken to them. Their captain was too attuned at times for her own good. Dorian was often several paces ahead of the game, and she rarely shared her insights until asked or needed. In truth, Dorian could not keep the Beings of the Key out whether she wanted to or not.

At the sixth hour, of the sixth day, of the sixth morning, Rahn awoke. She was startled by the slam of the door hitting the wall after it was flung open. She nearly fell to the floor from her crouch beside the bed frame. The Shee hobbled into the room, just being lit by dawn's awakening. The soft light filled the bottom spaces of the Caribbean filled air gliding in with God's waking breath.

The Shee mumbled something that Rahn couldn't understand. She said it again louder. "*Eig nack? Eig Nack?*" She gestured with her hands.

Rahn mulled it over in her sleepy mind. "YES!" She said, lightened. "Yes, he slept peacefully." She sighed. "Actually he slept like the dead," Rahn added under her breath, dismayed that Christian still laid in slumber.

"Mmh," the Shee grunted. The Shee moved a bowl back and forth between them hitting Rahn's chest.

Quickly, Rahn took it and immediately regretted having the bowl in her hands as she smelled the pungent odor. "I'll give him this. Thank you." Her nose crinkled as she stared at the soup like substance. It had the consistency of water and the color of muddy dog urine.

The Shee shook her head, grumbling as she walked out the door. Rahn watched after her, assuming that she was somehow picking on her or belittling her existence. Rahn had known the Shee for centuries. Dorian trusted her implicitly, but she always gave Rahn the creeps. The Shee was old beyond God, Rahn believed, surprisingly nimble for her centuries, but scary. You did not cross her. The first, and only time, Rahn had seen her defied, the person in question suffered fatally, and still resides in the Shee's museum of glass. No top, no bottom, just endless enclosure that can't be broken. Rahn shivered. *The poor condemned souls.*

"Drink this, my love." She held the bowl to Christian's pink, full lips. Just as the liquid slipped inside, her wrist was gripped viciously and held fast. His eyes fluttered open, vengeful in their stare, and focused on her. "Nooo…" she whined as the bowl flew across the room. "What are you doing!? Let me…" Alarm was in her voice. Rahn scrambled to try and save some of the remaining elixir but she couldn't escape Christian's death like grasp.

"*Neh, neh.*" The Shee waved her hand in the air motioning for Rahn to not do anything as she re-approached the bed. A crooked smile lit her face.

Rahn jumped in her skin as she noted the Shee's smile. It was simply terrifying.

"*Se grado pole fast nich mek nada.*" The Shee was so excited that she did a wobbly jig as she watched Christian.

"What!" Rahn was confused. "The mortal switch to ... No, no," She cursed under her breath.

"The transition to immortal is sometimes a long road."

Rahn turned to see the voice behind her. Von sat just inside the door of the balcony watching the scene in front of him. The Shee waved, excited that he had interpreted her correctly. To see such a small old woman excited could do nothing more than bring a smile to your face and a laugh to your lips. She looked truly mad. "How do you... Never mind. You can understand her?"

Von nodded.

"Thank god. What is she talking about?"

"*Eee nah moh. See ni dah. Konelo zara astra zoot machilo gadda. Lara doot pei nila oooseekiya.*" She grunted towards Von and motioned for him to tell the girl. The long dark sleeves of her garments swayed in the rising light as she pointed urgently, struggling for her words to be heard.

"The Shee says that Christian will soon be immortal. That is why his healing took so long and why his body slept for many days." Von spoke calmly as he watched everything before him.

Rahn looked down at Christian. He had rage in his eyes as he glared at her. He still gripped her wrist, but otherwise lay motionless. Rahn could feel the stirrings of sparks lashing into her body from Christian's form. The Shee grumbled something more.

"What did she say?" Rahn asked, distracted.

"It is time." Von looked her in the eye. "Sit tight, Rahn."

As the time approached the sixth hour, of the sixth day, to the sixth minute of his slumber, the sunlight stroked Christian from the window above his head. His whole body reached for it as it became fiery hot with the morning's glory. Rahn recoiled as his hand burned into her arm.

"Don't move," Rahn was instructed from the Shee via Von. So she bit back her pain and held fast to her spot.

"How is this possible!?" Rahn yelled over the torment of her body. Never had she ever been inflicted with so much pain.

Von's knowing eyes simply stared at her. They seemed to be saying, *how can you not know the answer to that question?*

"Do you not remember Christian's healing, Rahn?" Von inquired.

Von's voice hit her ears and exploded into her brain. Rahn couldn't think. She nodded. "Yes, of course I remember." Her voice was still yelling into a quiet room. She couldn't bear the stillness of the morning any longer.

"You and I both healed him. Two Elemental beings healed a mortal. Christian cannot come back from that experience untransformed." Von watched the room around them as the walls began to vibrate in the haze of the sun's splendor.

Christian's body flooded with sunlight. Starting at his head, his body began to shake and convulse all the way down to his feet as light surrounded him. He glowed with the birth of a new day. Then his body lay still, bathing in the light. As his eyes opened once more, an emerald radiance shot from them, enveloping the room. Rahn could barely take it anymore. She was almost burned straight through. The bones of her wrist felt charred. Christian turned to her and held her gaze. The pain faded to the background as he rose towards her. Holding her wrist, he laid it on the bed as his opposite hand slid to stroke the side of her face, burning the skin there as well. The light surrounding him filled to his heart as his lips came to hers. Light burst around them, blinding the pair from the sight of the other two in the room. The Shee and Von had to shield their eyes until Christian pulled away from her and the light sucked back into where his heart lay and calmed within his chest. He now glowed like an Urchin. Rahn brought her wrist up to examine it. A burnt hand mark disappeared from her newly forming skin.

"I am sorry, my love. I did not mean to harm you."

"Noo..." Rahn's voice trailed off as new pink skin filled the burn tracks. "No, it was beyond your control."

Christian stroked her face, her hair. "I thought you were lost to me."

A tear streaked down Rahn's paler-than-normal face. "I was so awful. I am so sorry, Christian."

"Sssshh." He held her violet stare. "Have you settled your vendetta?" He had no more time for nonsense.

She nodded. "I should not have been stupid enough to hold one in the first place. Your sister was right, although I find it hard to admit that. I behaved like a child." She paused. "It was my fault you were caught between two eras of time. I should have known that at some point you would not know how to get back."

"Then we can start anew?" Christian beamed at her, warming all the ice caps of her heart.

"Yes, my love, we can." Rahn left fleeting kisses across the new glow of his face. "What are you?" She asked alarmed. "Are you Urchin?"

The Shee grunted and mumbled to Von who answered her question. "He is Airin. It is a form of Urchin and Dragon because we both helped to heal him. A very rare combination to have, although I feel he will find camaraderie upon The Lady well enough."

"But, what gifts does he have? What will? What power?" Rahn was excited and slightly jealous at the same time. She wanted to know everything. Airin was something she knew nothing of.

Von eyed his companion. "That is not for me to tell. Soon enough Christian will reveal it to us all. We will leave you for now. Claim the new heart that beats within you, friend. It beats as fast as a Dragon's wings." Von reached over to lick Christian's cheek and was swiftly gone to seize a morning flight. The Shee nodded and hobbled out of the room slamming the door behind her.

• • •

The couple sat in silence. They assessed each other and took each other's measure. The tick of seconds turned to minutes, and the minutes turned to the bang of hours passing. Christian could feel the tingle of new blood racing through his veins. Although Christian's appearance had been altered only by the glow that now surrounded him, the armor of his skin had become impenetrable. His muscles bulged with new, indefinable strength, and his mind could be in many places all at once. He looked the same, yet felt completely different.

Finally Christian broke their silence. "What of Sebastian?"

"He is well. Dorian is having the men rebuild him a ship as we speak. She felt bad that The Alastar fell under her command. The new ship will either be one for Sebastian's personal use, or one to sail beside The Lady." Rahn sighed, staring boldly at him. "I believe she is leaving the choice up to him."

Christian stared at her in comprehension. His mind took a detour as the sunlight laid against his skin, catching his eye. In the shimmer of the light, scales could be seen iridescently reflected on his body. The rainbow of translucent color excited him. Christian couldn't wait to see what he was capable of in his new form. The grip of his fist felt foreign, as if the limb it was attached to was not his own. The sensation was welcome. Strength spanned throughout his body, starting at his heart.

"And Victor, what of him?" He paused. "I remember him being there when we exited." The memory came back fully wrapped in a surreal color. The world before him became more vibrant with every flutter of an eyelash. His vision charged forth with a clarity of sharpness.

"Victor is..." Rahn searched for him but could find no trace. "He is not here, with us. He is upon his own path. Perhaps someday soon you will see your friend again." She reclaimed the light of her lover's eyes. "Truly, I do not know what has become of him."

Christian shook his head. "It's no matter. Victor is resourceful beyond belief. He will be fine." The curve of his smile warmed her.

Rahn took a deep breath as she settled cross-legged in front of him. "We... I, I had held a vendetta against you for centuries. My imagined, unrequited love for you only drove me further into bitterness."

Christian gazed again down the length of his arm.

"Christian! Are you listening to me!? I am trying to apologize. An event which does not happen often, if I may remind you."

When Christian's eyes met hers once more, nothing else mattered in Rahn's mind. All the reasoning she had sought within herself dissipated into nothing of importance. "I have always loved you, Rahn. Over the years it changed and grew in different ways. I never stopped loving you."

Rahn held up her hand for him to stop. She had to get the words out, but had forgotten how to speak. "I know. It was in my own blind arrogance that I shut you out. I spent years wandering through throngs of people from port to port, trying to find something to make me feel whole again." She stared at nothing intently. "Then I met Dorian and my whole world changed. I had a purpose in life once again. She dismissed my brute behavior because she knew how to shape it. With every venture we undertook, I was pushed further into self-confidence and self-righteousness. The betrayal I felt from you only grew, as did my determination to find you in the present and destroy any semblance of a life you had built without me."

The vindictiveness that seethed from her eyes was enough to curdle one's blood. As the violet hue calmed and focused once again on Christian, the pain and hurt were gone.

"I have caused you far more pain than you have ever caused me." Rahn's breathing was slow, well-regulated. "I pulled you from your place in time and sucked you back to a dark past. But without you, I would not live to enjoy each day. I am grateful." Rahn hoped that Christian could forgive her.

He gazed at her, questioning her words. "What do you speak of?"

"Some Elementals have the power to relive time, to rewrite it. But with such power comes great loss. Eventually the gaps between past, present, and future close to reopen at other points in time. You were the only person who could save my mother and me, but we had to pull you from the future, your present, to do so. My mother opened the portal to your time. And with my help, she pulled you into the past. A trip you never even knew took place. When the portal my mother created that night finally closed, we were separated. What felt like years to you, has been centuries to me. But, there could be no one else but you, Christian."

"Centuries?" Christian's eyes grew large before he continued. "Rifts in time created by the continuum of our world create the portals?"

She nodded.

"Every time I sought you in Japan, I was transported back to a time where I wasn't even born?"

Again, she confirmed Christian's words in a nod.

"Incredible. Take my hand." Christian leaned forward and grasped Rahn's hand to sort through her memories. "Show me." And she did.

Upon every ferry, ship, wagon, horse, or boat that Christian had ever taken with the intent to seek Rahn and her family he had traversed through the ages. The entire sequence of events passed before his eyes as he watched from the beginning. He now understood why he felt so disoriented at times when he returned to a city he knew he had been to before, yet recognized nothing. He had been there, but in a different time, so little seemed the same. Places and people changed as he transitioned from one sphere to the next. Christian's heart skipped as the night flashed before him when he took Rahn to bed for the first time and solidified her place in his heart forever. He finally understood. That was nearing the last night of the portal.

Christian laughed with his whole heart. His body heaved forward with the mirth he now felt. He gazed at Rahn suspiciously. "I finally understand why my world seemed so different with every passing year but what I don't understand is why me?" His smile was bright and consuming.

Rahn caressed his face as only a lover can do, tender and kind. "Why you? You, because without you, my life could not inhabit this earth, I could not exist without you. The timing was all circumstantial. You were the one who mattered. You were the one who needed to be. If circumstance had been different and the timing off, I would not be here. You, Christian, are the fulfilling piece to the puzzle. Because of you, my future is certain. You were the only one who could have saved us, no one else would do." Rahn smiled, taking his face fully in her hands and drawing him near her.

"You know," his breath was warm against her skin, "this forgiveness you keep speaking of is tiring. I could not have chosen a different path to walk in this life, for all of them would have led me straight to you, no matter the century. I forgive you, if those are the words you need to hear. You are my whole heart. Without you, Rahn, my world would not exist."

Chapter

21

———◆———

AS THE WORLD FADED INTO DUSK, Seth watched the horizon from his little haven of shore. His heart felt the pain, as if it were his own, the moment Forte fell with his last breath. He himself died along with Forte, but was reborn anew as the moon's subtle kiss across his skin reignited his path. The ashes of Forte's corpse drifted upon the soft winds of the evening as his spirit sought Seth in vain.

The island Seth had claimed for his own was neither here nor there. It existed in time, but could not be found. In working with Ziah, Seth had grown stronger than Forte could have ever imagined. She taught him discipline and accuracy with his gifts. Amongst his new learning, Seth had nearly perfected the art of protection. Around his small piece of the world he had placed a dome of clear mist. Its purpose was to reflect the sight of others. Seth was safe, for now, from Forte's restless spirit.

As Forte died within him, Seth felt a great peace that he had never been allowed to feel before. But, as his brother's ashes settled upon the black sea, Seth also felt a fear, the extreme of which was unknown to him. Forte wanted the two of them to join and fulfill their soul pattern as one. But he also wanted to control Seth's body and mind into doing his bidding. Forte wanted to take Seth over and finish his ridiculous work.

Seth stood at the shoreline with the lap of the waves barely touching his toes. The sensation of freedom was calming to his spirit. The soft rustle of the palm trees behind him reminded Seth that he was not alone. He would not have to take on the brunt of Forte's menace solo. He simply needed help, and the right help, to aid him in finding Ziah in her watery tomb. As the waves continued to roll in, Seth let the euphoric sounds wash over him and wipe his slate clean. He knew he was more than deserving of a better life, a life without being under the rule of Forte's vindictiveness.

The retreat was small, and perfect. It offered Seth solace from the craze of his mind. At the island's heart lay a pool of crystal waters, with a waterfall that cascaded over the moss-eaten rocks. Beside this sanctuary, Seth had built his hut. It was a cabin-like structure with one large room functioning as a kitchen and living area with a sleeping loft located overhead in the vaulted ceiling. He had used all found objects in the hut's rustic, free-island feel. The island had been his and Ziah's secret place. It only made sense that it would be where he retreated to in hiding. Forte knew nothing about it.

Seth was biding his time. He had to let Forte suffer. He had to let Forte wander lost throughout this world until the timing was right. Seth wouldn't allow himself to bond with his entire soul – he couldn't. To become one with Forte would elicit a never-ending war as to whose personality would rule the shared body and mind. Seth thought too well of himself to allow that to occur. The moon's light calmed him as he moved to the center of the island and his waiting front porch. He did not burn a candle into the night. Seth simply appreciated the moon's full glow as it reached for the recesses of his tired body. His mind drifted over the pool's ever-changing current as his thoughts raced to Ziah's face.

Where was she?

Seth had pondered this question over and over without ever finding an answer. He had combed the sea and its lands far and wide without any trace of Ziah.

Was she still alive?

Seth knew that if Forte had killed his love he would have felt it. His heart would have felt as though it had been ripped from within his chest, tearing him to shreds at the impact. The velocity at which Seth would have felt Ziah's loss would have crippled him for life.

Seth felt inadequate because he could not find Ziah himself. He would have to outsource for aid in her recovery. His mind's eye found the women of The Lady, their faces in the shadow of the night. He cringed from deep within as his stomach churned in fear. Seth felt that the women of The Lady would not openly welcome him. He had to approach them with caution and tact if he ever wanted to see his requests granted. The echo of Seth's fist pounding into the armrest of his rocker bounced back to him from the waterfall. He felt so useless and insufficient. The woman he loved lay trapped in a cell somewhere, shrouded in an unseen fortress. He loathed himself. He had let Forte's reign grow too large and now he, Seth, was left to clean up the wreckage. Hours ticked away as Seth accepted the fact that he needed Dorian Lily's help. If he did ever find Ziah he would never hear the end of her mockery.

The only question that troubled his mind was how to keep Forte's soul out.

Chapter

22

———◆———

THE SEA BEFORE THEM was calm and clear. The turquoise depths portrayed a clear sandy bottom. The air was warm with a smooth breeze that refreshed the senses. Their bodies intertwined in the cool shade of the palms high above them, hiding them in a world of their own. Christian slowly looked over the woman lying next to him. She was perfect for him. She held no inhibitions as she lay beside him naked as the day she was born. Her pale skin glowingly glittered under the sun's light, accentuating the piercing slant to her eyes and the features of her homeland. Love filled their hearts as the sweetness of the day warmed their bodies, minds, and souls. The harshness of Rahn's masculine tendencies balanced the warmth of Christian's heart making them both whole.

"I spoke with Sebastian the other day and he said his vendetta against me has long been diminished and that he wishes only the best for us. He says the ill will he held for me was not of his own making. Apparently, it was created through the words of a tantalizing escapade and promises un-kept." Rahn laughed openly as Christian moved to lie atop her once again. "What have you to say to that?"

"Circumstance," Rahn laughed. "I wanted an accomplice in my journey upon the seas of revenge. I may have coerced him into joining me, for truly he had no reason for disliking you. Men are easily swayed when the correct terminology is spoken." She smiled. "You must entice them with adventure, wrath, war, vengeance, and an unknown element of excitement."

"Have you released him?"

Rahn sighed into Christian's anticipating face. She knew that her lover knew she had used her Siren gifts to her advantage in gaining Sebastian's help. "Of course I have! We remain friends because mortals are none the wiser after such instances."

Christian bent down to kiss her neck. "Good," he whispered. "Now, what about what I want?"

"What is it you want?" Rahn purred within his ear, tactfully intoning her voice.

He rose to his elbows to look down at her. "Do me the courtesy, my lady, of considering my proposal to spend the rest of our lives together. I would like to call you my wife – you only and only you – forever."

The lightness of love filled her voice as she answered him. "I will." Rahn brought him down to her to claim his mouth with hers. "On one condition..."

"What are your terms, pirate?" Christian teased.

"That we wed on The Lady's next voyage out to sea."

"Agreed," Christian beamed at her. "A woman after my own heart. I could think of no better place."

Rahn shook her head, brushing a fallen piece of hair from her lover's face. "I can't believe I allowed myself not to deserve you all those years. I love you truly, Christian, and no one else has ever come close."

He held her eyes with his. "My love, my wife," Christian spoke, smiling down at her.

Rahn could do nothing more than shine brightly at his embrace of her entirety. "My love, my husband," she spoke as if in a dream.

They had fought sword to skin for love, and won – never giving up. The love and affection of the one who knows you completely and accepts your every trait is worth fighting for. Thank goodness the pair did not have to fight alone, for that is a much harder and longer battle with ensured defeat. Slowly, Christian eased himself back within his lover's twine and they filled each other completely with passion, adoration, devotion, understanding, equality – and most of all, love.

• • •

For now, the Sirens' day could lay at peace. Dorian found solace within the laughter of her son, as freedom rang throughout the air upon the Dragon's wings. Rowan retreated inward, looking for answers to questions she did not yet want to ask. She feared that the answers lay within her, but she could not avoid moving forward. Rowan could feel a changing of the tides as they rolled in her direction. The ocean's tides calling her once more. The crewmen were busy laying out plans and making preparations for building Sebastian's ship, a promise well kept by the captain. Sebastian had decided to continue to sail beneath The Lady's colors. A grand moment of cheering occurred from everyone at this announcement.

Dorian sighed as she thought of Victor. He had returned home, once more, to his parents. He was going to wait for the most opportune time to return to her, to his family, to his life. To her core, Dorian knew Victor knew he still had many things to learn. She was safe for the time being, or so she thought.

As Dorian soared through the twilight sky with Jax snuggled into her chest, she felt a shifting of the winds. Upon the air floated whispers of vengeance.

The sun set on the Sirens' lives with a brooding squall building just over the horizon line, just out of sight. Forte's death was only the beginning.

Set sail in…

"The Siren's Sea: Redemption"

As the women embark upon their next adventure leaving what they know behind.

ABOUT THE AUTHOR

Clare Angelica was born in the New Mexican High-Country, but honed her skills writing in the shadows of Colorado's mighty San Juans. It was high-up in the Rocky Mountains, where adventure is equally boundless and the beauty is far less lonesome, that Clare began developing her first novel of intricate, mystical, and sea-faring people.

When Clare isn't out and about conjuring up inspiration from the loveable and nefarious characters in her own life, she is at home drawing from her imagination to bring the places, people, and stories to life.

Allow the story to capture your senses as you watch it unfold before you...

Enjoy!

Visit **www.ClareAngelica.com** to check out Clare's blog and to see her latest books!